Juan Pelleschi

Eight Months on the Gran Chaco of the Argentine Republic

Juan Pelleschi

Eight Months on the Gran Chaco of the Argentine Republic

ISBN/EAN: 9783337379421

Printed in Europe, USA, Canada, Australia, Japan

Cover: Foto ©Andreas Hilbeck / pixelio.de

More available books at **www.hansebooks.com**

EIGHT MONTHS

ON THE

GRAN CHACO OF THE ARGENTINE REPUBLIC

BY

GIOVANNI PELLESCHI.

London:

SAMPSON LOW, MARSTON, SEARLE, & RIVINGTON,

CROWN BUILDINGS, 188, FLEET STREET.

1886.

TO

MY MOTHER,

EUFEMIA PELLESCHI DEI TARUFFI.

TO THE READER.

THE present work is neither literary nor scientific. It is a plain account of what I saw, or believed I saw, in the Chaco, and of some of the feelings I experienced. I would not seek to embellish my tale, even had I the power, for fear of diminishing the faith of the reading public, which already seems to be small, in the narratives of travellers.

It is not for the purpose of excusing the many defects of the book that I add that every page has been written in snatches, if I may so express myself, in the rare intervals of leisure afforded me by the exercise of my profession, and almost always in country places, where, all the world over, there are few conveniences for writing. Hence a polished style was my least consideration. I therefore rely on the reader's indulgence, and I shall feel rewarded, if he thinks me an attentive observer and a faithful narrator.

On the one hand he must bear in mind the vastness and novelty of the scene. I use the word novelty, because travellers and writers of travels, of whom there have been many of late years, in this part of South America, have hitherto confined themselves almost exclusively to the southern territories of the Argentine Republic. That is to say, they have concerned themselves with that part of the Pampas which, until recently, was in the hands of the Indians, and with those portions of Patagonia still remaining in their possession. On the other hand, very few have dealt—and those not in any detail—with the Gran Chaco, which is the northern portion of the same Republic, and is of immense extent; the greater part being still in the possession of wild and independent Indian tribes. This I traversed in the discharge of my duties as an official of the Civil Engineers' Service in the Argentine Republic.

Although in the course of the book I shall place the fact in a clear light, it is well, nevertheless, to state in this place that the Argentine Republic must not be judged from the state of the Chaco. It must be remembered that this country, thirteen times the size of Italy, and with one-thirteenth of its population, exhibits the most opposite extremes, from the wealthy cities of the littoral, such as Buenos Ayres, in which a more splendid life can be enjoyed than in most Italian capitals, to the *estancias* and *ranchos* on the Indian frontiers, and the *tolderias* of the Indians. But I will treat of this in another work, if readers and the Fates are propitious to me.

GIOVANNI PELLESCHI.

Buenos Ayres, *March*, 1880.

CONTENTS.

~~~~~~~~

Part I.

FROM CORRIENTES TO THE FRONTIER.

CHAPTER VIII.

CHAPTER IX.

CHAPTER X.

CHAPTER XI.

CHAPTER XII.

CHAPTER XIII.

CHAPTER XIV.

CHAPTER XV.

CHAPTER XVI.

CHAPTER XVII.

CHAPTER XVIII.

CHAPTER XIX.

Part II.

FROM THE FRONTIER TO ORAN.

CONTENTS.

CHAPTER VII.

CHAPTER VIII.

CHAPTER IX.

CHAPTER X.

CHAPTER XI.

CHAPTER XII.

CHAPTER XIII.

CHAPTER XIV.

CHAPTER XV.

CHAPTER XVI.

Part III.

ON THE LANGUAGE OF THE MATTACCO INDIANS OF THE GRAN CHACO.

CHAPTER VIII.

CHAPTER IX.

EIGHT MONTHS ON THE GRAN CHACO

OF THE

ARGENTINE REPUBLIC.

———•———

Part I.

FROM CORRIENTES TO THE FRONTIER.

CHAPTER I.

PARANÀ—CORRIENTES.

AMONG the numerous causes that induce men to abandon their native country and their homes for a foreign land, perhaps the strongest is a longing for novelty and the wish to say, "I have seen." The fancies of youth and the restlessness of eager minds are fed by reading accounts of the adventures of travellers, which are all the more fascinating when they occur at great distances.

It may be imagined, therefore, that to me, who claim, like Terence's Chremes, that nothing in humanity is alien to me, the chance of being transferred from opulent Buenos Ayres to the midst of a wild community and a virgin country, and of observing on the spot the contrast between civilization and barbarism, between art and nature, was most delightful.

We are, then, on our way up the Vermejo river, that runs through the heart of the Gran Chaco, a territory four-fifths of which at least are still in the hands of the independent Indians, and continuing our way by the river Paranà after travelling 1500 kilometers north of Buenos Ayres, we reach a spot where this river makes a sharp turn to the east. Near the angle of this the city of Corrientes is situated, and is there joined by the Paraguay, flowing straight from the Equator.

B

THE PARANÀ.

Although for many persons the Paranà possesses no great attraction, to me it is most interesting. I will say nothing of the charm of what seems to be an artificial canal from the Tigre to the Paranà, its banks shaded with thickly planted willows that gently fan the sides of the ship, or of the houses and cottages built on piles, for fear of inundation; or of the islands surrounded by a labyrinth of narrow canals, and of flourishing plantations of peach-trees, orange-trees, and *seibi* that cover the ground, perfuming the air and delighting the eyes with their graceful white and red flowers.

I will say nothing of the feeling experienced by the unaccustomed traveller at the sight of the boundless pampas, which in almost an unbroken plain stretch westward, bounded by a high *barranca* (perpendicular bank) on the right of the river, nor of the submerged islands on the east, now covered with rushes, anon with young shrubs; nor of the interest excited by a curve in the shore, or an undulation in the landscape, or the whiteness of some house breaking the monotony of the horizon. I will say nothing of the intercourse between fellow-passengers as yet unacquainted with each other, carried on at first with formal reserve, and afterwards with ease and confidence. Nor will I describe the setting of the sun over the flat country, or his rising, or yet the brightness of the moon reflected in the rippling waters as the sharp prow swiftly divides them. These are poetical feelings appreciated in my own country, but considered foolish in others, where the only occupation worthy of human faculties seems to be that of acquiring and laying up money.

To me the Paranà is admirable for the immense masses of its waters poured through its numerous mouths into the Rio della Plata, and corresponding with an equal number of canals, once, twice, and three times as wide as our river Po, and navigable even by large ships for hundreds of kilometers. I am struck with admiration at its vast bed, as large as a great European State, with its numerous grassy and wooded islands, submerged in the time of floods, thus converting it into a sea. I marvel at its course for 300 leagues in a channel that would seem limitless were it not for the islands which succeed each other without intermission on right, left, and centre, and which still flows on, always deep, always navigable in some fashion for hundreds of leagues farther, receiving on its right the Paraguay, which is also navigable for hundreds of kilometers.

That the immense river and its islands, which from their extent would be capable of supporting millions of inhabitants and producing provisions for the whole of Europe, should lie absolutely waste and useless by reason of the depth of waters under which they are submerged during part of the year; that the vast western plain, with its pasturage, its forest, its sand-dunes, and its salt-mines, should, for the most part, and during the greater portion of the year deny one drop of water to man, beast, or plant, when it greedily absorbs all the treasure of the rivers and torrents flowing from the ridges of the central Cordillera and their dependent ranges, thus by an opposite excess rendering it uninhabitable to millions, adds to the impression produced on the senses, reflections which strengthen on conviction, that Nature proceeds by laws uninfluenced by care for that accident of her manifestations, Man, who nevertheless presumes himself to be the end for which all material creation has existed and does exist—was and is.

For half our voyage we coasted the province of Corrientes which lay on our right as we ascended the river, and we anchored at the water-gate of its capital of the same name. Let us take the opportunity of casting a rapid glance on the city and the province.

The latter is one of the richest of the Argentine provinces. It is watered by the Paranà and the Uruguay, which enclose it on three sides and form harbours to be cities in the future. These two rivers are navigable almost all the year by vessels of heavy tonnage.

On its territory, bordering on Paraguay, Brazil, Banda Oriental and Entrerios, *yerba-mate*, the tobacco plant, mandioca, and sugar-cane, grow in various degrees of abundance, and five million cattle find pasturage. In the interior are great lakes, including the vast and renowned Lake Ibera, which pours its waters into the above-named rivers on three opposite sides. In the extreme north there are dense forests of various kinds which gradually diminish in size and variety as they approach the south, where they consist almost exclusively of *ñandubay* about three yards in height, an excellent wood for fences, sheepfolds and garden palings, and largely exported throughout the whole Republic and elsewhere. The shores of the rivers and the islands are covered with willows, seibo, and other woods.

The population amounts to 150,000, about a fifth of whom are white—the remainder being Indians of the *Guaraní* tribe, who still speak their own language, as well as Spanish, which is understood by most of them. But it is very degenerate, not only in the vocabulary but still more in the construction, which constitutes the character of the language, and it is extremely complicated.

The climate is hot in summer, very mild in winter.

Rain falls principally in autumn and frequently in summer, and the fertility of the soil is not impaired by the long droughts of eight and ten months' duration that occur in the centre and north of the Republic.

On this account and because of the nature of the soil, I believe the province of Corrientes to be well adapted to agricultural pursuits, and capable of great development through its rivers. A favourable law regarding public lands was put in force at the end of 1869. It was framed by Dr. Justo, an eminent member of the *Nacionalista* party, who was subsequently, in 1872, made Governor. By this law, the land is divided into four zones, which are again subdivided. These are sold for payments spread over ten years at an equal annual rate, no interest being charged on the remaining purchase-money, and with a discount of five per cent. on what is already paid. If the purchaser is behindhand, for six months he pays interest at five per cent., after which, if still defaulting, the contract is annulled, and the sums he has already paid are returned to him, less eight per cent.

But the high price of land, and the fact that it cannot be obtained without special concession from the Government, throws difficulties in the way of poor immigrants, and of speculators on a vast scale.

Corrientes, the capital, is a port on the Paranà, a few leagues from its confluence with the Paraguay and about 300 from Buenos Ayres. It is situated in an undulating plain, a good deal above the level of the river, which is enclosed by a *barranca* composed of a soft sandstone called *tosca*, the upper part being apparently a stratum of clay. The soil, therefore, is artificial. The streets of the city are laid out in squares, the houses are seldom of regular elevation, and are usually built with porticoes. Many have roofs of extremely light and durable palm trunk.

This, together with the undulation of the soil, makes Corrientes much less monotonous in appearance than the other cities. Nor are ruined houses wanting, and others relatively ancient, with some remains of former buildings, and this gives the city an air of antique respectability, not displeasing to foreigners in whose own native land every ancient building has a history.

There is a national college and a club, and to judge by the number of members whom I met at the latter, the cultured class must be numerous.

There is a market ; that is to say, a market-place, where the Corrientine women squat on the ground selling oranges, nu - goes, bananas, sago, cakes, and soap, while they smoke thick and ill-made cigars, whose leaves peel off in the process. Their heads are muffled in small shawls that cover the breast, almost always nude as far as the waist, especially in summer. In general they are extremely ugly.

In the centre of the market-place is a shed where meat is sold by men ; this shed is about to be replaced by a regular market-house.

The Indians of the Chaco come into the harbour opposite the town, in canoes rowed by their women. Women are the labourers among Indians, and also among the lower classes of the Paraguayans ; in Paraguay, however, this is of necessity on account of the destruction of the male population in the pro- longed wars of the allies. Nearly all Indian women are ugly, the men are repulsive, and the whole race filthy. They crack the vermin infesting their tangled hair between their teeth *coram publico ;* a disgusting habit that also prevails among the inhabitants of Santiago and the neighbouring country.

The City of Corrientes should be called " San Juan de las siete Corrientes."

CHAPTER II.

To proceed.

We are not yet at the Vermejo,[1] but in the Paraguay; a red streak on our right tells us at twenty leagues distance that we are approaching it. As we advance we pass by Curupaity, memorable for its vigorous defence in the last war, and we touch at the village of Humaità—ranking as a city in the very poor Republic of Paraguay—with its church, formerly a solid building, but now shattered to pieces by the shells of the besiegers.

Here we came suddenly on a crowd of women muffled in *tipoys*, who solicited our custom, offering cigars made of *chipa*. They addressed us in the second person singular with "thee" and "thou." I must confess that it is pleasant to be so addressed. They have transferred this form of locution from Guaraní, their mother tongue, to the Castilian language. There is a classic and poetic savour about it, suitable to a sovereign people and to the passion of love, and it carries the mind back to Arcadian ages and to the Republicans of Greece and Rome, who, I may inform such of my readers as are unaware of the fact, always used "thou" in every class of society, as the Arabs, the Turks, and the Indian races in all parts of the world do at the present day. With regard to the Guaraní language, when first heard it seems like music itself, so full is it of cadence, reminding the hearer of the rhythm of Latin verse, but afterwards it becomes monotonous and fatiguing. This pronunciation prevails not only in Paraguay, but also in the Argentine missions, where I heard it, and such cadence or rhythm is an integral part of the language, which takes numberless variations in order to retain it, thus making it extremely difficult to acquire.

---

[1] Vermejo—vermilion. The town receives its name from the colour of its river, especially in the shallows.

If the traveller spends a night in Humaità, he will be struck by a blaze of light, which is quite dazzling in the midst of the prevailing obscurity, and by a clamour of harsh sounds, added to the barking of dogs, who rush threateningly from all sides so soon as he appears. The light and the clamour come from a shed, on which the following words are inscribed in capital letters : *Baile, almacen, restaurant de la marina, ala de billar y café ;* and they invite the public, both native and foreign, to follow their lengthily-worded programme all night long.

The public accepts the invitation. There you will find Paraguayan women muffled in *tipoys*, and the inevitable cigar between their lips, squatting round their baskets by the light of little hand-lanterns. They sell *caña*, tobacco ; *chipas*, oranges ; sweetmeats of *mani* and honey ; cigars ; and I know not what besides. Inside you will see a crowd of *señoras* and *caballeros* of every colour and every costume ; from the fair Scandinavian to the copper-coloured native and African negro ; from the black overcoat to the *poncho* of the creole, and to the sailor's jersey ; from immensely high boots to bare feet. Here you may take part in a French quadrille, or in a Milanese *schottische* waltz, or in the national *gato* or *zamba*, or you may watch the ballet-dancers, still wearing their hoods, as first they fly down the room, rushing, swaying to and fro, perspiring from every pore, and then quite gravely wave their handkerchief in each other's faces, pirouette on their heels, and bound away on the points of their toes, simulating entreaty, refusal, disdain, and reconcilia-tion. After this, you may see them bounding, like the agile sons of the north, and concluding with compliments and caresses, as they go through the *changez mains*, and *saluez la dame ;* then, in return for their kindness, you invite them to take a *copita* of brandy and a *puro ;* the cost of these constitutes the per-quisites of the liberal Amphitryon. The latter gives the use of the large room adjoining the drinking-bar. He has it whitewashed, and the sides painted with representations of a Garibaldian with sword drawn in the act of pursuing a Savoyard army with two flags, of an Italian officer and private also carrying a flag, of a many-coloured Amazon on a prancing steed, a Paraguayan woman, with her basket, her *tipoy*, and her bare feet, and lastly, pictures of scenes from the *cancan*.

I do not wish to speak unfavourably of this establishment, because six years ago, in my own country, in the valley of the Tiber, near San Sapolcro at the foot of the Appenines, they

danced thus, only it was the *trescone* and not the *zamba*, and with
the charge of a halfpenny for every dance, and a small glass of
zoppa for the lady. And there, as here, every one enjoyed himself,
and every one paid separately for his own amusement, regardless of those who would insist on finding the habits of Paris or
Buenos Ayres in every corner of the earth.

But with a westerly wind we have reached the mouth of the
Vermejo, and we are in Indian territory.

The Vermejo is a river, whose level course runs for a distance
of about 2000 kilometers over a geographical distance of about
700. It is extremely tortuous. At the foot of the mountains
it receives affluents which come from distances of 500 to 1000
kilometers, and descend from heights of four to five thousand
yards. In its level course it traverses the centre of the Gran
Chaco obliquely, from S.E to N.W. This river runs in a
deep channel, is between banks fifteen yards above the surface
of its shallows, and from eight to ten above the surface in the
central and upper part of its course, except, however, when it
flows over its own deposit, as is the case in the greater part of
the central portion. It is abundant in water and dangerous in
seasons of flood, but scanty in the dry season. It flows at the
rate of fifty or sixty cubic yards a second, is navigable for
part of the year, and would be so at all times with proper
steamers to do the works in the river that would prevent the
subdivision of its waters.

The flat country is rich in forests of hardwood, thickly clothing the banks of the river with trees, whose trunks are large
and high, but their branches few and poor. Towards the
mountains the woods assume all the splendour of an almost
tropical region. For a distance of 500 kilometers along the
Vermejo, as it runs from Paraguay, the country is inhabited by
the Tobas and Guaicurù Indians and a few tribes of the Chiulipos
and Vilelas. Then for about 1000 kilometers, measuring by the
winding of the stream, these are succeeded by the Mattaccos as
far as the frontier, beyond which they have also penetrated,
constructing small tolderias attached to some *estancia*,[2] or estate
devoted principally to the raising of live stock. Farther on
towards the north, are, besides, the Mattacco and Toba tribes,
the Chiriguas and the Chirionossos, and to the south, between
S. Fè and Santiago, the Mocovito Indians.

[2] *Estancia* signifies a large tract of land used for raising oxen, sheep,
and horses.

There is a story concerning the Guaicurù tribe, first told, I believe, by Azara, repeated by Arenales, and proclaimed at last in the churches. It is to the effect that they are becoming extinct through their custom of destroying their children, sparing only the youngest, so that in after years there would exist but one man, the last representative and champion of their race, as being of beautiful proportions. But this appears to me to be merely a legend or fable. The Indians are, in fact, much attached to their families, and especially to children, whom they spare when taken prisoners, without however reducing them to slavery, while they kill the adults in war, and even the women whom they have taken.

And why should they thus seek to become extinct? In order to avoid the loss of their independence? But if so, it would be simpler to destroy all the male children, instead of reducing themselves to ever-increasing weakness, and condemning their few descendants to a slavery more and more wretched, according as they become weaker and fewer in number.

It is to be remarked also that among these Indians slavery or anything approaching it is unknown, they are free as air, and the Guaicurù, even when conquered, can ally themselves with new friends and go and live among them, as the Chiulipos, who withdrew from the frontier, and made their home among the Tobas at the opposite extremity have done.

The story must also be untrue, because, in fact, the Guaicurù *are* the Tobas. The Tobas are a splendid race, tall, well-built, active, and courageous. I have seen and personally observed these facts.

On one occasion, after two months of difficult navigation, we reached a spot where a numerous *Indiada* [3] were gathered together.

A *ladino* (interpreter), whom we happened to meet, named Faustino, a deserter from the army, was gladly welcomed by us. He told us that these Indians were of various nationalities, and had met together in order to celebrate peace on the same spot where they had fought a few days before. We asked to what nation they belonged, and he replied that some of them were Tobas, *or* Guaicurù, and Chiulipos, and the others Mattaccos, among whom he himself was living.

On that occasion I saw an enormous Toba woman. We had

---

[3] *Indiada,* a large company of Indians.

made Faustino's friends draw up in a line, in order to present them with tobacco, and among them stood this giantess. She wore a mantle of beaver-fur, and was tattooed all over in patterns of a blue colour. This thick tattooing had the same effect as pittings of small-pox. She must have been nearly seven feet high. She remained silent and motionless, but became animated and almost smiling when she received attention, and seized afterwards on the little articles I gave her with covetous and ludicrous greed.

The Indians who were not friends of Faustino remained on the other side of the river, and would not approach nearer.

To return to the Guaicurù : they must have been a *parzialità*,[4] as they say here, of the same family as the Tobas, with whom they share a common language, and perhaps they gave the name to the *Indiadas* nearer to Paraguay. Afterwards, from the mixture of races, or from moving away, they were believed to be extinct, and in order to explain this, the exceptional case of destroying some children who have no recognized father was assumed to be the general rule. The custom alluded to prevails also among the Mattaccos, when the mother has neither kinsfolk, nor friend, nor tribe who will provide for the child.

In the same way, the Chiulipos and the Vilelas, who speak the same dialect, are no longer distinguishable, while, on the contrary, the Mattaccos, on contact with the Tobas, become enemies of the Mattaccos near the Christian frontiers ; nor will they be called Mattaccos, though they speak the same language, with very slight variations in pronunciation.

---

[4] *Parzialità* also signifies *family.*

CHAPTER III.

FIRST IMPRESSIONS—THE LANDSCAPE—THE PRIMITIVE INDIANS.

WE are still at the mouth of the Vermejo.

To find ourselves in the midst of savages, in an obscure region where the hand of civilization has never penetrated, and to know that hundreds of leagues lie before us, while we are ignorant of what, at any moment, a further step may bring forth, such conditions compel thought and reflection, and we watch anxiously, at every turn and at every instant, for some fresh feature of this new and strange life.

At one moment we see a bed of *tacuara* reeds 8 or 10 mètres in height, and with a diameter of 10 or 15 centimètres; at another a palm-tree with shoots 15 to 20 mètres in length, a crest of fan-like leaves, and lofty, upright, polished stems, around which the growth-marks of the fallen leaves show by the number of their rings the age of the tree. Its clusters of *cocchi* are unpleasant to the taste. These trees are few in number, inimical to all other vegetable growth, monotonous and sepulchral-looking. Another time we are struck by one solitary palm-tree, the pale green of its splendid curved leaves standing out against the deep gloom of the wood; or a dense forest of various growths crowning the edge of the high perpendicular bank, at the foot of which, on a narrow margin of shore, there is a straight row of the gnarled *ceibos*, with its crimson clusters of gracefully pendant flowers, the wayward nuptial bed of silent passions; and opposite these, a green shore which, surmounted by verdant meadows, recedes into the distant forests. These well deserve their name of Monti.[1] Meanwhile from a cave, excavated on the height of the bank, a water-wolf splashes through the current. The skin of this creature is of a dark green colour speckled with yellow, the

---

[1] In the Argentine Republic woods are called Monti.

legs are short and web-footed, and the tail terminates in a flapper or rudder which is often raised high, and the intelligent head lifted up from the water in the presence of danger. The sluggish *carpincho* also plunges under water when surprised in its hole, on a level with the surface.

An untrained eye is apt to confound the latter with the *suino*, whose bristles are white, thick, horny, and pointed, and which can be tamed with time and kindness. Its hide is excessively hard, the flesh, like that of the *carpincho*, is a most welcome change to sailors who are tired of dry, salt food At another time we come to a long grove of willows and aspens, overshadowing the river for long spaces, or to a thick growth of *bobos* a shrub yielding abundance of potash, and rapidly covering the ground from which the neighbouring waters have receded. Suddenly at a turn of the river we come upon a tiger who, for size, beauty and courage, is little inferior to his African brethren. He watches the unusual apparition and slowly retraces his steps, or dashes boldly into the river, defying the shots of his enemies, rendered harmless by his speed. In another place is a monstrous *yacare*, sunning himself on the shore, and careless of the bullets from our carbines that glance harmlessly off his scaly armour, unless successfully aimed by a good shot at the orbit of the eye, after which, if he seeks to drag himself under the water, he is drowned.

On a pleasant strand, we caught sight of a doe, which, surprised at the novel sight, fled swiftly across the country, while a stag who stayed to admire the reflection of his antlers in the clear water, fell a victim to his contempt of danger and furnished a sumptuous feast to the explorers. A pleasant morsel was added in the shape of the shining-skinned otter. His four front teeth are adapted by their length to secure his prey, when struggling in the sand, where with numerous companions he excavates his subterranean lair. He is merry and lithe in the water, and shows his enjoyment by bounding and splashing about.

From some distance off we can distinguish under a palm-tree a *tapir*, a heavy and slow pachydermatous beast, not much unlike a horse, to which he is compared in the Indian dialect, as the hippopotamus was formerly compared by the Greeks. On spying us out he raised his snout, forming a short proboscis, into the air, and shrilly summoning his inseparable mate, together they plunge into the river, for the accustomed bath, that

is necessary to them several times a day, in order to cool their.
natural heat. The wild boar and wild pig, though they may
appear somewhat similar to the tapir, are very unlike him in
habits. They rush in large troops through the thickest part of
the woods, a terrifying apparition to the traveller or to the
native who finds himself in their way.

We are now in the beautiful season of flowers, our souls
refreshed and our senses gladdened with the sight and fragrance
of thousands of orange flowers, that are blossoming even before
the bursting of the leaves. Here also is the yellow-spiked
arome ; the jessamine clothing the *palo-santo* and the *guayacan*
with its white mantle ; the *amenti* of the *algarrobo,* and the
various flowers of a thousand different kinds of *cactus,* some of
which surpass both in colour and shape the white and the red
camellia. Others are pale yellow, others again have their calyx
curved, containing the corolla which envelopes a *popoloso
genecco,* in which the seeds are fertilized that afterwards fill
the succulent figs.

Nor is the *chaguar* or wild pine-apple absent; it frequently
extends over wide spaces of ground, and is protected by plants
of old growth. From the centre of the parent trunk of all this
wealth of foliage that flings itself about curving and climbing,
with leaves of every shape, long, narrow, large, or deutelated,
each point furnished with a spike, there rises a short and thick
stem, crowned by a white cone, which is generally encircled
with horizontally disposed spears of a waxen red. These
drop off when fecundation is accomplished. The fruit is eaten
by the natives, and the leaf furnishes their only but admirable
.textile material. It supplies them with string, with which they
manufacture nets, bags, hammocks, or hanging baskets, and
lastly shirts.

Your greatest desire, however, is to see the Indians, and at
first you are divided between the hope of discovering dark spots
in the distance which the man on watch will tell you are they,
and the fear of finding yourself unexpectedly the aim of a
dozen arrows shot from the nearest wood—and if it were only
arrows ! This feeling is succeeded by a delusive confidence,
when suddenly a shout of "The Indians !" makes your heart
beat with various emotions.

The first seen by us were partly clothed, and some of them
wore hats, which they raised formally on our approach. They
followed us for a while, asking for tobacco and other things,

and continually appearing and disappearing at the openings of
short cuts on the farther side of the bends in the river.   They
offered us skins and feathers, and when we stopped in some
safe place, they even ventured on the boat, as if wanting to
take possession of it.   But there were only a few of them.
Amóngst them was a young and very pretty girl who brought
a deerskin for sale.   Her face was rather artistically tattooed in
blue.   There was also an Indian, with his hair drawn up behind
like a horse-tail, and with the true savage look in his eyes and
face.   He was naked, and seemed covetous, gesticulating with
energy.   On throwing them tobacco, they rolled down the bank
and swam to fetch it.

Two days later we met with another party of Indians who
were fishing with a sort of palisade two or three yards long
jutting out from the bank into the river ; boughs were carefully arranged against it so that the fish, meeting with resistance, are unable to escape.   The locality of these is admirably selected.   These enclosures point to the presence, or at
least to the proximity, of Indians, and do not increase our
sense of personal security.

They continued to follow us, but we did not stop our course,
as already we were beginning to be suspicious of them.   Some
of them articulated a few words of Spanish and Guaranì, and
being questioned in those two languages as to the whereabouts
of their companions, they shouted out, "Peleànno, peleànno
. . . . mucho . . . . allà," and pointed in the direction they
had taken.

These Indians, besides being absolutely ignorant, are unable
even to pronounce certain combinations of letters, such as n
with d, and therefore, almost always make use of the gerunds
of verbs, saying *peleánno* for *peleando* (fighting).   The question
arises amongst us, what is their real meaning?   Do they intend
us to understand that higher up there are many more of them
ready to attack us, or that they are fighting among themselves ?
But we are all agreed that there must be a large number of
them, that they are armed, and that we may expect some ugly
trick to be played on us, because for almost another 100
leagues we shall be in the midst of the Tobas, the declared
enemies of Christians, an indomitable, courageous, numerous,
and, worst of all, a well-armed people.   The word "Christian"
must be understood as meaning conquerors, for the Indians
concern themselves neither with Christ nor Mahomet, but only

with those who try to drive them from their land. Nor did they adopt the name in order to distinguish us from their other enemies; but it is in fact we who use it to describe ourselves by a name of more general application and of a wider meaning, which whether, for good or for evil, is no longer of these times.

We have frequently mentioned the Tobas, but whence is the derivation of the word? I have questioned the Mattaccos, the Chiulipos, the Chiriguanos, the Mocovitos, and the Tobas themselves, who never use the name. How, then, did they acquire it? I often put this question to myself.

I believe I may say that I have elucidated the mystery, and that I am the first to have discovered it. *Tobai* in Guaranì means *opposite*, and is composed of *Toba*, a noun, and *i*, a postposition (there are no prepositions in *Guaranì*). The Guaranìs live, and have always lived, on the left banks of the Paraguay and the Paranà rivers, and the Tobas dwell on the right bank, or just opposite them. They were therefore described by the Guaranìs to the Spaniards as being *Toba* or opposite. And the name remained among the Spanish conquerors of the Guaranìs as a geographical designation derived from a proper name. I consider this a satisfactory solution.[2]

[2] In confirmation of the above, I was told by Colonel Napoleon Uribrine, an Argentine officer who is slightly acquainted with the Guaranì language as spoken by the Chiriguans, that, at the time of M. Crevaux's fatal expedition, in which almost every soul perished on the banks of the Viloomayo, a river running parallel to the Vermejo, he was informed that all the Indians of the Gran Chaco are called *Tobas* by the Chiriguans: Now, as the Chiriguans, whether Christians or still living in a savage state, belong to the northern and western frontiers towards Bolivia, my contention is strengthened by their testimony.

The fact that so short a time elapsed apparently between the departure of M. Crevaux from Bolivia and his deplorable fate, leads me to the conclusion that his murderers were not true Tobas, but some other *Indiada* called Tobas by the Chiriguan Indian converts who accompanied the expedition.

The real Tobas inhabit the banks of the Paranà and Paraguay, from the frontiers of the Argentines and Santa Fé to the Tropic of Capricorn, which measured in a straight line from N. to W. comprises an area of from 100 to 200 kilometers.

CHAPTER IV.

PHILOLOGICAL DISCUSSION ON THE NAME OF THE TOBAS.

THE preceding etymology of the name Toba, as given by me, produced a dissentient letter from the Secretary of the Governor of the Chaco. The authority of the writer,[1] and of *La Tribuna*, the newspaper, in which his letter appeared, induced me to forward a reply to that journal, in which I alluded to several peculiarities of the Guaranì language, some acquaintance with which may not be uninteresting to the reader.

I will give, therefore, a summary of my reply, of which a translation also appeared in the *Patria*, a large-sized Italian newspaper published in Buenos Ayres. For the sake of brevity I will omit the arguments of my honourable opponent and that part of my reply relating to certain ethnical considerations without interest to the European reader.

La Patria says :—

" Signor Pelleschi derives the name *Toba* from the word *Tobai*, which means *opposite*, or *in front of*, and *i, in* a postposition, there being no prepositions either in Guaranì or in Chicciua.

"The Secretary of the Chaco writes in correction that *Tobai* means *fronte piccolar*, or a small forehead, and that *opposite* would be rendered by *cherobai* (*cerobái*). Signor Pelleschi replies as follows :

"'I do not deny that *Tobai* means *a small forehead* or *face* ; or its equivalent would rather be the Italian diminutive

---

[1] This was Colonel Fontana, who, two years after the author's journey, crossed the Gran Chaco from the mouth of the river Vermejo to the Christian frontier, following by land the banks of the river. He was wounded by the Indians, and lost an arm, and several of his party were killed in an attack made by the Indians on or near the same spot where they attacked the expedition to which the author was attached. See Chapter X., Part I. The same Colonel Fontana was despatched by the Argentine Government and the Argentine Geographical Institute in search of the remains of the unfortunate M. Crevaux.

frontina, from *Tbha* forehead, and the diminishing particle *i*, which may be pronounced either nasally or non-nasally ; but I contend that *Tobai* means *in front*, from Toba front or forehead, with the postposition *i*, which when pronounced nasally, signifies *in*.

" 'In order to prove this statement, I will make use of the very same example put forward by my opponents. They say that in front or opposite is rendered by *cherobai*. I contend that *cherobai* is a word composed of three words, viz. of *che*, meaning *my* when joined to a noun, but signifying *I* when used alone ; *roba*, which is identical with *Toba*, the *t* being changed into *r*, a very usual change in the Guaranì language ; *i* represents *in* ; and it means, strictly speaking, *in front of me*, in the same way that *tuba* in the Correntine or Guaranì language, becomes *tubè* in Ciriguano (both meaning *father*), and change respectively into *cherubà* and *cherubè* and even into *cherù* in order to express *my father*. Changes of this nature are frequent in Guaranì, and, together with the complicated conjugation of the verbs, offer almost insuperable difficulties to the foreign student of the language. For example, *in front of him* would be *gobai*, and *guba* means *his father*. Now who would imagine that *gobai* contains *Toba* and a *relation* and a *postposition* besides ? Yet such is the case, and these variations, together with certain subtractions, obey laws in the language, but laws so full of exceptions that they escape our observation and our memory.

" 'A noun is rarely used without its relation, because in fact the thing spoken of is seldom without relation either to the speaker, or the person addressed or some third person. The same rule obtains in Mattacco, the language of the independent Indians dwelling in the heart of the Gran Chaco. In my opinion this dialect belongs to the Guaranì family, and is consequently very difficult to learn.

" 'This is not the case with Chiccina and Arancano, which therefore, and also by reason of the simple conjugation of the verbs, appears to me comparatively easy. (Chiccina is still spoken in Peru, Bolivia, and in some parts of the Pampas and Argentine Paraguay ; Guaranì in the Argentine province of Corrientes, in parts of Brazil, and in Paraguay.)

" 'It must be remarked that the Toba Indians never speak of themselves under that name. The Mattaccos call them *Uancloi*, the plural form probably of *Uanc-lòc*, an ostrich ; an

C

appropriate designation for a tall, lithe race, while the Mattaccos are relatively short and stout. The Mocovitos, whose language includes many Toba words, call them *Ntocuit;* the Vilelas and Chiulipos call them *Huanicané* and also *Notocóit.* Now these Indians live on the other borders of the Tobas' territories. Moreover, it is well known that the names of peoples are generally given them by their neighbours. For example : the *Cafri* and the *Seres* (Chinese) actually do not possess in their language the letter *r,* which nevertheless forms part of the name by which they are distinguished, and the *Mohawks* have no *m.* *Normanni,* meaning *Northmen,* and *Austria,* a southern country, are simply names given by neighbours from the relative position of the tribes. Thus *Toba* will have been so called by the Guaranìs who dwelt opposite, and the word had the good fortune (for even words have their destinies) to be received and established by the Spaniards.' "

CHAPTER V.

THE CATASTROPHE ON THE "RIO DE LAS PIEDRAS."—THE MOUTH
OF THE TEUCO.—WIND AND RAIN.

Forty leagues from the mouth, at a bend of the river, where
on one side is a perpendicular bank, and on the other a charm-
ing grassy country, we saw two crosses, and a little farther
on, a third; pious mementoes of two unhappy incidents!
About three years ago a small steamer, the *Rio de las Piedras*,
Captain Wilken, with a crew of fourteen men, was attacked
and plundered by the Indians, who killed the captain and half
the crew, the remainder finding safety in flight while their
enemies were engaged in pillaging. Relying in the beginning
on the friendliness shown by the Indians and on the effect to
be produced by treating them with kindness and liberality, he
imprudently attempted to break through their lines, although
they were assembled in large numbers and consequently emboldened for the attack. He and seven of his companions were
despatched with clubs, while defending themselves on the deck,
the Indians seizing on the merchandise, arms, and ammunition.
Moreover, an ensign of the Argentine army, who some weeks
later was sent to punish the murderers, met with an unhonoured
death in the waters, being either sucked down by a whirlpool,
or snatched by a *yacare*, while bathing after the heat of the
day. We left these mementoes of the dead with sad hearts;
the circumstances under which we found ourselves contributed
to deepen the impression, and bidding a solemn adieu to the
spot which afforded us so impressive a warning, we continued
on our way.

We had now been travelling seven days, and had made ninety
leagues without having caught sight of the Indians, although
signs of their proximity were not wanting. On one occasion
we saw an Indian in the distance. He watched us from a
path in the wood and then disappeared. Our isolation seemed

alarming, and made us somewhat anxious. On reaching, however, a point where the two arms of the river that branch off 200 leagues higher up are reunited, we came upon some Indians fishing, who appeared to be taken by surprise; we saw them gather together and cross the river in their canoe, leaving behind them part of their booty, on which the *caranci* and other birds of prey descended greedily. Meanwhile a flock of red flamingoes, piscivorous birds, rose near them, skimming the water with their spoon-bills, and describing a semicircle with their long necks as they advanced.

Our little steamer has come to a difficult bit in the river, and we are obliged to tack; this retards our progress. We fear that the Indians will think we are frightened; they continually appear, vanish and reappear; they glance at us and then disappear once more. We advance, and just at a turning they show themselves among the trees and bushes, either lying at full length or sitting on their heels, some hidden and some half hidden. At first a few, and then on finding themselves discovered many more, take to flight, or rise to their feet, in uncertainty. We shout to them: "*Amicco, amicco*," and persuade seven or eight to draw near, some of whom know a few words of Guaraní.

We throw them tobacco, and explain that we want to navigate the arm of the river, and we understand them to say in reply that a few leagues farther up there is a waterfall and then a lake. I wish to go thither, but the river runs with a strong current in an extremely tortuous course, and resists our weak steam power. Meanwhile the Indians becoming suspicious, retire backwards a few steps, occasionally stopping, then fly out of sight, and from the bank we can see them further up, assembled beside a *tolderia* [1] at a bend of the stream. And I had armed myself for fear of them!

Being unable to stem the current, and there being on the other hand no object in so doing, we turned back and entered the other arm of the river. We cast anchor shortly and enjoyed a peaceful bath in place of the expected combat.

On the following day we came to another arm of the river a few leagues further up, and tried to explore it, but after about thirty kilometers we could proceed no farther in the steamer. Six of us, therefore, well armed, got into the canoe, and started

---

[1] *Tolderia*, an assemblage of *toldos*, or huts of the Indians.

up the little stream. The silence about us was profound, unbroken even by the fluttering of a bird ; only a white *yulo* more
than a yard high, and, as it were, impaled on a pair of legs like
stilts, with a long beak thicker than its head, was to be seen
standing motionless, watching the water for its prey. The
brackish waters ; the banks with moisture oozing between each
stratum, thus indicating the proximity of lakes and probably
some Indian dwellings ; the muddy bed of the river ; the land
covered with thick grasses and reeds, with a few tall withered
trees,—all these things completed a picture of desolation. At a
sudden turn we came upon a tiger[2] gazing at his reflection in
the water. He turned away, and was lost to sight in the woods.
Now and then we saw the smouldering ashes of a fire, some
remnants of victuals, a few stakes and branches that had served
as a hut, footprints on the ground, or some posts, mark to show
the middle of the channel, which becomes more and more
shallow, until at last we are forced to turn back. We land
first, however, and get ankle deep in mud, then we climb a
tree, and see forests in the distance, and the smoke of a *tolderia*.

But already we had not even a foot of water .... and a
few hours later we were back on board the steamer, and all of
us glad to meet again in safety.

But alas ! the arm of the river that we intended to navigate
contained only a third of its waters at that moment, and a little
later would contain only a fifth. And if hitherto our navigation
has been impeded, what will it not be in the 200 leagues that
remain ? We are provisioned for two months, while the rainy
season will not begin for seven! and we are in the heart of
the Chaco and in the midst of the Tobas !

It must be borne in mind that here in the Chaco, and
generally throughout all the northern portion of the Republic,
and I may say in all that part of this southern continent comprised between 40° and 30° lat., the rainfall lasts from December
to April, viz. during the summer ; occasionally it begins in
November, and may last until May, but this is exceptional and
depends on the direction of the winds. The damp, cold winds
blowing from the N. or N.E. or from the Equator fill the
atmosphere with vapour, while those that bring the rains are
dry and cold from the S. and S.E., or else come direct from

[2] The animal called a tiger in South America is really the jaguar.—
TRANSLATOR'S NOTE.

the Antarctic Pole, passing over the cold and arid tracts of
Patagonia on their way, or they rise at the Pole itself, driving in
heights above our atmosphere for forty or fifty degrees, and then
rushing down towards the earth's surface until they reach the
Equator as superficial currents of air.   This is my opinion, and
it accords with the theory of the general circulation of the
atmosphere.   I reject the theory that would assign a purely
local cause to these winds, although based on the fact that south
of the Republic the rainy season occurs in summer.

Nor can I think those writers correct who affirm that the
south winds are laden with rain, because, even were they so in
the beginning, they pass through an atmosphere continually increasing in heat towards the north, and thus acquire a hygro-
metrical strength so great as at last to render them dry.   Whereas
in these parts, for three or six days before the rains begin, a
hot and cutting wind, impeding the respiration, blows on us
from the Equator.   The temperature rises to 42° or 45° Reaumur,
and produces abundant perspiration even when we remain perfectly still.   It becomes impossible to rest, whether in bed, or
seated or walking, until, generally speaking towards the middle
of the day, the north wind begins to veer first to the east,
then towards the south, and, blowing chill and strong, drives
before it clouds of dust, darkening the very sky.   Then comes the
storm, the temperature sinks to 25° or less, and by condensing
the vapours in the air brings on the rain.   Whirlpools occur
at times.   On one occasion, on a December night, there was a
shower of fish, the larger ones, although they were mostly of
a size, weighing four ounces.   The biggest and smallest had
probably been deposited in various localities during the passage
of the wind.   These fish were from the neighbouring lakes.

CHAPTER VI.

AN ENCOUNTER WITH THE TOBA INDIANS.

WE have continued to progress slowly, making only a few kilometers daily, with frequent pauses while we extricated the screw of our steamer from the sandbanks that barred our way. At the end of a fortnight we perceived something white and motionless on the edge of the shore and near it a swarm of black objects. "Indians" was the cry, and "Tobas," as we approached nearer. The Tobas are recognized by a bandage or turban made of any sort of material and worn round the head, and also by their fine forms.

These men are beautifully proportioned. They are nearly all of tall stature and of a build that would make a man and a half among us, and bear themselves with a lofty air that is not displeasing. Their faces are not ugly, but of a kind that if placed over a figure in modern dress would extinguish any feeling of sentiment or love. They are at times insolent and rude. The white spot we had seen on the bank was the *ladino* or interpreter. He was dressed in linen trousers, and wore a military cap and brass buttons to match; the black moving points were the Indians. After exchanging some courtesies, four of us landed, and went among them in order to buy skins and curiosities. Among their number was a fine youth, with a pair of eyes of unmistakable strength and fire. He held a tiger-skin, with the claws intact. We wished to buy it, but he would not agree, and in the end the boy, imitating the spring of a tiger, thrust the claws in the face of one of our men. We smiled out of policy, but his companions burst into boisterous and malicious laughter, with intent to make us retreat. The thought of flight occurred to me, because, even when not chief in command, I have always held that in war the most necessary thing is to secure a safe retreat. The joke was becoming serious, and although the steamer was close at hand, it seemed well for us to retire.   There were no women present, and but few children.

To digress for a moment; the wearer of the military cap was a remnant of the great Paraguayan war, and on his buttons might be seen the distinctive marks of four nations and of Heaven knows how many regiments of different armies.   And, again, with regard to the bandage or swathe worn by the Tobas, a glance backwards will show it to be historical.   According to the historians of Perù—where every one knows the Spanish found a flourishing and civilized empire, and which, if I were disposed to institute comparisons, I should place in a corresponding rank with the period of our agrarian laws, and with primitive historic society and paternal government—the Incas, or reigning imperial family, introduced the use of the swathed head-covering; the colour, the material, and the size indicating the importance or privileges of the wearer, whether as an individual or as one of a class.   These historians also tell us that the *Inca capa*, the only *Inca* or Emperor, wore a headdress of massive gold an inch thick.

Now this custom must have pre-existed among some at least of the primitive peoples of the Empire, since we find it here in the *Chaco*, and we attribute to the Incas merely the law as to its use; their system being to regulate every person and everything by laws.

The Indians whom we have left had sold us some fowls.   The next day they returned in greater numbers with more fowls, and my reader can imagine how gladly we bought them.   The weather had turned cold and wet, and the Indians who yesterday were naked, were to-day, for the most part, clad in skins.   They were a picturesque sight scattered in groups on the shore, and not without a certain order, amid all the apparent carelessness. They seated themselves, in eastern fashion, on the bank, with their lances sticking upright in the ground at their feet, and bow and arrows at their side; with thick-headed clubs and a rope or band round their waist, with their netted shoulder-bags full of fish, rat-rabbits or rabbit-rats,[1] wild fruit, curiosities, in short of everything they gather together.   And it was curious to see them light their fire, broil their meat, eat it hungrily, and then entering the river, with head and body curved, reach out their hand and use it for drinking with wonderful

---

[1] Rabbits are never eaten in Italy.—TRANSLATOR'S NOTE.

aptitude. In so doing they recalled to my mind the pictures of Christ and John the Baptist standing in the waters of the Jordan, the latter clothed in skins and bearing a staff.

In order to light a fire, they proceed as follows : they take two pieces of stick, one of *cilca*, or of some resinous and porous shrub of the same kind, the other of hard wood. They sharpen the latter to a point, and rapidly twirl it between their hands on the other piece. The cavity thus produced fills with a fine subtle dust, the colour of ground coffee, which, becoming heated by the rapid friction, kindles as easily as a cigar or as saw-dust ; they then pile over it plenty of dry and easily inflammable materials, and blow upon it until the flame bursts out, when they can have as much fire as they want.

All this time there were no women to be seen. The glimpse we had had of the beautiful Indian girl had made us most anxious to see some others ; nor need our reader be in any way shocked at the wish, which was purely Platonic in all of us, while in some it proceeded from an intelligent curiosity.

During two or three days we were present at an interesting spectacle. The Tobas continued to arrive in increasing numbers, and finally the *Cacique*, or principal chief, came to visit them in the *tolderia*, which was situated about a kilometer from the river-side and close to us. He was accompanied by many other chiefs, and by numerous *Indiada* (Indian tribes). The women remained apart at some distance, but in groups, and indistinguishable. We landed on the bank, and the Cacique came forward and made us a speech through the interpreter.

He yelled like a madman, frequently slapping his thighs, and then shouting louder still. Each syllable was very *staccato*, so that the language seemed to be monosyllabic ; this, however, is not entirely the case. This mode of utterance is necessary to prevent one word from being mistaken for another, from which it frequently differs only by a slight shade of sound. He repeated the same things in different phrases, and made a long disconnected discourse. This custom seems to prevail among other Indians ; at any rate, in the Pampas, according to Colonel Mansilla, in his "Spedizione ai Rancheli."

He told us that his abode was near, that he and his were friendly to the Christians, and would continue to be so, and he invited us to come and visit him.

We replied that we could not at that time pay him a visit, that we too were friendly, that they must not fear us, and that, in fact, our friendship would procure for them cloth for garments and good things to eat. The great chief was tall and old, but robust ; his hair was white, an unusual thing, and short ; at his side stood an Indian with so expressive and pleasing a countenance that it was delightful to look at him. He transmitted his chief's orders, and gave him advice. He reminded me of the numerous country-folk in Italy, upright and well-to-do, with faces browned by working in the sun.

We proceeded to distribute tobacco and mandioca-flour among the crowd and the same, with a few additional presents, to the chiefs. Some resolution was needed on our part to give away anything in the way of food. But we bought fowls from them. We were informed that the Cacique's counsellor was the son of Colompotop, a chief celebrated for his fidelity and for the services he rendered to the Argentines in their war of independence. All honour to him !

When the dishes on which we had served the rations to the Indians came to be collected, one was missing. Complaint was made to the chief, and he immediately called to his companions who were going away, at the top of his voice, and seemed by his tone to be rebuking them. They returned, but we did not recover the dish.

Among these Indians are many Christian convicts, who have made their escape from Santiago, Corrientes, and Paraguay ; but they are not easily recognized, except by the hair on their faces. Men who have but a little white blood in their veins, and only a few points of the European type, become still less distinguishable in the costume of Adam before the Fall and after years of an Indian life. A youth, however, who had been stolen when a child had retained his natural light brown hair, and his face left no room for doubt as to his parentage. We called him to us, and he came : he pretended to be half-witted, but, on the contrary, was spying. The interest I felt in him at first soon died away, and every time I looked at him it was with a repugnance that I feel still. And yet people say that " *il sangue tira*," or blood is thicker than water. Another Christian was a chief. He was a certain Vincenzino, formerly the manager of an *estancia* at Santiago, where he was well known. He was a fine, tall man, sunburnt and with a short grizzled beard ; he looked like a diplomat. He had left his Indian followers, who were coming after to join the others. He uttered very few words, and affected to be unable to express himself in Castilian. This was an artifice to avoid rousing the suspicions of the Indians, by whom *Indianized* Christians are forbidden to speak in an enemy's language that is not understood by themselves.   Such Christians, therefore, remain mute and motionless as statues.   We gave Vincenzino plenty of tobacco, which he divided in equal shares among the Indians.   This is the general custom, and the obser- vance (or neglect) of it is the cause of the affection or dislike that decides the destiny of the chiefs.

I know not whether our good or evil destiny prevailed, but we were unable the next day to approach the shore where the Indians had assembled in great numbers,'and had waited, although the weather was wet, until eleven o'clock, the usual dinner-hour throughout the Chaco.   We had run aground on the opposite bank.   They departed in high dudgeon, and we heard them that evening at a little distance shouting their war-cry.   We did not see them again for several days, when they tried to kill us.

For many days we did not see a living soul.   At last, one fine morning, a swarm of Indians appeared on both sides of the river.   We were on the Toba and Mattacco frontiers, where various tribes had assembled for war.

Here we met with Faustino, who was destined to play so large a part in our life, and, alas! to sacrifice his own in our cause!   It was a glad day for us, and gave us at once a feeling of home.

It is well known that the Mattaccos are not hostile to the Christians, nor distrustful of foreigners.   Faustino informed us that they had lately been fighting, and had just made peace.   Each Indian nation has its own territory, and they will fight for a foot of land just as we do ; while to each tribe belonging to a nation, is assigned a certain portion of land, beyond which they cannot trespass without provoking war.   Wars are frequent on various pretences, and from the prevailing spirit of robbery. No sooner do they hear that another tribe is enriched in one way or another by the possession of animals or other property than they endeavour to surprise and plunder them.   Wounds, war-prisoners and loss of life naturally ensue, and these in their turn are the causes of future wars, which are undertaken with- out further explanation.   Every tribe employs a number of spies.

Fortune for a long time has favoured the Tobas, who occupy the best lands on the banks of the Paraná and Paraguay, being

about sixty leagues, or if measured by the windings of the
river, a hundred. By secret trading with Corrientes and the
Paraguayan Republic they have provided themselves with firearms.   Moreover, being farthest from the continually advancing
Christian frontier, they receive a considerable contingent of the
convicts of whom I have already spoken. In this way the
Vilelas and the Chiulipos have become mixed with them, and
the case will be the same with the Mocovitos, who live in the
south-west along the frontiers of Santa Fè and Santiago, and
whose language is not dissimilar, many words being identical.
The same thing will occur with the Mattaccos, who are contiguous to the Salta frontier on the west, and on the east to that of
the Tobas. Thus being straitened between two enemies, those
nearest the east allied themselves with the Tobas (among whom
we now found ourselves), and those on the west with the Christians, joining them in warfare. Nevertheless they all speak
the same mother-tongue and hold to it jealously, although with
some difference of dialect. For example, the Eastern Mattaccos always use *chiá* and *tzá*, pronounced *kiah* and *tzah*,
where those of the west use *ciá*, pronounced *shah*. Those of
the same tribe, however, make use of either expression without
experiencing any difficulty; they do so also with *chió, tzó,* and
ció, pronounced *kio, tzo,* and *sho*. For example, gamma is
tzonac, chionác or *cionác* (the last pronounced *shonac*) indifferently.

I have mentioned that the Mattaccos jealously preserve their
language. In almost every Indian dialect the new animals
introduced by the Spanish were accepted with their Castilian
names, pronounced as well as the Indian throat and the Indian
nature would allow.

The Mattaccos, on the contrary, sought for native animals
resembling the new importations, and if there were any, they
conferred on the strangers the same name accompanied by
a modifying particle, also belonging to the language. This rule
also they followed with regard to any new object. And they
showed acuteness in its application : thus they call a sheep,
tzonatác, tzonác, meaning gamma ; an ox becomes *chiuuassetac,
chiuuassét,* meaning a stag ; the horse is *jélalác, jélac,* meaning
tapir or *anta.* With regard to the horse, it will be remembered that thousands of years ago the Greeks, wishing to be-
stow a name on a pachyderm somewhat similar to the tapir,
called it a river-horse, i.e. *hippopotamus,* from *hippos,* horse ;

and *potamos*, river. Is it not wonderful that the poor, despised redskins should have reasoned in the same manner as the splendid genius of Greece! I also remark with gratification that the word *tac*, the modifying power of which I will explain later, would be better expressed by the Spanish *jota* than by the German *ch*. I must add in my own praise, that I took great pains to discover the relation between the new and the old words, and that each time I succeeded I experienced a real delight; and I may say the same with regard to the various pronunciation of the words.

CHAPTER VII.

PHYSICAL CHARACTERISTICS OF THE MATTACCOS AND OTHER INDIANS.

THE difference of size between the Tobas and the Mattaccos is considerable. In general the Mattacco is almost half a hand shorter than the Toba, without, however, being a small man when compared to us Italians. His chest is wide, he is bull-necked, with well-marked muscles; his limbs are strong, his head is large, his face is broad, with high cheekbones, and the upper jaw is deeply arched, like a horse-shoe.

The lower jaw is long and sloping, the forehead is seldom wide, and, generally speaking, partly hidden by the unkempt hair. The feet are well-proportioned, the hands small and wonderfully well-knit, especially the women's; the beard very scanty and kept shaven. Among their thirty-two teeth, the canine or eye-teeth seemed to me to be but slightly developed, and this would be explained by their habit of eating fish or fruit, and either very little meat or none at all; there are exceptions, however, to this rule. The teeth of the young men are fine and sound, but among the elders they are often ugly and decayed. The enamel does not seem to be precisely the same as ours; it resembles bone rather than ivory, and I think would have less resisting power. The gums are of a pale red, likewise the lips. Does their diet account for this? They eat no salt because they have none, but they are fond of it, and suck it like sugar when any is given to them. The lips of some appear swollen, prominent, and of a redder tint. The eyes are nearly always slightly oblique, slanting upwards from the nose, and almond-shaped; but some individuals have fine eyes, round in shape and placed horizontally. These latter are black with very blue whites, but in the oblique eyes the white is generally of a greenish colour, especially in the older people. The nose is broad, straight, not very prominent, and with wide nostrils, but it is not flattened. Indeed, they are seriously afraid of having flat noses, so much so that they will not eat mutton, which is supposed by them to cause flatness in that feature. This is a device of their medicine-men and soothsayers, in order to prevent the destruction of their few sheep, and also the consequent loss of the wool, which they weave and make use of in many ways. It is a pious fraud, resembling many that are taught by our holy religion.¹ And thus are men found to be alike in artifice and presumption in every clime and every age.

The hair is smooth, but in some few individuals I remarked it to be waving, if not curling, but I am ignorant whether this was natural to them or produced by artificial means; and I noticed incipient baldness in some. The adults have black or blackish hair; in the old it is sometimes, but rarely, white, possibly because very few attain to old age. The children up to ten or twelve years have reddish hair—a curious fact recalling the theory of De Salles, according to which primitive man was red-haired. This is an illustration of heredity. The hair is generally worn long and unkempt, but during periods of mourning it is cut off for a year. Nevertheless, they are eager to possess combs, the women especially. I recollect on one occasion being most anxious to obtain from them a spade or mattock made of *legno ferro*, in the shape of a double oar, with narrow, sharp blades. It belonged to an Indian, a friend of mine, whose wife was a handsome woman. I offered them a comb in exchange, but after thinking it over, the Indian would not come to terms, to the deep disappointment seemingly of his wife, who, however, persuaded him out of love for her to return the next day and offer spontaneously to make the exchange. My reader would perhaps approve of a little more generosity on my part, but had I freely given away the comb, I should have had nothing left to offer for the spade, in which I was more interested than in this naked Indian couple.

The above description of the Mattaccos will serve also for the Tobas, only that the latter are taller. I do not know whether their forehead is in fact broader, but it appears so, owing to their custom of drawing the hair back under the band they wear round the head. The same may be said of the Chiulipos and the Mocovitos, who together inhabit the Argentine Gran Chaco, north of which are the Bolivians, the Chiriguanos, and the Chirionossos.

The skin of all these Indians varies in colour from copper to clay, while occasionally some are spotted with black. The Chiri-

guanos, however, are of rather a lighter shade, approaching the
colour of bronze ; they speak the Guaraní language common to
Paraguay, Corrientes, and to part of Brazil, and dwell on the
Bolivian frontiers ; some of them being converts under the
missions, and some leading a nomadic life, remained under the
former Government and were banished with the Emperor of
the Incas, as we are informed by Garcelasso de la Vega, who
gives us some details on the subject which I will mention now
lest I forget them.   The Guaranis' and all these Indians of the
Chaco cannot count beyond five ; the Chiccinos on the other
hand and all the population of the Inca Empire can count indefinitely, as we do, and according to an admirably simple
system.   Now, the Ciriguani, although they speak Guaraní,
can also count indefinitely.   It is evident that they acquired
this faculty by contact with the Peruvians.   They cannot be
said to have learnt the art from the missionaries, because, if
such were the case, the Paraguayans would also have acquired
it, for we know them to have been instructed from the
very first, and to have established the now famous missions that were destroyed by the Christian governors.   As for
the rest, it must be remembered that along the coast of the
Pacific they are able to count indefinitely, and also among the
Chileni, a warlike and well-known race, who seem to have
extended through the whole of Chili, across the Cordigliera
mountains and into Patagonia and parts of the Pampas of
Buenos Ayres.   I infer this from the names of the Patagonian
Indiadas ; for I believe the Chileno word *Pehuen-ches* means
Indians of the Pine Forests ; *Motu-ches*, Indians of the Mol,
from *mol*, place of forage ; *Pilma-ches*, Indians of the Pilma,
from *pillota* or *pilma*, a game at ball ; *Carhué*, a fortified place ;
Leufoco, river-water, &c., which proves in my opinion what I
have stated above.   However, some of these names might also
be designations conferred on them by their neighbours the
Chilenos, without their being of the same tribe, as we have
seen in the case of the *Tobas*, whose name is a Guaraní
word, and as would seem to be the case with the name of the
Chiriguanos, which I derive from the Chiccina, men-of-the cold—
chiri, cold, and *guaina*, man, or, more strictly speaking, *lad* and
youth, as used among soldiers and in families.   And when compared with Peru, these tribes do in fact dwell in colder, or at
least, less hot regions.   The Chileno dialect seems to have
marks of affinity with the Chiccina and Aimará.　　　',

I must confess that my style is not consecutive, but the reader, if I have one, will forgive me. I am obliged to write in the intervals of my work, uncertain whether I shall be able to continue on the following day, hence I can follow no method, but simply write as circumstances or memory may suggest.

Concerning the Chiriguanos, I wish further to state that a custom prevails among them of wearing on the lower lip a small leaden tube not quite three quarters of an inch in diameter, passed through the lip, and held in its place by two little wings fastened to the inward end; while the outward side is engraved like a seal; this is worn as a mark of puberty. The wound in the lip is a painful sight when the tube is first inserted. If my memory does not deceive me, this custom also has been borrowed from the Chiancas, an Indian tribe living in Bolivia and, I think, near Lake Titicaca, or Cliff of Lead. The identity of so strange a custom authorizes the supposition that the Chiancas and the Chiriguanos, like the Guaranis, were closely related tribes. It is confined to the men. The women wear a white cloak and hood, called a *tipoy*, reaching from head to foot. This is of ample size, and is cut in front all in one piece like a dressing-gown. If I mistake not, Arago tells us that in Taiti the *poncho*-shaped garment worn by the natives is called a *tiputa*. The analogy between the name, the use, and the appearance of the article in question is very interesting.

I am glad to point out these analogies because it is popularly supposed and asserted that each tribe has a separate language, and in support of this assertion we are referred to the impenetrable forests, the unfordable rivers, and the impassable mountains. I, on the contrary, challenge any one to find regions more easy of intercommunication than these, where one may journey for thousands of leagues on level and treeless plains, or through woods where there are innumerable tracks even in the tropical regions; where the native Indians can swim like fish, and are actually amphibious animals; where the mountains are imposing, but few in number; and where there are populous cities in latitudes which would be regions of eternal snow in Europe. The truth is, each language is spoken throughout vast territories that are in many instances marked by no natural geographical divisions, and languages get easily grouped in one when belonging to a large family spread over immense regions. My belief is that in Chili, Perù, Bolivia, the Argentine Republic, and at any rate in part of

Brazil, viz. the South of the American Continent, there are two great families of languages, distinct as they are according to the two best known idioms, the language of the Chicciuas along the Pacific, and of the Guaranìs in the bason of the Plata.

Allow me to make two further remarks: the Chirionossos are said to be troglodites or dwellers in caves, fair, extremely fierce, with blue eyes; their women, too, have crooked feet turned inwards, so as to be hidden when they are seated. Both men and women are always naked. I have never seen them myself, but such is the universal account of these people. But are not these fair-haired, blue-eyed Indians like the fabulous Phœnix? A Chiriguano, who assured me he had seen them and fought with them, told me that their knees were turned backwards like those of ostriches! I repeat his exact words.

CHAPTER VIII.

AT CANGAGLIÉ—A HUNTING PARTY—A TOLDERIA.

To return.

We had remained on the spot where we had met with Faustino and various Indian tribes. The place is called *Cangaglié*, and is marked on all maps; it is historical besides, for a mission was established there, and another one fifteen leagues farther up, in the last century, and they were shortly afterwards destroyed by the Indians.

So many days had elapsed without our leaving the steamer for fear of being made into mincemeat by the natives, that it seemed well to take advantage of an opportunity that appeared safe, to tread once more on *terra firma*, and see something of the country. The information that there was a lake at no great distance determined us on getting up an expedition in search of sport.

Seven of us, therefore, went ashore, myself, Signor Natalio Roldan, Faustino, one of our men, and three natives. We entered on narrow footpaths, which are the high roads of the Indians. We were sometimes in the midst of grass so high that it concealed us completely; at other times on a perfectly flat surface, from the recent burning of the dry hay, and then the eye could scan a vast horizon. The least trifle arrested our attention, and seemed to have some great meaning for us. Meanwhile we saw nothing of the lake.

When halfway we came to a wild-gourd field. These are common in the Chaco. Near to it was a *madrechon*, or part of the channel that had been hollowed out years before by one of those floods that displace the river for leagues and leagues. In this same place we also lighted upon a Toba *Indiana*.

Oh, shall we see Indian women at last! and what will they be like?

Meanwhile our three Indians were quaking. "Tooba," said they, and seemed disposed to turn back. But we, on the contrary, remained firm, awaiting them, and resumed our fishing in the *madrechon*.

Ladies first. But what a disappointment! old, flabby, wrinkled, with shrunken breasts like dried figs; with squinting, greenish, half-opened, blear eyes, and with a few rags to represent fig-leaves. They were loaded moreover, with netted bags crammed full of filthy, stinking fish, that seemed like a mass of manure. They were on their way to the tolderia. They carried the bags or other load in the usual way behind the shoulders, held by a rope that goes round the forehead, and they looked like beasts of burden.

The women passed by, as if in haste, in a straight line. The men suddenly joined them, armed with their bows, arrows and lances, which they never lay down, and with the *clava*, a thick heavy club of hard wood, terminating in a larger or smaller head, which has caused the Mattaccos to call it *é-téc-tác*. I was struck at first with this name, which seemed to me an admirable imitative sound of the noise produced by the clashing of two clubs against another, but I discovered afterwards that it was a rational rendering of the shape of the weapon, signifying in fact, a large head. The bow and arrows are carried in one hand; the natives have no quiver, nor anything resembling one for their arrows.

They halted for a moment, and exchanged a few words, then a large number approached nearer, observing us, and we determined to push on for the lake, which we found at a distance of three kilometers from the steamer.

This lake was more like a bog, and full of rushes, reeds, and aquatic plants, with a muddy bottom. There are numerous lakes of the kind, all within certain limits, and called by me on another occasion *oscillations* of the river. They are portions of the channel, hollowed out in the season of floods, and in the course of years they have gradually filled up with water, until they are permanent shallows, in which the rain-fall and the floods lie stagnant.

In the beginning those that were of the same depth as the river were called *madrechons*. Both lakes and *madrechons* dry up in part, and provide good localities for fishing. On this account the Indians are in the habit of halting on the banks during their nomadic marches.

After some sport with water-fowl, we resolved, as it was getting late, and on the advice of our three Mattaccos, to retrace our steps. These men, although friends of the Tobas, were excessively afraid of them. They are friends, rather from necessity than choice, and their connection with the Christians is displeasing to the Tobas.

I was anxious to learn a few Toba words, and this seemed to me a good opportunity for the purpose. One morning, therefore, I got an Indian on board who knew both Toba and Mattacco, and with the help of Faustino, who knew Mattacco and Spanish, I began to set about my task. At the first word a Mattacco chief, who was observing us, came up, and, rebuking my two instructors, placed himself opposite us, so as to hear all that passed. After a few more words, I gave up the lesson, for I began to doubt the sincerity of my interpreters, and I never found an opportunity for resuming it. The *cacique* was carrying out the Toban law.

The next day we began, with the help of Faustino, to prepare an expedition to Rivadavia, a district near the frontier, about 500 kilometers from where we were. Our object was to obtain additional provisions and a reinforcement of our numbers. Three of our crew, well-armed and resolute men, taking with them a horse and a small amount of food, were to proceed under Faustino's guidance, to the confines of the territory menaced by the Tobans, and there were to be introduced by him to his friend the chief, Pa-i-lo, who would furnish them with a guide as far as the frontiers. The expedition would be ready to start in three days.

One of our three Mattaccos was the famous cacique whom we called *Mulatto*. In the last war he was said to have fought singly three of the enemy, and to have vanquished them. A short time before he had suddenly come upon a tiger in the forest. He just escaped its spring, and, clutching hold of its two fore-paws, stood on the defensive. His wife meanwhile unexpectedly came up, and striking the creature a blow with a club, laid it lifeless on the ground.

There are many fierce tigers in those parts. Only a short time before a tiger had suddenly sprung on a poor Indian deaf-mute, who was gathering wood near the lake where we had fished and shot, and, after mangling him horribly, would have devoured him, had not his companions, on hearing the noise, rushed up and put the brute to flight.

Tigers are one of the most serious dangers of the Chaco, both to Indians and Christians, but principally to the former, from the absence or scarcity of firearms. They are a perfect scourge to the cattle on the *Estancias*. There are many tiger-hunters in Christian Chaco, who breed hounds expressly for the purpose. When once started, the tiger is pursued by horsemen and dogs until he either turns at bay in a thicket or at the foot of a tree, or else climbs the trunk. A carbine, or more frequently a lance or dagger, puts an end to the combat.

A tiger sometimes waits for the discharge of a volley from the guns, and if he does not drop dead, springs at once upon the enemy. During my residence in those parts, two famous tiger-hunters were found dead, with their heads mangled by the teeth of some ferocious beast. Such an one will spring on the crupper of a horse, and nothing but a sharp dagger, perfect self-possession, and herculean strength, can in such a case save the hunter. Every owner of an *estancia* is a tiger-hunter.

A certain Signor Diaz, living on the frontier near the Tenco, had a short time previously killed his fourteenth tiger. Another estancia-owner, a certain Celestino Rodriguez, a fine-looking old man, had his nose deeply scarred by a wound from the claw of a tiger whom he had encountered alone and on foot. It was fine to hear him tell the story, and to see him show how he drove his dagger into the belly of the brute, whom he had already wounded, and who was then standing upright before him, kept at a distance by his strong arm.

The skin of a tiger, killed at no great distance from me, measured when fresh nine hands, from the root of the tail to the nape of the neck. A *cebado*, or man-eater, will spring on you at once, without waiting to be attacked.

In truth, the tiger [1] of the Chaco, is little inferior to his brethren of Africa, whether for ferocity, size, or beauty.

We were coming to a Mattacco tolderia, and so great was our wish to see something of the home life of Indians that we determined to make the journey thither on foot. After walking about a league, we came to a wood reaching down to the water side. Under the guidance of an Indian, we followed a steep footpath that at last led us to the tolderia.

While on our way we could hear the sound of the wood-cutter's axe, the clamour of their *cine*, or women, and the voices of the children singing over their games. We were much impressed

---

[1] I give the *jaguar* his popular name of tiger.

by these tokens of a life of which we were as yet completely ignorant. We were five in number.

On our appearance in their midst there was a general disturbance; some running to seize their arms, some to conceal themselves in their huts, and others to escape to the forest. They shouted "*Chihucle, Chihucle!*" meaning "Christians, Christians!" But, on recognizing our guide, who was one of their own people, they became quiet, and drew nearer to us, the men standing round in a circle, and the women in a group apart.

We had brought tobacco with us, pieces of cloth, and little fancy articles, partly as presents, but especially in order to obtain sheep and poultry.

With the greatest difficulty we succeeded in obtaining two or three fowls, partly because they possessed but few, and partly because we had no interpreter, Faustino having left us in order to meet the expeditionary party, of which I have already spoken, at the frontier.

I turned over the leaves of my note-book, in which I had jotted down Faustino's lessons; but even when I could make these people understand a few words of mine, I could by no means succeed in understanding any of their words to me. We thus got through a couple of hours.

This tolderia was bounded on three sides by the forest, the fourth was open country, the river was at a distance of half a kilometer. It is customary, probably with a view to security, to establish the tolderias against a wood, in which to escape if surprised by the enemy, who would be unacquainted with the forest paths; and in close proximity to water, both for fishing and for drinking and bathing purposes.

These Indians are said to be very dirty in their persons, but I doubt the accuracy of this assertion. I have seen great numbers of them in summer taking the greatest delight in plunging into the water at certain fixed hours, both men and women, but each sex apart. This seems to point to a settled habit rather than a momentary caprice, moreover they are frequently in the water when fishing. True, they have a dirty appearance, first on account of their dark skin, and then from the scars produced by tattooing, and the scorching rays of the sun that dry up the cuticle, especially on the shoulders. Moreover, tramping naked and barefoot on the mud, through bushes and forests, and lying on the bare ground, they naturally become travel-stained, just as each one of us who can

wash countless times in the day, if we chose, would do.   But I
assert that their habits are not dirty.

A tolderia consists of a greater or lesser number of huts,
built of willows fixed in the ground and the upper part
enlaced in the form of an arcade.   They cover this with such a
quantity of straw that it looks more like a waggon, so loaded
that the wheels are hidden, than a hut.   They fling on the
straw from a distance with wonderful accuracy, all the more
wonderful that this work is done by the women.   When
finished a *toldo* is strong enough to support the weight of a man
on the roof, and is impervious to water.

Each cacique, or chief, has his own group of toldos apart from
the others.   At times the chiefs assemble in great numbers,
especially when intending to make war.

Toldos are, in general, so low-pitched that one cannot stand
upright within them, but they vary in length according to the
size of the family or the number of kinsfolk who are to assemble
in it.   The longer toldos are generally slightly curved, and
have two or more doors, or rather entrances.   These are almost
always provided with a wing to the windward side, fixed up
somewhat in the fashion of a folding screen.   It is necessary
to stoop on entering.

There are various parts in a toldo, viz. the cooking-place, and
the place where the inhabitants live, sleep, or wash, &c., but
there is no partition-wall between them.

The kitchen is merely a level space whereon the fire is kindled,
and this is only done when the weather is cold, or in the case
of mourning, by the woman, who for one year does not go out,
or let herself be seen, or speak, except when absolutely necessary.   It is customary to cook the food out of doors, before the
entrance.   Every family has a kitchen.

The living room is that part of the hut in which the Indians
live, and where they keep their clothes and skins, when they
have any, to stretch themselves upon.   They wear them afterwards when they go out if the weather is cold.   They hang up
their various appendages, such as bags, nets, &c., and some of
their weapons, all over the walls.   Sometimes they place
four pitchforks about a foot in height, at the four corners
of the bed, across these they lay two planks, and then as
many rods or switches as will make a kind of wattle, on which
they stretch their mats and skins.   They make use of this bed

in summer principally for the sake of coolness and to escape insects and venomous reptiles. A similar custom exists among the Christians, only they use *forconi* instead of *forconcini*, about a couple of yards high, as a protection against tigers. I have slept on all these beds, and I can assure my reader it is merely a question of getting used to them ; sleeping on the ground is nevertheless more comfortable. When the Indians change their quarters, they set fire to the huts.

In Mattacco there are two words for house: *háuét* and *hepp* (the *h* being pronounced as in English or German). Now *hépp* means smoke, vapour, and mist, and is likewise moreover Mattaccan for steamboat. Now, is not the analogy complete between the Mattaccan and Italian languages in this instance ? We Italians name the family or the home *fuoco* and *focolare*, and we call a steamboat *vapore*. Here, therefore, we perceive another link between Aryan and Mattacco man. A tolderia is *héppéi* in Mattacco, the plural of *hépp*, and *Huna kel-la hép-péi*, "Let us storm the tolderia," is one of their war-cries. The *k* is strongly emphasized, and produces quite an imitative harmony.

As for the plural forms, I should state that these Mattaccos possess various declensions of nouns and all of them inflected, whilst the Guaranìs, the Chicciuans, and the Chilenos add to the singular form a particle expressing the idea of plurality. It is certain that the Chicciuans are more civilized than the Mattaccos, and so are the Guaranìs, if we may judge from their kinsmen the Chiriguanos.

Now to a student of philology an inflected language would appear to represent a more advanced condition of speech and consequently of civilization. But in this instance we have a clear and luminous contradiction to such a theory. We must be on our guard, therefore, with respect to absolute theories in matters of philology, both for the present and for a long time to come, during which the study of Indian languages in the old and new worlds may remain as imperfect as hitherto.

They stick their lance upright in the ground opposite the entrance to the hut, and place their arrows and bow against one of the walls. This gives a martial aspect to the scene, which is attractive. The huts are not built on a geometrically straight line, yet between one row and another they endeavour to leave a broad space representing a street.

It is delightful to see their fires while they are cooking. They boil. various kinds of roots and vegetables, in separate earthen vessels. They prepare a species of bean and a kind of potato that are both excellent.

The *Chenas* or women wash the kitchen utensils very carefully after using them. And when the hour of meals draws near, which in the tolderias is generally at 11 a.m., and again at 6 p.m., they appear with a spit laden with fried, smoked, and dried fish, in order to stimulate the appetite. Game or wild fowl or rabbit as a frequent addition to the meal, these are all very rich dishes, and the absence of salt makes them less acceptable to an European accustomed to its use from infancy.

The Indians feel gratified when a Christian is civil to them, and does not show contempt for their surroundings. When therefore the inhabitants of the tolderia had become familiar with me, I sauntered in and out, examining their food among much hearty laughter from them, while I repeated several times *hiss, hiss,* meaning *good, good.* But one must eat with the forks provided by Nature, except in the case of broth, which is eaten with the shell of a large oyster, found in great abundance in numerous lakes.

But I found drinking from a hollow gourd with a very dirty rim the hardest trial to my politeness? I shut my eyes, and a few seconds later opened them again, proud and triumphant !

On this occasion they were anxious to see our firearms discharged before we took our leave, and to please them we fired two or three times in the air. The shrieks of the women and the wrangling of the boys over the cartridges are things to be remembered. How wonderfully human beings resemble each other, whatever the amount of their civilization !

I was forgetting to mention that the width of each toldo does not exceed six or seven feet. .

CHAPTER IX.

THE CHENAS.

LET me say a few words concerning the *Chenas.* Mattacco women are in general rather short, but this does not prevent their being often very attractive and well-shaped when young. Among themselves they are seldom clothed, but they wear garments, more or less, before strangers. For a few days we had a married couple on board with us. The wife merely wore a short pair of drawers such as we use for bathing, and as she was young, well made and very handsome, some of our Argonauts, anchorites by necessity, found the trial rather dangerous.

To see this couple, nine parts naked, seated on a bench among the cylinders and pistons of the engine, and remaining motionless for hours, was to be forcibly reminded of the Garden of Eden.

When with strangers the Chenas are silent and impassible, but among themselves as noisy and gay as children. And this is the character of Indians on the whole.

The Chenas have a curious way of holding their hands when standing upright. Having no pocket in which to thrust them, nor fan or other ornament to play with, they cross them on their breasts, which thus serve as a support to the arms crossed above them. This habit would seem likely to lengthen the breasts, but it has not that effect. They are wide, certainly, but shallow and straight when young; but after suckling children they become wrinkled and shrunken and extremely unsightly. It must be remarked that both men and women age very quickly and bloom early, and to this must be attributed the absence of white hair among them, although from the appearance of their face and body they might be of the age of Methuselah.

I have noted the shape of the breast, because in other parts of the country the women are said to throw the breast over their shoulders in order to give suck to the infant they carry on their back. This is certainly not the case in these parts.

Women and men alike have an abundance of smooth hair; the former wear it rather long, but not extremely so; it is shortened, partly by being tangled over the head so as to screen the eyes and forehead from the sun, and partly by being cut.

The jawbones of a fish called *palometa* are used as scissors, both for the beard and the hair. These bones are furnished with a double row of very sharp teeth, those in the upper jaw locking with those in the lower.

The *palometa*, *raya*, and *yacaré* are the terror of bathers in the river, and in the lakes and *madrechons* belonging to it. The *palometa* uses its tusks to tear out pieces of flesh. It is a flat, oval-shaped fish, holding itself upright in the water. The *raya* or *razza* is a flat, circular fish, with three points in the tail, the one in the centre is furnished with a sting that inflicts most painful and dangerous wounds, and is used by the fish when attacked. It suddenly turns over and gives a blow with its tail. Some of these fish measure a yard in diameter; they prefer the calm and shallow parts of the river, and therefore remain near the banks. The *yacaré*, a species of crocodile, will treacherously snap off the leg or arm of an unfortunate bather, and then drag him to the bottom of the river and devour him.

Bathing, therefore, which is a necessity in the suffocating heat of these climates, is constantly interrupted by the presence of these anthropophagi.

The Chena after marriage is faithful to her husband out of affection, through training and from fear. Frightful stories are told of the vengeance of husbands, who have the right of life and death over their unfaithful wives. If these are girls, the husbands may be and usually are generous. There is no doubt that they would feel sympathy towards the Christians were it not for the prejudices of race; since the poorest Christian is always in a position to make better presents than the richest cacique.

The women are fond of ornaments and dress, but their habits are not adapted to wearing petticoats or stays, and in place of these they wrap cloths round the waist, which they keep on by a cord tied round them.

They arrange these cloths so as to display their fine figures without impeding freedom of movement, although one does not notice this at first Their garments consist of cloths, and when they possess any, they put them all on at once, whether summer or winter, partly because of their wandering life, partly from choice, because they are careful people, and seem to verify the proverb, "Quel che para il freddo para il caldo."

Both sexes are fond of variety and of bright colours, especially red. Nevertheless they prize white materials very highly. The Chiriguans wear white hoods, but, as I have already said, they live nearer the equator. When they wear anything over the shoulders, one arm is usually left uncovered. They like the shirts worn by Europeans.

They make themselves ornaments of skins and pieces of oyster-shell with more or less claim to elegance of shape. The girls wear a kind of leather bracelet until they present it, as I have been told, to the first recipient of their caresses. They make shirts of thread, doubly woven, and very, very narrow, but elastic; these have the appearance of petticoats, they are sleeveless, and are decorated in various ways with bits of oyster-shell; they are worn principally in battle, and as a protection against thorns in the forests, but they are a scarce possession.

Other ornaments are composed of feathers, especially ostrich feathers; they are worn on the forehead, the waist, the shoulders, wrists, and ankles. These are more especially used by men in battle, or at festivals, and when in attendance on their sick, as I will presently relate.

Some others are woven from the wool of their few sheep, and arranged according to the natural colours in stripes or squares. They have no knowledge of ornamental design.

For weaving they plant four stakes in the ground at right angles; on these they place pieces of wood on which they stretch the threads of the web, and fill in the woof by means of a splinter of palm. They have no knowledge of the shuttle. Weaving is *potzin*, the loom is *noccalei*, and the thread *huolei*. These words, having absolutely no affinity with Spanish, are sufficient proof that the art originated among themselves.

We must not, however, rely too implicitly on the resemblance or non-resemblance between words, in forming an opinion on this subject, because, as I have already stated, the Mattaccos always endeavour to avoid the use of foreign words in expressing new ideas, but rather adapt their own expressions with certain modifications. In this instance, however, such is not the case. Another reason for changing words may be their inability to pronounce them as we do, besides their custom of giving them a form suitable to the nature of their language.

For instance, Mattaccos cannot pronounce the letter *r*; other Indians, e.g. the Mocovitos, pronounce it in the throat, like the French ; they are besides unable to join *b* to *d*, and to pronounce, for example, *Pablo* (Paul).

The alterations thence arising are very curious. For instance, in this district there is a principal chief or cacique called Pe-i-lo. I tried to ascertain the meaning of the name, because it is a custom with the Indians, when they reach a certain age, to call themselves by the name of an animal or plant. Now, Peilo means *Pedro* (Peter), and Pedro was the name given him, nobody knows when, by the Christians, and repeated by the Indians that he might be recognized by the former. In the same way *Pablo* is altered to Pa-i-lo ; and *cabra* a goat, to *ca-i-la*, their intention being thus to reproduce the genuine foreign word.

To students of the parentage of languages this is a lesson on the apparent similarity between sounds and written words.

All heavy work, such as building the toldos, making the earthen pots, cooking, weaving and gathering roots, falls to the share of the women, whose business it is also to make the nets. The part of the men is to hunt, to fish, to make their arms, and to fight, while both sexes undertake to *melear*, that is to seek for honey in the woods, where it is extremely abundant, and to gather fruit. This labour in common is probably because the season of the maturity of the fruit and the gathering in of the honey being short, it is necessary to employ as many hands as possible, so as to obtain a larger quantity.

Before making the nets it is naturally necessary to make the thread or *nignhioi*. This is obtained from a *bromeliacea*, called in Chicciua *chaguar*, a name that is now used by the Christians also, and in Mattacco *húié*. The leaves of this plant are macerated for a short time, and then combed with an oyster-shell. After this they are laid in the sun to dry and bleach ; and lastly is the fibrous part combed, by holding the mannella in the left hand, and with the right drawing it over one leg, on which is sprinkled a little powdered chalk called *maccotac-muc*, to preserve the skin from injury.

The thread thus made is used for their nets, and also for making cord, which they call *nignhioiless,* meaning a family or gathering together of threads.

Some of the men are very skilful in manufacturing weapons, and exchange them for other articles with their comrades. They make them of the hardest and heaviest wood, and use the sinews of ostriches or strips of leather for bowstrings. The arrows, of willow, with heads of hard wood, are frequently covered with bone and cut into notches like some fish-hooks.

.

CHAPTER X.

A DESPERATE ATTEMPT.

AFTER we had spent some time near the Mattacco tolderia of Cangaglié, and had much intercourse with the Indians, we became quite fearless, and went about unarmed, but this was within a little of costing us dear.

We had returned to our steamer one evening, and a crowd of Mattaccos had assembled at the river-side, when all at once the *Chenas* began crying out, " Uanc-lo-e, Uanc-lo-e ! " meaning Tobas, and fled in all directions, some of them taking refuge with us.

Such are the *friendly terms* among these Indians, that a visit from the Tobas is a terror to them.

But on this occasion nothing further happened, and the alarm passed off.

The next day the Toba *ladino,* he of the white continuations, reappeared on the scene after an absence of two or three weeks, and with him came a troop of Tobas, among whom various hang-dog countenances belonged to *Indianized* Christians. These were amply clothed with one or two ponchos on their backs and their hands were concealed.

They came forward boldly, and one of them said in pure Santiagueno : " *Deme camisa pá mi señora ?* " and on our reply that we had none, he suggested that we should give him "*pañuelo pa su señora.*" But we would give him nothing, and just at that moment having succeeded in overcoming a *mal paso,* we steamed away, leaving them on the shore.

We thus quitted the tolderia, having already taken our leave of the inhabitants : a portion of whom, however, accompanied us on that and a few following days. Among them was the cacique *Mulatto,* whom I have mentioned before ; he was at that time friendly to us, out of self-interest, but afterwards he killed Faustino, who was his son-in-law.

The next morning we came to a narrow bend, and were obliged to stop for a time, in order to wear round it. It was 9 a.m., and although in the winter season, the heat was unbearable in the sun, therefore I sat on a carpet in the shadow cast by the helm towards the west, a scant shade in these tropical regions. At my feet were Mulatto and the Adamite couple lying extended on the carpet. I was anxious to learn a few words, and put many questions to them; but they never moved, and answered me with a smile that I could not interpret.

All at once, when I had risen to my knees to inquire the names of an earthen vessel, and of a pipe that I pointed out to them, and was just re-seating myself, several shots were fired. At first all was surprise and uncertainty, but the balls whizzing close by made us aware of our danger, and "Tobas, Tobas!" was the general cry. We flew to arms, and the Corrientes helmsman with another man sprang on shore, their muskets in their hands; but the enemy took to their heels through the forest.

It turned out that the Tobas, knowing the locality, had arranged an ambuscade at a point whence they could fire on us at close quarters while we were stuck fast; and this in fact had occurred. Some misfortune would have ensued only that our steamer made a slight movement towards rounding the point. The Mattaccos on board were well aware of all this!

A ball grazed the bench on which I was seated and my own shoulder, passed through the double wooden partition of the little shed, struck the wheel of the helm and splintered it, and finally embedded itself half an inch deep in the jamb of the little door. I have kept it in remembrance of the occasion. The helmsman and I escaped as by a miracle, due to the slight movement of the vessel.

The muskets were breech-loaders, and probably had been pillaged from the *Rio de las Piedras*, of which I have already spoken.

The rest of the day passed somewhat gloomily. I received the congratulations of those on board, on having, as it were, received a new lease of life. I comforted myself with this belief; I thought that having escaped so imminent a danger I should be unlikely to fall a victim on another occasion, just as when the next number to one's own is drawn in a lottery, it is improbable that one's own number will be drawn afterwards. The impression produced on us nevertheless by

E

the danger we had run quenched our habitually good spirits, and lessened our appetites for the remainder of the day.

The hostility evinced made us thoughtful. We were still in Toba territory, although among Mattacco *Indiadas*; our vessel made but a few kilometers each day, and sometimes none at all. We were in the very heart of the Chaco, where the *Indiadas* were numerous and continually increasing on account of a war then in preparation against the Mattaccos on the Christian frontiers.

We were warned every day that the Tobas were about to attack us, but had not the courage to do so. Meanwhile we were obliged to keep a strict look-out. Signor Natale Roldan and I generally shared the watch from midnight until 2 a.m., but our enemies did not attack us again.

Those long winter nights máy be imagined by the reader. Even after days of extreme heat they were cold, and sometimes wet. Other circumstances were not cheering, and our provisions were rapidly diminishing !

It was not possible to go with our guns in search of game in the midst of the enemy. Occasionally we contrived to kill a *charata*, something, between a fowl and a pheasant, but our staple food was fish. Poetry, however, that consolation of the exiled and the unhappy, came to our relief.

We discovered a musician, singer, and guitarist, on board with us. He was an Andalusian mason, called Don Felix, and almost every night we had some music. His répertoire was scanty, and I can still recollect two of the verses, as follows :—

> Si una vez en el mundo adoraste
> Y en el caliz de amor tu bebiste,
> Ah ! porqué compasion no tuviste
> De un amanto al jurarte su fé !
>
> *　　　*　　　*　　　*
>
> Me despierto y te busco á mi lado . . .
> No te encuentro y maldigo á mi suerte ! . . .
> Ah ! mil veces prefiero la muerte
> Al vivir separado de ti !

The notes of the instrument, vibrating for the first time in those atmospheres, the glorious vault above us, shining with a light almost as bright as that of day, or glittering with innumerable stars, made a deep impression on the mind. And a similar effect was produced by the vast country surrounding us, and the immense fires kindled by the Indians, which we sometimes perceived like a full moon on the distant horizon, and sometimes heard the crackling and bursting of the burning bush, like a discharge of artillery, and then we could feel the heat of the flame as it blazed out, and found ourselves in the midst of smoke and burnt straw driven over us by the wind! We seemed threatened at times with some inevitable misfortune.

The mysterious dark forests against the darker background of the fields; the solitude, the danger, the uncertainty, the distance both of time and place between ourselves and those we hold dear;—all these things stirred our souls with thoughts—half sweet, half sad! . . .

CHAPTER XI.

SUCCOUR—EIGHTY-FIVE LEAGUES ON HORSEBACK.

AH! it was a touching and beautiful scene! At a turn
in the river were five Indians hastily advancing. "Captain!" I call out, "news! news! Here are Indians coming quickly." For in fact it is not their habit to move fast,
although they are great walkers. They advanced straight along
the shore, arriving opposite our steamer where she had
stuck fast. They wheeled half about in military fashion to
the left, and informed us by gestures that further off there
was relief, in the shape of cows, horses, and soldiers, on
their way to us. We gave a whistle from the engines, and the
loud and prolonged sound was answered by a discharge of
fire-arms at a very short distance, and in a few moments
more three, ten, twenty naked or half-naked Indians rushed
out from among the trees and shrubs that clothed the bank.
Moving impetuously forward, adorned with feathers, and armed
with lances, lithe and soldier-like, they drew up in line on the
shore. Our ambassador with his *guardamonte* came next,
mounted on a mule, and then two soldiers and three cows, and
horses and Indians; the whole forming a picture on the
river-side that might well be represented on the stage. For a
week we have been without meat, and for two months we
have eaten it salted; our peas and beans are already exhausted,
and our dietary reduced simply to fish and some few wild-fowl we
contrive to snare; we are in a wilderness among savages who
are gentle, ferocious, and perfidious by turns;—let the reader
imagine therefore how heartily we welcome the succour that
we expected indeed, but not so soon. In a few minutes an
officer with two subalterns and other soldiers come up. We
despatch the canoe, and they draw near in order to get on
board. But what is this? I feel my heart-strings tightening.
By the side of the officer I see the *ladino*, who, formerly a

soldier, has already twice deserted, and now finds himself for the third time in the hands of those who may order him to be shot to-morrow.

For forty days he has been, as it were, sharing our life; after deserting he hunted with the Indians, learned their language in his three years' sojourn among them, and served them faithfully all that time. It was through his influence, when our progress was impeded after a navigation of forty days, that we were able to obtain permission from his friends the Indians to send an express to the Christian frontier, a distance by land of 100 leagues, to ask for help, which came to us in six and thirty days. And then he has been my teacher of the Indian language all this time! Oh, may we be able to save him!

*   *   *   *   *

Poor Faustino! our compassion harmed thee! It diverted from thee the punishment due to military discipline, which would, however, have restored thee to the society to which thou didst claim to belong, but it caused thee to fall a victim to the ferocious jealousy of thy unbaptized companions. Envious of the affection we all showed thee, and of the gifts we offered thee, although thou in thy generosity and according to custom, shared them with thy comrades and with thy partner, a daughter of their tribe; fearful lest thou shouldst depart from the equality that is so dear to them, they put thee to death. They first transfixed thee with darts, then when wounded and already unable to resist, but suffering and conscious of their tortures, they cut thy throat. Still unsatiated, the monsters became inhuman! After decapitation, they hung up thy body by the feet, and they used thy unshorn head for a cup, from which, when full to the brim, thy former partner will drink during their orgy, while the fermented liquor drops from the locks in which she has so often entwined her hands when soliciting thy caresses!

But if he who leaves behind him an inheritance of affection finds joy in the grave, and if the tears of the survivors like drops of dew on the awakening flower are refreshing to the dead, as our poets have sung, then art thou indeed happy! For thy friends, numbering three times seven, in misery will weep over thy dreadful fate, and will keep thee in dear and holy remembrance; thou who wast rejected from the company of the baptized, because thou couldst not endure the in-

human rigour of their law. Oh, civilization has its tortures
too! and I groan as I render this tribute to thy memory,
thou who twice wert outraged and contaminated by the lash
that scourged thy body in the name of *civilized* law! Thou,
Faustino Diaz, who wert trumpeter in the 12th Regiment of
Dragoons, an orphan from thy birth, twice flogged ; ever a *pariah*
among thy own people, a victim among those thou hadst
chosen for thy people, a friend in need to us wayfarers in
the midst of thy murderers !

*   *   *   *   *

We had spent seventy-two days in navigating the Vermejo,
when the long-wished-for relief arrived. Three days later we
began our land journey through the Indian territory, with a
very small supply of provisions, and we had also to leave some
for the men who remained on the vessel.

There were ten or eleven of us. After a forced march of
110 leagues, we came to a tolderia called *Chaguaral*, of which
the principal cacique was the same Peilo, besides eleven other
caciques. We had already left behind us another less important
tolderia called Cruz Cheka, at a distance of seven leagues.

We surprised the Indians standing in the water, fishing.
They were Mattaccos. This tolderia is situated on a beautiful
lake on the borders of which are the toldos, extending for about
the length of a kilometer in front and two or three rows deep.

A large number of them were standing in a row, fishing,
uttering loud cries, and stirring the water as they advanced ;
from time to time they almost immersed themselves in the
water ; then raising themselves again they shook the nets, and
struck them so as to stun the fish they had caught.

These Indians have various modes of fishing. That of the
palisade I have already mentioned, it works in the same way
as our weels. Then there is that of a separate net to each
man. It is fastened at both sides lengthways to sticks which
are held one in each hand. The net is two or three yards long
and about one yard broad; they open it, dip it in the
water, raise it again with the two handles held close together, and then capture their prey after stunning it with
blows. The name of this net is *hut-tanac*. There is another
mode, also with a net, but one of a larger size, from eight to
fifteen yards long, and carried by several men. It corresponds
with our sweep-net, and is called *huec-lu*.

They use arrows, moreover, and short lances. The latter are

pointed with metal, like our own lances. They let fly the
arrow by means of a bow, but they simply hurl the lance.
They do this repeatedly in battle. The bow is *letzég*, the
arrow, *lutéc*, the lance, *hén.* Finally, they also make use of the
fish-hook, *timec.*

Their food consists principally of fish, game being extremely
scarce ; the fruit season lasts only for a few months in the
year, and is at times very deficient. They keep but little
cattle, because they mutually rob each other, and slaughter the
few beasts that can accommodate themselves-to a nomad existence. For the same reason they do not sow, excepting a few
gourds, water-melons, and Indian corn, all of which spring up
quickly. But even these are grown in very small quantities.

We passed the night near the tolderia, at a distance of
about a kilometer. Towards evening we invited the caciques
to come to us; they were placed in order, and Signor Natale
addressed them. He explained to them, through an interpreter, that we were their friends; that they should not
molest him, and then our steamer would remain ; that they
should rather help him, now that he was near their tolderia ;
that they should give him fish and other things ; that the
captain would give them tobacco, pieces of cloth, and shirts ;
that he would immediately despatch Peppe, one of his men
then present, to bring tobacco and cows to the steamer, and
that two cows should be killed for them. He accompanied
with words and gestures the speech of the *ladino*, repeating
as he held out his arms and lifted two fingers : " Dos guassettas
. . . y tambien giuqquás . . . giuqquas . . . guassettas
. . . dos !" viz., meat and tobacco, pronounced rather in
Christian fashion, since the Mattaccos would say, *Chiu-uassetas*
and *iuc-quas.*

Meanwhile, I heard one of them muttering, and inquired
of the *ladino* what he was saying. "He says they are fine
promises, but that you may not afterwards keep them."
Decidedly, these children of the wilds are not stupid.

One of us presented a pretty young girl with several little
ornaments. Her face, arms, and part of her chest were painted
blue. He told her father that she must keep them for
notchequa or *nockicqua* (*notchequa*, means "my wife") on his
return in a few months.

At nightfall four of us went to the tolderia, and paid a visit
to Pa-e-lo, to whom we made presents as well as to his wife and

daughter. We wished afterwards to visit the *notchequa*, but she and the family had courageously hidden themselves. They were afraid that the proposal might be carried out, and flattered themselves, as we do in Italy, that now the favours had been obtained, they might laugh at the saint who had befriended them.

We passed the night in our beds (i.e. the coverings of our saddles and our travelling-blankets), sheltered by the ample foliage of an aged algarrobo.

During the first hours of the night it was beautiful to watch the numerous distant lights of the toldos, and to hear the confused sound of the women's and children's voices dying gradually away, and succeeded by a profound and solemn stillness, strangely broken every five minutes by the cry of " *All' erta !* " from our sentinels. And there was a spiritual beauty also in the contrast between this handful of men armed with the power of civilization and the numerous tribes of savages among whom we were encamped, and who, although both willing and able, had not the courage to attack us.

On the following day, after journeying a few leagues, we found ourselves near an ancient mission, now destroyed. An Indian who had accompanied us for the purpose, guided us to the spot.

We crossed the former channel of a river that is now at four or five leagues' distance, climbed a bank, and entered the wood on foot. Plants were growing on the site of the former habitations of men, and by their profusion made up for their want of size. We saw mounds of earth, some of them still having the appearance of walls constructed of unbaked bricks. We discovered some door-posts. The place where these Indian converts had their dwellings seemed to have been surrounded by a low rampart.

We questioned our Indian, who told us that his father had heard from his grandfather that, in former times, men with long robes lived in that place, and that one very tall and stout man seemed to be the chief. These men, he continued, sowed and had already acquired much cattle, when, after the lapse of a few years, the Tobas suddenly attacked the settlement and destroyed everything. The same thing occurred, he also told us, to another colony of converts near *Cruz Chica*. He added that these men were good, that they had many Indians under their charge, and that they gave them meat and other things.

Before undertaking our march by land, a bronze bell (*to-tah-tec* in Mattacco) had been brought on board, about forty centimeters in height and twenty-five or thirty wide at the base. It had been exposed to the fire, and a square piece had been taken away. It no longer possessed either tongue or ears. It is now to be found in the museum at Buenos Ayres. "Sic transit gloria mundi!"

We resumed our way, guided by sun and compass, through tracks made by the Indians, sometimes passing through wide meadows, and sometimes through thick and thorny woods, where we tore both our clothes and our flesh, and were compelled to a continual exercise of equestrian gymnastics, on account of the narrowness, and sinuosity of the paths, encumbered as they are by the trunks and boughs of trees, and intended only for travellers on foot. At one time we found ourselves in a bog; and at another we were struggling through a dense plantation of *bobos* and willows. We followed the long and narrow path with heads bent and knees closely pressed to our horses. The way was irksome, but not difficult, and led to the banks of the river, or to a *madrejon*, of which these trees are the immediate precursors.

Our object was always to reach a piece of water, where we could obtain fish, and allay the thirst of men and beasts. Sometimes we would travel a whole day before finding one, and if we reached it late, farewell to any success in fishing.

Those among us who were best mounted took advantage of it to press forward, for our small store of provisions would be exhausted in two or three days.

We came unawares on water the first night, a serious occurrence! On one occasion we missed each other in the dark, and were separated! We kindled fires that our companions might at least follow us. and late at night we reached a *madrejon*. Overcome with fatigue, we threw ourselves on the ground, careless of food.

We frequently came across ant-hills. On a favourable site there would be hundreds and thousands of these sugar-loaf mounds, generally much more than a yard in height and a couple of yards in diameter at the base. They were about two yards distant from each other. No ant was to be seen outside, but a regular labyrinth of beaten tracks half a hand wide. Within the woods, however, there are cone-shaped ant-hills, not more than two-thirds of a yard in height, and from four to six in diameter, with glacis outside each entrance like a fortress. And on the bifurcations of trees we often saw other ant-hills in immense numbers.   Ants in these parts are a perfect scourge to agriculture. Their presence in myriads of millions sufficiently explains the existence of the ant-eating bear.

We had now come to the 20th of September.   What thoughts and emotions this anniversary awakens in the breast of an Italian !   I was living in the desert, but my heart and spirit were in Italy and at Buenos Ayres, with my fellow-citizens.   At first I thought of the contrast between the life and gaiety with which the day would be celebrated in the public places and in the homes of my countrymen, and the wretchedness and desolation in which I should spend it.   Then I immersed myself in the political, social, and religious considerations appertaining to the deed so joyfully commemorated on that day.

And my hand, following on my thoughts, sought a pencil with which to trace my impressions and reflections and transmit them as the voice of one crying in the wilderness ; but on that day the ground was both table and chair for me, my breakfast had consisted of a little fish broiled with salt, and obtained after two hours' fishing ; I had made both my dinner and supper off a cup of sugarless tea, and had made a splendid day's journey on horseback beneath a sun that gave 72° in the shade, although it was still winter !

For Heaven's sake, when you travel, rely only on what you carry in your knapsack.   Leave trust in the providence of nature to the birds of the air and the beasts of the field.

After journeying in this fashion for ten days and eighty-five leagues, we reached the Christian frontiers, and made our triumphal entry into Fort Gorriti.

CHAPTER XII.

A FRONTIER FORT—ARGENTINE SOLDIERS—INDIANS AND CIVILIZATION.

" WHAT is a fort ?" You put this question to me hearing of our arrival at Fort Gorriti.

In the first place (I am speaking of the Chaco), a fort consists of a picket of soldiers, next, of a few straw-built huts to afford them shelter—mud huts would be luxurious ; and lastly, but not always, of a ditch that surrounds all or part of the rectangular area containing picket and huts. The number of soldiers composing a picket varies from fifteen to thirty. The huts are separate ; i.e. there is a hut for the officer or officers, a hut for the privates, a hut for the sick, and a hut for those under arrest. The material of which they are built is not always straw, but for the most part reed-canes, either placed upright or horizontally ; the roof is of mud.

You can judge whether the wind and the rain find their way through. A private, if he wishes, can have his wife with him. The bed for officers, soldiers, and wives is nearly always a hurdle laid on two supports, or a network of leather stretched on a four-legged frame, with skins and coverings above. But it is still oftener the ground, for the garrison is frequently sent out on expeditions of some days' duration, and the forts (I speak of those in the Chaco), are fifty and eighty kilometers apart.

I shall never forget one visit that I paid to a fort, down in a very lonely place on the frontier near Teuco. The picket consisted of twelve or fourteen soldiers, but six of these were on patrol duty, two were ill, one was out on service, a couple of old men from the *Puna*, i.e. the mountain of Jujuy, were disabled, so that they could go nowhere except on horseback : there remained only the lieutenant, a couple of soldiers, myself, and two of my men.

The exploring party had been gone three days, but did not

return at the appointed time ; we began, therefore, to be
anxious. Two men were sent out to gather news, but returned
having learnt nothing. A little later the dog that had accompanied them came back, but it was already evening and the
patrol party did not return. We were now decidedly uneasy,
and three of us were detached to search for them, leaving four
of us behind. Meanwhile a storm was rising. The wind began
to blow, the leaves to rustle, the sand to fly, the clouds to
gather ; the atmosphere became cold and the sky dark, and still
they did not return. Frequent and long flashes of forked
lightning revealed the distant horizon, and the thunder rolling
indistinctly sounded like the distant discharge of artillery, or
the dull sound of an earthquake.

The wind rose yet stronger, a few heavy drops began to fall,
the boughs of the neighbouring trees, violently agitated, clashed
together, and the old wood breaking away produced sounds
that seemed like human utterance . . . while we remained
there in ignorance of the fate of our companions, not knowing
whether they had been taken by the Indians, or whether the
latter, under cover of the wild night, were not preparing to
attack us who had remained behind.

The hurricane burst at length in all its fury, the howling
wind, the brilliant lightning, the claps of thunder, the rattling
rain, the rent and breaking branches, the shrubs torn up by
the roots and flung about the plain ; the crackling of the cane-
reed walls, the sudden gusts through the shutterless entrances
and through the openings in the walls ; the solitude, the
threatened peril,—all these were deeply impressive. In such
moments of anxiety the hand unconsciously seeks the trigger
of the revolver, and at every flash of lightning the eye keenly
explores the scene. But the tempest passed away, the heavens
became serene and shone bright with stars, the purified atmosphere breathed freshness and strength, and shortly afterwards
we were joined by our missing and saturated companions. . . .

As for the Argentine soldier, one must see him on the
frontier to admire and love him. From the lowest private to
the colonel in command, his life is one constant abnegation of
self.

Cast upon the desert, in the midst of dangers, always in action
and always most keenly on the watch, liable to fall by the
ignoble hand of a savage, he does not possess one of the com-
forts of civilized society, to defend which he lives in a lonely

building, forgotten for the most part by the happy inmates of the gilded homes of the higher bûreaucracy.

His pay is often deferred for years, and is diminished by half on account of the usurious interest charged for a bottle of brandy to warm, or a shirt to cover him.

Flesh meat, I may say, is his only food; neither bread nor wine nor vegetables . . . Ay, he is the scapegoat of the society that he defends.

Well, you will see him resolute at his post; and no curse will he utter against his ungrateful country. And while you find in the common soldier obedience that surprises you, you will also find amenity, generosity, and frequently, among the officers, education that you must admire. And thus, where it was least to be expected, you will find the time pass pleasantly amid the kind attentions shown to you, the discussions in which you will take part, and the elevated sentiments you will discover.

Among those noble soldiers of the State, who live for years in the midst of the most mortifying privation, fatigue, and danger, you will discover a strength that you would hardly expect to find. You will find men quite indifferent to the inclemency of the seasons, satisfied with any kind of food; able to live for whole days on horseback with impunity, or to journey on foot like Indians. They endure all this to a degree that is unknown in other localities, except perhaps in the Banda Oriental, and in one or two southern provinces of Brazil; they are soldiers who could pass from a peace to a war footing without being conscious of a change.

The army composed of such soldiers, strong in its iron discipline and its glorious and immortal traditions, is capable of grand and stirring actions. During its sixty years of existence it can recall among its leaders a San Martin, a consummate tactician and strategist, who crossed the Andes; a Belgrano, skilful in organization; a Lavalle, lion-hearted, the Bayard of his country's liberty; a Lamadrid, a Las Heras, and a Paz, whom Garibaldi has declared to be one of the first generals of the world. And among its anniversaries may be counted the glorious day against the English in Buenos Ayres; the Passage of the Andes; the victories of Suipacha, of Tucuman, and of Salta; and those of Chacabuco and Maipiu in the campaigns of Peru and Chili. It remembers the day of Tacuary in Paraguay, more glorious than a great victory; and the triumph of Ituzaingo over the German battalions in the pay of Brazil, although these had been inured to war and victory in battles against Napoleon. It may boast also of the independence of its country, as the result of its own deeds exclusively ; the only nation in the South American Continent touched with Carthaginian courage.   I say nothing of contemporary men or things, on account of the well-known rule, nor of that splendid day in the last Paraguayan war, and the admirable attitude of the troops during the painful civil dissensions ; but I must declare that the people and the army of the Argentine nation have a right to call out to strangers as their hand closes on the hilt of their sword, "Beware of it !"

For my own part, I can never forget the generous services rendered me by valiant and chivalrous officers from Cordoba to Oran, and the pleasant moments I have passed in company with the loyal soldiers of this nation ; and I have thought it a moral and social duty to pay this modest tribute to their fine qualities. My words, however humble, may yet find their way across the ocean.

There is a large Mattacco *Indiada* near Fort Gorriti, divided into three tolderias.   These Indians are civilized, and the caciques receive rations from the Government ; the others make shift in the usual way.   These are they who, during the harvest and preparation of the sugar-cane, work for hire on the *Estableci-mientos* or *Haciendas* for making sugar in Oran and the valley of San Francisco, and do a good stroke of work.   When the time comes that the surplus of this and other products can be offered cheaply and with facility, the labour of thousands of Mattaccos and Chiriguans can be utilized, and one of the first conditions of a splendid development be secured.

The Indians go in large numbers to these establishments. The manager visits the tolderias, eight or a hundred leagues away, and treats with the caciques as to salary, which consists of six Bolivians, or twenty-four francs a month and food, the latter is a mere trifle.   The salary is paid in kind, clothes and pro-visions, being rated generally at an exorbitant price.   The Indians come back discontented, and with the intention of never return-ing to the work, but the next year all is forgotten, or necessity obliges them, and they begin again.

These Indians of the frontier, as well as those living farther within Christian territory in the pay of some *Estancia,* preserve their spirit of national autonomy, their habits, and their religion, and remain independent, without, however, failing in any way towards the laws of the country, except that of not doing evil to the Christians, who on their part, without having recourse to law, know how to give tit for tat, while on many occasions they resort to arbitration. Among their own people their caciques are more than masters, and rule everything without interference.

The nomad Indian does not feel drawn to our civilization. And why should he? Would not the change be altogether to his loss?

While independent he may suffer some hardships at certain seasons, but he can compensate himself at others, and he is free; he is a sovereign citizen in his tribe and equal to other citizens; he does not tolerate an injury, and is free to revenge himself; and when among Christians he is respected because independent.

But what would become of him if he came amongst us? He would be a *pariah* in his adopted family, a slave, in fact, if not directly belonging to an owner, who, by involving him in debt, becomes the master of his liberty, and in the end owns all his labour, because a *peon* (day-labourer), if a debtor, cannot leave the service of his master unless he has personally paid his debt, and cannot obtain an augmentation of salary because he is not free. If cast out by his master, he soon falls, either from some failing, or from want, or by choice, or through public events, into the ranks of the army or the National Guard, under an iron discipline, without pay for a year, liable to the degradation of flogging, and uncertain thenceforth as to when he may be able to leave it. As a citizen, he would be an object of contempt to the white man, who would only consider him as an electoral instrument on the day of election, and afterwards as a being naturally inferior to himself. No, no! the Indian does well to lead a nomad, savage life outside the pale of our religion, and to preserve his independence or die. Woe to him, if he change his mode of life!

CHAPTER XIII.

MARRIAGE CUSTOMS.

To those who are unacquainted with the Indians, their life might seem to be both morally and materially barren. But such is not the case; the savage loves, hates, has ambitions and joys, encounters peril and acquires glory. He has a religion, and he has fears. Faustino used to tell me when I questioned him on the inner life of the Indians, that every human affection was experienced among that primitive people just as among ourselves.

The love of women is one of their strongest passions, and although to Christians the women may seem too much over-burdened when carrying heavy weights by the side of a man who bears his arms only, yet they are not worse treated than the immense majority of women among ourselves. The few exceptions with us are those women who do not work because they pay other women to work for them.

Moreover an Indian never makes a journey without the intention of securing food, and is never free from the possibility of attack. How could he procure the first or encounter the second while bearing a heavy burden?

The part taken by an Indian woman is in perfect accordance with her social wants and physical attributes. She does not hunt, or fish, or fight, but she attends to the house, the kitchen, and the family, and is remarkably active.

By turns she fetches roots and fruits from the woods, combs the *cháguar* and spins, makes nets, and weaves, cooks, arranges the house, makes fermented drinks for the men, takes care of the provisions, helps her partner to sow, drops the grain into the furrows of the very few fields that they cultivate, and then in due season gathers in the harvest. And she is a mother.

In all the tolderias in which I have stayed I have wondered at the multitude of occupations of the women in our rustic abode. They are always at work. *Tzina* and *chiequa* or *chequa* is Mattacco for woman, and *chequa* means wife as well.

An Indian may have more than one wife, but he seldom keeps them in the same hut. Their number depends on the means of the husband for maintaining the various families. Wealth though of an unstable kind can exist among nomadic tribes, in the shape of skins, sheep, and the aptitude for work or plunder that a man may possess.

There are very few, if any, caciques with one wife only. A wife may be repudiated, and then she becomes her own mistress again, but she seldom marries a second time, because she has nearly always lost the attractions of youth, because she hopes her husband may take her back, and because she would be ashamed to marry again before all her tribe.

To repudiate a wife, moreover, is almost always a cause of quarrel and vendetta between families.

In districts such as this one, where the women quickly lose their attractions, and where the men are decimated by continual warfare, polygamy becomes a social necessity for the tribe, or the place would be depopulated, and a physical necessity for the men and the numerous women, who must otherwise remain celibate. Nevertheless *traviatas* and prodigals are not wanting, and are called *amoeccue*.

The Indian is jealous, and cruel towards a woman whom he believes to be unfaithful. On the occasion of our visit to Pa-e-lo's tolderia, there was a woman who had not extricated herself, her husband thought, with sufficient promptness from the caresses of a soldier. We could hear her husband beating her within the toldo and threatening her with death. "*Nu-a-i-lon-là*" ("I will kill thee"), he muttered between his teeth. And another time, we knew of a woman who when her husband had been two years absent married another man. The former lay in wait, watching, ran after her, overtook her and kicked her in the abdomen before the Christians could come up to prevent him. The woman did not die, and when cured returned to live with her would-be murderer.

When an Indian wishes to marry, he paints his cheek-bones, lips, and the cavity of the eyes with red. He makes his proposals accompanied with gifts to the lady of his heart, and if she accepts him, he bestows on her a dower of such property as he may possess, viz. sheep, fowls, skins, &c. If the respective families approve the match, the new-married folks dwell with one of them; if otherwise, they remove to another toldo, and often to another tolderia.   When consent has been obtained the nuptial ceremony consists in the consummation of the marriage. This custom of the husband bestowing the marriage portion, may appear strange to us who are used to the contrary, but even among ourselves and among various Indo-European peoples, it has been and still is at times put in practice.   Thus, for example, in some cases there is the *controdote;* the Lombard law recognized the *mundium,* the right of guardianship that passed from the father to the husband by reason of a sum of money paid by the latter to the former ; and among the Romans was the *coemptio,* i.e. the *emptio,* or dower, exchanged reciprocally between husband and wife.

In ancient India it was the custom for the husband to endow the wife with money and cattle ; the same custom seems to have prevailed in ancient Greece, judging from a passage in the Iliad ; among the ancient Finns, and the Turks and the Turcomans of the present time, the bridegroom purchases the bride, and on this subject see De Gubernatis' " Usi Nuziali."

I repeat it, these Indians are men, and behave like other men.   Among the Chiriguans, when a man wishes to ask for a girl, he puts a bundle of wood at her door, and a roebuck or some other eatable ; if the girl on the following morning is to be seen lighting the fire and preparing the dinner with the presents of her lover, it is a sign that his proposals are accepted, and he goes to share the meal when ready.   A similar custom is said to prevail with other tribes besides the Mattaccos, but from the inquiries I made on the subject, I am led to contradict this statement.

The custom recalls one that exists in Pinerolo, where the girl goes to light the fire when her lover is to her liking—not to do it, when she is called, is equivalent to dismissing the suitor ; there is another in Abruzzo Ultra Primo, in accordance with which the youth carries to the girl's door at night a log of oak called *tecchio;* if the log is taken inside the dwelling the youth may also enter, but if not there is nothing for him but to remove it secretly, and take himself off.

In India, if the bridegroom was a Brahmin, he gave a cow to the bride ; if an agriculturist, and trader, a horse.   In the time of Tacitus, this custom of giving a cow was prevalent in Germany and appears continually in Isvezia; likewise the giving of a cock.   (See De Gubernatis.)

The Chiriguan caciques, however, possess a privilege; that of not being refused by the object of their predilection. They consider, in fact, that such preference is of destiny. The cacique reveals his wishes by offering to the girl a piece of meat or other food. The girl cooks it, and table and home become common property. The caciques, especially the principal chiefs, who rule over several tolderias have at least one wife in each.

Two or three days after childbirth, the mother and the infant are washed. The lying-in rarely lasts longer than this.

Those who are bent on discovering Christianity all the world over, profess to see an imitation of baptism in this exclusively hygienic custom.

The father recognizes his paternity, and taking the child in his arms says, "This is my son."

In some tribes it is customary for the husband to lie down on the bed, as an act of recognition, and among the Chiriguans he takes his place by the side of his wife and for three -days receives every attention, as if he were the new-made mother !

After this he rises from bed, but does not travel nor work until the end of seven days, when the wife also rises and washes. During this period, the married pair take nothing but water, and *mote* and *maza-morra*, a liquid food prepared from Indian corn, and bean-broth ; no flesh-meat.

A man has frequently two or more sisters as wives at the same time. And I believe I may assert that sometimes a father and daughter live in conjugal relations. If no one comes forward to adopt the offspring of such an union, the mother is allowed to destroy it.

Indian women are skilful midwives, and are employed even by Christians ; they are said to recognize the moment of crisis with great sagacity, that they then support the patient in a more or less upright position, and also it would seem shake her, without however causing her any pain. The action is accompanied by words to which the Indians ascribe great virtue, and still more the Christians, who do not understand them. The usual thing !

You must not think, however, that all their love-making is conducted solely in pantomime of a more or less expressive nature. They have words and expressions well adapted to courteous intercourse, and of these they make use. It is well-

known that the Guaranì language is harmonious, too much so,
indeed, when spoken by themselves and the Chiriguanos, whose
native tongue it is; but even the Mattaccos, the Red Mattaccos, who are lowest in the anthropological scale of the Indians
of South America, possess harmonious expressions and courteous
ideas corresponding therewith.

I remember on one oocasion there was a beautiful Indian
girl on board, who remained silent and impassible, not to say
gloomy. Faustino whispered to me, "Say *am iss* to her, ex-
pressively." And I said softly in her ear, "*Am iss.*"   In spite
of herself an imperceptible smile parted the lips of the handsome Indian, for I had said to her, "Thou art beautiful!"
Another time I had been present in a tolderia at the treatment
of a sick man by Indian doctors. A young girl was also present,
the most beautiful Indian I have as yet seen.

A lieutenant came up and said to me in a loud voice, "*Que
buena moza, ché?*"   "*Como no!*" answered I. And the girl
in the half-light murmured, "*Teniente toc tzi-la-tà,*" i.e. "It
is the lieutenant who is handsome."   But she said it so
gracefully, in a half-ingenuous, half-coquettish way, hiding her
face behind the shoulders of another girl, and with a sudden
flash of her eyes, that from my soul I envied the handsome
lieutenant.

The following is a dialogue between a youth and a maiden :—

He. "Who will that pretty girl be who will charm me so
greatly ?"

She. "Who will that youth be, to whom I wish so well?"

The above is a nonsensical ritornello that seems much used.

Then drawing nearer to each other,—

He. "Every time I see you I long to carry you off; who
knows that one day you will not fall in my arms?"

She. "Who knows? Let us go walking together!"

He. "If you wish me well, let me caress you!"

She. "If you wish me well, you would not caress me : you
have a wife."

He. "No one can say a word to me; I am alone; and if I
were not, I would not speak thus to you. Farewell! I go
away to-morrow ; I shall be two years away."

She. "Oh! I am sorry! I shall miss you!"

He. "Do not get married during that time. I will bring you
a necklace, a head-covering, needles and thread. Farewell!"

She. "Farewell. Come back soon."

I refrain from giving the original Mattacco for fear of being wearisome. But does not the above dialogue contain the very same sentiments and expressions that would occur to two persons of our own race?

A wedding according to rule is celebrated by drinking spirit made from the husks of *algarrobo* and *vinal*, and wild honey.

CHAPTER XIV.

FERMENTED DRINKS—NATURAL PRODUCTS FOR DOMESTIC USE.

THE algarrobo holds the same place here as the chestnut-tree in Europe, by reason of its usefulness to those peoples who dwell in its vicinity.   I have found it on heights varying from 100 to 400 yards above the level of the sea, and geographically situate between 30° and 15° S. lat., between the slopes of the Cordillera and the sea.   It is averse to humidity, which drives it from its natural altitudes and latitudes, and on the other hand, I have found it growing in an exceptionally dry and cold climate at 700 metres above the level of the sea ; invariably, however, on a plain.

The algarrobo grows in the woods in these regions, but also itself forms complete woods, and it blends abundantly with other trees.   In my opinion it is of the most widely extended growth, and deserves on this account, and by reason of its importance, to give its name to a forest region or zone.   It exists, in fact, in equal abundance in the woods of those parts of the country that emerge from the waters after the seasons of flood, and in the woods of the alluvial coasts of the actual rivers.

The timber of the algarrobo is excellent for the greater portion of covered buildings and for carpenter's work, but it has generally the defect of being short : a dark resin flows from the trunk, which is utilized by the Indians, but not by us ; the fruit grows in a shell which contains a sweetish flour, which is used in the making of bread and fermented liquors.

There are two principal kinds of algarrobo ; the white, which bears shelled fruit resembling our white bean in colour and size, affording an excellent beverage, and could yield flour also ; and the black, bearing shelled fruit like our broad bean, and yielding an inferior drink, but a most excellent and abundant flour, with which they make bread called in Chiccina *patai*.'

Both varieties have leaves simply composed, i.e. of so many pairs of leaflets along the axis and with thorns.

The making of patai, is a peculiar and according to our notions a repulsive process. The dried pods of the algarroba are placed under a wooden or stone mallet, worked by a long handle; when thus beaten the algarroba falls into flour without bursting its seeds, which are extremely hard. The flour is then sifted with more or less care, and is pressed into an earthen pan that has been previously heated in the sun or by the side of the fire. The mouth of the pan is then covered with fine sand, and it is exposed again to the heat of the sun or to that of a slow fire. In ten minutes the patai is made, because the only object in heating it is to dissolve the honey contained in the flour, which remains hard like cement when the honey has cooled. After this fashion they make loaves from four to over seven pounds in weight, and carry them in saddle-bags on the cruppers of their horses. They are thus supplied with a most nutritious though somewhat surfeiting food. It is not unlike pounded chestnut. You hold a slice to the fire on the blade of a knife, and draw back a delicious mouthful both in odour and taste.

Aloja is the Spanish word in these parts for fermented liquor; in Chiccina it is called *chicha;* in Mattacco, *huna;* in Mocovite, *na-na* and *nanna;* in Vilela, *tsucque.*

The mode of manufacture, both in Peru and among the Indians, is by masticating a portion of the substance and mixing it with the whole. This causes fermentation, for the saliva, as we know, contains *diastasia,* which being thus placed in contact with the cotyledons of the seeds converts the amilaceous substance into *glucosio,* or sugar of grape. The seeds are thus rendered soluble in water, and produce alcohol when fermented. The Indians are ignorant of these matters, but they are very observant, and have discovered the effect of a process which is highly nauseating to European lookers-on.

The very same method is followed in China for bread-making, and in the East Indies for the manufacture of spirituous drinks. And among ourselves, who is ignorant of the habit of wet-nurses and nursing mothers of chewing the pap before giving a spoonful to their infant? Notwithstanding the ignorance of those who employ this method, and the ridicule and nausea it excites in eye-witnesses, it tends to a most useful end, and is ratified by science.

Bowls of wood or cocoanut are kept in the toldos, in which

the Indians, who are chewing all day, spit out the husks.
At a certain hour, the women and children set about
breaking and chewing the seeds, and the babies amuse themselves by snatching handfuls in their little plump fists, and
hiding them in their mouths and spitting over and over again
into the bowls.   Frequently, too, the adults assemble for the
purpose, and then the preparation of aloja serves as an occasion
for rejoicing.   The unmasticated part is pounded in a mortar
made invariably of *yuchan*, a tree which I will describe.   The
whole is placed in a cylinder made of the trunk of the same tree.
Sufficient water is added to make two or three barrels of aloja at
a time.

In twelve hours the aloja is made, and is of a sour-sweet taste
and a yellowish colour.   Its tartness stimulates the appetite.   I
prefer it to any other drink, wine included.   If taken in quantity
it is inebriating, but the effect soon passes off and does not produce sickness.   At least this is the result of my observation of
others.

The season of the ripening of the algarroba corresponds with
that of the *vinal*, which is less good, but can be used to make
aloja.   Next comes the *chañar*, the fruit of which is sweetish,
small, round, yellow, and nut-like ; it is eaten raw, and is also
boiled and a syrup made from it, pleasant in flavour and with
medicinal properties, according to these tribes, for relieving cough
and asthma.   The trunk and leaves of the *chañar* when young
are almost like those of the tamarind, but the branches resemble
the eucalyptus.   A little later than the algarroba comes the
mistol, corresponding to our jujube-tree, or *Rhamnus-zizyphus*,
although with a slight difference.   The fruit, mixed with algarroba, is used to make patai ; and it is preserved besides, tightly
pressed down in skins.   At the same season, some sooner some
later, all the other fruits ripen, whereas in the colder Chaco
they come to maturity in October and December (the spring
and summer months), and farther south, towards Tucuman,
from November to February.

The fruit season, especially an abundant one, and if we
include the time during which some of the fruits can be preserved, lasts from four to five months.   It is the Indians'
carnival.

In order to preserve the algarroba they construct small huts,
which they raise on four supports, for the purpose of ventilation,
and to preserve it from ants and other insects.   It is pretty *to*

see these little cupolas rising above the toldos like our belfries. Each tolderia prides itself on displaying a greater number than the others. They preserve vinal, and some other roots and fruits, that can be or ought to be cooked in a dry state, in the same way.

When the aloja is ready, which should be about 11 a.m., all the men assemble round the cylinder of *yuchan*, sitting on the ground like Mussulmans ; and with two or three empty gourds reach the liquor and hand it to each other, conversing meanwhile on their affairs—such as battles, harvests, news of any kind, gossip ; and laughing Homerically over a curious adventure or a play upon words. This lasts for three or four hours, or even longer. When the liquor is finished they consume the solid matter that has remained at the bottom ; the women and children take no share in the proceedings.

They esteem the algarroba very highly ; a celebrated head cacique called *Granadero* by the Christians, on account of his height, and *Chiatzutac* by the Mattaccos, in allusion to his size and nation, replied when asked how he was, " Bien yo, yo rico, yo teniendo, mucha algarroba yo rico." They are stingy, too, with regard to algarroba and aloja, and will not exchange it, except under extraordinary circumstances, for other things ; nor will they invite any one, except grudgingly and with much ado, to drink with them.

One morning I found a crowd of about forty Indians round a *giuccian* of aloja. On seeing me they all cried out : " *Iuan !* *Iuan !* " (" Gianni ! Gianni !") " *júc-qu-ás, júc-qu-ás* " (" tobacco, tobacco "); and I replied, " *Hué-ni-tde, nikioc-lá-pac* " (" I have not any ; I will give you some shortly"). They then invited me to drink with them, but, on my first refusal, they did not ask me a second time, and the cacique said, " *No hijito, no ; nosotros tomanno, tu dánno tahuaco* " (" No, my son, no, we will drink ; you shall give tobacco "). We were exchanging courtesies— rather Indian ones certainly—but courtesies, nevertheless. Wishing to please them, I then endeavoured to say a few words in their language, and finally took my leave, saying, " *Amecná, nu jopil nuháuet, nutpinlá pác, niochioc-lá júc-qu-ás* " (" Good-bye, I am going home ; I will soon return ; I will give tobacco"). They were all delighted, because I had used their language, and had promised them tobacco, and they shouted, " *Amecná, amecná ; tapil ccaelitt* " (" Good-bye, good-bye ; come back soon "). I returned two or three hours later with my wallets crammed full of cut tobacco, and found them still drinking. Scarcely had they perceived me when they reminded me of my promise, which I thought they had forgotten in the fumes of drink. I distributed it among them ; but when all was finished, they still asked for more. At last I held the bags upside down, crying " *Namhuen, namhuen* " ("I have no more"). Convinced by my eloquent demonstration, they concluded with " *Hée, hée*," meaning, " Very good." But they did not renew the invitation to drink.

Indians make a very poor mouth, and are grudging of their belongings to Christians ; if you will believe them, they are as poor as Job !

A remark just occurs to me that I will note, although out of its place, lest I should forget it. Children up to eight or ten years of age have such large stomachs that they have to be bandaged at the height of the navel, but the size diminishes gradually, and in manhood their figures are remarkably slight.

I think it opportune to remark in this place that the algarroba belongs to the family of our carob-tree (*Ceratonia siliqua*), and the scientific name given it by botanists is *Prosopis algarrobo*. It is of immense importance in the domestic economy of savages and of the inhabitants of the desert country. It therefore claims our attention. Its foliage extends to ten feet or more in diameter, but is not very dense, either from the small number of leaves, or still more from their highly indentated shape. Nevertheless, it affords a plenteous shade. The bark is very rugged, resembling that of the vine.

The vinal (*Prosopis ruscifolia*) is a low tree, but with ample foliage; it is remarkable for thorns ten or fifteen centimeters in length, which inflict most dangerous wounds. The leaves are about the size of acacia leaves, but more pointed and rather rough. They are said to be an efficacious remedy for weak eyes. ·

The scientific name of the chañar is *Gurliaea decorticans*, that of the mistol, *Zizyphus mistol*.

All these fruits are eagerly devoured by cattle, and algarroba and vinal are excellent for fattening horses and cows.

The plum-tree grows wild, but it is scarce, at least so far as I have seen. The flavour of this fruit is pleasant, all the more so from the absence of the cultivated plum in these parts.

During the Aloja Carnival frequent quarrels take place. There is much fighting, and some deaths occur, not only among the Indians, but also among the Christians of the Chaco.

I will now say two words concerning the *yuchan* (*Palo briacb*), and the *Chorisea insignis*, which might be called a cotton-tree. The shape is peculiar. The trunk resembles an oil jar, that is to say, it is small at the base, large in the middle, and small again at the bifurcation of the branches. The diameter of the trunk attains two yards; it is full of knots, and is four or five yards in height, when full grown, and is often united with another as far as the base. The foliage commences with two branches only, which are afterwards subdivided, and form an ample canopy, eight or ten yards or more in diameter. The leaves are like those of our nut-trees, but rather smaller, and of a beautiful colour.

The bark is cut into strips for binding; it is also used for roofing, for wrapping and tying up rolls of tobacco, and for other like purposes. From the trunk the Indians make their canoes in one single piece. To do this, they need only scoop it out with an instrument of some kind, the wood being soft when fresh cut, and becoming harder than cork, although of the same nature, when dry. The Mattaccos call the canoe *cuo-kiac*, meaning a duck.

The special value, however, of the yuchan lies in its fruit, which resembles a lemon in shape, colour, and size. When ripe (from November to January, according to the locality), the fruit divides in four, and a feathery tuft unfolds of perfectly white cotton that gradually falls from the tree. An open lemon is the size of a large doubled fist. The tree bears hundreds of these all the year round.

The Indians make some use of the cotton, the Christians none; nevertheless, in Catamarca, where there are a few of these trees, I saw some white goods manufactured from it, that ranked first in the Cordoba Exhibition.

There are immense numbers of yuchans in the Chaco, standing amongst the hard-wooded trees in the lands liable to immersion. If an industrial use could be made of the cotton furnished by the yuchan and the chaguar—the latter affording material for cordage, and both trees extending over immense districts and requiring no cultivation—a very valuable trade would be inaugurated.

Another very interesting tree, both for its domestic and also, perhaps, for its industrial uses, is the *pacará* (*Euterolobium timboiva*). This is a magnificent tree, and one of the most beautiful for height, size, and foliage. The leaves are like those of our sorb-apple, but are larger. It belongs to the *mimosa* family.   The fruit is oblong in shape, its colour a dark chestnut, about an inch and a half in length, and it contains from twelve to fifteen per cent of saponina.   It is used for cleaning clothes and woollens.

In order to conclude where we began, I will add that the Indians drink largely of the liquors used by the Christians, and will eat hemp until they are stupefied.

CHAPTER XV.

WAR.

THE Indians delight in warfare. It is necessary to state this, because they fight very frequently, and are in a state, if I may permit myself the expression, of continual scuffle.,

One war follows on another, that the vanquished may take revenge for their losses, and the victorious gratify their increasing taste for successful battle. To have fished, hunted, or gleaned on the territory of others, is sufficient reason for a war, or to have to revenge some injury, or, in short, any hope of plunder.

War, however, is not carried on strategically, one battle following another until the enemy is no longer able to defend himself; it is rather a system of attacking the tolderias by surprise, and plundering them of goods, cattle, children, and sometimes of women also.

For this reason, in wooded districts, the tolderias are always built with two sides against the forest, for refuge in case of assault. It is impossible for the enemy to follow in pursuit through a labyrinth of foot-paths known only to the inhabitants of that particular tolderia.

In order to reassemble afterwards in a common meeting-place, the inmates guide themselves not only by the indications of footmarks, but they also twist off small branches or tufts of grass at cross-roads, to give warning to their companions who are on the look-out for these previously concerted signals.

Another mode of communication is that of lighting fires. During our march through the Chaco we were always surrounded by fires at a greater or less distance, occasionally of immense extent. And often, when we thought we had been completely isolated, we found our arrival at some Indiada had been expected, and that the order of our march was well known.

The Indians employ numerous spies and explorers; the

Mattacco word for the former is *niguaiecque*, and for the latter *guéicass*.

They seem to have one elementary notion of military tactics, since they have a cacique-general, ordinary caciques, and chiefs of half-cohorts. The first is *Canniat tizán*, the second *canniat*, and I am ignorant of the Mattacco for the third. The caciques-general are elected from the second grade, and these again from the chiefs of half-cohorts, who are themselves chosen by the people, generally from the sons of deceased chiefs, if grown up, courageous and good. The same passions are aroused in these elections as among ourselves.

Moreover, another order of persons exists called *nee-yat* corresponding with the Spanish *caballero* and the Italian *galant'uomo*. Thus Christians, who appear to belong to this category, are called by them *nee-yat*. Analogous distinctions probably exist among other Indian tribes. In Peru, and wherever the Chicciua language is spoken, caballeros are called *viracoccia* and *ueracoccia*.

On the election of a cacique-general, the electors, if able, come and visit him, and on such an occasion the usual eating and drinking takes place. A cacique-general usually rules over several tolderias at some distance from each other. *Tzi-ckiac* is the Mattacco word for his visits to them. The authority exercised by the cacique-general over the Indians of the Chaco is purely military; in time of peace they scarcely exert any active power, unless with regard to foreign affairs. As to these they receive information from the tribes living near foreigners, both in arranging any business, or in contriving a war or a peace. No one, however, is bound by their acts, and the common people, the *mob*, are free to refuse to make war, although their pride seldom allows them to abstain from it.

When a cacique wishes to make an attack he asks the opinion of the elders, and of persons of influence, and if they approve, he invites all who will to follow him.

Sometimes the respected chiefs of various tolderias agree together long beforehand on a proposed attack. When we reached the tolderia of the *Ciaguarál*, we found an assembly of twelve or thirteen caciques, all of them Mattaccos, and expecting their allies the Tobas, in conjunction with whom they shortly afterwards invaded the territory of some other Mattaccos, who, three months before, had inflicted a defeat on them.

On starting for war they utter threatening and joyful shouts;

and stain parts of the face and body with black, and sometimes tangle still more their entangled hair, till they look like *troubled spirits,* to use the expression of an Indian Christian. At the moment of battle those who possess any feathers fix them on their heads, their waist and even their ankles, giving the preference to red and yellow ones. If they wear any clothing it is bound tightly round the waist, and when actually fighting they utter loud cries.

The custom of painting the body for war is found among all wild tribes, and was practised by the peoples whom the Romans called barbarians. According to Claudian, for instance, the Sicambrians painted their faces bright red before battle.

The caciques are entitled to the post of honour in the thickest of the fight, resulting always in the death of some of them. If the invaders are victorious they plunder, and pursue the women, children, and cattle, and on departing set fire to the tolderia.

No quarter is given to the combatants, and they seldom spare the lives of the grown-up women, fearing them either as spies, or as unlikely to train properly the children they have carried off, and if they are old, despising them as useless. But they take the children under ten or twelve years, to bring them up as warriors or as wives for the benefit of the tribe.

These customs should not appear more barbarous to us than those of the Scythians, who in the times of the Romans dwelt between the Don and the Danube, and were accustomed to kill their prisoners in order to spare themselves the trouble of guarding them in their nomadic life. And what have we to say when the Romans, after their conversion to Christianity, threw their prisoners into the circus to be tormented by wild beasts amid the insults of the populace. Listen to the compliment contained in the panegyric repeated by a great Christian personage to Constantine the Great, the Victor Emmanuel of Christianity. "With the blood of the Franks you have increased the splendour of our games; you have given us the joyful sight of innumerable prisoners torn to pieces by wild beasts; and the expiring barbarians were still more outraged by the insults of their conquerors than by the teeth of the brutes or the agony of death."

I recall these things to prove that in every time and place human nature is the same.

By these expeditious means the Indians avoid the shame and dangers of slavery, which moreover would be incompatible with their wandering life, their continual wars, the scarcity of their food, and finally with the independence of their own character, which leads them to inflict or suffer death rather than endure slavery. Nevertheless we may consider the extraordinary effects such customs produce on the existence and distribution of tribes, since a succession of victories on the part of one, or several allied tribes, may involve the complete destruction and disappearance of others.

Whosoever kills an enemy wears as a trophy, if he has time to secure it, the scalp with the hair, the ears, and possibly a fold of skin from the back of the neck. He forms it to the shape of a cup by means of a bulrush or a flexible twig which he binds and stitches all round the edge ; then, while still bloody, he fills it with liquor, and holding it by the hair passes it round to his companions, who empty it as they drink in honour of the victor and in scorn of the vanquished. Another way is to hold the scalp by the edge and pour out the liquor in drops over the hair and jaws.

One of these scalps came into my possession. It had formerly belonged to a Toba cacique killed by a friendly Mattacco during the attack that was being prepared when we reached the Ciaguarál.

This custom of scalping prevails among all the Indians of these parts, and also among those of North America. More strangely still, it existed among the Scythians.

The Germans used to drink out of the skulls of the enemies, they had slain. And who has not heard of Alboin, the Lombard, who, thirteen hundred years ago, made his wife Rosamond drink from her father's skull ?

This custom of the Indians recalls a scene to my remembrance that demonstrates the cunning of these savages.

On one occasion, I accompanied the colonel of the regiment stationed on the frontier, in one of his periodical visits. Close to a fort where a tribe of Indians dwelt, the son of the cacique-general came to pay us a visit; the father did not come himself, because the colonel, he asserted, should first call upon him. But he sent us a present of some excellent aloja. As he had just returned from fighting the Tobas, we asked him whether he had brought back any scalps. And the Indian, by way of excusing his cruelty, replied, "The Tobas take scalps from the Christians, and we from the Tobas."

On that occasion, seeing me in European dress in the midst of so many military men, and treated by the colonel with great politeness, they said among themselves,—

"·Who can this be ?"

And the more knowing ones replied,—

" Oh, *some* President ! "

I felt on hearing this as if I were among a crowd of our own people.

It is a custom of war among these Indians to begin their undertakings at the new moon. They attribute to it apparently some superstitious power; they do not, however, make night marches, for fear of vipers and tigers.

We find a similar superstition among the Spartans, and we know from themselves that in the war with the Medes (491 B.C.), they were not in time to relieve the Athenians and Plateans, who under Miltiades won the famous battle of Marathon against Darius, King of the Persians ; the cause of the delay was their waiting for the full moon, on which account they did not arrive until the day after the battle.

I have already mentioned that their arms consist of the bow and arrow, the lance and the club. All these are of wood. They do not use metals because they have none, and would not know how to work in them. They esteem very highly any nails or knives or tinned boxes they happen to possess. They make use also of *las boleadoras*, a kind of sling.

They carry on war at hundreds of leagues' distance, traversed entirely on foot, and with relative rapidity. For the Indians are stupendous walkers. Naked, and hence light-footed, and in constant practice they cover the ground quickly without appearing to do so ; they are barefooted, and therefore it is less needful to raise the foot high.

The chiefs do not fail to harangue their troops before battle, and at the moment of attack their leader shouts, "Comrades ! here we are ; fight courageously ! *Do not fly even if the enemy tramples you underfoot !* " An expression that seems to me full of energy and truth, relating as it does to a hand-to-hand struggle.

They revile the dead body of an enemy. Besides cutting off the head, they tear out the heart, mutilate the various members, and outrage it in a thousand ways.

I am ignorant whether these tortures precede the death of the prisoner, or whether they are satisfied with cutting his

G

throat like a sheep's, before mutilating him. They acted as follows towards Faustino. First they pierced him with arrows so that he fell to the earth unable to defend himself; then they seized him while still conscious and cut his throat, then they cut off his head, hung the body to a tree by the feet, and went away having stripped him of everything.

The following conversation took place between two Indians after a battle :—

First Indian. " Now I will tell you what happened on our return. All at once I heard some one behind me, shouting, ' The enemy are killing our comrades down there, in the hollow.' I cried out to my men, ' Stand fast ! they are killing our comrades ! Do not fly, stand firm even if they trample you underfoot.' "

Second Indian. " Oh, how I wish I had been there ! The misfortune was that I did not see you when you marched."

First Indian. " You would have seen ! We set at them with our lances and clubs, and killed ever so many. Oh, we took our revenge ! So now I am quite contented ; we are even now. We scalped some, cut the hands off others, tore out the hearts of others, or mutilated them ; and cut off the heads of many."

And he continued minutely describing all their achievements.

They seem to ascribe some virtue to the limbs of an enemy. I remember on one occasion having brought with me three Mattacco heads, taken from a spot where four years previously two score of them had been taken prisoners and then massacred. The floods had carried away all but the three I succeeded in obtaining. I brought them a distance of ten leagues to my *ranche* on the frontier, where I put them in my room, under the little table that served me for a desk.

One stormy night I heard a voice through the open door. The poor light of my tallow candle dazzled my eyes, and thus prevented me from seeing a black figure in the darkness of the background. " *Quien es ?* " I cried, instinctively seizing the revolver on my table. " *Amicco, amicco ; no mas*" (" A friend, a friend : nothing else ") ; and a Mattacco cacique drew near, followed by a companion." "*Que queriendo, amigo ?* " (" What do you want, friend "), I continued. " *Toba etec* " (" The head of the Toba "), replied he. I took up one of the skulls and gave it to him, saying, " *Toba catchia* " ("Wicked Toba "). The Indian clutched the head almost convulsively in his left hand, and thrust the

The Mexicans and the Peruvians, however, who are strongly constituted as nations and far advanced in civilization, have reached a second stage, that of the worship of stars and idols, from which the powerful civilizations of Asia, Greece, and Rome, of the last of which we are the immediate heirs, was developed among ourselves.

We stand at the junction of this second stage with a third, higher than it, and which affirms an impersonal First Cause, Eternal, Almighty, the Creator of all things, and to this we have added the Evil one, the Incarnation, worship, priesthood, churches, saints, amulets, the threefold kingdom of the extramundane life. These few allusions are intended to prove that we are all brothers during the first stage of apparitions, ecstasies, exorcisms, and good and evil angels on the right and left hand of every individual of our poor humanity.

It is difficult to learn the creed of Indians from themselves; for while they entertain a profound contempt for the religion of Christians, they are afraid of the ridicule, the threats, and the questionings of their presumptuous and intolerant enemies.

Faustino, a Christian who had returned to the Indians, when asked the reason of some religious observance, used to reply, "Ignoro, señor; yo no pregunto nada, porqué los Indios desconfian mucho."[1]

I am about to give an account of what I learned from their own lips after endeavouring to inspire them with confidence by my behaviour, by presents, by frequenting their society, and (I ask absolution from his Holiness) by having agreed with them in thinking their attachment to the religion of their fathers a fine thing (orthodox style), by blaming the attempts of the Christians to convert them, by contemning the scorn with which these latter treated them, and, lastly, by joining with them in a hearty laugh at all the Christian absurdities.

Let me explain. I hold the religion of my ancestors and parents in profound respect; and now that my years are beginning to increase in inverse ratio to my teeth, I greatly regret having angered my loving mother when a boy by showing myself careless of her pious request and unwilling to comply with her wish that I should pray on the rosary for the repose of our departed friends and neighbours. I blush when I remember

[1] "I do not know, sir; I ask no questions, because Indians are very suspicious."

that in my youth I thought it clever to go out of my parish church when mass was half over, shocking the kind and worthy prior and the devout country-folk, while it would have been so much more simple to have stayed away altogether. I feel gratitude towards the good Fathers, that will last while I live, for the instruction they imparted to me during many years; yet all my repentance, blushes, and gratitude fail to inspire me with any zeal for the machine that calls itself Christianity, or with any anxiety for the conversion of these innocent and free unbelievers, who would find their chains of slavery riveted by baptism.[2]

I know this to be true. It will be objected that looking at the matter from a merely human point of view there must be progress for these savages in entering on civilized life, even through the portals of Christianity, and that the crossing of races is a progress for the whole of human society.

I reply to this that we must not hasten to the conclusion that the crossing of races so remote would be a social progress; rather is it to be feared, that the result would be a non-reproductive hybrid like the mule; and the fact that the natives of this continent are continually bewailing a few drops of Indian blood in their veins, seems to corroborate my view of the subject. With regard to the tribes themselves, what benefit would they derive from entering our ranks? Their birth and colour would be the first hindrance to their happiness, and even if we grant that they would share equally with Christians in the advantages of their new social conditions, it would always be true that only a microscopic portion of these would afford them pleasure, the rest would be a heavy burden, as is the case at the present moment with the proud descendants of Christian civilization.

Ahót is the Mattacco word for spirits, the Vilela word is *cokss*.[3]

These are subterranean spirits, but they wander about the world at night, entering into houses and also into persons, gene-

---

[2] The fate of the prisoners taken by General Rocca in his expedition to *Rio Negro*, which resulted in the conquest of 15,000 leagues by the Argentine Republic, proves to demonstration the accuracy of this opinion. The expedition was undertaken after the above lines were written.

[3] The *h* in *ahót* must be aspirate and nasal. This is a frequent sound in the Mattacco and other dialects. But of this I will treat later.

rally causing sickness. The *ahóts* ride on the wind, and are either themselves the storm or are accompanied by it, dancing in a circle round tolderias, toldos, and individuals that they wish to hurt. The most terrible *ahót* is small-pox, against whom the wizards are powerless. When it appears in a *hauet-ei* (tolderia) the Indians hurry away from it, often leaving it in flames behind them and abandoning their sick. The disease is very destructive, owing rather, in my opinion, to want of care, which is impossible in their houses and with their clothes, than to want of domestic or personal cleanliness, which seems to me to be sufficiently attended to. Nearly every case is fatal, which accounts for very few Indians being pock-marked.

Each man has a spirit, that after death is united again, beneath the earth, to its companions, and enjoys among them the same consideration he enjoyed while living among the inhabitants of his tolderia. For this reason they hold a special religious rite for their dead.

Although the *ahóts* are fond of roaming about, nevertheless they remain near the spot where the bodies that contain them are to die.

The spirit of the person who dies away from home, and who cannot be buried in his own country, wanders solitary and sad among strange spirits.

I inquired of my cicerone why these unfortunate beings were destined to so cruel a fate, since, without fault of theirs, they died, and their bodies were buried away from their own people. He answered me thus: The bodies being left far away from their kinsfolk and from the members of the same tribe, was a sign that they had not been loved and esteemed in life, hence the other *ahóts*, when they see a stranger appear among them, reason thus: these persons, whom neither their earthly kinsfolk nor their tribe honour with fraternal burial, cannot, by this token, have received love or esteem, therefore they deserve nothing;" and they leave him alone. I repeat the gibberish of the *ladino*.

I was reminded of the Latin tradition recorded in the golden verse of the Æneid when Æneas, having gone down to the Elysian fields, meets the shades of the unburied wandering round the Stygian marsh without being able to cross over :—

" Son of Anchises! offspring of the gods!
(The sibyl said) you see the Stygian floods,

The sacred stream which Heaven's imperial state
Attests in oaths and fears to violate.
The ghosts rejected are the unhappy crew
Deprived of sepulchres and fun'ral due,
The boatman Charon : those, the buried host,
He ferries over to the farthest coast ;
Nor dares his transport vessel cross the waves
With such whose bones are not composed in graves.
A hundred years they wander on the shore ;
At length, their penance done, are wafted o'er."

And I remembered the respect in which the grave is held by almost every nation, and the consequent intolerance of some grotesque and barbarous religions.

The beliefs I have mentioned are the basis of their cere-monies for healing the sick and burying the dead.

Before describing these, however, I should notice a kind of worship rendered, especially by the women, to some of the heavenly bodies, viz., the moon and the morning star.

At the rising of the moon, the women issue forth from their toldos, and holding each other by the hand, dance rapidly round in a ring, jumping and crying out in honour of the silvery planet.

They do the same on the appearance of the star in the east, praying it to be favourable to the algarroba harvest, and to that of the other fruits of the earth.

It is a custom also for men and women to arise from sweet repose at midnight, and all to dance together in a circle, jumping and shouting, to propitiate Heaven.

At the eclipse of the sun or moon they assemble in the same way and implore the cessation of the inexplicable phenomenon, but in this case it is an *ahót* whom they fear and propitiate.

I know of no other acts of adoration but these, and they denote an approach towards Sábaism or the worship of the heavenly bodies. But it is curious that the sun is not included among the objects of their worship or their exorcisms. Our interpreter, Faustino, however, informed me that they assemble to implore his reappearance when he has been hidden by clouds (a very rare occurrence in these regions) for any length of time, or if a storm lasts too long ; but even so they are rather conjuring the *ahót*, who has withdrawn the bene-ficent planet from their sight and from their unclothed bodies.

We see by this that among these Indians, too, the women are the first to worship, and that like the women of olden Pagan times, they recognize in the pale moon an object more consonant with their condition, and therefore more able or more willing to protect them than the sun, who is too unlike themselves, and who awaits the adoration of men, slower to fear, to hope, and to pray.

In no place have I seen idols, notwithstanding a diligent search, and my guides have always denied the existence of any. But idol-worship would not seem foreign to their character, and in addition to the partial adoration of the heavenly bodies that I have mentioned, it is probable that certain natural objects offering special characteristics of a terrifying, benevolent, or mysterious nature, are looked upon by them with feelings not far from worship.

Braly, an engineer, who has travelled in the Chaco as far as *Rio Salado*, assures me that the Mocovitos of that region never forsake the spot where an aerolite has fallen with loud crash and dazzling light.

This gives credibility to Azara's statement, according to which the first conquerors of Paraguay asserted that the Guaranìs who inhabited that country worshipped an enormous caged serpent. This was probably a species of boa, called here *ampalagua*, and equally remarkable for its size and gentleness.

I am not disposed, however, to accept as true the assertions of Garcilasso de la Vega, a descendant of the Incas, according to whom the peoples who were conquered by the emperors, his ancestors, were plunged in the grossest idolatry, worshipping imaginary monsters, the most disgusting animals, and small inanimate objects. Garcilasso, who was piously attached to the memory and traditions of his forefathers, although he concealed his feelings, sought to show the complete civilization of their immense empire, now vanished, and lent a willing ear to the national legends that might support this claim. But the grand civilizing action of the Incas, the promoters of the worship of sun and moon, of whom they claimed to be the sons, requires no such contrast to show it forth ; it will always be evident in the stupendous achievements of their labour and skill. Woe to the vanquished ! And the injustice of the Incas towards conquered nations was inflicted with usury upon themselves by their foreign conquerors, who, in the name of the true God, destroyed their palaces, temples, public works, and institutions, loading them with contempt and anathema.

However this may be, the wandering life of the wild tribes of the Chaco would seem to exclude idolatry.

And in fact how could wandering tribes carry with them idols of large size. In any case, they were obliged to exclude large or heavy burdens, and those that would be endangered by falling. Again, how could they respect their gods if carried on horseback in awkward positions; or how preserve the prestige and terror of mystery in the midst of removal? And how could each one attend to his own daily bread on the march, and also to the misfortunes of his gods and priests who may have been taken prisoners and destroyed on the way by the enemy in ambush?

Hence idolatry must be practised towards objects of small size and requiring little care ; but these are the last to seize on the imagination, and we can only conceive them as the fringes of a larger vestment, and as a passing caprice on the part of those not satisfied with the ordinary worship, like the luxury of the lesser intercessory saints in the houses of the great.

The facility with which the Indians abandon their tribe, their cacique, and their sorcerers, is now a well-ascertained fact, and when added to the utter absence of prestige in the two last, except in time of battle or of peril, is a confirmation of the above argument.

CHAPTER XVII.

RELIGION. (*Continued.*)

WITH these Indians God and devil are one, and are called by the one name, which, as I have already said, is *ahót* in the Mattacco language.

This lack of distinction frees them, at least in language, from the vice of intolerance, which is so prevalent among ourselves. Thus their name for our church is *tohuó-hotó-hi*, the literal meaning of which is "that which contains the *ahóts*," that is, the *ahóts* or Christian gods.

Moreover, they give the same name to a burial-ground, and in this they resemble the inhabitants of these countries, in which it is called a Pantheon.

And with regard to this expression, remark the destiny of words! Everybody knows that in Greece the Pantheon was a temple dedicated to all the gods, as the word itself explains, for *pan* indicates totality or the whole, and *teon* expresses divinity. It was next applied to the temples where men were set up, who, for their great deeds, were looked upon as demi-gods, and, finally, since mythological ideas waned, it has been used by us to describe the burial-place of famous men. And to this end, some celebrated buildings, renowned by beauty or historical traditions, have been devoted, viz. the Pantheon in Paris, and the Church of Santa Croce in Florence.

In the Chaco and throughout the whole of the northern parts of the Republic, where the inhabitants are more democratic, more on an equality, more ironical or ingenuous, they give the name of Pantheon to a piece of grassy ground surrounded by a hedge. This place is open to tigers and dogs, who, by turns, hold high festival on the fresh-buried corpse of a white man, a negro, or a leopard, but never certainly on that of a Greek demi-god or a divine modern!

On account of this, the word Pantheon will, some day, convey a contemptuous meaning.

The *ahóts* have the power not only of entering into individuals and bewitching them, and of becoming incarnate—allow me the neologism—in the elements of harm, such as tempests, the small-pox, famine, &c., but they are also able to inflict wounds and especially with arrows. It seems, however, that they only inflict these arrow-wounds directly against the will of the sorcerers, who, in Mattacco, are called *ha-ia-qüe*, and in Cheereguan *ippaia;* and this is the case also with the *hualicho* of the Araucans, who have, in fact, a word to express this action, viz. *cúglin.* In Mattacco it is *ióco.*

It is intelligible that the wizards should have selected the arrow as the weapon of the spirit of evil, because it is the only one among those used by the Indians that has any semblance of mystery or witchcraft. Being a projectile it can be shot from any direction and from afar, the archer remaining unseen.

The Indians have great faith in this power of their *ahóts.* A ladino of mine, a certain Taio (so called on account of a cut, *taglio,* across his face), an Indian, told me the fóllowing story in order to prove to me the power of the *ahóts* and the ignorance of the Christians in denying their existence. Once upon a time a tribe had just returned from a sugar-factory in the province of Salta. It was the algarroba season. One night the people were making merry, singing and dancing. All at once they hear a Christian approaching and singing as he comes; they hear the clattering of his horse's hoofs and the jangling of his silver spurs.

As soon as he comes up he draws rein, reproves them for what they are doing, and wishes to prohibit them from continuing. The people are displeased at his intrusion, and tell the *háiagué* to send him away.

The *háiagué,* not succeeding with fair words, tells the Christian who thus persists in interrupting and profaning the feast, " Now you shall see if we are such poor people ; you shall see what the *ahót* can do."

He stoops down, covers himself, and cries to the *ahót,* " Send an arrow into that Christian, and show him whether we are quite such a helpless people."

" It is well," replies the *ahót.*

All at once a noise is heard from below as if a stick had been snapped. It was an arrow.

The Christian suddenly fell from his horse. He was dead !

The *ahót's* arrow had killed him, because he had disbelieved in the *ahót*.

The whole tribe swore they had witnessed this.

When he had ended his story I thought to myself : what difference is there except in the proportions, between the credulity of these people and that of the Hebrews, who believed in the destruction of Sennacherib and 185,000 Assyrians in one night by an angel of the Lord, when he was about to lay siege to Jerusalem ? or that of the Spanish conquerors of Mexico who, according to the historian Gomara, chaplain to Cortes, vanquished innumerable enemies by the apparition of *Señor Santiago apostol sobre un caballo tordillo* at the head of the Spanish troops ?

And this was but a second edition of the good angel in golden armour on a white horse who enabled Antiochus Eupator to overcome Juda some thousands of years before !

These savages have as much foundation for their belief in these idle tales as we have for believing in ours. They, too, have the phrases *it is said* and *I saw it*, repeated by thousands. They have facts accompanied by circumstances, and they take the latter for the cause of the former, just as we do. One miracle is as good as another.

It is curious that the object of recognition, if not of adoration, is the principle of evil, because, after all, the *ahót* is a maleficent power, able to work evil. If we consider this recognition as the dawn of a religion, we must concede that the point of departure is the fear of evil and the desire of averting it.

We find the same beliefs prevalent in the other wild tribes of America as among these Indians of the Chaco, although in some, in North America, they also acknowledge benevolent powers or invisible beings, called *manitos* and *ockos*.

Concerning these spirits, they argue ingenuously but wisely enough. Why trouble oneself, they say, about a being who, by his nature, is beneficent ? He cannot harm us, because if he is good he cannot wish us evil.

It must be admitted that every religion has something of

original sin, if I may so call it, because they all teach and enforce expiatory sacrifice to appease the divine anger.

If we make our examination of conscience, can we say we have any love of God? We have fear certainly, notwithstanding the tenth commandment; and, in fact, our preachers always inculcate the *holy fear* of God.

To any one who should affirm the contrary we should repeat the words of the Saviour, "Blessed are the poor in spirit, for theirs is the kingdom of heaven."

Among the Indians of the Chaco who retain some traditions of the catechism taught them by the missionaries, there is a ceremony, perhaps the only religious one, that seems a parody of a Christian observance. From time to time they all assemble round the elders and chiefs, the women on one side, the men on another. In the middle, on a mass of flowers, they place an *ahót*, that is, a boy, a future sorcerer; meanwhile they talk, smoke, and drink, and say they have been at mass.

The wizards do not fail to converse with the child-god, and to communicate the replies they receive from him.

In these, as in other ceremonies, the wizard is continually bowing down, covering himself, talking towards the ground, under which are the *ahóts*. He speaks to them with his natural voice, and answers either in a shrill or a deep tone, according to the disposition of the *ahót*, and the crowd believes that the latter is really answering, not understanding that it is the trick of a ventriloquist.

We see that even before revealed religion, impostors have not been wanting, to cheat fools.

The stupidity of fanaticism, not to say ignorance, has discovered a mysterious communication of baptism in the custom prevalent among savages, *ab antiquo*, of washing the bodies of their infants. But this custom is simply due to the absolute necessity of cleansing a new-born babe.

I have frequently mentioned the wizards or sorcerers as being mediators between the *ahóts* and the living. They are also physicians or medicine-men, and priests besides. I will now explain how far they are physicians.

The association of religion with medicine seems to be of constant occurrence among primitive peoples, and among the lower classes of society at the present day. In this fact there is food for philosophic-historical reflection. It certainly existed among the Indian tribes of America, as we learn from their history. Oviedo calls our attention to it as occurring in *Spagnuola*, and Robertson, the historian of America, explains it shortly in the following words : " Superstition in its primitive form, springs from the natural impatience of man to free himself from present evil, and not from fear of the evil awaiting him in a future life. Thus it was engrafted at first on medicine and not on religion."

Among ourselves great numbers of persons who place their faith in witches and sorcerers, believe them not only to be the best doctors, but to derive their power from intercourse with invisible beings of their own kind. Every one is acquainted with the tragedies that have always accompanied, and always will accompany, such superstitions by which we are linked to our uncivilized brethren.

I have not found that the superstitions of these Indians lead them to deeds of cruelty, nor have I read of their so doing among the other American tribes. Cruelty seems to be the exclusive privilege of religion.

In fact, the Mexicans, the Bogotans, and even the Peruvians, who possess a regularized religion, viz. that of the stars and of some few idols, delight in acts of the grossest cruelty as propitiation to their deity, to whom they offer human sacrifices. With regard to the Mexicans, we even know the number of their victims at certain epochs. Las Casas, who is very compassionate to the Indians, whose faults he seems always anxious to extenuate, tells us, nevertheless, that the number of victims immolated to the Mexican god, *Huitzlopotolili*, was not less than 20,000 every year, and that at the inauguration of the great Mexican temple, a generation before the conquest, 80,400 men were sacrificed. The republics of Tlascala, Ciolula, and Hetzotziaco, on the borders of the Mexican Empire, had marked out a zone on the frontiers where every year they were to make raids for the purpose of securing prisoners, young and, if possible, unwounded, in order to sacrifice them when fattened.

According to Garcilasso, Manco Capac abolished human sacrifices in Peru. Nevertheless, if we may believe Acosta, children from four to ten years of age were sacrificed on solemn occasions, and, according to Garcilasso himself, who endeavours to minimize the customs of his forefathers, *zancú*, a bread made of maize, and kneaded by their nuns with blood from the forehead and nostrils of children, was supplied to the imperial table at the solar pasch of *Raymi*, just after the solstice of June.

And among ourselves do not we begin with the sacrifice of Isaac, which, take it as we will, is that of a father offering his son to a god who has required it of him? And Jephthah's daughter sacrificed to the god of victory against the Ammonites? And Agag, king of the Amalekites, who, when a prisoner of war, was sacrificed to the Lord by the hands of the high priest Samuel? And the priests of Baal, who flung children into the red-hot idol? And the King of Moab, who sacrificed his son to idols to deliver himself from the besieging Hebrews?

As signs of the times we have the sacrifice of Iphigenia, daughter of Agamemnon, and Curtius plunging into the gulf.

What is the Redeemer who must be crucified to propitiate the God of humanity? What are fastings, hair-shirts, and penances, all the paraphernalia of mortifications to appease the anger of Jehovah?

I ask the question: If a conqueror had come back from another world four centuries ago and had seen the *autos da fé*, would he not have mistaken them for Mexican sacrifices?

Yes, in truth, cruelty is the privilege of all religions. It owes its origin to dogma, and its power to governments.

But when the day is come on which philosophy shall replace dogma, and worship be sustained by the wholly interior adhesion of conscience to truths recognized by the intellect or intuitive in the mind; on that day the infamy and disgrace of religious cruelty will disappear from society.

On that day Humanity will have overcome the waves of idolatry and of dogma, and will have reached the shores of the empire of humanity. With intellect magnificently enlarged, strengthened by trial, and gladdened by the future of love, work, and peace that lies before it, it will look back on the seething billows and on that far-distant shore, where its youth was passed, in ignorance of the fierce contests of life and of the heart-corrupting subtleties of the intellect. There, during childhood, she had been untormented by the wrath of the gods, and thence she will understand that her very simplicity spontaneously bestowed on her that tolerance and that peace which she will now have acquired through ages of sanguinary strife, and will draw from thence a proof of her own innate virtue and a pledge of the new future—the noble, strong, and glorious future of Science.

CHAPTER XVIII.

THE INDIANS AND THEIR DEAD.

NEAR the city of Santiago dell' Estèro I saw the tumuli, and the vessels contained in them. They are situated on the banks of a former channel of the River Dulce. A great number of these curious relics of the past have been found; these are of various dimensions, some of them being sixty centimeters in height and forty in diameter. Some are unglazed, others are glazed and ornamented with twisted cords and linear geometrical designs. The body and colouring are both very good.

The ashes or bones of the dead are contained in these receptacles. The soil below the banks, from which only a slight undulation separates them, is clothed with ancient algarrobas and with other plants indigenous to the present alluvial soil, the alluvium being produced by rivers that are hydrographically disposed at the present time. On those lands that are formed by emersion or are of an alluvial nature from climatic and hydrological conditions belonging to an earlier epoch, as, for instance, the glacial period, other kinds of plants grow. I state this from personal observation and with perfect confidence, and I have also mentioned it in my official reports.

There can be no doubt that when these burial-places were constructed, the river flowed at the foot of the bank, this being the first condition of life, sought by civilized and uncivilized humanity alike, all the world over, and, as all the antiquity of that period shows, we may safely conclude that even then special care was taken of the dead.

In Calingastra, in the Cordillera of San Juan, sepulchres are found in the shape of wells, not walled, because the soil remains solid of itself, and covered with a flat stone. At the side of the corpse various objects are found, especially a species of deer, and it seemed to me the dog also. A piece of polished stone, like an open fan, was found in one : this may have served as a mirror. Similar ones were also in use among the Etruscans, and I remember that in one of their sepulchres at Sovana, in Maremma Toscana, P. Busatti, the civil engineer, found a silver mirror that was shown to me. It was superbly engraved with a design representing, in my opinion, the judgment of Paris.

An Indian mortuary chamber, containing several bodies, was found in another part of San Juan, near the *Sierra de Pié de Palo*, beside a heap of stones (*pintadas*).

Stone sepulchres (*guacas*), in the shape of small ovens, such as are used in country parts, are found in the Salta and Jujuy Mountains in Puna. They contain as many as three bodies clothed and hooded. These are in a sitting posture, and sometimes there are jars by their side containing gold and silver. At the present day the Collas, Christian descendants of the Indians dependent on the Emperor of Peru or the Incas, seek out these sepulchres and gather up the bones to give them a Mass, as they say; but greed has nearly always been beforehand with them, so that although the bones are there, they find none of the precious objects which had been buried with them. The kind of garments in which the bodies had been clothed cannot be distinguished, because no sooner are they exposed to the air than they crumble into dust.

The Chiriguans, in the Bolivian Chaco, enclose their dead in a jar which they bury beneath their own *rancho*. They have thus one and the same home for the living and the dead, and whether as cause or effect, or both together, the Chiriguans are not nomadic. They ornament these jars with great care; the kind of jar and of decoration depends on the means of the family. The clay is baked, and the glaze, made of an ill-smelling red bitumen, is put on either before or after firing. In the former case the colours are brighter and clearer, but in the latter more lasting.

A fire is, in some cases, kept burning for a month over the buried jar. Where this is done, it is assuredly to destroy the pernicious gases that escape from the body during decomposition.

The poorer Chiriguans, who do not possess jars, inter the corpse[1] in a hole underneath the *rancho*, which they vacate until the effluvium has ceased.

The bodies of those who have been put to death for repeated murders are thrown into a field or burned.

Some Indians, among whom are the Cherionossos, dwelling on the borders of Bolivia and Brazil, bury their dead among trees. To this end they seek the thickest part of the forest, and having pitched upon a giuccian-tree,—the trunk of which is shaped like a jar, and is of cork-like texture—they empty it and place the body in the cavity, covering it up securely that vultures may not disturb or devour it.   One of these sepulchres was found when a road was opened to Fort Sarmiento.

The Mattaccos bury their dead, and some tribes on the Toba borders burn them, a custom observed by the Tobas themselves.

We may infer that the ideas by which the Mattaccos are governed in their funeral ceremonies are common to the other Indian tribes with whom they are in continual contact, either as allies in war, or as enemies, and belief in spirits is the same.

Now, the Mattaccos, as I have already said, believe that the souls of the dead do not find peace if their bodies are not buried in ground belonging to the tribe.   I do not know whether an exception is made for warriors dying in battle.   Thy hold, also, that the soul, which they call *hésech*—while they call the body *tzan*, and the dead person *ahót*—will not be able to join its comrades if the body has not first suffered decomposition either by fire or by air.   Until then, they say, the soul wanders round the family *rancho*, and is seen lamenting.

These apparitions of grieving souls are the subjects of many of their narratives, and of a great part of their conversation, and, it is probable, excite as much terror among them as with ourselves.

It follows, of course, that when an individual dies at a distance, his kinsfolk and the inhabitants of the tolderia go forth to seek his remains, in order to bury them in the territory belonging to the tribe.   But to people who travel on foot the carriage of a corpse would be a serious matter, since they must often traverse hundreds of kilometers.   They wait, therefore, until the tissues of the body have perished, and then carry home the bones.   This is in no way prejudicial to the deceased, because his soul cannot descend under the earth until decomposition is complete.

Meanwhile, if the death occurs in the morning the body is placed in a grave the same evening ; if at night, then the next morning.   But it is not covered in ; branches are merely laid over it to prevent tigers, dogs, and birds of prey from feasting on it.   When decomposition is over it is either burned, as I have said, or finally interred.

When an individual dies away from home the corpse is wrapped in a net, and is placed in a tree with the necessary coverings, as usual, for protection. The next year, or at some indefinite period, provided always that only the skeleton remains, the friends of the dead man fetch the bones away and carry them to the *rancho*, where they receive proper burial.

In whatever spot they may place a corpse they invariably leave beside it a gourd of water, and for this reason. Scarcely is an individual dead when other dead persons come to pay him a visit, and as both he and they may be thirsty, water is left in order to assuage their thirst. Any one aware of the importance of water in these regions will understand the value attributed to this gift to the dead, and will find its explanation in the fraternal and hospitable spirit that outlives death itself.

But whatever may be the reason of this custom, which exists in one form or another among other uncivilized tribes, we cannot fail to be struck with the analogy between it and the traditions of the Greeks and ancient Romans.

Every one knows that it was the custom in Pagan times to place a piece of money in the mouth of the dead, that they might pay Charon for ferrying them across the Avernus. The Egyptians enclosed ears of corn and other things for the use of their dead, and these grains having been found when the tombs were opened, have served to prove how enduring is their vegetative power, for they take root and bear fruit when sown in the earth.

Nations who burn their dead—a custom which we are at the present time endeavouring to revive—burn food with them also ; this is mentioned by Virgil when describing the last rites rendered by Æneas to his friend Miseno, whose body was consumed on a funeral pyre :—

> "Then on a bier, with purple cover'd o'er
> The breathless body, thus bewail'd they lay,
> And fire the pile, their faces turn'd away
> (Such reverent rites their father used to pay).
> Pure oil and incense on the fire they throw,
> And fat of victims, which his friends bestow.
> These gifts the greedy flames to dust devour :
> Then on the living coals red wine they pour."

We remark another analogy in the custom prevalent among the most remote nations, of covering graves with a heap of stones. In fact, among the Manzaneros—"Araucanian Indians living between Limay and Neuquen, on Argentine territory, on the eastern slopes of the Cordillera,"—this practice has attained such proportions that travellers have mistaken some of these tumuli for small natural eminences. Among ourselves it is customary for those present at a burial to throw a clod of earth into the grave, and to do the same at the foot of those crosses by which the wayfarer is reminded of the last resting-place of some fellow-mortal. The custom must have flourished centuries ago, for Dante, speaking in the person of Manfred, says,—

> " Yet at the bridge's head my bones had lain,
> Near Benevento, by the *heavy mole*
> Protected."

The universality of the practice renders the explanation of the construction of the Pyramids for the purpose of sepulchres still more plausible. They are merely colossal exaggerations of the *heavy mole,* and the custom must have been generally prevalent in the land of the Pyramids.

The belief that the dead feel a need in the other world of those things they enjoyed while in this, besides having been traditionary among every people in both hemispheres, has led to some cruel customs.

We all know that among the Brahmins in India it was, and still is, customary for the widow to cast herself on the funeral pile. It is true that in order to lessen her sufferings narcotics are administered to the victim.

In the New World, those nations whose religion included caste used to sacrifice human beings on the tombs of the great, viz. their servants, officers, and favourite concubines, who considered it an honour to be thus chosen.

It is stated that at the death of the Inca *Huaina Cápac,* one of the greatest emperors of Peru, 1000 victims were immolated on his tomb! And what must have been the number among the Mexicans, to whose deity human sacrifice was daily bread, while the flesh of their prisoners of war was daily consumed by themselves? To complete the likeness between the two worlds, while Asiatics gave narcotics to the doomed widows, the Natchez Indians of North America stupefied their victims with tobacco.

If we compare the results of this superstitious belief concerning the wants of the dead on nations possessing religion and civilization with its results on those possessing neither, i.e. savages, the balance of humanity is in favour of the latter. These are all equally poor and ignorant, and content themselves with the humble and innocent offering of a cup of water and perhaps a handful of algarroba, without even the holocaust of an animal, which, according to Leviticus, is "an offering made by fire, of a sweet savour unto the Lord!"

The poor Indians of the Chaco are unable to make themselves interesting on the death of their kinsfolk by wearing handsome black garments, as do Christians, or white stuffs like the Chinese, they show their grief after their own fashion by shearing their head, the only part they habitually cover. The women, instead of hastening to display their sorrow in the temples and public places, take refuge in their toldo, avoiding any contact with their friends, remain silent, and attend with more than usual care to their domestic duties. They mourn after this manner for a year, during which time it is indecent for them to marry again. If they must go out they always walk apart, and should they be met by any one they cover their face ; they refuse to converse, and avoid any occasion of speech. It has happened sometimes that travellers have chanced to come across these silent women in a suspicious place, and being ignorant of this custom, have ill-used and killed them.

To cut off the hair has been considered even among the nations of Europe as an act of sacrifice and mourning. Among the barbarians who invaded the crumbling Roman Empire, the lover used to cut off his hair on the tomb of the beloved one.

In addition to this they make a lament, sung to a monotonous, inexpressive air, which seems to be conventional, accompanied by the sound of the *pimpin*, which, as I believe I have already said, is a kind of mortar formed by means of instruments and by fire from the trunk of a tree. It contains water, and is covered with a skin stretched like a drum-head. They strike upon this with a hollow gourd, in which they place grains of maize or algarroba nuts.

The lament is carried on at fixed hours, but the widow or mother wails almost continually, even when walking out in the streets on her various duties. The deceased is followed to the grave by his kinsfolk and friends, and if he is a popular cacique or a well-known sorcerer, by the whole tribe.

Caciques and skilful sorcerers always hold a high position among the *ahóts* who have been expecting them, and their influence in the other world will be in proportion to the consideration they have enjoyed among their neighbours, as demonstrated by the funeral ceremonies. When one of them is dying, the Indians assemble round his home and beg him to intercede with the *ahóts* down below, that the *ahóts* of the whirlwind, of disease and of famine may spare their toldos and visit those of their enemies.   The dying man gives them his promise, and, in return, his fellow-citizens pay honour to his funeral rites, and thus augment his beneficent authority over the *ahóts*.

And what else do we ask from those of us who die in the odour of sanctity, than that they should become intercessors with heaven for us pilgrims in this valley of tears ?

Men are drawn together by sorrow, and the harmony of human nature in act and word, in hope and in fear, is never so fully manifested as beside an open grave !

CHAPTER XIX.

MEDICINE.

IN the Chaco there are both medicine-men and medicine-women, but very few medicines. Treatment is entirely empirical on account of the ignorance and superstition of the inhabitants.

We may wonder that the tribes of the Chaco have discovered no remedies, but this is accounted for partly by their low order of intelligence, and still more by their superstitions respecting disease.

They believe that a malady is produced by an *ahót* who has entered into the sick person. Their only idea, therefore, is to drive it out by means of their sorcerers.

Hence only their magicians or priests, by whichever name we choose to describe them, can be their physicians. This superstition of theirs is a consequence of the desire in man to rid himself of a present evil, and of his ignorance of the means of so doing. The cunning innate in mankind is the medium between ignorance and superstition.

They acknowledge, nevertheless, their want of real remedies, and the superiority, in this respect, of Christians in whom they have great faith as physicians; while the lower orders of Christians, on the contrary, believe in the Indian wizards and sorcerers.

I have known owners of *estancias* who have sent for Indians to cure them.

The very poor exorcise the *ahót* by shouting and dancing, and by the breathing and spitting of the sick person himself. They accompany their exorcisms, however, by some homœopathic prescriptions, such as dieting, baths, etc.

Their faith in their conjuring is not diminished, however, by recourse to Christian remedies.

On one occasion, when, the steamer having stuck fast in shallow water, we remained on board and were surrounded by

Indians, a group of them approached with a sick man, that we might cure him. We had no interpreter on that occasion, and I took advantage of the little knowledge of the language I possessed, and contrived to make out that the man had been bitten by a viper, and that they were asking for " *chiaskiétach- kia*," a cure for a viper bite.

We had a small medicine-chest with us, and we all of us decided on treating him with ammonia. It was of the highest importance for us to succeed in this affair so as to acquire prestige and gain friends among these Indians, who, a few days before, had fired upon us from an ambuscade at close quarters.

The cure, however, proceeded very slowly, and there were moments during the first three days, an eminently critical period, when we were greatly alarmed, because the swelling of the injured leg began to extend to the groin and abdomen, and had it reached the region of the heart all would have been over for the patient.

During the treatment, which was strong enough for a horse, the patient drank nothing but water, and at night, when all the ship's crew were sleeping, the medicine-men began to chant, " Húu, húu, húu—hée, hée, hée—Hí, hí, hí,"—" Húu, húu, húu," from time to time spitting and blowing like bellows on the wound and other parts of the body. They spent whole hours in this way.

I was in the habit of sitting up late into the night, both to take my turn in watching the invalid, and to secure some quiet hours for study, and I frequently drew near them. At first they would instantly cease, but after a time, encouraged by my " *Hiss, tzilatác, bene, bello*," and by my respectful manner, they would continue in my presence.

At last, after twenty days, the sick man was cured.

An extraordinary method of cure is that practised for wounds made by the ray-fish. These are horribly painful, and even cause death. The treatment consists in holding the wounded part, usually the ankle, over the smoke of burning logs of *palo santo*, an extremely resinous wood, and afterwards a woman at her lunar period sits astride over the limb. I have been assured by Christians who have tried this remedy that it is efficacious.

All treatment, however, to be of any virtue must be under the direction of a wizard, or, at the least, a witch.

Not every one can become a wizard or medicine-man; and as the treatment is paid for according to the disease and the person, aud the pay consists of skins, animals, food, and other things, the profession affords opportunities for deception and trickery. Moreover, to exalt thoir prestige the practitioners surround themselves with mystery.

Thus in the Granadero tolderia the Indians tell of a youth, who had already entered on the career, who disappeared in boyhood and returned again after spending two years underground with the *ahóts*, who had taken him away in order to teach him the art, and inoculate him with the virtue of medicine-man and priest.

Apropos of trickery, I found myself once in evil case. I went to visit the cacique Granadero, who had just recovered from a long illness. I carried with me, as usual, a pocket writing-book and a pen. Granadero comes up and asks me what they are. Thinking to please him I take up the pen, and am about to write, but at that moment I perceive Granadero grim and threatening. His medicine-men had cured him shortly before from the *ahót*, who had tormented him for a long time, and had extracted pens and pencils from his body, under which exclusively Christian forms the *ahót* had bewitched him.

The Indian women seem to have undeniable skill as midwives. They perceive with extraordinary accuracy the moment of child-birth, and then, lifting up and supporting the patient, they shake her, accompanying the action with the usual conjurations until the end.

But a really interesting spectacle is to see a cure effected in the midst of a tolderia. One night I was camping out near one of the settlements when I was aroused to curiosity by the sound of many loud voices and the echoing of heavy blows on the ground. Relying on my friendly relations with the people, I ventured to go out and ascertain the meaning of the noise. In the midst of the tolderia, in a sort of open square, I saw a circle of black figures lighted up here and there by the flames of the great fire : these were women and men sitting on their heels, silently smoking. Within the circle four robust men were run-ning backwards and forwards in a space of about eight yards. Ostrich feathers and little bells were fastened to their ankles, wrists, head, and waist. In their hands, which were always lifted up in gesticulation, they held small gourds, half-filled with grain, and these being shaken added to the din. They rushed about shouting and yelling, panting and sweating, thrusting out their legs, stamping hard upon the ground, and then raising their voices in ludicrous and horrible fashion, holding their arms high in the air, bowing their heads and curving their bodies. By turns two of them would stop short, and squatting on the ground shake their heads rapidly from left to right, backwards and forwards, groaning, blowing and spitting on the back, legs, head, and face of two sick persons who had been placed in their midst.

The two patients were suffering horribly from the *ahót* of rheumatism, who had entered into them, and the conjurers were endeavouring to liberate them by means of these infernal jigs. They would not attain their object as long as they could not succeed in tiring out and intimidating the *ahóts*, who were maliciously dancing the same jig at the same moment underground, so as to intercept by their noise any communication with the *ahót* of the malady in question. The best medicine-man is he who springs highest, shouts loudest, and stamps most heavily.

The spectators remain to do honour to the treatment and increase its efficacy, but not without fear that the *ahót*, on quitting the body of the sick man, may enter into theirs.

The scene convinced me that among Indians physicians earn their bread by the sweat of their whole bodies; that among them, too, impostors, by dint of deceiving others, end by deceiving themselves, and that the mob was sincerely persuaded of the truth and efficacy of the conjurations employed.

And I am moved to a smile of disdain and compassion when I remember the charlatans, the holy water, the devil, the exorcisms believed in by the people of all classes among ourselves; but then the smile dies away upon my lips.

CHAPTER XX.

SOCIAL CONDITION—PHILOLOGICAL REMARKS.

THE Indians of the Argentine Gran Chaco must unhesitatingly be classed among the most barbarous people of the earth. Let me explain. When I say that they are barbarous, I do not mean cruel. I have sufficiently shown in the preceding pages, that highly civilized nations far exceed these children of nature in cruelty and ferocity. By barbarians I mean *savages*, viz. a people with few or no laws, with few or no institutions, with few or no industrial pursuits—a people, in short, very inferior to us in their equipment for the battle of life.

Various details that I have already given are sufficiently convincing on this subject, and further indications that I shall point out will confirm my statements.

All philosophers are agreed in assigning a distinctive character of inferiority to a nation, in proportion to its ignorance of numeration ; I do not mean written, but oral numeration.

Darwin, in his "Origin of Man," cites the inhabitants of Tierra del Fuego, south of the Magellan Straits, as being in the lowest stage of civilization, because they are unable to count beyond four. This is intelligible, for if speech correspond with ideas and wants, how few of either can they possess who are unable to go beyond the number four !

Now none of the Indians of the Argentine Chaco can count beyond four, whether they be Tobas, Mattaccos, Vilelas, or Mocovitos, whether they be victors or vanquished in their internecine wars.

The Guaranis, likewise, who have long inhabited and still inhabit Paraguay, part of Brazil, Corrientes, and Misiones, and in all probability still more remote parts of the so-called Argentine Mesopotamia, can only in their own language count up to four. The case is the same in other parts of the American continents.

In Patagonia, however, according to the Argentine traveller, Señor Lista, they count up to ten progressively. The Guaranis have the expression ten or twenty, but they borrow it from the hands and feet, saying *two hands* for the number ten, and *two feet* for twenty.

The Pampas, who are not less uncivilized than the Patagonians, and at about the same depth, I cannot say height, as the inhabitants of the Chaco, can, however, count indefinitely, like their brethren the Araucanians or Chilenos.

The Peruvians, next neighbours of the Chilenos, and who, as I have previously stated, formed the great empire of the Incas, called by them *Tavantin-suju*, or the four quarters of the world! also count indefinitely ; likewise the Aimaras, who live in the city and neighbourhood of Paz in Bolivia, and who probably, before being conquered by the Chicciuas or Peruvians, extended as far as Catamarca, and perhaps Jujuy, as denoted by some of their words, such as *marca*, *pucará*, *huma-huaca*, which would be in Aimarà language, *people, fortress, spring of water.*

All those nations who inhabit or have inhabited the Pampas, the two declivities, Atlantic and Pacific, of the Cordillera, and the table-land of Bolivia, owe their aptitude either to the stage of civilization they had already reached, like the Peruvians and the Chilenos, or to near connection and frequent contact with them, as was the case with the Pampas. While the lower numbers differ notably in the different languages, some of them higher than the numbers four or ten resemble each other, and their construction obeys the same rule. This reveals the unity of the source whence the knowledge was derived.

I do not think it opportune to dilate in this place on the subject ; I hope to do so on another occasion, and then I believe I shall be able to show the parentage of the languages of different nations in this part of the continent, although widely separated by locality and by their various degrees of civilization ; but I will give one proof of the influence of contact among these peoples, which I think has not been hitherto noticed.

Those Guaranis who count, as I have said, up to four, dwell on the left banks of the Paraguay and the Paranà. They were surrounded and confronted by peoples who also counted up to four. The Chiriguanos, on the contrary, who are in fact Guaranis separated from the other savage tribes, either previously to the Spanish Conquest or after the arrival of the Spaniards ; in any case dwelling on the borders of the ancient Peruvian empire, as the historians of the conquest testify ;—the Chiriguanos, I say, by contact with nations who could count indefinitely, and who, moreover, were notably advanced in civilization, can count indefinitely also, although, as I have shown, they are at a stage of civilization very inferior to that of the Peruvians.

This fact, taken with the other that several of the higher numbers, such as *hundred* or *thousand*, are alike in many dialects, and again to the notorious superiority of the Peruvians in civilization and in war, at least during the four centuries prior to the Spanish Conquest, by means of which they had acquired an immense territory, larger than that indicated by historians ;—all these things, I say, make me think that the art of numeration was imparted to the tribes of this part of the continent by the Peruvians, who moreover were acquainted with the mode of determining numbers by a system of *knots* which they termed *quipu*. (We must regard this system, which according to some historians was also possessed by the Mexicans, as the first step towards writing, since it served to fix ideas by signs.)

The Chinese, if I may be allowed the digression, had a similar system handed down to them from the second semi-mythological Emperor of China, *Soui-gin-ke*, the same who discovered fire, taught commerce, and established government among his people, according to the annals of the Tribunal of History, that admirable and entirely Chinese institution, which dated from many thousands of years.

It must not be thought, however, that this serious inferiority in the power of expressing numbers has a corresponding inferiority in the rest of the language of the inhabitants of the Chaco. Not so; their language is as rich as that of any other people. If they are deficient in certain expressions of abstract ideas, it is because the idea itself is wanting to them ; but their language is able to express new ideas and new things *ad infinitum*. It has tenses, moods, persons, number, and finally cases for verbs and nouns, which render it very complicated.

Nor are general names wanting, such as fish, tree, bird ; and they also have augmentatives and diminutives, which lend themselves readily to express new things by names of their own, which they seek to preserve as much as possible.

I have already mentioned that certain animals imported by the Spaniards are called by the native name of a somewhat similar animal, with the addition of a distinctive particle; thus, the Mattacco word for horse is *yélatách*, meaning *great tapir*, from *yélach*, tapir, and *tach* an augmentative particle; a sheep is *keónatách* from *keóná*, deer, and so on. If there is no name in their vocabulary for an animal of the same kind, or if they have already made use of it, then they take the foreign appellation of the new object, pronouncing it according to the physical capacity of their throat, and the nature of their language. Thus they call a goat, *ca-i-la*, and Pedro, *Pe-i-lo*, for being unable to pronounce the letter *r*, or the letters *bl* and *dl*, they substitute for the former an *l*, and for the latter an *i*, *Pedro* and *Pedlo* thus becoming *Peiló*, with the accent on the last syllable in accordance with the nature of the language. When this law is recognized, several Guarani words are found to be the equivalents of Mattacco words, by merely changing the *r* into *l*; and the same with some Spanish words.

But I admit that the principle was not easy to find out, although now that it is explained it seems a very simple thing.

Since I am on the subject of language, it occurs to me to take exception to an opinion that appears to have been put forward by eminent philologists.

We are told, if I remember rightly, that there are three distinct stages in the formation of language : the monosyllabic, the agglomerate, and the inflected. The agglomerate is the process by which, when we desire to express a modification of a thing, we use the word expressing the thing and another word expressing the idea of the modification ; on the other hand, by inflection is meant modification by a variation in the form of the word expressing the thing.

The inflected period in a language does not always correspond with greater intellectual progress in those who employ it. If such has been the case among Asiatics, it is not so here in America, as I will proceed to show. The fact is, that if there be a people lower than others in the scale, the Mattaccos are that people ; now the Mattacco language is exuberantly inflected, while numerous neighbouring tribes and numerous others more civilized than they, are partly in the agglomerate period. For example : the Chicciuans use the word *cuna* to express the plural, this word does not mean *many*, but it conveys a notion of dignity or superiority ; the Guaranis use *hetá*, which means

many; the Chiulipi *hu-ué, much;* the Cileni, who have also a
dual form, make constant use of various particles; the Lules
use a word meaning *much:* all these words are added to the
singular.

The Mattaccos, on the contrary, have no less than four declensions, all of them inflected, and one that they make use
of by agglomeration, *ntók,* meaning *much.* The inflections are
ss, ess, i, and *l* (like *ll* in Spanish. Examples: horse, *jélatach,*
horses, *jélatáss;* this *tóch,* these *tochéss;* post, *ac-ló,* posts,
ac-lo-i; man, *icnú;* men, *icnúl,* or *icnuil.*

As to their verbs, besides an auxiliary *oit-tac,* that is the
same for all tenses, and means when used alone *I will,* they
employ the following inflections; he comes, *nóm,* he came,
nommé, he will come, *nom-là;* there are many besides these
that I have not yet discovered.

Meanwhile it may be affirmed that the native American
languages are not strictly in any one of the three stages into
which we divide the growth of languages, and on the contrary,
they include, so to speak, all three.

The so-called wealth of the language of wild tribes has given
a supposed-to-be powerful weapon into the hands of the
philosophers of Revelation, who find in this abundance of grammatical form and of vocabulary a proof of the divine origin of
human speech. But independently of this consideration, and
proceeding logically, I ask why these savages cannot count?
and why do they learn to do so as they become civilized? If
the art of enumeration is one result of an improved and progressive intelligence, why should not grammatical form be
another? It is certain that numeration is quite as difficult
as grammar; and we see it to be, as a fact. The difficulty of
written numeration has proved so lasting that, from the small
cords of the Peruvians and the tablets of the Chinese to the
Roman numerals and Arabic figures, whose marvellous simplicity we have reached after traversing the three stages
attributed to language, has been a progress of many thousand
years.

Next, as to the boasted riches of ancient and primitive languages, for example, the Vasco and American, that have separate
forms corresponding to every relation of time, place, person, or
sex, I have my own opinion. I believe that those languages
are linked to ours, for instance, to the simple and clear English
language, as an alphabet of 40,000 letters might be to one of

I

twenty or thirty, or as in numbers the system of juxtaposition and Roman figures is to the Arabic.   I contend, moreover, that all these innumerable forms, that are like so many figures and symbols particularized and localized, are a consequence of an inferior intelligence not yet sufficiently awakened and developed to adopt the relations expressed by the relative position of words in the period.   In the same way, an individual might be capable of comprehending what is signified by 1, 0, and a separate sign representing one hundred, two hundred, &c., but would be unable to reason, that 1 with two zeros might equally well express a hundred without the necessity of writing the word or placing a hieroglyphic against it. Certain intellects are strong as to memory, but slow in ratiocination. We ought to say of languages what we say of machinery : "That one is the best that gives the same result with the least expenditure of force." The English, who are expert mechanicians, have a very simple language.

CHAPTER XXI.

SOCIAL CONDITION. (*Continued.*)

THE embryonic state of numeration is repeated in all the other manifestations of intellectual and material life among the Indians of the Chaco.

We have already noticed their want of religion, which is still in the state of mere superstition. And although we must regard religions, in so far as form constitutes their substance, as a collection of absurd and even cruel ceremonies, often the result of unconscious, because habitual imposture (see the discourses of sacred orators of various sects), still the absence of these forms accurately marks the absence of civilization also in the history of a people, because it proves them to be incapable of constructing the complicated, formidable, and portentous armament and equipment of religion.

I wish it to be understood, however, that the opinions I express on religions have nothing to do with the speculative idea which directs them, and which makes them worthy of respect, nor with the historical reasons that determine them, and in which they find their power ; nor yet with the social functions they fulfil, and in which they find a motive for their expansion, and for the resistance they offer to the inevitable changes of time. But it is lamentable that mankind has not yet learned to look for the development of its historical causes and the fulfilment of its social functions apart from religion, because the coming out of it involves later so much cost and hardship that it makes one curse the benefits received at its hands in former times. I wish to say this with all possible respect for the faithful towards all religions past, present, and future.

The Indians distinguish the seasons of the year only by the various harvests. Thus they speak of the epoch of algarroba, of the mistol, of the cova, &c. How would it be possible, in fact, for them to divide the year into months or moons, if they cannot, count beyond four? This also implies, *à priori*, that they have never cared to comprehend the laws of the earth's movements, or of the apparent movement of the sun.

It is curious, however, that they divide the day into an immense number of parts, which they express according to the height of the sun, and which take the place of our hours. They recognize also various constellations such as the Pleiades, Venus, the Milky Way, and the Centaur. They have no word, however, to express a year.

The Mattaccos have a word, *ch-lupp*, that means epoch, and which is of indeterminate period, like the epoch with us; they use the word *i-quá-la*, sun, to express a day, and *i-gue-lách*, moon, for a month. Their language conforms in this to the universal language of the nations; with us it has remained and is genuine in the language of poetry, while in the vulgar tongue it has undergone so many transformations that at last the words used as equivalents have become independent of their original meanings, sun and moon.

Now whether they liken the moon to a lamp, or, as is more probable, a lamp to the moon, the fact remains that they call by one and the same name the moon and a light.

Not so, however, with fire, to which they seem to attribute some special property, for the Chiriguans condemn those to be burned who have died in evil repute. The Tobas, on the contrary, and some Mattaccos, burn all their dead indiscriminately. This latter practice may be explained by their desire to attain as soon as possible a favourable condition for the deceased person, who, so soon as all his flesh is consumed, is able to join his companions under the earth.

Although they possess no knowledge of either phosphorus or sulphur, nor even of steel (they have not even stone in these parts), yet they can kindle a fire when they please. I have already related how by rapidly grinding one piece of wood on another, until a powder like ground coffee, which does not kindle, comes from it, and adding some very combustible material, on which they blow, a flame is produced, and then as much fire as they want. One, at least, of the pieces of wood they use is *chilca*, a small and fragrant tree, both resinous and porous, which is plentiful throughout the Argentines.

It is generally believed that each individual Indian does everything by himself, and singly, and hence, it has been argued, the slowness and delay in their actions. This, however, is not the case. Although a nomadic people, they nevertheless understand the division of labour, and among them are weapon-makers, canoe-builders, makers of nets, weavers, &c., who barter these goods to their comrades, receiving other articles in exchange. Thus they have a beginning of arts and industries, but in embryo. Nor are the right words wanting to describe them; they consist, in Mattacco, of the word expressing the object and of a particle denoting the function. *Hi* (*h* nasal) denotes possession or deposit; *guu*, production or manufacture; *kiá* indicates means of obtaining, viz. those who procure certain things. For instance, fish is *jach-set*, fisherman *jach-set-kiá;* an arrow is *lútek*, makers of arrows *lutek-güu*, possessors of arrows *lutek-hì*. And by means of these particles, the first time they see a travelling-trunk or a birdcage, they name it at once *imai-hi*, that is, a guard-garment, and *huentié-hi*, a guard-bird.

One of their most advanced industries is that of weaving, in which, as I said before, they do not use a shuttle but a splinter of palm-wood, with which they draw the woof together by hand; and another is the manufacture of nets, which are sometimes fifteen or twenty yards long.

But their most remarkable and elegant manufacture is that of bags, in which the meshes are like rippling hair, and so elastic that a small one will acquire considerable size, according to its contents, while the network will remain sufficiently close to prevent their escape. They make use of designs, but exclusively geometrical ones, such as parallel lines, triangles, and squares.

Their canoes deserve special mention. They are made in one piece from the trunk of the large, cork-like giuccian, roughly hollowed out, and then launched.

The tools used by the Indians are, in the first place, the shells of a large kind of oyster, like those vulgarly called cockle-shells in Tuscany; these are found in great quantities in the lakes of the Chaco; tiger-teeth; very hard wooden stakes; and the jaw-bones of fishes, such as the *palometa*, with which they also cut their hair and the little beard they possess.

Far from being ignorant of potters' work, they are less inferior to us in ceramic art than in any other.

The cooking of food no doubt contributed greatly to the birth of this industry, but reverence for the dead has been the determining cause of its development and comparative progress.

In effect, the Mattaccos, Tobas, Chiulipi, and others, who do not put the bodies of their dead in jars, use rough and unvarnished vessels for cooking, but those who dwell at Santiago, and the Chiriguanos in Bolivia, while they use some for pitchers, have others besides, very highly glazed, painted, and ornamented, in the largest and handsomest of which they enclose their corpses.

The water-jars are nearly always made with a narrow neck in the thickest part, through which a cord is passed; this is fastened in front and secures the jar on the bent shoulders of the bearer. This fashion of carrying burdens is far less graceful than our peasant women's way of bearing them on their heads, and makes the bearers look like beasts of burden; but it may, perhaps, be a more wholesome mode.

They neither understand nor practise agriculture, yet they sometimes sow maize (native to America) and sugar-cane. When they think it is fit to eat, they gather it in. They do not grind the maize, but eat it with sugar, fresh boiled or roasted; the harvest, therefore, is reaped little by little, and lasts for some time. A hard wooden spade, shaped like an oar or like a lance-head, is used at seed-time; the man digs the ground up, the woman scatters the seed and covers it, and all is done. They sow in ground that has been burned, and is fresh from recent rain.

Harvest is reaped in common, but they are tenacious of the produce. While we were living on board, with provisions almost all exhausted, and longing for fresh meat and vegetables, for we had been more than three months without any, a gift of ears of corn and of sugar-canes was received with great joy from some friendly Indians—friendly, but who afterwards murdered our interpreter. The sailors discovered where the maize and sugar were growing, and went secretly and took some. The next day they returned to the spot on the same errand, but found the corn and sugar-cane cut, or plucked up or destroyed, in short utterly useless. And not one of those Indians showed himself again.

It would seem, too, as if the Christians did not wish the Indians to be agriculturists. I was assured that the former having found fields sowed by the Indians of the frontier—friendly Indians—destroyed them all, and that from that date the Indians of those parts have never cultivated a foot of ground. Such conduct springs from a motive of self-interest, and seeks to prevent the Indians from taking possession, that would be recognized as legitimate by Argentine law, of fertile land which the border Christians look upon as future prey for themselves.

They are not traders; how could they trade without either agricultural or industrial pursuits, and themselves a nomadic people on a footing of perfect equality? They barter, however, on a small scale, exchange being the primitive and embryonic form of commerce. They do not even possess any words corresponding to purchase or sale, and to express these ideas they would seem to have gone to school to an economist in order to learn the *do ut des*, the formula of barter; the Mattaccos for instance, when they wish to say *we sold*, say *atkioc nikioc*, i.e. *give to me, I give to thee*.

They have consequently no money; but they constructed a word for expressing it when they saw ours. The Mattaccos call it *tdoc-kynat*, signifying skins of metal, *kynat* being the generic name for any metal whatsoever. No metal of any kind exists on the table-land of the Chaco.

Nevertheless the inhabitants of the Chaco possess a certain kind of money, in embryo as usual, in a material which is valuable on account of its extreme scarcity. The plant that supplies it is called *urucú* at Santa Cruz, in Bolivia, and when the fruit is boiled for a night and a day, it deposits on the surface of the water its colouring matter, which forms itself into balls of different sizes. The colour is obtained from the rind of the fruit, which is the size of an orange. Black rinds produce a black dye, orange-coloured produce red, and white ones, green. The two latter fruits are the size of a nut. All three are different species of the *urucú*. This shrub is of the height of a man, the fruit resembles a pomegranate and opens when ripe.

This substance although grown and manufactured in Bolivia, circulates among all the Indians of the Chaco, and is used by them to stain themselves red as a sign of love, black in sign of fear, and green for ornament. The colours can be washed off with the greatest ease.

Apropos of ornament, the Indians of these parts are more or less tattooed. I have seen tattoo to a great extent on famous Toba warriors and especially on women. It looks like the marking of small-pox, and is in geometrical designs. It is effected by pricking the skin with a big thorn dipped in an acrid milky substance, that leaves an indelible mark wherever it falls, and which is absorbed into the epidermic tissue. This substance is found principally at Santa Cruz, in Bolivia, and is called in Guaranì, as is likewise the plant itself, *i-güo-qui.* It is a climbing plant, with clusters of white flowers, and with a round fruit from which a powder escapes when it bursts open. In order to obtain the *igüoqui*, one of the clusters is broken off before it is ripe, and a milky fluid exudes from the stem, this, during the operation of tattooing, is kept in water, that the milk may not escape. One of these shrubs was seen by a Chiriguan, twenty miles from the Christian frontier, on the Vermejo river, at a spot called *Luna Nueva.*

Another custom closely allied to that of tattooing, the end to be attained being the same, is that of the depilation of the skin, which is universal in the Chaco and possibly also among all the Indians of the New World.

It is practised with a view to ornamentation, but perhaps the real cause is health and convenience. Perhaps, also, they wish to distinguish themselves in this way from the other animals which are hairy.

Meanwhile, whether they are so originally, or whether the effect has been produced by the gradual selection, consequent on this custom, Indians are almost entirely hairless on face and body, and with very few exceptions they voluntarily remove the little hair they have.

Notwithstanding the completeness of their language, I have been unable to discover any songs, or music of any kind. All I know of among the Mattaccos is the following attempt at verse, sung, heaven knows how, by the Chenas. It reveals, however, a notion of rhyme—

> "Bonica, nambonica,
> Se-lé-etié-nó ;
> Bonica, bonica,
> Nambonica, nambonica."

"The meaning is : It displeases me, it pleases me, that thou shouldst embrace me ; it displeases, me it displeases me, it pleases me, it pleases me." Nor have they dances ; for their wild whirligigs hand in hand cannot be called dancing. They are modest, however, for the men and women whirl round in separate rings, not touching each other.

In short, all that is imagination, or is called religion, or poetry, or *cancan*, is completely wanting in these wild tribes.

CHAPTER XXII. .

SOCIAL CONDITION. (*Continued.*)

DOES a want of imagination imply also a want of heart? It has been frequently stated and repeated again and again that the ties of blood are neither strong nor tenacious among Indians, and the assertion is based on observation, on reasoning, on the want of offspring, and on the practice of concubinage.

I think this too hasty a judgment. Accustomed as we are to Christian traditions, which, by the way, form an exception to the great majority of others, and which are in some degree balanced by hidden infidelities, and by the shameless immorality of prostitution, it seems to us that if a woman is not united to a man by all the sacraments of the Church, and if she is not the only one, every proper feeling must be destroyed.

The contrary could be demonstrated; but I will limit myself to the Indians, among whom, although polygamists, I have seen instances of the greatest conjugal tenderness.

One Indian whom we had on board with us, and who had a beautiful and youthful companion, watched over her and worshipped her like the Virgin. The Indian who had been bitten by a viper, and whom we cured on board, was joined by his wife, who nursed him for twenty days, never once leaving his side. The cacique Pasquale, whose old and ugly wife was carried off in a sudden raid, prepared an invasion, followed on the tracks of the enemy, fought like a lion and recovered his companion. These occurrences took place under my own eyes and within a short space of time.

When an Indian introduces himself to you and asks for anything, he never forgets his children, his wives, or his parents; and if he receives anything divisible he shares it, not only with his family, but with his comrades.

I have always seen mothers most affectionate to their children, and it is well known that the wars between the different tribes, and murder among the inhabitants of the same tolderia, are always acts of revenge for offences committed against comrades or kin. What greater proof of affection can be given than this ?

"But they are cruel, and kill their prisoners of war!" We can hardly reproach them for this, since, until recently, we did the same ourselves. We did it on an immense scale at the time of the Spanish Conquest towards these very tribes, and we do it at the present day, when we can do so safely and without risk to ourselves. Only a few short years ago Austria, the chartered gendarme of the signatories of the Berlin treaty, habitually shot the defenders of their country when prisoners of war.

This custom of killing their prisoners is one of necessity for the personal safety of the Indians, who are, through their nomadic life, in constant danger of sudden surprise ; moreover, it frees them from the shame of slavery which is unknown among them. The custom is also of the greatest importance on account of the alternation of victory among the tribes, by which the superior of the two, either in strength or in intellect, takes the place, for a while, of the vanquished, and thus affords an opportunity for that process of natural selection which is the scientific basis of Darwin's theory, and to which is due the gradual improvement of races belonging to the organic kingdom for whom the battle of life resolves itself into *mors tua vita mea.*

Are these Indians cannibals ? This question invariably occurs in connection with savages.

In America anthropophagy has been held in honour by Jews and Samaritans, by barbarism and civilization. The Caribbean savages and the non-civilized Mexicans lived principally on human flesh. The mild Peruvians did not abhor to mingle human blood with their Paschal feast. They steeped their maize bread in blood taken from the forehead of children.

But among the former, cannibalism was limited to prisoners of war, and—death for death—it was considered more merciful and more advantageous to let them first enjoy themselves and grow fat, in order that later they might grace the conquerors' table.

Thus the Chiulules and the Tlascalans, who aided the Spaniards at the siege of Mexico, were horrified that the latter should, through hunger, have eaten the flesh of their own comrades who had fallen at the siege. We are told, moreover, that anthropophagy had a share in the immense number of human sacrifices at Huitzlopotolili, where the priests, like the Levites of old, had select portions of the victims reserved for their own table.

Here in the Chaco, even if these customs existed *temporibus illis*, which cannot be considered as certain, cannibalism either does not exist at the present day or is minimized.

I say nothing of the custom of drinking *aloja* from the skull of a murdered prisoner, converted into a cup propitiatory of vengeance and victory, but I will relate a circumstance which will afford other data.

I had just arrived in Buenos Ayres when I was commissioned to go to the Chaco and divide some land on the Rio Salado. At that time the journey from Cordoba to Santiago was made entirely by coach. Being ignorant of the customs and even of the language of the country, I was prepared for an unpleasant journey, when I happened to meet with a Brazilian of French parentage, who was going to Santiago in order to arrange for the purchase of a large number of mules from the Taboada.

He was an experienced traveller, a Frenchman, and amply provisioned, and the prospect of his companionship was most agreeable. We soon made friends, and the six days of the journey passed away delightfully.

On our parting at Santiago he said, "Friend, if you spend some months in the Chaco, I hope we shall meet again; and as I shall have a great number of mules, I shall also have plenty of excellent provisions. If we meet we will spend a couple of days together in honour of the occasion. We will have good cheer and good wine, which, by that time, you will need."

I hailed the augury, and we parted. Six months afterwards (the whole of which I had passed in the woods and about the lakes of the Salado), on a day of unexpected and pouring rain, falling in advance of the rainy season, and which came down continuously, I found myself, with a few followers, separated from the rest of my companions. Our footmarks being effaced by the rain washing the hard, burnt ground, my men would not consent to turn back in order to find our party. I wandered about, trusting to chance, wet through, and for four and twenty hours without food or fire.

All at once I heard a discharge of firearms, then silence.

"My comrades are letting me know where they are," I exclaimed, and advanced in the direction of the sound.

Then a box of matches on the ground caught my eye.

"What can this mean?" I thought to myself. "We have no boxes like that."

On going farther I found some clock ornaments, a rifle, and a blood-stained sword. Then my hair stiffened, but I proceeded with my men.

Suddenly I caught sight of two, and then three, blood-stained bodies; they were still warm, horribly mutilated, the faces soiled with blood and dirt, and had been disembowelled.

I hastened to wash the face of the corpses and—my heart still aches at the remembrance—I recognized my fellow-traveller, the Brazilian, with whom I had interchanged promises to meet again in the Salado! Ah! I cannot forbear from tears.

Having dug a grave and placed each corpse on a cow-hide, one above the other, I buried them in this humble fashion, with the utmost reverence.

Meanwhile, a band of Mocovitos appeared on the opposite side of the river, who, struck their mouths with their hands, and uttered loud shouts as they drove before them a large herd of mules; then, turning towards us, they scornfully saluted us, holding up the smoking and still bleeding entrails of our friends.

The Indians had dogged the Brazilian's steps, and when he had hastened forward with his men and some of the less tired mules, and was stopping at the *fogon* for *maté*, they had fallen upon him, killed him, and stolen the mules.

The Brazilian had defended himself, it appeared, like a lion, and when at last he was overpowered they had disembowelled him for their horrible feast. For it is a part of faith with these savages that the heart of an enemy who has died bravely fighting imparts valour to those who partake of it.

The above was related to me by the engineer, Braly. And such scenes as these are of frequent occurrence in the Chaco! They are in contradiction to the opinion of some persons who consider the Indians an inoffensive people. Not more than two months ago a band of this very tribe withstood more than fifty Christians, among whom were soldiers and National Guards, and put them to rout with the loss of more than two-thirds of their number.[1]

We are very far, however, from endorsing the exaggerated accounts of Padre Lozano and many other travellers who have written on the Chaco, probably without having stayed there and without any acquaintance with the Indians.

I have seen them drink the blood of animals killed for our use with avidity, but they do not make flesh-meat their exclusive food, as some writers have stated; on the contrary, their food consists principally of fish, game, roots, and wild fruits, with which, and with the honey found in abundance in their woods, they also make fermented drinks, as I have already described.

It would, however, be unjust towards these Indians, if I omitted to relate a circumstance that does them honour.

The reader will recollect that our steamer had been left with the crew at the point where we had been joined by the relieving party, together with whom Roldan and I rode on horseback as far as the Christian frontiers, a distance of eighty-five leagues. Among those who remained behind was Don Felix, the Spanish mason, who used to entertain us through the night with singing and playing the guitar. This man became tired of life on board, which was duller than ever after our departure, and his *ennui* at last reached such a pitch, that, at his own request, and to avoid some untoward accident, the captain of the vessel put him ashore and bade him God-speed.

The poor fellow had soon consumed the small amount of provisions he took with him, and found himself alone and unarmed in the midst of the greatest dangers, and altogether without food, for it was not yet the fruit season. He wandered about in despair, and, endeavouring to reach the frontier, made his way up the river, sometimes walking along the shore and sometimes forcing his way through the sharp brambles of the woods that lay between one point of the river and another. He could of course have returned to the steamer after the first day, but like every true Spaniard, he was too proud to appeal to the compassion of any one who had insulted him.

Every day the situation became worse; sometimes confused by the labyrinth of little paths before him, he would

[1] To this must be added the encounter with the Fontana expedition, and, subsequently, the massacre of Crevaux's.

find himself shut in by dense woods without apparent way of escape, and then with the strength of despair he would plunge through the jungle, and, wounded and bleeding, would reach the river-side, where only hunger awaited him.

This existence lasted for two months, during which he met no living soul, though such a meeting would have been probably an additional peril. He lived on roots, leaves, and even on grass. Only once did he meet with a tree whose fruit was unknown to him, and he ate as much as he could of it. But this was as a drop in the ocean, and his anxious and vain search after another caused him desperate fatigue.

At last a day came when completely exhausted, absolutely without food and incapable of further exertion, he dragged himself to the river-side. He bent down to drink; but was unable to rise again, and remained there in the full rays of the scorching sun, like a dead body.

How long he lay there, and how he escaped wild beasts or *yacarés*, cannot be known; but it may be that twenty-four hours had not elapsed, when a confused sound struck upon his ear, and dusky figures seemed to be encircling him. He made a slight movement to repel them, and fell back into unconsciousness, which lasted until he felt water being thrown over him and heard the murmur of a monotonous chant. On opening his eyes he found himself surrounded by Indians, both men and women. He was lying on a skin, and was being watched until he should return to life.

This was an ineffable moment. There was joy in the consciousness of renewed life, and terror of greater and more atrocious evils than he had yet encountered. He made signs that they should bring him a packet he had with him and found it untouched. He made them open it, and divided among them the white cotton goods it contained. Then he asked for food, and ate of the coarse food of these savages until it sickened him. He remained with them a few days, and as soon as he was able to sit upright, begged them to take him to the frontier, promising that they should be rewarded for their trouble.

One day an uncertain rumour reached us, that a Christian had lost his way in the wilds and had been found by Indians, and presently we saw him appear at the door of our *rancho*. He was tied on his horse and supported by two Indians. He looked like a ghost, was unable to articulate a word, and his eyes had an expression of horror. At first we remained motionless, in spite of our desire to help him ; then we approached, and slipping he fell like a bundle of clothes into our arms, wept, and cursed !

On going out fishing one morning, the Indians had noticed a motionless human body afar off on the strand ; they drew near, and knew it by the clothes and hair to be that of a Christian. Instead of robbing and murdering him, they tended him as we have seen. Then they sent word to the frontier, more than thirty leagues away, that, if not molested, they would bring a Christian in. On their arrival they were deservedly rewarded.

This miraculous escape, however, was near being of no avail. Although we nursed the invalid to the best of our ability according to the place we were in, his stomach refused or rejected every kind of food ; he became weaker each day, and his case at last seemed desperate. At this juncture a Bolivian gentleman, a trader, arrived in the place, and suggested a plaster of meat, vinegar or wine, and I know not what besides, to be applied to the pit of the stomach, and whether by effect or chance, from that night, which seemed likely to be his last, he began to mend, and the cure was commenced which three months after was still incomplete.

Any one who dwells for a certain length of time among Indians, will be led to remark the absence of any deformity among them. Some travellers have argued from this that the Indians, like modern Spartans, destroy their children when born with any defect. Several historians are of the same opinion. But although I can confirm the fact, I explain it by the physical and social conditions of the Indians. The freedom of their life, the sufficiency, in general, of their food ; and, whatever the pious may say of it, the custom of their women to wear no clothes, and, consequently, no ligature round waist or chest ; and the climate, which is healthy, at any rate for them—are material conditions which contribute to the rarity of bodily malformation in their offspring.

On the other hand, the continual state of warfare, the frequent and sudden attacks, the custom of giving no quarter, and the danger from wild beasts and reptiles, must quickly put an end to the imperfect among them, who are deficient in the elements of the struggle for existence. Deformed children, moreover, are probably exceptions to the custom by which the children of the vanquished are spared by the victorious enemy, and are brought up in his tolderias to be the future warriors or mothers of the conquering race.

The absence of deformed individuals is sufficiently explained by these considerations ; there is no need to attribute to the Indians the custom of destroying their new-born infants, or of suffering them to perish ; and for my own part I can bring forward a positive fact in contradiction of such alleged customs.

In the very heart of the Chaco I came across an Indian deaf-mute of the age of thirty. Now if there be a defect that renders a man useless and unfit for the society of his fellows, it is surely his ; but it may easily occur under the most favourable physical conditions, when it is the result of inter-course between persons too nearly related in blood, which is not infrequent in these parts. I shall not, I think, be contradicting myself when I say that I have been told that among the very rare physical defects to which these Indians are liable, deaf-mutism is the most general ; at the same time I must mention that I have never seen a case of cretinism or of goître among them, though both are very common in the northern and western parts of the Republic.

. To conclude, however, my story of the deaf and dumb Indian. I only heard and saw him when he had been attacked and horribly mangled by a tiger while gathering wood, an additional proof of the increased difficulties of the struggle for existence in these wild regions when any of the senses are wanting. We were called in to cure the poor fellow, but he objected strenuously, having full faith in his sorcerers. So true is it that everywhere and in every condition of society, misfortune is the most solid support of superstition and of her civilized sister, religion !

Notwithstanding all this, however, these same Indians have assured me that sometimes mothers will let their children perish when there is no father, or other person who will recognize them and assume the burden of their maintenance.

But such cases must occur very rarely, and do not invalidate our arguments concerning deformity when we remember the striking solidarity that exists among the inhabitants of the same tolderia, and still more strongly among blood-relations. Such cases may, indeed, happen, and not seldom in years of famine, which however can never be very sharp on account of the variety of food, and the truly wonderful abstinence that they can practise when urged by necessity, and for which they make up with usury in a season of plenty.

Their elasticity of stomach is really extraordinary, when idle it consents to an extreme sobriety, but in the open air, the pursuit of game and fish, the work of the harvest, and the travelling necessitated by these things and by their wars, joined to iron health and strength, may be stuffed to any extent.

Either from identity of race, or more probably from a similar mode of life, the same alternation of the severest abstinence with enormous voracity is found in the *gaucho*, and in general among all the inhabitants of the *campo* in the Republic, and probably among other nations under the same social conditions. So it is, the same causes will ever produce the same effects.

These Indians are tenacious of equality. They do not admit distinctions; and the women are the first to combine against those among them who, by natural gifts or their husband's partiality, obtain special favours and ornaments.

I cannot forget a lesson which I had on one occasion. *Tajo*, who instructed me in the Mattacco language, has a beautiful young wife of gipsy type, with a certain distant resemblance to one of the handsomest women in Buenos Ayres. He was very fond of her, and it occurred to me that I could not do better for him than to present his wife with some ornaments and articles of dress. The husband joined me in doing the same, so that the girl was able to dress and adorn herself better than all the others.

When she appeared among her companions in an almost Oriental costume of varied and brilliant colouring, the admiration was general, but so also was the protest.

I was in the tolderia once, and asked to see the beautiful Mattacco in her new dress; this I considered was my right, but I never succeeded in obtaining it. The Cacique had forbidden it, because the other women complained that so much finery humiliated them; and, for the sake of peace, the poor beauty had been obliged to distribute her dresses among them, and to wear the few things she retained one at a time and very seldom. There are sumptuary laws even among savages !

K

CHAPTER XXIII.

SOCIAL CONDITION. *(Continued.)*

Is it really true that these Indians abandon themselves without measure to sexual passion ? and that they exhaust their dynamic and reproductive powers by abuse, as has been frequently stated ?

The explorer who finds himself for the first time in presence of these daughters of the forests in a state of nature, without veil or garment of any kind, may find this novel spectacle of nudity full of danger and almost irresistible ; but in fact it is not and cannot be so, in the ordinary intercourse of daily life.

Habit weakens impressions, and consequently the stimulus to the passions—which, moreover, are not excited by meretricious and bold caresses, or by irresistible coquetry.

The primitive clothing of these Indian women, always in one's sight, the menial offices they fulfil, and liberty, cause the appetites of man to be satisfied by their exercise in such due measure only as contributes to health.

As a matter of fact, who is ignorant of the attraction of forbidden fruit ? But this is a thing unknown to these ingenuous children of nature. On the other hand, how could the orgies of luxury take place among a people so poor and so simple ?

Moreover, we must bear carefully in mind that all which is deadly to man, cannot be attributed to him as original or permanent; how then has it been formed and multiplied ?

When therefore we attribute vices to the savage, we should reflect that either the observer may be mistaken from preconceived ideas against a state of life so different from his own, or that those vices have been introduced by contact with other people, and are foreign to the very nature of savage life.

It has been said of the American Indians that they have revenged themselves for the Conquest and for the small-pox, that we brought among them, by bestowing on Europeans venereal disease.

I believe this to be one of the usual statements made on insufficient grounds, and easy to disprove. I have heard of learned works in which the scourge in question is referred to a very remote period. Popular feeling (often fallacious) refers its origin to France, and historians solemnly fix the date as the period of Charles VIII.'s invasion of Italy. In Leviticus, chapter xv., are the following words :—

"When any man hath a running issue out of his flesh, because of his issue he is unclean.

"And this shall be his uncleanness in his issue : whether his flesh run with his issue, or his flesh be stopped from his issue, it is his uncleanness."

I leave to annotators the true signification of these words.

Meanwhile this scourge is unknown among the Indians of the Chaco, or it is unknown at any rate where Christians have not introduced it. And although this may be explained by saying that a new malady disappears or becomes weaker when once it has gathered in the victims predisposed to it, nevertheless the facts are as I have given them. This is the scientific theory, and in my opinion it is supported by the modern school of medicine, and seems to be in accordance with Darwin's theory of Selection. Moreover, where this disease exists, the Indians do not escape it ; while the Africans are either exempt altogether, or suffer from it far less severely, as every *gaucho* can testify—the various races existing in the country having afforded opportunities for making these observations, which I note here for the benefit of those who may happen to have overlooked them.

It is known, but not sufficiently known, that these Indians are nomadic ; it is not a custom with them to keep domestic animals, the few they do keep are an exception that proves the rule.

Even at the time of the Conquest the Spaniards were surprised by the want of domestic animals among them, and this want, which prevails throughout the whole continent, is a characteristic that from Robertson to Humboldt, and down to the very latest explorer, has arrested the attention of historians and philosophers.

Nomadism still, as formerly, exists in Asia, but domestic animals, such as the horse and camel, have always been well

known.   But the Laplanders, the Samoyedess, the Ciutci,
and the inhabitants of the Kamtschatkan Peninsula, have
domesticated, the former the reindeer, and the latter the dog, to
draw their sleighs.

To what then must we attribute the undoubted inferiority
of the nomadic Americans?   Not to an innate incapacity
certainly, which at first sight might appear a simple and convenient solution, because in that case Greenlanders would not
have kept domestic animals, since American Esquimaux, who
are of the same race, make no use of them, although the bison,
a species of bull, inhabits the polar regions and can be
domesticated.

Nor, on the other hand, does the domestication of animals
present such difficulties as to require a very elevated capacity
in man, since these nomads have succeeded after some attempts
in domesticating them, and the Indians of the Chaco do in fact
habitually keep ostriches, *chugnas* and *charatas*, or wild fowl, and
we know that mute dogs were found domesticated among them.

I believe that the fact of the absence of domestic animals is
due to three circumstances peculiar to this continent and its
inhabitants, viz. their physical conditions, their social conditions, and the scarcity, if not the actual absence, of animals that
can be domesticated.

Everybody knows that the cold on this continent, for easily
explained physical reasons, is much more intense than in the
same latitudes of the Old World.   Thus the temperate zone is
far more circumscribed here than there.   This has rendered the
care of animals difficult, and the means of feeding them extremely
limited, among the inhabitants of the cold regions of North
America, where the bison is found.

But these difficulties apart, the social state of the American
nomads makes the preservation of domestic animals almost impossible.   For a time the same nation occupies or has occupied
immense districts, yet that nation may be divided into small
tribes to whom belong relatively small portions of land, and
these tribes will wage continual war upon each other.   It
follows that the first condition for rearing animals, or for any
other peaceful occupation, i.e. security, will be wanting.   At
this very time the Indians of the Chaco, although they know
our domestic animals and attempt to rear some of them, only
do so on an insignificant scale, because the fact of possessing
.them is an incentive to neighbouring tribes to attack and

plunder them. If their social state had reached to the point of teaching these Indians to dwell together in large populations, then, although nomadic, and in spite of continual war, they could always, in case of invasion, have placed their animals in some safe spot of their enormous territory.

Finally, the scarcity of tameable animals has made it easier to do without domesticated animals, and this in its turn has rendered large social aggregations less inevitable. This scarcity is a notorious fact, and an irresistible proof is furnished by the Peruvians, who, though owning a religion, a government, and agragrian institutions, yet among the larger animals have tamed only the llama, which for shape and strength may well be called the camel of the Andes. On the other hand, the Mexicans, albeit they have a government, and may be called civilized, and also the Bogotans, have only domesticated animals such as we should keep shut up, viz. rabbits and poultry, because there are no other animals that can be tamed.

The same Peruvians who domesticated the llama, of whose flesh and wool they made use, and who also utilized it as a beast of burden, as those at the present day in Bolivia,[1] had to content themselves with hunting the sheep of the country, the fine wool was then, as now, greatly appreciated, and this may be the reason that these animals cannot be domesticated. The hunts took place at certain fixed periods, and, by order of the Inca, a great number of persons assembled and enclosed a large extent of precipitous country with a thin rope supported on stakes. The sheep would rush together and huddle in a small space, for to them the smallest obstacle that they could clear at a single bound appears insurmountable. Then the hunters, drawing in the rope by degrees, a large number of the animals, finding themselves thus enclosed between the rope on one side, and a precipice on the other, are easily captured. The chase was restricted each year within certain limits, and thus the danger of extermination was avoided. A similar plan is pursued at the present day, and although without limitation of zone, the race of sheep does not seem to diminish.

We see by this that, had there existed any other tameabl animals, they would have been reduced to servitude, and we must conclude, by analogy, that where this has not been

[1] The llama, when trained as a beast of burden, carries only a weight of four arrobas, i.e. fifty kilograms ; while a mule can carry twelve, that is, one hundred and fifty kilograms.

done, animals must either have been non-existent or scarce in the highest degree, which we know, in fact, to have been the case.

The result has been a very sharp line of demarcation on this continent between its nomad savage races, and those who have devoted themselves to agriculture; while in the Old World there is an intermediary state combining the nomadic and the pastoral life.

The absence of this intermediary state is sufficiently explained, in my opinion, by the non-existence of domesticated animals, or of animals that could be domesticated. Hence I believe it would be a mistake on the part of any one suddenly finding himself in presence of agricultural nations, such as Peru, Mexico, and Bogota—surrounded, nevertheless, by multitudes of barbarous tribes—to attempt to explain the anomaly by a reference to the history of Asiatic races, and the hypothesis of an invasion by the people of another continent, who would suddenly have introduced and enforced their own pursuits in these regions. The explanation is to be sought, on the contrary, in the natural causes we have laid down; and so far as Peru is concerned, I believe I may affirm, with due knowledge of the facts, that the language spoken there officially in the time of the Incas was kindred with that spoken by the savages.

But if we admit the kind of *Deus ex machinâ* of a supposed invasion or immigration by a people of the Old World into the regions inhabited by the above-named nations, the question arises, to what are we to attribute the civilization of Peru and Mexico? These are countries where we find institutions of which some appear to be copied from those of the peoples of the Old Continent. We find, in fact, planets, gods, temples, priests, nuns, and caste. At Mexico a calendar that Humboldt found to be similar to the Egyptian; at Cuzco, in Peru, a period of years almost equal to that of the Hebrews; strings for counting, like those of one time in China; a pedagogic government; a periodical distribution of land; an assemblage of marriages made publicly by the Inca, recalling to one's memory the pedagogic governments and the agrarian laws of the Old Continent, the jubilees of the Hebrews, and the marriage customs of the Assyrians.

The question is one that arises, and has always arisen, in the mind of every thoughtful man, but the solution is difficult. Some of the greatest historians answer it in this way. "The regions occupied by those empires enjoy a beautiful, but enervating climate, therefore their people will more readily accept the discipline of civilized life. A conqueror, or a victorious people, can subdue them and rule them with despotic sway, ferocious at Mexico, mild at Cuzco, but invariably terrible. Human genius, which is everywhere human, will develop here in the same way as elsewhere ; hence civilization and likeness to the peoples of the Old World."

I do not fully endorse this reasoning, especially the first part. I regret that I am unacquainted with the physical conditions of Mexico, but I know those of many parts of the Empire of the Incas, and I find in them the natural explanation of the fact.

That empire resulted from necessity, not from the enervation of its inhabitants.

Throughout the whole of Peru, on all the western slopes, and on almost all the eastern slopes of the Andes, and in Bolivia, life is not possible for man, or even the lower animals, without agriculture, and agriculture is impossible without irrigation.

These two facts oblige man to remain in one spot and in association, and hence to live under laws, and to constitute and build up successively arts, discipline, religion, and government. Despotism explains nothing. Proud nations and weak ones have alike endured it ; they endure it now, and will endure it in the future, without therefore becoming inferior to nations under liberal rule. In the Chaco, on the contrary, in the Pampas, Brazil, and North America, the soil spontaneously brings forth fruits, roots, and food for quadrupeds and poultry, while the rivers and lakes afford an abundance of fish. Hence the necessity for union and co-operation ; here are peoples who will probably be destroyed by others, who have been forced into civilization by necessity, and have thus obtained the weapons of victory, in preference to becoming slaves to labour, for which there is no need. Nevertheless, in the greater part of these regions the climate is favourable and less enervating than in Peru, Bolivia, and Mexico.

Now let us imagine that either for the purpose of making war, or from the need of expansion—those two most powerful causes of emigration in masses—a people have penetrated into Peruvian territory (and we shall soon witness such an occurrence), and after increasing beyond the scanty resources of that poor soil, ask from the earth, by means of labour, the food that is needful, and that cannot be sought in other parts inhabited by numerous, prosperous, and powerful enemies.

This beginning is, in my opinion, so certain, that if historians had been acquainted with the necessary physical conditions of these regions, they could not have adopted any other ; and I am disposed to assert that even in Mexico the conditions of soil and climate are such that life and production can only be supported by labour.

The analogies of institutions and customs with those of the former peoples of the Old Continent, while they do not prove that they are the result of invasions on the part of those nations, yet suggest to us in some of their details the personal action that may have been exercised by any individuals cast upon these shores by the wrath of the ocean, and who remained on them. And I also think that they may be the result, in a great measure, of human genius, the harmony of which is thus revealed through space and time.

But if we grant a material union, or, at least, a prehistoric intercommunication, beyond the memory of man, between the two worlds, then we must declare the immense inferiority of the Americans. This inferiority was either original in the races composing the population, or was caused by the material conditions of this continent. The inferiority, moreover, is shared by all species of American animals.

To the physical and natural sciences, and that little loved one, philology, is reserved the solution of the most important of all problems, the great problem of Humanity.

Part II.

FROM THE FRONTIER TO ORAN.

CHAPTER I.

THE FRONTIER—ARRIVAL.

THE frontier ! We have only crossed an imaginary line, marked at intervals of forty or sixty kilometers by the blue and white flag floating from the ramparts of the moat-encircled fortress—but by how great a distance, moral, political, and social, are we not separated from the Indian territory we have just left behind us !

In other parts of the world one may travel for hundreds of miles and pass through a dozen different countries, and yet find everywhere a society which has the same traditions, customs, and appliances of civilized life, and forms with those a *de facto* confederation closer than can be effected by written constitutions. But here, separated by a few steps only, is the naked Redskin, with his bow and arrow, on one side, on the other the soldier, in variously-coloured uniform, armed with his breechloader. On the one the natural law of retaliation, and of compliance with innate tendencies; on the other a written code, equal and superior to those of the most advanced nations, compiled by such jurisconsults as Velez-Sarsfield and Tejedor, whose names are known throughout the whole republic of science ! On one side the spontaneous and terrified adjuration of evil and of phantasms ; on the other the artificial, incomprehensible Christian theogony. On one side nomadic races expecting from inviolate nature spontaneous fruits, and happy in a state of poverty equal for all, and in the savage independence consequent upon it ; on the other the agriculturist, the shepherd, the mechanic, the merchant, the magistrate, poor and rich, master and servant !

We reached Fort Gorriti about 10 a.m. We know already what a fort is, but I will add that forts are almost always named after some distinguished citizen. On asking after the captain, who was a friend of Signor Roldan, my fellow-traveller, we were informed that he had recently been transferred to a place called Rivadavia, at twenty kilometers' distance, in order to assist at the provincial legislative elections, which threatened to be stormy.

Roldan had a brother at Rivadavia; we lost no time, there-fore, and although we had been in the saddle for above five hours, we mounted fresh horses, and accompanied by an ensign and two men, we set off with slackened rein. After a gallop of two and a half hours through an exuberant growth of algarrobo, vinal, chebracci and giuccian, diversified here and there by pasture land, enclosed sometimes by a hedge, we reached the settlement.

No one expected us; moreover, it was dinner-time and Sunday; the few streets were therefore deserted, nor did the clatter of five horses in a place where no step is taken except on horse-back, and at the close of a day of elections, attract attention. We arrive at the corner block, and at the place of business of Roldan's brother; the doors are shut, we knock, nobody comes. We find our way to the piazza, this is likewise deserted; then we bend our steps towards a leafy giuccian tree, loaded with bursting fruit, all clothed in its tufts of white cotton.

We reach the house; Roldan ascends the steps, knocks— and the two brothers are in each other's arms! They are speechless with emotion, and can find no other expression for their delight than repeated embraces, until they exclaim in turn, " Brother, we have met at last ! "

The captain and the others long for their own turn, and a series of embraces, hand-shakings, interrupted questions and anticipated replies is commenced, amid a friendly rivalry of eagerness, and demonstrations of affection.

Every eye is wet, except perhaps mine. I am still in the saddle, waiting for an invitation to dismount, with legs dangling, body curved, head bent, shoulders up to my ears, and hands on my saddle, while I watch the scene with dry eyes, and deep in thought I contemplate things present and past, and in the far-off distance. It was a scene that lasted perhaps five minutes, but was indefinite in time and space and substance to me. I know not what happened to me, but never have I felt so lonely as at that moment in the midst of that joyful gathering. Was I mortified at being left out by all those good people? Was I grieved at counting for nothing in their joy?

And then, my thoughts suddenly reverted to my paternal home, to my aged mother, my beloved brothers, and the friends and inhabitants of my native village. And suddenly it seemed as if I too had lightly bounded up the hill, had knocked at the door of my home, and had been answered by a cry of joy and delight; and that I found myself encompassed by my loved ones, called by my boyhood's name, and apostrophized in a thousand exclamations. All this seemed to be happening in the hall of the house, while the neighbours stood grouped round the entrance, telling each other the news, beckoning to me with their fingers, and talking about me. And then it seemed to me that visitors began to arrive, and that in the little drawing-room there was a great crowd of persons, and a constant succession of questions, a continual influx of fresh visitors, with greetings, questions, answers, and exclamations as before. And then all at once a dense cloud chilled me to the heart, as I recollected the burial-ground where so many of my house are at rest !

"The Señor National Engineer," explained Signor Natalio Roldan, as he introduced me to his brother and the rest of the family.

We shook hands, and I dismounted.

CHAPTER II.

RIVADAVIA.

THE settlement of Rivadavia consists of about twenty houses situated round a square and along the neighbouring streets. It is laid out on the same plan as all the towns and districts in America, i.e. straight streets about nine yards in width, intersected at distances of one hundred and thirty, by others at right angles, thus forming quadrangles. The land thus enclosed between four streets is called *manzana*, that is, a table.

In new districts and the new parts of towns, for which a great future is in store, the width of the streets has been increased to fifteen or twenty yards.

The houses are built of unbaked bricks, made of clay or other plastic earth, and worked with ground straw, dried in the sun. These are called *adobe* in Spanish. A similar system has been found to exist among the Indians of Peru, except that the *adobe* are round instead of square. The same clay serves for mortar when a little less stiff, and for plastering the walls. A coating of whitewash over the plaster completes the business, and gives the appearance of a house built of better materials.

When I say better materials, I must explain. For houses of one story only which have no great weight to sustain, and are not to be used for the same purposes as higher houses, the *adobe* is serviceable in these hot climates, for it necessitates thick walls, and is a non-conductor of heat. But from another point of view there are so many objections to it, that the habit of employing it can only be explained by the necessity of economy, or the inability to procure other material. For these reasons the cities of the Republic, including the old town of Buenos Ayres, are built of *barro*.

The roofs are thatched with straw, and for the most part, are daubed over with several coats of clay called *barro*. The straw resembles that of our straw hats when untwisted, and is plentiful throughout the Republic.

The interior arrangements are extremely simple. The rooms are few in number ; sometimes there is only one. With rare exceptions there are no windows ; on the other hand there are plenty of doors, some on the street, some at the back of the house, opening on to a covered *coridor* or gallery. Detached houses also have these galleries or verandahs as a protection from the sun, while in summer they are used in preference to sleeping-rooms, for the stifling heat within the house and the insects of every description that swarm in the straw of the roof and the *barro* of the walls oblige one to sleep out of doors.

The kitchen is always detached from the house, to which also belongs a courtyard or garden, called *patio* and *era.*

Another mode of building consists in enclosing a space of any width that is desired, of one or two yards in depth and about one yard in height, with movable planks. The soft earth is then pressed down in layers at the foot of these partitions as well as on their surface as fast as they are built up, alternating the joins of the blocks. This system is adopted more especially in the west of the Republic, and must, in my opinion, have been acquired from the subjugated Indians of the Peruvian Empire, which was dominant there also, although historians make no mention of it.

Near the town and in the country, standing isolated and apart, are numerous dwellings, called *ranchos,* built in various ways, but mostly of wood, or cane reeds, and over this either boughs or *barro.* These *ranchos,* now so well known to travellers in America, and to those who write or read concerning them, are run up as easily as they are afterwards abandoned, and they are the dwellings most generally met with in the vast country districts of these regions.

Since we are on the subject of houses, I will say a few more words. An *enramada* is a house with a roof made of branches fastened at the four corners to stakes of wood—and there is also the *galpon.* This serves principally for stores, but as it is necessarily of large size, it can be used for any purpose. It consists of a large gable roof with sloping sides, covering an extensive surface. The two sides sometimes reach almost to the ground, the narrow ends remaining open. At other times the space is enclosed by walls, or in some other way. A *galpon* must necessarily be large and in an airy situation. A church, for instance, makes a model *galpon;* I speak of the churches in these parts, when there are any. It is a storehouse for men or for goods; both the name and the construction are Chicchuian, and both have been adopted by Spaniards, among whom the word is now current, and is used to express a magazine or a stable-yard, &c.

Estuncias are all alike; there is the house with its corridors for the owners, the *galpon* for a magazine, the *enramada* used as a kitchen, and *ranchos* for the labourers.

Rivadavia (so named after the great historian of the Argentines) is not an agragrian settlement; no seed is sown; one might say, not a bushel of corn is raised; and it is not even military. Perhaps it will become so, or it may have been thus intended; at the present time it consists of a restricted population at headquarters, with a municipality extending over an immense district of perhaps a couple of thousands of inhabitants, living at distances of fifty kilometers and more. But a day's journey on horseback seems a trifle to any one accustomed to long distances.

One should, however, see the strength of passion out here, the agitation, the scandals!

In one of the intervals of my journeys I found myself at Rivadavia on Christmas Eve, *noche buena,* the good night, as they call it here. A family of the name of Riocana made ready a room with flowers, plants and fruits, arranged a manger in imitation of the one in which it is supposed Christ was born and invited us to celebrate the festival. The Roldans, the captain, myself and a few others were present, and we all sang a hymn to the Infant Saviour, magnifying His name, and repeating after each verse,—

> " Albricias! albricias! albricias! se dén!
> El nino Jesus ha nacido en Belen! "

the meaning of which is : "The firstfruits, the firstfruits are offered! The Child Jesus is born in Bethlehem." [1]

What were my thoughts at that moment? I was thinking of her who gave me birth, and of her joy, could she have seen me then from a distance of 7000 miles! How greatly my piety would have pleased her!

[1] The real meaning of *albricias* is drink-money given to the bearer of good news.

The owners of the house expressed great pleasure at the company of the aristocracy of the place, as they called us; But this was not exactly accurate, because the colonel of the National Guard and surveyor for the province would not condescend to associate with the Uriburistos (so called from the family name of Uriburu, the leaders of the opposition to the Government); and the justice of the peace acted, or rather did not act, in the same way. He was an honourable old man, formerly a Senator of Congress, and now from reverse of fortune had taken refuge in the Chaco, where with the help of his excellent wife he was endeavouring to make a provision for the present and future wants of a large family. Such reverses are often seen in America, and such courageous spirits also. Happy is the country where work and ability are appreciated in no matter what position in society.

On the next evening there was a French and Creole ball, in the same room, with the little manger still standing. There were refreshments in plenty, brandy, cognac, *mate* barley-water, and grapes. A guitarist supplied the music, which the Creoles accompanied by songs, when not engaged in conversation.

Meanwhile the ball went on, with the thrummings of the guitar, the false, harsh, nasal notes of the singers, and the jumping and tripping of the *gato* and *zamba;* wine circulated freely, and many were the *obligos* enlivening the conversation This custom of the *obligo* is a serious one indeed!

A *caballero* carrying a glass of spirits gracefully approaches a *señorita*, and says with a bow, "*La obligo, señorita*," and drinks from it, on which the young lady must do the same. She then reverses the process with "*Le obligo, caballero, hasta concluirlo*," and for the one mouthful she has taken, the cavalier must empty the glass.

It is easy to imagine the scenes that frequently follow on country balls such as this one, and the obligations that a girl may contract. But people must have amusement! And I do not think La Rochefoucauld was in the wrong when he said, "He who has no follies is less wise than he thinks himself!"

On leaving the ball I came on a different scene. On the other side of the street, opposite my room, the only one on the *cuadra*, dwelt a shoemaker. For several nights a faint light had shone from his window, and on the preceding night, until three in the morning, when I fell asleep, I could hear his wife every now and then calling in a sad voice, "Caballero, Caballero." I could not understand how she could call her husband *Caballero*, but I heard afterwards it was his family name.

The next morning the room opposite was open and elegantly decorated. It seemed to be prepared for some festivity, but I took little notice, as I habitually refrain from occupying myself with my neighbours' affairs.

That night, on returning home, I saw a bright light in the house opposite ; it was crowded with men and women ; there were sounds and cries and *obligos* without cessation, accompanying Creole dances. I approached, and there in the middle of the room on a wooden couch covered with a soft white cloth, and amid wreaths of wild flowers, lay the corpse of a little child ! It was the shoemaker's little daughter, and the festa was the *velorio !* I was horrified !

This scene lasted all night and the next morning, until the hour of burial, with only one interruption. This was when drink had so softened the father's heart that he could not preserve the customary composure, and he broke out into tears, cries of agony and imprecations, and would have destroyed everything! But it did not last long. With us, also, when an angel dies, we ring not the passing-bell, but a carillon !

Meanwhile I cannot sleep, partly from the noise, but more from disgust.

CHAPTER III.

THE ELECTIONS.

THE elections held on the day of our arrival were subsequently annulled by the provincial Legislature for informality. It was therefore necessary to proceed to new elections within a certain time. The Government, which had been defeated on the first occasion, endeavoured to influence the coming elections by appointing local authorities devoted to it, and of determined character. Salta, the capital of the province, is about 600 or 700 kilometers from Rivadavia, a nearly desert land lying between them; this can only be traversed on horseback, and in fine weather the journey there and back takes twenty days.

One day we received news of the death of Dr. Alsina, the head of a great party; and at the same time the National Guard was ordered to assemble under command of its chief officers at certain appointed spots. The apprehension of possible disturbances consequent on Alsina's death appeared to explain this unusual call to arms. In obedience to orders the National Guard and the indispensable horses were soon assembled at about ten leagues from Rivadavia. Meanwhile it began to be whispered in the town that this call to arms had a bearing on the elections, and was intended to secure the votes of the electors belonging to the National Guard through the influence of prestige and discipline, and through them the votes of others. On Saturday there arrived a *chasque*—Chicciuan for messenger—informing us that the troops were already within five leagues, that they were being feasted on *asado de vaca con cuezo* (beef roasted without removing the skin, a very favourite dish with the natives), and, excited as they were with spirits and tobacco, would all vote for the Government candidates; also that on Sunday morning they would come, a few at a time, so as not to attract attention, into

cuero.

L

Rivadavia, where they would vote in a body in presence of their superiors.

The alarm of the opposite party may be imagined on finding such a trap set for them, with the certainty of defeat, because the Government and the Legislature were on the other side. Besides, it seemed clear that this system of conducting the elections was against the spirit, if not against the letter, of the electoral laws, which required that public notice of elections should be given at least a week in advance. No such notice had been published at Rivadavia. The captain of a fort twenty kilometers off was immediately sent for, that he might use his influence to prevent this scandal.

Early on Sunday morning an unusual stir became perceptible. At intervals of a quarter of an hour or half an hour, parties of two, four, or six horsemen came into the town. Horsemen with fluttering *ponchos*, with ample and many-coloured *chiripas*, with fringed *calzoncillos*, with long and clattering spurs, boldly riding their mettlesome steeds. The open *poncho* frequently disclosed the glittering hilt of a *facon* (a weapon between a short, broad sword and a dagger) that, according to the custom of the country, is worn at the waist, sticking upright in the *tirador* (waistband). Others, holding their *ponchos* by the borders, endeavoured to conceal some larger weapon. All made for the same point, whence by degrees rose a clamour that increased with the fumes of drink and with the company.

About nine o'clock a half-ruined *galpon*, formerly a church, was thrown open, and disclosed the Electoral Board composed of *Situazionisti*. (We called the partisans of the Government, and therefore of the *situation*, by that name.)

This was the critical moment. The Opposition had assembled in a house, but were afraid of taking action. Should they protest? They had let the time pass for doing that. Should they vote? This would be to sanction their own defeat. Remain passive? But this would be to yield the victory, which must, on the contrary, be theirs, were the proceedings regular.

At last it was resolved that they should present themselves, holding the law in their hand, and endeavour by persuasion to get the elections prorogued; and, if this failed, stop them by force.

Persuasion was a rather serious undertaking, although the law was clear, and was in print on the papers they carried; then to use force was the alternative, and would probably end in the massacre of the protesting party.

The official took opportune measures. With two orderlies who had accompanied them, and three other soldiers who were passing through on business, one of whom was my Indian teacher, he made up a force of five, and stationed them in readiness to act on the first signal. Then he with eight or ten others issued from the house, and, making a circuit, re-entered the *galpon* through a door at the back, and confronted the Electoral Board, who, surprised and confused by the audacity of the Opposition, were at a loss how to proceed. I stood apart, watching the drama.

After a few short moments of amicable discussion the dispute waxed warm, and was supplemented by shouts, gesticulation, and invective.

"But this is a *pronunciamiento !* " cried the president to the captain.

"*Pronunciamiento* indeed!" replied the latter; "do you think that because I am a soldier, I am not a citizen as well?"

"This is an attempt against the majesty of the law!" exclaimed the secretary, addressing himself to Natalio Roldan.

"It is yours that is an attempt!" returned Don Natalio. "The law is on our side; look at it!" and he held out the sheet in his left hand, tapping it with the right.

"Now we shall see!" exclaimed the commissioner, and he ordered the electors of the National Guard to advance in line, while he and the captain left the enclosure, and those who remained engaged in discussion.

Shortly after this a group of National Guards were seen advancing on foot, ten abreast, from the back of the piazza, armed partly with carbines and partly with *facons*. On a whistle from the captain, the five soldiers stood in readiness.

The National Guards advanced about twenty steps, and a second whistle from the captain brought up the soldiers from one side of the piazza, where they were stationed, to the church.

"Forward, forward!" shouted the Commissary to the Guards, who had already formed into four bodies of two ranks each. A third whistle brought the soldiers between the door-way of the church and the National Guards, who were half-way across the piazza.

The Commissary and the captain standing side by side formed a curious contrast. The latter had laid aside his sword on entering the electoral precincts. The former in *poncho* and *chiripa*, the other in a plain tunic worn with some elegance,

and wide cavalry trowsers.   Both carried revolvers.   The
Commissary was furious at his position having been taken with
so much ease ; while the captain was as calm as if on parade.

The commissary shouted, " Forward, boys ! up with your
facons ! "

And the captain, "Present arms ! carry arms ! "

The National Guards waver.   They are on foot, as are the
soldiers ; they come in order to vote, not to kill, or be killed
with Remingtons discharging fourteen shots a minute.

The commissary vociferates : "Forward, friends ; don't be
afraid !—out with your *facons—al de*—(he meant to say *degüello*,
the act of cutting the throat).

" Ready ! " cried the captain at the same moment, and five
rifles were levelled in readiness for the word " Fire ! "

It was a solemn moment !

There, like a point in the vast square, stood the little troop of
five foot-soldiers, in linen clothes, rough highlows, and red caps,
armed at all points—breech-loaders, cartridge-belts—slender,
upright, resolute, and ready to obey the orders of the elegant
officer standing on their right.

Here, a parti-coloured crowd of peasants, in ponderous *ponchos*,
or large cloaks, held together at the edges, *chiripas*, and white,
fringed *calzoncillos*, with wrinkled boots, and tattered hats, of
various shapes, and worn in different ways, like men always
on horseback, and who have only just dismounted, and stood
awkwardly on their feet, balancing their carbines, and holding
their unsheathed daggers in a hundred different attitudes.   At
the back of the *galpon* were a number of *caballeros* in two files,
one in front of the other, with uncovered heads, composed, but
resolute of mien, but scrutinizing   countenance   and   calm,
observing by turns the adversaries in front and the troops in the
square.

All the rest of the square was empty, and the doors of the
few houses near were either shut, or, if slightly ajar, disclosed
upon a dark background white-robed female figures, who revealed their presence and their fears by the stealthy movement
of the doors.

The silence was sepulchral !

It seemed as though we could hear the beating of our hearts.
And how all hearts were beating at that moment, on which hung
the lives of scores of fellow-citizens, of comrades, of friends, of
relations !

But suddenly the National Guards, already wavering, broke —some stood firm, some, with their faces to the enemy, drew back. There was confusion in their ranks. The Commissary's orders by voice and gesture are no longer obeyed. The entire column retreats, disperses, and abandons the square when confronted with those five rifles that, at a moment's notice, would have scattered death and destruction around. It would avail nothing to recall them ; victory is on the other side, on the side of principle, said Roldan. On the side of discipline, of improved firearms, and of courage, say I.

I do not wish the reader to retain a bad impression of the National Guards. They were numerous, it is true ; but half of them at least were at heart on the side of the Oppositionists ; and all of them knew that the latter, who were there before their eyes, had come to prevent an act that they declared to be illegal, and which the Situationists made to appear so by the unusual, furtive, and scheming manner in which they managed it. Moreover, their arms were inferior, and then they were fathers of families and owners of property. How could they be expected to fight, or to wish to do so ?

At this point some one says to me, " This is all very well, but in the meantime this is the beautiful Republic ? Abuses, civil wars, anarchy, misery ! You require a Dictator, not a Republic ; or, better still, a king ! "

I do not think so. In politics accomplished facts must be taken into account. Now the Republic is a fact, and its historical reason appears to me to reside in the other fact, that its independence was achieved outside of, and in opposition to, the monarchy. If the Bourbons, when Napoleon drove them from Spain, had retired to South America, and had there placed themselves at the head of the movement of independence of the mother country, they would probably have taken root, as the House of Braganza under similar circumstances took root in Brazil. But the Bourbons were too much in love with the vast and glorious kingdom of Spain, containing as it did double the number of inhabitants of the whole of Spanish America, the population of which was at that time three parts Indian, and they knew not how to practise the cheerful self-renunciation of the House of Braganza, when driven from their modest Portuguese throne.

The House of Bourbon, with the authority of tradition, with prestige of service rendered to those countries, might, with the aid of other elements, have constituted an aristocracy of birth and wealth to be the base and nucleus for the concentration around itself of the followers who would by degrees have arisen in the different parties, and to discipline and educate them. This we may believe, and it was much to be desired.

But the contrary took place. Independence became possible, and therefore inevitable ; but it was vigorously resisted by Spain. In order to attain it, the people rallied round the most conspicuous individuals, and by them were led to victory. Afterwards, there being no superior centre of attraction, each wanted to preserve supremacy, and this was only possible, firstly, with the independence of the great territorial historical and natural groups, historically or geographically ; and secondly, by the federation, in all these new nations, of the provinces that were distinct, either by their physical or social characters, or by the part they had taken in the war of independence.

The ideas of '89 had indeed taken hold of those classes who had directed and inaugurated the war of liberation ; but the physical and social conditions of these countries were and are little adapted to such ideas, because their chief men were and are inspired to abdicate a part of their liberty in favour of a conventional personage, not supported by services rendered. How then could a new dynasty take root ? How the old, since they had shed their blood to free themselves from it, and had conquered. To attempt it was to ensure ruin. This was proved in the case of San Martin, the great Argentine commander, who was suspected, and perhaps not unjustly, of attempting it on behalf of another ; and, again, Bolivar, the great Columbian general, who was accused wrongfully, I think, of attempting it for himself.

These countries, therefore, separated by immense distances, by great natural demarcations, and by the limits of colonial administration, felt the necessity of separating into different nations, and when the Republic was constituted they became federated on a basis of the widest political and administrative liberty.

Was this federation an evil ? Was this basis of liberty an evil ? The occurrence of an historical fact is difficult without the operation of potent reasons, which, while they have made it inevitable, make it also a substantial . good—if, indeed, the expressions bad and good can be used in reference to political necessities.

It must also be observed, that if we only recur in thought to the times when the political and social centres were separated one from another by hundreds and thousands of leagues and by intervals of months of travel, before railways, telegraphs, or even stage-coaches and mails had shortened the distances or facilitated communication, federation was a primary fact, which was written in the constitutions; and because it was a fact, it was also sanctioned in the constitutional laws. It may come to pass that in time, with improved communications, and altered relations, federation may disappear; it is certain at any rate to be modified, first in the actual relations between the provincial and national Governments, and next in the written laws. But then and now it was and is so. The same law is imposed by similar physical conditions, upon Brazil, where notwithstanding the monarchical and imperial form, the provinces are true confederate States, constituting an immense empire.

The necessity and hence the excellence of the federal order is granted; but it is denied that written institutions, however liberal, have been or are good for these people, who are not supposed to be ripe, as it is called, for liberty. To this I reply: The evil is not in the laws, but in the social conditions. If liberty is, in fact, illusory among some nations, it would be so to a still greater extent under a Dictator or a despot. If the thirst for command agitates the whole country at election time, and frequently renders them either violent or fraudulent, this very thirst has made and would make it quarrel with the ruler who was not made one by election.

If the Government, in order to keep power in its party, corrupts or coerces the electors, the same Government, if absolute, would certainly, in order to prevent revolt, corrupt and coerce the citizens.

But we have had peace; with peace, prosperity; and with prosperity, the possibility of attaining true liberty.

We have also had frightful tyranny, and with it the reverse of the medal. Under the social conditions of these countries, a Dictator or a Life President, in order to free the country from electoral agitation and from the anarchy of liberty, would be quickly transformed into a merciless tyrant, who would repress his quarrelsome fellow-citizens in their distant provinces by means of a crew of satellites more brutal than himself. Rosas was an instance of this. And then, besides the danger to peace, is the education of citizens to be counted as nothing, and free activity in all, for the moral and material progress of the country ?

However much these institutions and countries may be traduced, the fact is, that power alternates between the two parties ; that no citizen abandons his country in despair on account of the eternal persecution of authority, which is curbed by its precariousness. And according as wealth and political education progress, the people become more and more the sovereign power ; while in the solid reality of the constitutional guarantees, and in the wide horizon now open to all, each citizen becomes a better and a happier man.

Lastly, even when the tendency of a governor is towards an abuse of his power, the institutions of the country virtually exist. Then will the remembrance of fraud and violence endure in the minds of the citizens, and when the day of reparation comes, society resumes the suspended tradition with the mere disappearance of the despot, and continues to confirm and assimilate it.

To conclude, a periodic electoral agitation, in order to gain the magistracy, is better than permanent political agitation in order to obtain the control of the vote, where that manifestation of the popular will does not take place.

CHAPTER IV.

POBLACIONES—MISSIONS—CIVIC GOVERNMENT.

From Rivadavia I was to go to Oran, a city of 4000 inhabitants before 1871, when it was destroyed and depopulated by an earthquake. The distance geographically is 200 kilometers; but as I was to visit on my way that point of the River Vermejo where it divides into two branches, the distance I should have to cover on horseback would be doubled, and, including the return journey, quadrupled.

At the fork of the river, the stream on the right retains the name of Vermejò, that on the left taking the name of Téuco, from *Téuch*, a word meaning river in the language of the Mattaccos who live on its banks.

The two branches run with many windings to a distance of fifty kilometers, and in a direct line for a distance of 400 kilometers, thus forming a large oblong island, its width being one-tenth of its length. It begins at about 100 kilometers within the frontier, and ends at the mouth of the Téuco, 300 kilometers below the frontier.

In the Christian territory westward from the frontier the banks of the island and those on the farther sides of the two arms of the river are partly populated, i.e. they have been sold as allotments or *presellas*, consisting of a certain number of provincial half-leagues, equal perhaps to 1200 *hectares* under condition that the purchaser shall build a *rancho* and set up a *poblacion*, that is a family with some cattle. When the *poblacion* is on a large scale, from the number of animals, and the extent of land, and consequently, with a large dwelling-house and outbuildings, it is called an *estancia*.

Some of these *estancias* are also met with beyond the frontier within a radius of four leagues (twenty kilometers), the farthest spot legally under the inspection of the patrols (*comisiones*) from the Forts; beyond this distance the *estancieros* are deprived

even of that amount of protection.   The love of gain, however,
induces the owners of *estancias* to push still farther forward, if
the bordering country (*campo*) affords good pasturage.

I leave you to imagine the kind of life led in these parts,
surrounded by savages and wild beasts, at long distances from
the nearest inhabited districts, and hundreds of leagues from
any town.   And nevertheless I have met with ladies in these
estancias.   I can assure you that the Argentine lady is inferior
to none in the world, in her spirit of self-sacrifice as a wife and
a mother, and her admirable domestic qualities.

It will easily be understood that individuals of certain classes,
such as medical men, priests, and gendarmes, are rarely found
out here, or, generally speaking, in the heart of the Argentine
countries.   But life seems none the worse for their absence.
For the doctor, there is sometimes a substitute in the *curandero*
—but almost always in a sufficiently salubrious climate, wholesome, though plain food, and a frame trained to this kind
of life.   The gendarme is replaced by the strong hand of the
master over his *peones* (labourers), and by the few opportunities
for evil-doing, with the exception of quarrels, and then the
guilty party can always lay his hand upon a horse and escape.
The priest's place is perfectly well filled by the moral sense
innate in man, and practically exhibited when required by the
exigencies of human society, which depend in their turn on the
state of that society, whether the fact be or be not pleasing to
the advocates of an absolute morality, armed at all points, pre-
existing in the head of Jove.

And then, too, the priest does not come to these parts, because he does not find it profitable either for himself or for his
Church.   But in order to preserve appearances, he sends missionary brothers, who are as incapable of teaching savages one
step in civilization, as the Indians are incapable of appreciat-
ing their good intentions.

On this subject a large part of the public is in a state of
mental aberration, and some of the governors enact a ridiculous
part for their benefit.   It is believed, and the belief is encouraged, that one barefooted friar is worth a battalion of
soldiers, or a police station, and funds are provided and
expended on this account.   But it is not so.

Savages understand nothing about incarnations, transub-
stantiations, immaculate conceptions, and indulgences.   And
should they, when those who are born amidst these beliefs'·

either laugh at them or become mad on the subject? The idea of reward and punishment in a future life, by which they might be elevated and morally improved, is not new to them; they already possess it, as we have seen. Hence it is more natural that they should remain in the faith of their fathers, and it should be considered more moral also, by those whose morality consists in the impossibility of believing what one no longer believes, or in cheating and lies. The savage will learn the new religion, that to him is no religion, as a business, and according to the measure imparted to him. Where is the education in this? Where is the march of civilization? We cannot make much of having taught him to gabble the creed, or be sprinkled with holy water!

A battalion, on the contrary, by preventing robbery, obliges the savages to work for their living, and the station offers relief and help, in the day of want, that comes even to the nomad! Meanwhile the hope of gain attracts them to the new life, from which they are not able to withdraw, and into which they will enter as one of its necessary parts on the day that the inevitable progress of the superior race must despoil them of the lands that they do not cultivate. This is education! This is civilization!

The missions may supply convenient resting-places for travellers, as in Africa, or afford opportunities for useful scientific discoveries, if their members can be imbued with the scientific, instead of the religious spirit; but until then, I cannot see what results they have to show, with the exception of some acts of charity and courage, such as the rescue of prisoners, a truly noble and holy deed. Among all the Indians of the Pampas, not one has joined us through the attraction of religion, and the same is the case with the Chaco Indians. If a few score live near the *estancias* and work on them, it is because the land was formerly theirs, or because they felt attracted to the new life and became unconsciously bound to it. If some hundreds go to the sugar *haciendas*, it is because paid labour is more attractive than idleness and misery. Let us enclose them within the circle of civilization, and they will come to us quicker than if enclosed in a circle of friars. And if this is not sufficient to absorb them within the period judged necessary by civil society, invasion and force must be employed, not preaching. The missions please neither savages nor citizens; but they are liked by governors, who use them for the purpose of deceiving the people as to their devotion, and foreigners as to the mildness of their rule.

Meanwhile there is strong antagonism between the *pobladores* and the missionaries, and some years ago a regular pitched battle took place between them, resulting in the burning of the settlement and the destruction of the inhabitants. A monk, whose name I forget, wrote a pamphlet on the subject at Genoa, on his return to Italy. The divergence of the course of the Vermejò subsequently destroyed two new houses (I have already explained what these houses are) built by these same missionaries, and the neighbours declared and still declare it to be the *finger of God!* Is that finger, then, a two-edged sword? Eventually, at the time of electing a Deputy to Congress, the *estancieros* of the Rivadavia district united their votes, in order to return a candidate who had assisted them in their legal struggle before the Salta tribunals, consequent on the battle I have already mentioned; and at the present time, as I am writing, this same gentleman, Dr. Oliva, has been elected Governor of the province.

If the priest be wanting, so also must the marriage ceremony be wanting, which is celebrated here by means of the Church exclusively. But the concubinage prevailing in the *campo* is caused rather by the unwillingness of the man to contract marriage than by the absence of the priest, because from time to time some priest makes an excursion into the country, not unprofitable to him, if he be a poor man; and, on the other hand, it would be no great thing to ride some score of miles for once in a way, as in fact any who care about it do. It would be wrong to attribute the same immorality to this custom, as if it prevailed among ourselves; the circumstances being totally different, whether as regards means of communication, social conditions, or the race itself. While the unmarried man who comes to these wildernesses is nearly always white, or presumed to be so, the woman, on the contrary, is almost always an acknowledged half-caste. Now this constitutes a social inequality that very few have the courage to face. The lower orders—I use this term unwillingly, but in order to make myself clearly understood—consist of a breed almost entirely native. Therefore the custom of concubinage is the quickest and the least costly. We must add that it preserves freedom, which is precious to a people who have it ever before their eyes in immense and solitary lands, and among whom the women age very rapidly! The Argentine laws, however, have looked to this, and have decreed that a natural son shall inherit name and property in the same, or almost the same, manner as a legitimate child, and that he shall have the right to verify the father. The learned jurisconsult, Velez-Sarsfield, who drew up this law, was equally great in head and heart. The social disorder, therefore, that might perhaps be dreaded among ourselves only appears here on a small scale in consequence of this provident law—which, moreover, promotes fruitful unions and the blending of races, and thus contributes to the increase and improvement of the population, objects of the highest importance in a country such as this, of which it has been well said, *to govern is to populate.*

Nor do the women live in a state of humiliation. There are few countries in which women are more respected than here. Whether from Spanish traditions, or from habits formed under the social conditions of the country, when the population was only one-fifth of its present numbers, and each individual became of increased value in the solitude of country life, women possess extraordinary influence, and are loved and respected by men. During the atrocious civil wars that distracted the country for the first fifty years of its independence, woman was alternately the guide of a man's life and the companion of his misfortunes. Hence the participation of women in the very springs of politics, which, while it may seem imprudent, nevertheless excites the admiration of foreigners.

The respect and consideration for women that exist in the upper classes of society are also found among the people, either from the force of example, or from innate custom produced by the causes I have mentioned. One example will suffice.

One of my servants, acting as guide, was a poor country labourer, a married man with a family. After a couple of months' absence, he asked me to write in his name to his wife. Not quite knowing how to begin the letter, I asked him to tell me. After a moment's thought he said, "Write, '*My esteemed lady!*'"

This kind of *tone* is mutual—I do not say among the classes privileged by wealth and education, for there it is a matter of course, but among the lower classes and even among the Indian nomads. The very prostitutes conceal and dislike their mode of life. The calm and apparently impassive Indian nature conduces to this outward bearing, which may be called irreproachable.

Their manner of walking is generally majestic; and their way of holding their arms, which has so much to do with the elegance of motion, is nearly always absolutely correct. Two Indian sisters, wives of the same Indian husband, who had settled among the Christians, made such an impression on me when they came with him to Rivadavia, that I took them for two ladies in disguise, so correct and elegant were their manners, although they were seated on the ground in the shade of a tree at the side of the street, and busy over a child of the husband's and with various little domestic duties.

In order to understand all the contingent value of any civil institutions whose social and individual influence is so much extolled, and also the conditions of their merit, it is necessary to have been in places where they do not exist or act in a contrary sense.

CHAPTER V.

DEPARTURE FROM RIVADAVIA—FEATURES OF THE COUNTRY.

IN the middle of October we set out for Oran. *A* few *vecinos* accompanied us for half a league, and then Signor Natalio Roldan and I continued our way, attended only by the Santiagueño[1] and the Chiriguan, who rejoiced in the name of Sardina!

On entering the territories of the savages we found ourselves on a vast wooded plain sloping imperceptibly from west to east.

Yet on this immense table-land there are frequent and unexpected breaks in the ground. These are due to the action of the waters, aided by the friable nature of the soil through which they wander. The forking of the river has been repeated over and over again since the primeval times, when the immense plain first came into existence, and the abundant waters flowing over it formed for themselves channels in which they were confined.

Only five or six years ago Rivadavia stood on the brink of the river; now it is half a league away and is reached by a series of steps or terraces. The ancient bed of the river has become an immense natural tank, retaining the water all the year round, and replenished afresh during the floods. It is the favourite haunt of the yacaré, a kind of crocodile. Deposits of mud will gradually fill it up ,and the level, being thus raised by a succession of layers, will remain dry, first in the season of drought, and later during the moderate rains. Finally, with the lapse of ages, joined to the deepening of the river's course, it will remain dry even in the great floods, unless the overflow, being impeded by banks formed across mouths belonging to a former period, it becomes first a lake, then a *bañado*, and lastly a marsh.

[1] Inhabitant of the province of Santiago.

Such is the genesis of the existing alluvial lands. They are due to the working of causes still in activity, and which every year are forming a more extensive and closer network, in the meshes of which the primitive soil, broken up into islands of different size, is enclosed. This soil, so long as it endures, will retain its own altrimetrical, physical, and vegetable characteristics. The waters will not overcome it, though they never cease from their operations, sometimes carried on with insidious caresses of the clay foundation of the perpendicular banks, and, by continual lapping, bringing it down, bit by bit, into their bosom ; at other times, turgid and impetuous, they seek to destroy it by force, assaulting, dragging, demolishing, until, laden with its ancient forest-growth, they whirl it into their seething currents.

The rings of the net already formed are subject to similar action ; for the river, conscious, as it were, of its irresistible strength, both for building up and for destroying, seems to take pleasure in undoing its own work, and substituting other work for it, tracing with its spume, more powerful than adamant, a fresh network above and across the former one, which is unfitted to resist the attack on account of its brief gestation in the bosom of the waters.

And as it will cost nothing to the land that in the beginning afforded an asylum to the waste of waters to receive on its soil the axe-defying quebracho and the giuccian, with its produce of white cotton, these trees will accompany its infancy while the waters are coiling about like monstrous serpents. In the same way, without cost, the later inhabitants will enjoy the fertility of lands producing the algarrobo, the chañar, and the nutmeg, with their delicious fruits ; and the medium lands will freely provide for health and cleanliness in the growth of the splendid and elegant pacara, with its saponaceous berries ; while the more recent soil hastens, with child-like grace, to adorn the paths with poplars, willows, and silvery-leaved shrubs that grow in countless profusion along the wooded banks.

Alluvial action is very powerful, and exists on an extensive scale. During our journey we frequently came across dried-up channels, sometimes many leagues in length, that had been full of water three or four years previously. And it is certain that if suitable engineering works are not carried out, the existing arm of the river that retains the name of Vermejò will soon form, along its whole length of nearly a thousand kilometers, a series of tanks that will themselves undergo the transᴸ, formations I have described. Fort Aguirre only a short time ago stood on the right bank of the Téuco, from which it is now half a league distant, and a "madrechon," or natural reservoir, has taken the place of the river.

The alluvial lands, formed by the existing currents on which, as being the most ancient, the highest and driest, the algarrobo flourishes, are always lower than the primitive soil, where the quebracho and the giuccian grow; thus forming a kind of stair, never less in depth, I think, than a couple of mètres. The steps of this stair are, of course, not always very distinct, for the length of time in which atmospheric agencies have beer at work has allowed the parapets to slope, and time has filled the space between the two soils with detritus from the surface, as is easily understood. But the perpendicular banks of the river afford clear evidence of the facts I state, and I do so with the greatest confidence, although based only on my own observations.

Occasionally, in the time of great floods, the algarrobo lands are under water, but never the quebracho; the former lie at a height of six or eight yards in the centre and west, and eight to twelve yards and more, eastward, in Paraguay, for about thirty leagues from the mouth of the river.

This first stair is generally succeeded by others before reaching to the river, and, as its course is more or less circuitous, the bank on the outer side is almost always perpendicular, and of greater or less height according to the nature of the soil. The inner side of the curve is alluvial.

Now this alluvial land is nearly always in steps or terraces, and seems as if butting against a high bank. One can actually see these steps in process of formation by the river, which is very muddy when swollen, besides which the friable soil on the exterior side of the curve is easily disintegrated, and thus the absolute, and even the relative position of the steps, is frequently and rapidly changed. This occurs when a huge mass of earth falls over into the stream, especially when trees are carried away with it, or when the unevenness of the river-bed fails to offer a equal and homogeneous resisting power. In that case the terrace becomes still more irregularly formed.

Thus we find that the steps or stairways in the bed of the river are owing, not to one year's work or one single flood, but to the normal and continuous action of the stream in ordinary seasons. These steps, however, are shallow, and the terraces very narrow. They can be levelled with little trouble.

M

Those terraces and stairways which, from their size, are important features in the aspect of the country, are due to the heavy floods which for considerable distances deposit wide terraces four to six yards high, their width being increased by the *débris* of a former smaller terrace—other lesser ones are due to the ordinary floods.   Now, a different degree of productiveness may be said to correspond with each terrace, because the composition of the soil in each must vary according to the known laws of deposit, and on account of the depth of the water and their longitudinal distance from it, which is a considerable element in every respect in this country, where the climate is so dry that agriculture is almost impossible.

To give an idea of this, Rivadavia is, or rather was, at a distance of half a league from the river.   In that space there are, as it were, four stairways, with terraces six to eight hundred yards long covered with algarrobo, and soils of all kinds, marshy, dry, sandy, and clay.

Madrechons, lakes, and swamps, all formed by the same force, constitute with the terraces the only features of the soil that break its monotony, and partially alter the uniformity that results from uniformity of climate.

CHAPTER VI.

ON OUR WAY TO ORAN—THE RAINS AND AGRICULTURE—A LEPER.

WE proceeded onwards across the immense level plain, broken by the natural accidents I have described, and clothed with woods, varying according to the nature of the soil, but so frequent that they seemed to be the same, only with darker and different shades alternately predominating.

Every eight or ten kilometers we came to some *rancho* inhabited by the *pobladores* of the estate, and less frequently to the dwellings of the *estancieros*. Our march was arranged so as to bring us at nightfall to a place where we could get water and pasturage and a place of safety for our horses. On drawing near such a halting-place, one of us would go forward, and riding up close to the stockade that always surrounds a house in the *campo* would clap his hands together, and on the appearance of the owner salute him with the words :—

" Ave, Maria ! "

" Ave, Caballero ! "

The customary courtesies were then immediately exchanged, and our wants were named ; the traveller remaining on horseback until the sacramental words, " *Bajesé* or *apeesé*," that is, " Condescend to dismount," authorize him to put his foot to the ground.

Not to wait for this invitation would be uncivil and presuming, and would be offensive to the master of the house. Moreover, the dogs that are always growling round the *estancias* in large numbers might make one pay dearly for such a breach of good manners.

When we have entered the enclosure, and are seated in one way or another, we are questioned as to whence we come and whither we are going. We speak of the drought (*seca*), and of the locusts, the two great scourges of the Republic, of the pasturage, the cattle, and the harvest.   Meanwhile *maté* is handed round, the horses are led to the *potrero* (an enclosed feeding-place), *asado* is prepared, and beds are got ready.

My fellow-traveller was shorter, stouter, and fairer than I, and looked the more important of the two.   Consequently, whenever there was a bedstead, that is, a hurdle of cane reeds, or a network of leather fastened to a frame supported on four posts, it always fell to him, and he, as an experienced traveller, never declined the honour.   For me there remained only the ground, as hard as bricks, on which I stretched the *montura*, i.e. my saddle, for a bolster, the *carona* or leathern horse-cloth to keep me from the damp, the *pellones* or sheepskins with the wool on, that form the cushion of the saddle, for a mattress, and the *coperte del campo* for blankets.

But sometimes we shared alike, and then I experienced a certain pleasure, because, as we all know, "an evil shared is half a joy," and because equality is the ideal of mankind "ever by envy or other hatred moved."   However, when the contrary was the case, I easily resigned myself, well knowing the hopelessness of contending against nature, who had chosen to favour my friend.

When the *asado* was ready, it was brought in threaded on a wooden spit and placed in the midst of the circle, each one of us helping himself with his knife to *churrascos*, small juicy portions, smoking hot.   Earthy, yellowish, oleaginous, tepid water from the neighbouring tank, a mouthful of Cognac or brandy, a cup of tea or coffee, and a cigar accompany and crown this frugal repast.

Flesh-meat was seldom wanting, because, when travelling, we generally came to one place or another where it was slaughtered ; not, however, that this country is the California of flesh-meat, as supposed, and as indeed it was at one time ; quite the contrary ; a fat beast here in the Chaco, where the meat is the most savoury of any in the Republic, costs not less than twenty or thirty scudi, without the skin.   And the meat is far from being so fat, savoury, or nutritious as in Europe !   Beasts are slaughtered from time to time in every *estancia*, and the flesh cut into the thinnest possible strips ; these are dried in the sun or at the fire, either with or without salt.   The meat when thus treated is called *charqui*, from a Chicciuan word used in almost every part of the Republic ;—a proof that the custom in question was known to the aborigines.   When dried in this way, it shrinks to about a third of its bulk, and if the weather is not damp will keep for weeks.

But what I may truly assert to have been wanting was bread. In the whole of the Chaco proper not a hundred sacks of grain is harvested. The cause is simple enough. The climate is so dry during the growth and ripening of cereals that they almost always fail, if not artificially irrigated, and on this table-land, with rivers running in very deep channels, that cannot be accomplished without mechanical means or an extended system of canals, for which the time is not yet come.

Flour is therefore purchased at a distance, and brought in from time to time on mules, for the most part from Catamarca, Rioja, and even farther, a distance of a thousand or fifteen hundred kilometers.

This dryness of climate is so disastrous that even maize, which is indigenous in America, is frequently ruined by it, although sown expressly in the bed of former tanks, near running water, and although it comes to maturity in forty days.

I affirm that agriculture in the centre of the Chaco within a limit of four to five hundred kilometers in breadth, and of some thousands in length, is the most hopeless of pursuits, and it would be the greatest imprudence in the world to undertake it. And this because of the unfavourable dryness of the climate.

Within the boundaries, however, of the Paraná and the Paraguay the climate is less unfavourable, on account of the close proximity of immense masses of water which advantageously affect the climatic conditions prevailing over this portion of the continent. The district in question is from fifty to a hundred kilometers in width, and of the same length as the unfavourable district mentioned above. Here agrarian colonization might be attempted by men possessed of large capital and clear judgment, who would refrain from importing families accustomed to the high and frigid peaks of the Alps into these tropical climates and low-lying lands. Such immigration has been and is still practised, with very serious and grievous results to individuals and to the colonies.

And since I am on the subject, let me proceed. Considered from an agricultural point of view, we may remark on the west of the central district another district bounding it on that side, as the coast bounds it on the east. It lies against the mountains that, starting from the Paraná and Paraguay, rise at a distance of 1000 or 1500 kilometers from their left banks, and follow a corresponding course. In this district, on the skirts of the mountains, the numerous and not very deep water-courses, and still more the sloping nature of the ground, would easily admit of water being brought from short distances for the purpose of irrigation. The Chaco is situated in latitudes where the cold south-east winds are always and necessarily reacting on the warm and comparatively moist winds blowing from the Equator; hence the atmosphere becomes cooled, and with diminished temperature is unable to hold in suspense the same amount of vapour, which consequently escapes suddenly in rain.

In order, however, to produce this phenomenon, since the south-east winds increase rapidly in temperature as they approach nearer, the moisture of the equatorial winds must be such as to saturate the opposite winds that have slightly risen in temperature as they travelled, but have received no increase of moisture on their way, because they have only passed over an enormous and arid territory; and they must also be so laden already with humidity that the atmosphere will be saturated at the same moment that its temperature falls by contact with the winds from the south-east.

Now these circumstances are not of very frequent occurrence, but the contrary; hence rain falls very rarely, except during the last months of summer and the first autumn months, when the difference in temperature between the two winds I have mentioned is very much greater. But even in these months there is little rain in the centre of the Chaco, because the equatorial winds are not so laden with moisture as to be unable to endure a fall of 15° or 20° without breaking into rain, while they are sufficiently hot for this great fall to cause by reaction positive hurricanes, known as *tormente di terra*, of such violence as to drive away the previous atmosphere from before them, as they sweep over the huge plain.

In the western district against the mountains, it happens instead that these hurricanes suddenly meet with an obstacle in the hills, and saturate the atmosphere, which, aided by the cold of the high mountain peaks, 3000, 4000, and 5000 yards in height, discharges the condensed vapours in rain.

This effect in the western district (or *della falda*, as it is called) may easily occur, and thus we have rain there, although not very often, at other seasons besides those I have mentioned. Together with the facilities of irrigation already indicated, and the almost tropical climate, this would conduce to prodigious fertility. The width of the district, however, is very limited. It is only from five to ten leagues broad, according to the height and configuration of the mountains, and only commences when these have attained a height of 2000 yards, because only then does it begin to possess numerous perennial streams of a certain volume. It must be remembered that in these latitudes there are no eternal snows at a less height than 5000 yards ; this is attained by Mount Zenta, the highest peak in the chain from which flows the Vermejo.

I have made a rather long digression over a handful of flour, but have not useful books been written on the history of a drop of water? And I have much more to say on the subject, but I reserve it for another time, should an opportunity present itself. What I have already said will, in that case, serve as an introduction, for repetition helps us to understand new and distant ideas.

To return to our subject, viz. bread. Here in the *campo*, and with few exceptions in many of the cities of the Republic also, the bread is baked in small separate ovens, generally built of unbaked brick, and in the shape of half an orange. The heat is consequently only sufficient to bake small rolls or buns in the shape of shuttles, and these are the loaves. Being made of very hard and little-leavened dough, they crumble almost into flour a few hours after baking. Nevertheless, when fresh the bread is good, although it lies like a ball in the stomach. When hot, the scent is most fascinating to a frugiverous European, existing on flesh-meat in a tropical climate.

But I was destined to endure the tortures of Tantalus concerning that bread. One morning we were passing quickly by a spot where three women in white gowns with sleeves, the only garments worn in such heat, were making loaves of the whitest flour. I, who had the greatest craving for bread (for my comrade and our two men were Argentines, and consequently satisfied with meat), halted for a moment to buy a couple of francs'-worth. The women were very well behaved, therefore I was not annoyed at having to wait a little. But when I opened my saddle-bags to have the bread put in, I saw that the woman's hand was thickly covered with a kind of ulcer then prevalent throughout the whole of the Chaco! What could I do? Disgust was stronger than hunger, and greatly disappointed, although laden with bread, I rejoined my companions, who

made merry over my piteous silence and the bread-hunger I had
never felt so strongly before!

This loathsome malady was a kind of leprosy, and it attacked
immense numbers of people that year.   It was said that excoria-
tions suddenly developed into it.   Some deaths took place.   It
was attributed to the extraordinary dryness of the year, owing
to which the water had become impure, the air more epidemical,
cleanliness more difficult, and food absolutely destitute of
vegetable matter, while the heats were the same as ever, and, as
some persons added, to a universal taint of syphilis.   It was
expected that the epidemic would cease at the season of rains.
I had the good fortune to escape, although not a little afraid of
the complaint.

CHAPTER VII.

DISEASES OF ANIMALS—FORAGE—DISTRIBUTION OF HERBACEOUS FLORA IN PASTURE-LANDS.

INCREDIBLE but true! One of the most difficult things to find in this country of horses by the million is a good mount. And this is intelligible. No one either lends or gives his best, especially in horses. Contentedly, therefore, we mounted our sorry jades—*mancarrones*, as they are called here—and not without embellishments of sores and galls. Our two attendants were old hands, and knew how to put their steeds discreetly on their mettle, although heavily laden with our belongings. But I must candidly admit I have little skill in horsemanship, notwithstanding five years' practice, and I could not succeed in raising the spirits of mine, or of any one of mine, for I changed sundry times during our journey to Oran. It was dreadful!

In the beginning I had rejoiced at the look of a fine *tordillo*, i.e. dapple-grey horse, that was offered me. But I was doomed to disappointment! He proved to be *achuqchado*—that is, he had eaten a sort of grass that apparently fattens horses, but destroys their wind. This grey had been running wild for many months, and when he was caught was found in the state I have described. There is no other cure than to turn him into a wholesome pasture, and work him, a little at a time, for some months.

But *achuqchiatura*, so called from the symptoms exhibited by the animal, which trembles as with ague, or, as it is called in Chichucha, *chuqcho*, is nothing when compared with a terrible disease of the shoulders called *deslomadura*, resulting almost invariably in death.

It shows itself in two ways: the one is by rapid emaciation, weakening the horses so that they lose their sight, and at last fall and cannot rise again; the other by a kind of paralysis of the hind-quarters, beginning in that part of the animal between the haunches and the ribs.

In both cases, but especially in the latter, they drag their hind-legs after them, and when no longer able to stand, fall down dead. It is said that the flesh on the quarters of these animals is found, on examination, to be putrid, full of matter, and stinking; and if eaten by dogs or lions, they swell up, emit a horrible stench, and burst.

The disease carries off whole herds of horses in a short time, and sometimes mules also, and the complete disappearance of these animals from the Bolivian province of Cicuitos, adjoining the Argentine department of Oran, is said to be due to this malady. Cicuitos formerly abounded in *caballadas*. It is curious that strong and well-fed horses are said to fall victims to it rather than thin and weak ones. It is supposed to have been imported from Brazil through the Bolivian provinces of Santa Cruz and Cicuitos; appearing first in one place, then in another, then back again to the first, and continually extending farther, until it becomes a matter of the gravest importance.

Certain phenomena partly explain the disappearance, sometimes rapid, sometimes slow, of many fauna and flora—such as flaccidity of caterpillars, and the *oidium* and *phylloxera* in the vine.

Horses and mules are subject to another disease called *tembladéra*, from the shivering with which they are seized. It must not be confounded with the preceding one, although some of the symptoms are similar. *Deslomadura* attacks Creole horses in preference, while imported animals do not suffer from it until they have been a year or more in the infected district.

The contrary is the case with *tembladéra*, which is said to be caused by antimonial vapours absorbed by the animals during their passage through certain districts. The road through the Argentine province of Catamarca, which is travelled by mules on their way to Andalgalá, laden with minerals excavated from the mountains of the province, runs through some localities of the kind, and is strewn with carcasses.

Deslomadura shows itself after the rains, and especially in those districts submerged during the full floods and exceptionally arid in the dry season. There is no known remedy; blood-letting is of no avail. Brine plasters and friction with tiger's grease are said to be useful; but recovery is so rare that one cannot safely attribute it to any particular cause.

The existence of the fossil horse in South America might lead us to suspect that dominant diseases such as we have

described may have totally destroyed the race in very remote
ages. This should be a guide and a warning to breeders to
preserve these invaluable animals, which were imported here
from Europe at the comparatively recent period of the
Conquest.

And à *propos* of the diseases of animals, the Oranese have
assured me, that north of Oran, where the ground is already
rising some hundred yards, that is, to a height of 600 or 700
above the level of the sea, although the pasture-land is of the
usual kind and remarkably fine, it is no longer possible to raise
cattle. They do not breed, and die in two or three years
time. This is in the mountainous district, not on the plain
properly called Chaco.

Since I am on the subject of cattle, let me say a few words
on their food-stuffs here in the Chaco. They are all, of course,
natural, and consist of grasses, shrubs, and trees.

Among those with tall stems, *mimosas* supply the largest
amount of food. Their leaves are eaten by goats, and their
fruit by beasts of large size. The carob-tree or *algarrobo*, the
cassia or *tusca*, the *chañar*, the jujube-tree or *mistol*, the *duraz-
nillo*, similar in shape to the peach-tree, called *durazno* in
Castilian, supply forage. The Algarrobo, the Vinal, the Tusca
and the Tatané with their pods, the Chañar and the Mistol
with their fibrous integuments supply fruit which is eaten
so soon as it falls, and forms a splendid food for man as well
as beast. These fruits last for three or four months, beginning
with the Chañar and Mistol, followed by the Algarrobo, whose
fruit is more abundant and of a finer quality and ripens
in succession ; the Tusca and the Vinal coming last of all.
The time of year for these excellent food-stuffs corresponds
exactly with the time when forage is scarcest, or fails utterly
through prolonged drought, the rains not beginning to fall in
the regions where these trees abound, until the latter half of
summer, as I have stated already, while the fruit ripens in
these latitudes during the greater part of the first half. Yet in
districts far from the river and deprived of lakes, the want of
water devastates the cattle at these seasons and annuls the
benefits of this easily procured food—moreover, in some years
the food itself is scarce.

Cattle are sometimes obliged by want of water to have
recourse to leaves of the cactus plant or prickly pear ; and not
cattle only, but men also, as it happened to myself. At first this

seems like assuaging one's thirst by eating ham, but afterwards one feels it slightly alleviated. In time of famine stale bread is good.

The principal shrubs affording forage are the following :—the *suncho* and the *bobo*, also called the white willow. They grow on the flat banks of rivers, scarcely out of the water, and produce a yellow fat, less prized than white fat; the *garravato*, a kind of mimosa, with branches almost creeping along the ground and covered with short but formidable thorns like the claws of a cat, whence its name; the evil-smelling *calakchin*, which is highly fattening, but imparts an unpleasant flavour to meat and milk; and the *chuqcho*, which, although eagerly devoured, weakens the animal, as I said before.

But the natural pasturage, here called *pasto*, affords the principal support to cattle, and is divided into *pasto duro*, i.e. hard or strong food, if the grasses of which it is composed lasts more than two years, and *pasto tenere*, or soft food, when they are annual or biennial.

There is a great difference between one *campo*, or extent of ground, and another. The one, covered with algarrobo woods, &c., and with few and scattered herbs, will support only five or six hundred head of cattle on the square league; the other, consisting of pure herbaceous pasture-land, will feed from two to three thousand. Both may be equal in richness of soil, but the first will support about one-fifth of a head per hectare, and the second an entire head. The explanation is obvious, grass will grow very little, if at all, under trees.

The natural distribution of pasturage offers a splendid lesson to the attentive observer on what may be called *vegetable selection*. It is confirmed also by the distribution of tall-stemmed plants, due apparently to the single fact of the difference of age in the soil, after allowing for latitude or its equivalent, viz. height above the level of the sea. Not that this lesson may not be studied in our own country, where, if the materials for it do not exist, their absence must be attributed to the violence of man; but here we have it pointed out and repeated on a vast scale over an immense and unbroken plain, where, the indications being more marked, more simple, and more certain, because they are absolutely natural, the lesson is more eloquent.

We have already hinted that notwithstanding the uniformity of the plain or country over which stretches this vast extent of forest, which must be looked upon as the northern continuation of the grassy pampas of the south, there are, nevertheless, various accidental irregularities due to the action of the waters, the deposits from which have been unequally distributed. These irregularities hold the original plain, as it were, in a net, whose meshes are constantly becoming thicker and closer along the rivers, within a zone of some leagues on either bank, in which the river has oscillated since its beginning. This is called consequently the *zona di oscillazione*, although it is in fact undefined, and is always augmenting on account of the facility with which the original soil is permeated by the river.

Well, then, in one and the same latitude, and at levels differing from each other by a few feet only, you will see as many different pastures in the same district as will correspond simply with a scale of a few feet.

Why so? Because that scale represents a different period of formation; not, of course, a geological period, but one of those into which the existence of the river has been divided up to this very day. Consequently there is not only a difference of duration, during which any given fibrous growth may easily have predominated and imparted a particular character to the pastures, but, more than this, there is a difference in the component parts and in structure, which causes varying conditions of growth.

I am aware that I am saying no new thing; but I believe that in general little attention has been given to this subject, and I write for the generality. Learned men, if I have any among my readers, will find their opinions confirmed by observations made in the presence of these vast solitudes.

While navigating the Vermejo, the first thing that struck me was the presence of clover along the dampest parts of the sloping banks, where the crumbling soil belonged to the most ancient period. I thought the seeds might have been brought thither by the river, which higher up in its course might have run through fields of clover; but, on the contrary, the forage grown in the mountainous districts is the medicinal trefoil, of which there was no trace here, nor did I see it during my ride of 160 leagues through a territory, half Indian, half Christian, and thus was led to conclude that the trefoil I mention is indigenous. The Mattacco Indians call it *chiù-asset-locq*, i.e. stag-forage. This may be a secondary reason for the name given by them to a cow which is also a ruminating animal, *chiù-nasset-tàch*, i.e. a large deer. In Chichuio, trefoil is called *mosco-jujo*.

Clover, which is a biennial, grows spontaneously in the dried-up shallows, and on the banks of the lakes, tanks, or ponds, as well as on the banks of the river itself. We found it most serviceable during our journey across the Indian territory. I saw scarcely any on the Christian country. I attribute the scarcity to the cattle, who are fond of it, although I found it bitter to the taste, and who exist in great numbers among the Christians, while the Indians hardly own any. There are two principal kinds of trefoil. The importance of this food, in an agragrian point of view, must be my excuse for having dwelt on it, and I must add that 1500 kilometers south there are natural fields of clover on this same river Negro, and the same are found on other rivers of the Pampa and in the Chaco.

In solitary districts enclosed by forests covering the country there are fields of *simból* which, from a distance, might be taken for corn. It is a gramineous plant and grows to more than the height of a man on horseback; it is perennial, and even when burned grows again. It reigns as a sovereign, despotic and exclusive, but it cannot escape the caresses of the *tramontana*, a climbing plant that entwines it, and, mingling its own leaves with those of the *simból*, affords a most appetizing food.

On land almost equally dry and high there are vast meadows consisting exclusively of *aibe*, a bush supplying a hard and bitter food, never eaten but from necessity, and in its natural state, but it does not fatten or give a factitious fat; it has the appearance of hay.

On level but somewhat high ground we find the *coda di volpe*, or fox's tail, which is equal for fattening to the medicinal trefoil.

We find also in succession the *paglia rossa*, or red straw, growing to a height of over a yard and a half, and used also for thatching roofs; two kinds of Afata, remarkable for their large rhomboidal leaves—this is a favourite food, and fattens well—and a trailing plant called *erba poglio*, with a thick, broad, round leaf, provided with thorns at the axis. It is eaten only out of necessity, but is held to be a remedy for ague (*chuqchó*), pains in the stomach, and boils.

The best food is perhaps the *pasto crespo*, so called from its

crisped appearance.   It is eaten both in a green and dry state.
It attains to half a yard in height, and likes a dry soil.

The white and red dog-grass, on the contrary, prefers a
rather cold soil, compressed, beaten, and hard.   It appeared to
me to be more abundant in the western country.   It is an
excellent food for cattle here, just as it is at home.

The following plants grow in low and moist ground :—the
cebadilla or *orzuola,* i.e. barley, the reed-cane, the clover, as I
have already said, and the *camalote,* a large-polled willow, almost
a trailing plant, and yet growing higher than a man.   It is found
in fens and in very wet ground, such as the lowest islands,
and entangles itself in such a way that when washed away by
the great floods it moves in masses like little floating islets.

There are many other herbs and small plants that I have
forgotten, but of those as well as of the others that I have
mentioned, the most characteristic by situation, extent and
appearance are, in my opinion, the Simból, the Aibe, the
Pasto Crespo, the Cebadilla, and the Camalote.

A plant, useless as forage but characteristic in other respects,
is the *cortadera,* so called from its hollow-shaped leaves, which
are very long and notched at the edge, and which cut like a
sharp saw.   From the centre of the thick bush springs a long
reed like those in marshes ; it is four or five yards in height,
with a handsome tuft at the top.   Each shrub is of great height
and size, and stands out distinctly from the others.   It grows
on the low parts of high table-land, where they are washed by
the rain-courses.   The size of these shrubs, their large numbers,
and the great extent covered by them, constitute, together with
the river deposits, an actual formation as they push forward,
their foliage and structure offering an adequate resistance to
the force of the waters, by which they might otherwise be
washed away.

The *nio* is remarkable for its poisonous properties ; it is fatal
to horses and cattle who eat it, but at the same time affords a
proof of their intelligence.   For if the herd is new to the locality
where it grows, some animals invariably fall victims to the
poison, but after a while they recognize the danger, avoid it, and
in some way convey the warning to other cattle who arrive
there subsequently, and who apparently do not touch the herb.
The Nío is found principally in Tucuman and in Jujuy.

Land differs greatly in value, not only by reason of the
quality and amount of pasturage, but also on account of situa-

tion. The provincial government of Salta has a law by which
certain lands are given as *mercedes,* i.e. gratis, with an annual
charge of 4.80 per thousand on the reputed value. The
provincial square league is valued at 6000 francs, and is equivalent
to about 1350 hectares, or 5000 Spanish varas. An obligation
is also incurred of raising a house within the year, and putting
at least fifty head of cattle on the land.

Other land is put up to auction, and has hitherto fetched a
very low price. In the department of Oran, near the frontiers,
it has been sold at 250 francs the league. Some *campos* taxed
at 500 Bolivian piastres, equivalent to 2000 liras, failed to find
a purchaser at 100 Bolivians. In better and less exposed
situations they have fetched 200 Bolivians, and as much as 600
in the department of Anta.

The land when purchased has no further burden than the
land-tax, which is now 4.80 per thousand. The owner is not
obliged to place people on it.

For the purpose of official taxation, cattle are valued at the
average price of ten Bolivians, or forty liras, per head. The
value of an ox-hide varies from six to twenty francs ; its weight
is in general 35 lbs., or one *pesada,* equal within a little to
sixteen kilogrammes. A cow-hide weighs about 22 lbs., or ten
kilogrammes.

The expenses, legal and otherwise, of obtaining possession
amount to 500 Bolivians per league. The spit costs more than
the meat !

The wild cattle of the Chaco are the finest, largest, and best
for eating of any that I saw in the Argentines, and this not
only on account of the breed, but also because of their feeding ;
some of the imported calves attaining to a superior development
in this region. The climate, and possibly the food afforded by
the algarrobo and other plants, may contribute to this, for
mutton here is so savoury that it seems to resemble beef—at
least so it appeared to me.

The cattle wander quite at liberty, the owner's brand being
duly registered. It is impressed with hot iron at the age when
the males undergo the usual operation, which is effected by
twisting and crushing. *Estancieros,* however, who own fine
pastures, enclose their *campo,* if able to do so, by a dry hedge,
but this is frequently burnt down by accident or malice. But
almost always near the house in every *estancia* there is a *potrero,*
or enclosed pasture of good quality, intended specially for

horses. Notwithstanding the great distances and the immensity of the woods, it is rare to lose an animal, unless killed on the spot by the thief, because the owner's brand is known and easily recognized by all the inhabitants of the district. And as every one rides about a good deal, it is difficult to escape meeting, sooner or later, with some one who will deem it his duty to inform you that he has seen an animal with the brand of such or such an owner in the *estancia* of another. Moreover, if an animal has been sold, it should bear the brand of the original owner, reversed, under the old brand, and the new owner's mark placed upright. Thus even stolen hides may be recognized.

Cattle-breeding is still the best business in the whole Republic. If no epidemic occurs, capital is doubled in three or four years. Hence the colossal and increasing wealth of some great *estancieros*.

CHAPTER VIII.

A NIGHT AT THE MOUTH OF THE CHAPAPA.

AFTER five days' journeying we reached the river at a place called Bella Vista, where there was a boatman and his *chalana*, i.e. a narrow, flat-bottomed boat suitable for floating over shallows. Thence we were to go up stream for about thirty kilometers until we should reach the bifurcation of the river, which it was one of the principal objects of my journey to survey.

Along the whole way we had met, at the end of three days' journeying, with only one little settlement, consisting of a few wooden and *barro* houses, called Villa del Carmen ; the usual leprosy was prevalent, and we had crossed a region of former channels of the Rio that are still deep, although dried up. Two, four, or eight years ago, the river rushed impetuously through channels that are now sand-pits, and did not even spare the two Missions established at Sauzal, but washed them away in its whirlpools—providentially, says vulgar report. The Missions have been re-established two days' journey lower down, near Rivadavia, at a place called Pozo del Tigre. When I passed them, the fathers in charge—there were but two, I think—were absent ; nor were there any *tolderias* of Indian catechumens, so that the mission seems to be of a somewhat intermittent character. Moreover, the fear of another flood has made them seek for higher and firmer ground, which is likewise less damp.

The whole length of the route I saw neither priest nor friar, and only one on arriving at Oran. It is true that these parts are not adapted for a profitable propaganda, because the Indians decline to be converted, and the population is scanty, poor, and scattered at great distances. The clergy, therefore, muster their forces in the cities, where, since the suppression of religious orders in Italy, they have largely increased, and acquire greater influence every day, partly by the traditional ability of this powerful ecclesiastical institution and partly by the talents of some of the fathers. Among these I cannot refrain from mentioning Father Pio dei Bentivoglio, a man of letters, a philosopher and a gentleman; Father Georgi, orator, musician, and architect; the Fathers Donati Marco and Porreca Quirico, models of charity and humanity, who more than once have risked their lives in endeavouring to rescue Christian prisoners from the Indians, and in braving the pestilential diseases that have ravaged the country.

I am of opinion that through one of those numerous inversions of things that cannot fail to strike a philosopher-historian, the Catholic clergy are gaining in America in the same proportion as they are losing in Europe; although ultimately the destiny of both continents must be substantially the same, in this respect as well as in all other social conditions.

Starting from Bella Vista, we four began to descend the river; the two men being *Carontos*. At times the waters flowed over an immensely wide bed, which so diminished its depth that we were obliged to land, in order to lighten the boat until the difficult bit had been overcome; and at other times the stream rushed through a deep and narrow gorge, and disaster seemed imminent. We soon recognized that the river voyage we had undertaken would be long and dangerous, but what could we do? We could look for no help in the deserts through which the river flowed.

Close to a spot called *Pozo de la Oréja* (Well of the Ear) we saw some Indians on the bank. Thinking we might obtain assistance from them, we drew near. But not one would come with us for all our promises of gifts and our assurances that we should turn back after a few days. Their invariable reply was that their enemies were a little lower down, and that they feared an attack. Some bloody fray had probably taken place, and they feared the customary Biblical and Indian reprisals.

Groups of Indians are often met with on Christian territory; on the frontiers, however, they live either in the midst of the riverside forests, or are attached to some *estancia*, where they work for the owner when required. But they invariably retain their own religion and their own ways and customs, and public rumour does not fail to accuse them of being the authors or instigators of robberies and murders that are laid to the charge of Christians. When I passed through, there had lately been an attack by Indians in which one Christian youth had been slain and some cattle stolen. Similar accidents are unavoidable in these parts.

A little later, at eight or ten kilometers from Bella Vista, we remarked a *rancho* on the bank, and our spirits rose. But we could obtain no assistance, the owner being away. The horizon, however, seemed to be clearing in the direction of security.

We continued our way down stream. At one point we saw three oxen sticking in the mud; the endeavour to assuage their thirst had destined them to a terrible death. Troops of vultures were collected on the neighbouring trees, awaiting the banquet provided for them by the cruel fate of these poor animals. But either from cowardice, or preference for putrid meat, none of the foul birds attempted to hasten the end. A little lower down we caught sight of an Indian through the thick foliage of the wood. He stood as it were in a frame, just like the illustrations in books of travel, bow and arrows in the left hand, lance in the right, and club at his belt. We invited him to join us; but he refused for the usual reason—fear of enemies. Then we told him of the oxen in the mud; he replied he dared not go to them, because it was late and he was afraid of tigers.

Finally, at dusk, we reached the bifurcation of the river, at the point called *Boca de la Chapapa.*

We had not even a dog with us, hence our sleeping at night was rather a serious matter, on account of wild beasts. Making, however, a virtue of necessity, we lighted big fires, and spread out our couches in the usual way on the edge of the river, at a spot some distance from any tiger track.

The next morning we were startled by the furious barking of dogs, and a moment afterwards, at the distance of a few yards, we saw a large tiger plunge into the river, and swim rapidly across. A pack of hounds were in pursuit, and behind them a group of horsemen at full gallop, armed with lances, carbines, and daggers. They crossed the river and began to gain on the fierce brute; he had been seized by the dogs before he could reach the shore of the other arm, and had turned at bay, half sheltered in the thicket at the foot of an old tree. The hunters came up, and before the creature could spring forward he was brought to the ground by a musket-shot and then finished with a spear through his heart. A brief and fortunate conflict.

This tiger, one of the largest in the neighbourhood, was the same that a few weeks before had been pursued by two famous tiger-hunters. Their aim had failed, and one escaped by flight, while the head of the other was so mangled, his eyes being almost torn out, that he expired shortly afterwards. Signor Vianello, a captain in the mercantile marine, had the skin.

Tigers habitually follow one track, as do most wild animals. This is detected by the tiger-hunters, as the track of a hare is by sportsmen.

The return journey was much more difficult, as we were going against stream. Moreover, the weather was threatening, and we had no protection against rain. We set off, hoping to reach the *rancho* at *Pozo de la Oréja*, but at nightfall we had made but half the distance. The situation was becoming serious. A suffocating heat had been succeeded by a south wind which was fast covering the sky with clouds, and was blowing with increasing violence. Our men told us to hasten all our preparations for sleeping and eating, for the rain would soon be upon us. We halted, therefore, at the first convenient spot, fixed up a kind of tent over the boat with our *ponchos*, and arranged a sleeping-place at the bottom, where we were packed like anchovies, side by side.

We cooked some pieces of fish, and had scarcely had time to make a little tea, when down came the rain, preceded and accompanied by a furious and chilling wind, and we understood that a Toledan night was commencing for us.

A most wretched night! The recollection depresses me even now, although the memory of them is supposed to be the consolation of past fatigues.

We were in the midst of the wilderness, in utter darkness, amid the warring of the elements, the shrieking of the wind, the beating of the rain, the rolling of the thunder. Between the claps we could hear the roaring of the swollen and angry river, and the noise made by parts of the banks breaking away and tumbling over into the water, and in the glare of the lightning looking like enormous masses that must overwhelm us. It was horrifying. Then the rain dripping from the tent on our bed-coverings forced us to remain completely motionless, so as to prevent its reaching our persons. At the same time we had to contend with the wind, which blew first on one side of the tent, then on the other, and against the rain, that rushed through every aperture, threatening to inundate us. Then, too, there was the contention between sleep, a still more imperious tyrant than fatigue, discomfort, cold and constant resistance. Meanwhile, there was no sign of intermission in the hurricane, nor any prospect of repose.

At earliest dawn we proceeded on our way through ceaseless rain. We selected the least wet of our clothes and put them on like *chiripas* and *ponchos*, as the best way of keeping the damp from us. Towards noon the rain ceased, but the weather remained threatening, and we could not even manage to break our fast with tea; we longed to reach the *rancho*. But we came to a spot where it was no longer possible to breast the current that threatened to overturn us at every bend of the river, and we were obliged to land. Each of us made a bundle of his clothes and away we went, completely naked, our bundles on our shoulders, following the edge of the stream and towing our boat along the best way we could.

Still fasting, we arrived at nightfall at the *rancho* of *Pozo de la Oréja*, leaving our boat half a kilometer off. Meanwhile the cold became so intense that the Chiriguan who had been despatched to fetch the clothes left in the boat was seized with cramp and would have died, had we not sent a horse to fetch him back. I leave you to imagine the impression produced on us by that *rancho*. There was a splendid fire to dry us; a boiling hot *asada* to restore our strength, and the lattice-work of boughs fixed at about a yard and a half in height, so as to diminish the danger of tigers, seemed like a royal bed to our wearied limbs.

The next day we returned to Bella Vista loaded with fish, of which thousands had been washed ashore.

"These are fine stories to tell when they are over." Quite so. If they were not followed by a train of colds and catarrhs that hasten by a quarter of a century the approach of an ailing old age, with the prospect in addition of passing, like a broken-winded horse, from the stables to the knacker's cart.

CHAPTER IX.

THE PASSAGE OF THE VERMEJO (OR VERMILION) RIVER—THE
DELTA—EROSIONS AND FLORA.

WE have arrived within a few leagues of the mountains in
which arise the streams that, after a long course through the
various valleys lying at their feet, unite and form the Vermejo
river. We have followed the river throughout almost its
whole course, and have reached a suitable point for studying
its hydrography. It is therefore time that we should pause
awhile, and, mentally retracing the route we have pursued, take
this opportunity of sketching its history, its present, and its
future. The analogous conditions of other rivers of this region
renders the study which we are about to undertake still more
profitable, because they give its results a general application.

We can easily imagine an epoch when this immense plain
was, so to speak, the sister, and even the twin-sister, of the
Pampa. These two plains of somewhat similar aspect extend
throughout the continent, from Magellan to the Equator. The
repeated alternations of submersion and emersion, of which
there are traces in the stratification, which retains marks of a
vegetation distinct from that of the higher land, and visible in
the perpendicular banks of the river, suffice to destroy any
hasty hydrographical theory, such as a preordained difference
in the vegetation of each stratum.

At a later period the plain became extended and slanted
imperceptibly from north to south in the same direction as the
course of the great rivers, the Paraguay, Paraná, Uruguay, and
Rio de la Plata, and stretched out either east or west, according to the distance of the Andes range, or of the mountain
ranges opposite them; never, however, to a greater extent
than 200 or 300 yards in a length of 700 or 1000 kilometers.

At that epoch the Mar Dolce, that in later times was called

by lying greed the Silver River (Rio de la Plata), was twice its present size, the two tributaries of which it consisted combining in one full stream along its whole course, while at a subsequent period they were again separated, and remained distinct and apart among the numerous islands they encircled, although circumscribed in their flow and subdivided by many an outlet.

Then, the waters rolled precipitously through the narrow rocky channels and steep mountain passes, and sought their level as they flowed over the vast plain beneath, wandering happily over the gentle slope that drew them to the east and south, while this twofold invitation was seconded by the irresistible laws of nature ; and thus flowing neither directly east nor absolutely south, they yet turned much more in the former than in the latter direction. And in this same direction, and following the features of the soil as produced by the very waters themselves, and at times actually coerced by their own products, they excavate an ever deepening and narrowing channel, with a maximum of regularity and a minimum of force.

The soil, which is still recent, especially when it has been elaborated in a short time, and in shallow waters, is therefore, when brought to light, insufficiently compact, becomes easily divided by the action of the current, which at one moment subtle and persuasive, and at another swollen and impetuous, seeks to force open a permanent channel.

In the early but brief period when the waters lay level on the plain, the floods may have contributed to form a covering to the immersed surfaces, but the channel of the river soon became sufficient for its wants, compensating in width for any deficiency in depth, until equilibrium was restored.

On the first occurrence of inundation, the soil being unable to resist the lateral pressure of the current that was unchecked by the very slight declivity of its course, afforded at once an ample space for innumerable windings, and from the first moment that the bed of the river sufficed to contain the mass of waters, the process of disintegration on one side and of deposit on the other was set up, the latter being inferior to the former both as to level and as to bulk.

Hence the extraordinary tortuosity of the rivers of the Chaco, and of this river Vermejo, the windings of which measure 320 leagues over a geographical distance of 130. Hence the terraces ; hence the inevitable lowering of the absolute level of the land when the rivers shall have completed the disintegration of the primitive soil, and shall have substituted a soil composed of their own deposits, the highest points of which are at present two yards lower than the opposite soil. Hence the alluvials which have formed the islands of the Paranà and the Uruguay, and which follow on the deposits or *deltation* of the mouths of those rivers, and will end by filling up the estuary of the Plata.

The development of the rivers, their depth, and the friability of the soil give rapid extension to this process, and great results must ensue in a relatively short time, geologically speaking.

In fact, if we may suppose (and the hypothesis is rational) that the lateral erosion of the primitive soil proceeds at the rate of two yards a year along the whole course of the river, the soil subtracted annually by the Vermejo alone from the territory of the Chaco would amount to 6,400,000 cubic yards, equal to an island ten yards deep by 1000 in width, and with a frontage of 640—that is, one of the largest islands in the Rio de la Plata. We can now understand that the disintegration of the mountains in the *deltation* of the Paranà and the Rio de la Plata does not equal in importance that of the plain, and the importance of the latter is increased when we reflect that the process is being repeated under similar conditions by the Pilcomayo and the Salado, the other two rivers of the Chaco.

According to this hypothesis the surface of the basin of the Vermejo plain, which is equal to 9000 square leagues, will have lost two yards in level 70,000 years after its emersion, and will then have yielded 450,000,000,000 cubic yards, which will represent an island ten yards deep, 500 kilometers long, and ninety kilometers wide, i.e. twice and one-fourth the surface of the estuary of the Rio de la Plata, which contains nearly 20,000 square kilometers. In other words a mass of earth sufficient to fill the estuary four times over, supposing the average depth to be five yards.

Nor is this all. This disintegrating action of the river tends towards changing the character of the vegetation in the Chaco, because, according to my experience, the plants growing on the primitive soil or on the emerged lands differ from those clothing the alluvial lands, the former belonging, generally speaking, to timber-giving trees, such as the quebracho, the urunday, and the palo-santo. But we will revert to this when treating of the forest flora.

The change which thus takes place without the agency of

climate affords us an excellent explanation of analogous conditions in Denmark with respect to the pine and the oak, which
have been replaced by the beech, the last named even retaining
the name of one of its predecessors.   The cause is usually
referred simply to change of climate, while the renovation
of the superficial stratum may have largely contributed to it as
well as the law of natural affinities.   Hence a detailed study of
the Chaco, with particular reference to relative altimetry and to
the amount of vegetation, might supply us with the chronological
data of the period in which this territory first made its appearance ; data no less certain than those adopted in respect of other
regions by such geographers as Morlot, Forel, and Arcelin.

In fact, if we assume a lateral disintegration of the *bordo firme*,
or primitive soil, at the rate of two superficial yards a year along
the whole course of the river for 320 leagues over the plain, we
obtain a complete change of the surface of the Vermejo country
and a lower level for the soil in 70,000 years from its appearance.
And if we suppose that at the present time the surface we are
treating of has risen to one-half of the whole, as is in fact the
case, more or less, we still find that the age of the Chaco territories amounts to not less than 35,000 years.   In any case it is
my opinion that the first appearance beneath the light of the
sun of these lands that are now called the Gran Chaco from a
Chicciuan word [1] does not date back to the glacial epoch.   The
existence of that epoch on this continent and in these latitudes
is, to my mind, an indubitable fact.   In the neighbourhood of
the Acconquica Mountains, in the provinces of Catamarca and
Tucuman, and at a height of 2000 or 3000 yards above the
level of the sea, latitude 27° S., I saw huge masses like high
hills clothed with thick and ancient forests, but with all the
characteristics of Morenica formation, and I observed also single
masses on high and isolated peaks.

Following the river back from its mouth to the mountains, the recent perpendicular banks disclose a formation of
the strength of fifteen or twenty yards in the first cutting of the
geographical length of thirty leagues, and of the strength of ten
yards, and even less as it reascends.

---

[1] According to a dictionary printed at Lima in 1754 *chacu* means the
hunting of wild beasts.   In the Chaco itself I was told that *chacu* means
a place where animals are confined.   The *pobladores* say habitually
estos chacos for " these fields."   In the Italian edition *chaco* is rendered
by *lake*.

This formation rests upon a substratum called *tosca*, of a soapy and partly magnesian nature, and consequently not easily friable. This is revealed in the lower parts by small streams of water, which give place to the rapids or natural cataracts (*arrecifas*) at seven or eight points. .

Tosca, sometimes of a bluish colour, at others somewhat red, has a tendency to splinter into small scales, and might be termed magnesian schist. The scales are very soft. In other districts there are *toscas* of a different kind.

The formation above the *tosca*, and which may be called the visible part, is again subdivided into stratifications from two to four yards in depth, those strata nearest the bottom and towards the mouth of the river being finer, more clayey, deeper in colour, and consequently more compact, while the upper strata, as we ascend the river, become fainter in tint, coarser, less clayey, less compact, and of a sandy nature, in accordance with the mechanical laws of deposit.

I say deeper in colour and consequently more compact, because colouring depends on the presence of metallic oxides, and every one knows the agglutinative force of these latter.

On the other hand the parallelism between these stratifications and the uniformity in every sense of the inclination of the surface, point to a common grand cause of origin, which has acted at intervals between one and another emersion, during which each would become clothed with vegetation which would at a later period be submerged in the waters, and give place to newly formed surface.

These operations must have occurred when the climate of these regions was in the same relative condition as at present, because the vegetation was evidently fine and multiform in the lower cutting, and there was a surface of dark earth or *humus*, produced from its accumulated residuum, as at the present time, while both are scanty in the centre until close to the mountains. In the same way the dark part of the lower stratifications, corresponding with a former vegetation, lies relatively high, while it is thin and sometimes almost imperceptible in the centre, where the climate at the present day is likewise arid.

And then, as now, there existed alkalis in the earth, which are indicated by incrustations and nitrous efflorescence on the uncovered parts of the banks, the same elements are exhibited at the present day in the *salnitrali* frequently covering the sur-

faces less elevated from the water, and by the growth of *jumes*
and *cactus* on the higher ground, and of *bobos* and other
shrubs on the low-lying soil scarcely out of reach of the
current. The ashes of all these plants yield an abundance of
potash and soda that hitherto has only been used for domestic
purposes.

Thus we find the same climate and the same materials
then as now, and the same conditions at the period of the
formation of the deepest strata as at that of the actual alluvial
lands.

Yet this identity of original causes is not accompanied by
identity in floral phenomena. We have pointed this out
already. Because the physical conditions of the soil, which, if
we except extremes, are the most influential in determining
vegetable life, vary according to the amount of the deposits
and according to the length of time during which all the energies
have been in action. The result of these same energies alters
the chemical order of the elements to which they are due, either
by chemical reaction, or by the products of vegetation giving
back to mother earth the aliments received from her, transformed and enriched by new ones absorbed from the atmosphere.

Hence the variety of the herbaceous and forest flora that
respectively cover similarly situated soils. Hence the aptitude
for new growths, and for agriculture, varying according to the
above-named conditions.

Such is the past history of the Vermejo. What of the
present?

The work of ages is still going on—erosion on the one hand,
and alluvial formation on the other, in the shape of terraces,
and the later floods either carrying away the previous deposits if
these lie in their way, or adding fresh deposits, if the former are
only reached by exceptionally full floods. As we have already
mentioned, the alluvial soil brought by the river is a couple of
yards lower than the original soil, which is known in the locality
as *bordo firme*, and is never inundated by the floods.

Some of the alluvial soil is several yards in depth, although
deposited as it were almost instantaneously, so great is the
quantity carried by the waters, and washed down almost in one
mass from the surrounding land, of which a large proportion
is crumbling. Other alluvials are again deposited over these,
without obliterating them, and it is not unusual to see *bobos*,
very straight poplar-like shrubs, with their leaves silvered on

the lower side. These trees are of rapid growth and burgeon after four or six years, hardly before, if an abundant supply of water be wanting. Their boles traverse three or four different layers of alluvial deposit ; their roots therefore are three or four yards below the surface of the ground.

After this fashion does the river, year by year, pursue its task ; causing changes of every kind, as it alternately flows along the banks of the *bordo firme*,[1] or over its own alluvial deposits. The number of these changes, their symmetry, their correspondence with the disintegration of the land, the constant deposits, and the consequent steps or terraces, cannot fail to make a deep impression on the spectator, notwithstanding that he understands the inevitability of them, from physical and mechanical laws.

The Vermejo divides into two arms ; the stream on the right-hand, which in the greatest droughts carries one-fifth of its waters, is much more winding in its course than that on the left-hand, named the Teuco, which carries the remainder. The cause of this inequality is simply the inferior flexibility of the larger mass of water, and in the lesser influence on this of the numberless accidents to which the river is exposed ; while its course being not so tortuous, it consequently spreads out less, and hence the zone in which the river exercises its erosive and sedimentary action. The state of fulness, moreover, in the smaller stream being proportionately more abnormal, the accidental channel formed during the shallow season is altogether inadequate at the season of fulness, and the waters therefore force into existence an adequate channel, and in so doing destroy many sinuosities formed in the time of shallows, and thus contribute to greater changes than would take place, had the bed of the river been at first less winding and less uneven.

We may therefore assert, however paradoxical it may seem, that the displacements of the river—or I will say of rivers—are, under like circumstances of easily disintegrated soil and heavy floods, in inverse proportion to their mass of water. This is demonstrated by the magnificent Paraguay and the gigantic Paraná and Uruguay. I do not say this of the Rio de la Plata, which is principally governed throughout its immense course by the tides. The ebb and flow of these are perceptible for some scores of leagues from the mouth of the river, and the case is the

---

[1] *Bordo firme*, as it is called, is land that is never submerged by the floods ; I have rendered it sometimes by *emerged land*.

same with the Uruguay and Paraná. Yet even so, these rivers are not exempt from the law of perpetual displacement which is inevitable from the crumbling condition of their banks. It is certain that if we could compare their course to-day with that of a century ago, or more, we should notice remarkable changes in the line of their shores, independently of the effects produced by the *deltation* or *depositation*, as I will call it, of sediment from the rivers of the Gran Chaco, which tends to lengthen these rivers at the expense of the Rio de la Plata as well as to choke the greater part of this latter and the other rivers.

In the landslips of the *bordo firme*, as well as in those of the alluvial soil, an immense number of trees are precipitated into the water and remain fixed, either on account of their foliage, or because the greater part of those of the *bordo firme* are much heavier than water. Immovable banks impervious to water are thus very frequently formed ; the stream therefore rushes to the sides and forms a new channel.

Sometimes one of these trees, either falling singly or becoming isolated on its short journey, remains head downwards, and its trunk, not being strong enough to form a bank, becomes, if unseen, the most terrible enemy to the keels of boats. These trunks are called *raigones*. In any case it is a satisfaction to know that it is extremely rare for a tree to be carried any great distance by the stream, or for timber to float, on account of the manner of its fall.

In other respects the soil forming the bed of the river is, by reason of the timber that has fallen on it, or by geological accidents, more capable of resisting the action of the stream than is the soil of the banks to resist the friction of the lateral currents. The waters therefore overflow and form almost innumerable shallows, which, however, are easily cleared by means of spirals or steam-wheels.

The bottom of the river-bed is at present crossed, as we have said, by seven or eight veins of chalky magnesia, difficult to corrode. These diminish the amount of water, and cause *rapids* and cataracts (*arrecifas*).

All these features render navigation so difficult, that it is only possible in vessels of light draught, and during the season of deep waters. To these causes of the division of the river into two branches, we must add another important one.

The limits within which so far the Vermejo has oscillated, may be considered to include from ten to fifteen leagues in width; and as this increases, a somewhat analogous course is pursued by the Pilcomajo (*Bird river*, in Chichuan), running north of the Vermejo. At no distant date, perhaps, a junction may be effected between the lower parts of the two rivers. The uniform level of the country will facilitate this.

The land watered by the Vermejo may be estimated at 13,000 square leagues, of which a fourth part is mountainous, and the remainder consists of plains.

The mountain portion, or higher basin, is comprised within lat. S. 21° to 25°, and within three degrees of longitude; the lower portion, or basin, is comprised between the Equator and 27°, i.e. within three and a half degrees of latitude, and five of longitude.

The lower Vermejo crosses the Gran Chaco from north-west to south-east for a geographical distance of 130 leagues, between the *Juntas del San Francisco* and its fall into the Paraguay. It runs a course of 320 leagues, making a curve about every quarter of a league. It is confined on the east by Chaco Central, which lies between the Vermejo and the Pilcomajo.

The comparative narrowness of the hydrographical basin, with its six degrees of latitude, and the uniformly eastward position of the mountains from north to south, cause the volume of its waters to depend on a very usual order of climatological phenomena. The rainy season occurs only in summer, from December to March, and the melting of the snow on all except the very highest mountains occasions heavy floods, which are succeeded by extreme droughts in part of winter and spring.

During the time of floods the masses of water are enormous; in the middle of the dry season—that is, in the month of July—I measured eighty cubic yards per second, and in the next drought, in October, fifty cubic yards.

At about fifteen leagues from the *Juntas del San Francisco*, which are situated at the foot of the mountains, the river divides into two branches: the one on the east, or left hand, is called the *Téuco*, from the Mattacco word meaning "river;" and that on the west, or right hand, retains the name of Vermejo, *Téuch-tach*, or "Great River" in Mattacco. When I was sailing in those waters, the Téuco contained four-fifths of the total bulk of the stream, and the rest formed the Vermejo.

The two arms of the river, with a distance between them varying from five to ten leagues, are reunited after a course of 200 leagues, at a distance by river of ninety leagues from the spot where it empties itself into the Paraguay. This spot is called *Boca del Téuco*.

During this last course of ninety leagues, corresponding to fifty leagues in a straight line by land, we come to parts that look like artificial canals ; in these places we find for the most part the clay banks I have already mentioned ; here, too, the river runs deepest.

At 140 leagues by water from the *Boca del Téuco*, and following the banks of the river, is Rivadávia on the present frontier, and ninety leagues further on *las Juntas del San Francisco*, near which, at eight leagues farther north, is Oran.

In all this long distance from the fall into the Paraguay to the *Juntas*, there is not one single hill !

The water is brackish, on account alike of its scarcity and its muddiness ; on the other hand, it contains an immense variety of fish, thus providing the inhabitants of the country with unfailing and palatable food. Some kinds weigh from twenty-five to thirty kilograms, without counting the *yacaré* or crocodiles that weigh two or three times as much.

Is this river navigable ?

With a steamboat drawing one yard, it would be navigable for at least half the year, with no further trouble than forcing the flow of water through one arm only, which arm should be the Téuco, since it already bears four-fifths of the whole bulk of the river. The cost of such an undertaking, together with the annual expense of maintaining it in working order, would amount, I calculate, to a sum of 23,000 scudi.

In order to make navigation possible throughout the year, a system of dredging away the sandbanks must be brought into operation, the *tosca* must be destroyed, and the *raigones* cut away. These works, supposing the dredging machines to be used for hauling, when not wanted on the river, would absorb about 50,000 scudi per annum. In all, 70,000 scudi per annum.

I do not speak of locks or weirs. The expense would be too great at such a distance for commercial enterprise.

There should be also a system of steam transports of various draught for serving the markets. Those of one-yard draught and of eighty tons' burden should ply between the Foce nel Paraguay, or the cities of Humaitá or Corrientes, and Rivadávia on the Christian frontier ; others of half a yard draught and thirty tons' burden, between Rivadávia and *las Juntas del*

San Francisco, or practically Oran. It is useless to dream of sailing-vessels in such a sinuous, deeply-lying river, with its banks crowned with woods and swarming with Indians.

The cost of a voyage from Corrientes to *las Juntas* and *vice versâ*, including interest on the value of the vessel and its fittings, and the redemption of mortgage, would amount, allowing for the highest charges, to about 4000 scudi, with which a 160-ton burden could be carried at a rate of twenty-four scudi and three-quarters. Supposing the Indians to remain harmless (and an adequate system of national defence could be promptly organized), the above sum would be reclaimed to two-thirds. Full particulars of this plan are stated in one of my official reports.

At this cost, increased by the annual charges for maintaining the river, which we have estimated at 70,000 scudi, a large proportion of the South Bolivian trade, and part of the trade from the north of the Argentine Republic, would find its way along the Vermejo and the Paranà. The marvellously fertile province of Oran would develop on a large scale the agricultural industry for which it is adapted, and of which there are examples in the valley of San Francisco, where their important establishments for the manufacture of sugar for local consumption exist. The Gran Chaco, that immense forest region full of precious materials for civil and maritime building purposes and for valuable cabinet work, and inhabited by scattered tribes of wandering Indians, and isolated by its very immensity from the rest of the world, would, by means of this central artery, throbbing through thousands of kilometers, be placed in immediate and easy contact with the emporiums of consumption, of production, and of civilization.

Five hundred thousand scudi wisely expended, and the navigation of the Vermejo would be a splendid success.

CHAPTER X.

AT FORT SARMIENTO—HOSPITALITY—TWO BIBLIOGRAPHICAL
OPINIONS.

FROM Bella Vista, where the end of our last chapter left us, our
route lay directly N.N.W. to Fort Sarmiento, so named in
honour of the former President of the Republic. It is the headquarters of the *Comandancia* of the dragoon regiment that garri-
sons the whole frontier, a length of 500 kilometers.

The climate becomes less dry as we approach comparatively
near to the mountains, and the land being more under cultivation the chebraccio and the giuccian become scarcer, and the
chañar, the giuggiolo, the vinal, and the carob with its hanging tufts of half-ripe pods begin to abound. This fruit excites
equally the appetite of both horse and rider, who amicably unite
in stripping the boughs, the one with his teeth and the other with
his hands. The meals thus taken in common with one's horse give
rise to very curious and awkward scenes, when, owing to the
strong resistance of the berries, the bough gives one a violent
box on the ear, or, almost unseating the rider, puts his bones out
of joint, twists his muscles, and flays his hand. The horse next,
having recovered the shock, plants his head between his legs,
sniffing round after the scattered fruit, and forces his rider to
begin his equestrian acrobatics all over again.

It will be understood that our horses had no resemblance to
those poetically celebrated Arab steeds, who, returning to the
inn after a long and weary day's journey, will not even look at
the food provided for them until called to it by their master.

The rain that had fallen two days before had revived the fields
and refreshed the foliage of the trees, and purified and cooled
the air, so that heaven and earth alike seemed to smile on the
travellers.

In these tropical climes, after the brief winter sleep, a little
rain is sufficient to awaken all nature to an exuberant vege-

tation, but, alas! it is equally ephemeral, if not continually replenished by the life-giving moisture. The drought that for some months yet follows on the early rains blights the promise of the fields, and the burning heat of the sun increases in power, until at last the plentiful waters of the latter half of summer force into sudden and exuberant growth the grasses and herbs that in a few short hours will conceal, beneath a sea of redundant vegetation higher than a man on horseback, the fields that only a little while before were absolutely bare. These rapid alternations and this sudden and marvellous exuberance have frequently led travellers to form erroneous opinions as to the productiveness of regions such as these, if unacquainted with the annual cycle of the climate, and with its regular and successive phases. To acquire a knowledge of these facts in any given country is the first duty of the conscientious traveller who wishes to describe and to judge with accuracy.

Thus journeying, we arrived after a long day's march at Fort Sarmiento. This fort is situated near a tank, by which it is supplied with water, sometimes good, sometimes bad, depending on the dryness of the season. But within the last few weeks a well has been sunk in the very middle of the piazza, and another at a short distance, and Fort Sarmiento is thus superior to any other houses or villages within a circuit of 100 leagues. And yet there is water to be had at a depth of fifteen or twenty yards. But what is to be done if the thing has never been seen to be done? There is no well in Rivadavia, and the municipal authorities have discussed the subject, I know not how often, without ever coming to a conclusion, although it is a public work of the highest importance to the country.

The population of Fort Sarmiento is essentially military. Vast barracks, some houses built of *barro*, including a handsome one belonging to the commandant, and others of timber, all of them thatched with straw and mud, surround the piazza. These and a few more scattered round constitute the whole village, which is inhabited by the soldiers, their wives and children, and a few tradesmen and their families. It is customary here for soldiers to be accompanied by their wives, to whom Government allows half-rations. There is nothing more picturesque, and sometimes a little grotesque too, than an encampment or military march in time of war, above all when the camp is broken up. How often have I not longed for a De Amicis to describe these and many other scenes!

A delightful surprise awaited us at Fort Sarmiento, and made our three days' visit seem like a country holiday.

The commander of the regiment was Lieutenant-Colonel Emiliano Perez Milan, a brave officer, who on one occasion was struck by a ball in the knee when leading his soldiers to the attack during the war in Paraguay, and immediately on his recovery rejoined his regiment. On another occasion, his men having mutinied, he left his bed before daybreak, seized a revolver, and wrapping a *poncho* about him, faced the mutineers alone, and disarmed them.

As I was already known to him, and he was besides a friend of Roldan's, we were received with the greatest hospitality. How comfortable it was! What a contrast to the *Boca de la Chapapa*, and to every other place we had visited the last five months! The house was large and cool, there were beds, there was water from a well, there were pleasant meals, with bright, youthful company and gentlemanly men, and—there were also savoury and varied dishes. Two kinds of soup, one of which, called *locro*, made from maize, was excellent; an *asada à la crioglia*, cutlets à la Milanese, and algarrobo *aloja*, prepared by the skilful hand of our hostess; wine and beer. There were roots also and some few dishes of green vegetables —too delicious in these regions where kitchen-gardens are not! And then some sweets, either of milk and honey, or of preserved apple-quince. or of some other kind; and, last of all, a cup of magnificent Yunca coffee, and a scented Havana cigar. Could more be desired? I felt like a prince, and I thought princes could not have a better time of it than I. Moreover, in the hottest part of the afternoon beautiful earthen vases were brought in filled with old aloja, amber-coloured, crystal-clear, sparkling and cool; and a little later we had our choice of tea, or *maté*, or both!

In the evening of this delightful day there was a military ball. Everything is military here, and once again the fair Tucuman ladies bore away the palm from their Argentine sisters, as did the officers from the citizens, whose claims as guests were quite eclipsed by their gold lace. The ball was held on a clearing covered by a straw roof, and with the four sides open.

At about a league away the colonel had set up a tan-yard, that we went over. A flint hatchet had been discovered there during excavations for a well; and, to my great disappointment, this had been given a few weeks before to the official paymasters from Buenos Ayres, who had returned thither. The search for fossils in these parts might lead to great discoveries, especially in the direction of the Oran Cordillera. I remember seeing some years ago, in a precipitous part between Oran and the Juntas of San Francisco, some bones of a gigantic animal that according to the inhabitants of the neighbourhood no longer existed. Other explorers have remarked similar fossils in the north, in the river-gorges of a road leading to Bolivia, superposed on a stratum of chalk. This stratum is probably the continuation of a chalk formation that I remarked at the foot of the Precordillera, farthest east between Cordoba and Oran, extending for about a thousand kilometers and forming banks of great size, and high hills that seem once to have been the coast, when the present Argentine table-land was covered by the sea. A true geological horizon is thus presented to us.

Near the tan-yard (*curtiembre*) there were many wild mulberry-trees, or *mora*, as they are called here. They grow in large quantities in the woods between this neighbourhood and the slopes of the mountains. The mora attains a very great height; the trunk is of close fibre, and is used for articles of furniture and for carts; the leaf resembles that of our mulberry, but is smaller; the fruit is the same as ours; a milky fluid exudes from the stalk when the leaves are plucked.

The tan is made from the bark of the *cebil*, a large tree like our sorb-apple, but with smaller leaves. It grows at first on the plains immediately contiguous to the mountains, and extends to a considerable height up the slopes. The extent covered by this tree, its importance and its characteristics are sufficient reasons for taking it into account when determining the distribution of the flora. There are two kinds, the *white* and the *red*. The timber is not adapted for building, but is used for ploughs and carts; the bark resembles cork, and that of the *red* is preferred, as being less knotty, for the knots cannot be split through, and therefore the timber is less good. The bark contains from 14 to 15 % of tannin. The worst is that the tree dies when stripped of its bark; and in Tucuman, consequently, where there are many tan-yards, the *cebil* is beginning to be very costly, especially as its growth is not at all rapid.

As we are on the subject of tanning, I will add that the leaf of the *Quebracho Blanco* (Aspidosperma quebracho), which abounds in the Chaco and in the forests of Santiago, contains

27·50% of tannin ; it is not, however, so far as I know, made use of on any large scale, although it has the quality of not colouring the hides, like the *cebil*, and acting, therefore, as a corrective of the latter.

But to return to Fort Sarmiento. Besides all the delights I have mentioned, there was another, the crown of all. This was a fine library belonging to the colonel, full of military and other histories, of works on science and literature, and of those handbooks that make science popular by presenting it under an attractive form, such as the works of Mantegazza, of Flammarion, and of Jules Verne. Writers such as these are the evangelists of science, and however loudly learned pedants and sophistical teachers may declaim against the usurpations, the transfigurations, and even the inaccuracy of these authors, the fact remains, that through them and by their means the public learns and enjoys the truths of science distilled in their laboratories, where but for such writers they would remain inaccessible to the people, who would not appreciate them if not presented under an attractive form.

When wandering in foreign countries, one always seeks, especially at first, for something that appertains to one's own native land. I looked round, therefore, for Italian authors. One only had the honour of being a guest, but to me and to the owner of the library he was a host in himself. I speak of Cesare Cantù and his " Universal History " (*Storia Universale*) in a handsome Spanish translation.

I have met with this history in all parts of the Republic, thanks to the public circulating libraries, that, during the presidency of Sarmiento, were extended in every direction with the aid of the National Government, who granted in every case a sum equal in amount to that collected in the neighbourhood. They are now ruined by the mismanagement of taxes, and are struggling with numberless local difficulties, the chief of which are the long distances.

I have often wondered why Cantù is not even a senator, and then I have reflected that he must have declined the honour, because it would have been a disgrace to Menabrea at least, if not to Cairoli and Depretis, not to have offered him a nomination. I am aware that he has been accused of historical inaccuracy on certain very intricate questions, but I, who cannot unravel them, am struck with admiration, not only for the gigantic lines on which his work is laid, but also for his lucid and beautiful style. I learned more of the history of American independence in twenty pages of his work, than in any special history of the subject.

It is said that " he has not the philosophic mind." I grant it, but he is a model of the grand historical style, in the distribution of subject, the grouping of facts, in conciseness, in clearness, and in the literary style which is so greatly appreciated in other authors.

" But his history is written in favour of the Catholic Church." I remarked this myself, and I have never been able to forget the kind of subterfuge made use of with regard to a letter on the analogy between Christianity and pre-existing Buddhism written by a missionary named De Giorgi to the Propaganda at Rome. Cantù transcribes it, either in the appendix to one of his volumes or among his authorities, but in Latin ; and, however familiar the style, it is not easy, and the greater number of readers will not take the trouble to make it out. On the other hand, he translates many other documents. But after all, this is only one of the many sides of the work, and although open to criticism, as are some other points, the larger remaining portion does not thereby lose its value.

Besides, are there not numberless historians who devote their skill to the service of a cause ?—and who, nevertheless, are approved by the majority of readers ? It is merely a question of sympathy with the writer's views. Now let him who is without sin cast the first stone.

In the public library of a mining district I met with another book by an Italian author ; the " Lezioni di Geologia," by the Abate Stoppani, a well-known name in Italy. To a vast scientific erudition, he adds a style so splendid, that it is a real creation applied to the discourse on the earth.

I feel that I owe much to Stoppani, although I do not even know him by sight. The full discussion of, and his own views on, the circulation of the atmosphere as based on the theories of Dana and Maury, and his hypothesis on the upheaval by consensus of the mountainous systems, have been to me as a mariner's compass among the climatic and geographical phenomena I have observed in my explorations of the Argentine regions.

The hypotheses of parallelism in the upheavals, deduced from the fact of the relative position of the Lebanon and the Anti-Lebanon, of the Alps and the Pre-Alps (see the " Nuova

Antologia" of four or five years ago), explained by the comparison of a carpet which, when pressed down on one side, moves in parallel folds, is in my opinion confirmed on an immense scale in the book of nature by the aspect of several mountain chains that in the centre and north of the Republic are all parallel with the Andes, with which they may be said to form the Argentine Cordillera, which includes both narrow valleys and wide plains.

This parallelism and simultaneous action struck me yet more forcibly when walking in S. Luis Street, Mendoza, in company with the engineer Ceresetto, a former disciple of Stoppani's, I perceived that the road, 200 kilometers in length and running in a straight line from east to west, traversed a series of hills, the direction of which was from south to north, like that of the above-named mountains. This disposition of the hills (the wrinkles in the carpet) continues in diminishing as it reaches their sides, which form a chain as far as the Desaguadero river, that flows in a northerly direction, and the undulations are distant from each other in inverse proportion to the height of the *Sierra S. Luis* and to the chain of the Andes. This undulation is the true cause of the collection of the waters in the Bacino, as it has been instinctively named by the people. The volume of water, however, is very insignificant, and is not to be compared with that which descends directly from the Andes and waters the plains and cultivated fields before uniting with the river.

I do not venture to suggest the perusal of the whole of Stoppani's work. It consists of three volumes, of which two are in large octavo. The type is clear, but extremely minute, and the notes almost microscopical; these two volumes contain more than two thousand pages. They are fatiguing to read, notwithstanding the author's sparkling style; but the first volume (I am speaking of the edition of 1873 or 1874), which treats of "Terrestrial Dynamics," and which is the shortest and perhaps the best, should be in the hands of every student before the conclusion of his college course, because the topics of which it treats should form part of the curriculum of secondary studies, like physics and other natural sciences. And it would be difficult to find the subject more clearly treated.

"This work, then, is of surpassing excellence?" Yes, it is a great work, but, being human, it is not perfect, though it may seem rash in me to say so. To sum up, I have read it through, and some parts of it more than once, and am therefore in a position unusual to critics, especially the great ones. But to return. I do not enter into the science of it, for I know nothing of that; let me speak of what may be called the literary side.

To begin with, the author is too argumentative. It may seem strange to call this a fault, but I consider it one in a scientific work. The eagerness of the author to demonstrate his conclusions, his enthusiastic, nay, almost irritable advocacy of views which, if true, are true, and which, if not, can be made so by no effort of rhetoric, does not appear to me a good scientific method. It must at first confuse the student, sometimes annoy him, and often compromise the author.

The very honesty which leads the writer to correct in the edition I have mentioned some conclusions to which he had come in an earlier edition, is apt to shake the confidence of the reader, and, if he is a pupil, to expose him to severe mortification.

The student, as such, espouses his author's cause, and supports all his teaching through thick and thin, and then some fine day may find himself confuted out of the mouth of his own master! The latter, in his turn, cannot but find himself trammelled by the previous hot polemic, and the confidence he had inspired lessened by his change of sides.

There are, moreover, two other serious defects, which to my mind are anti-scientific: these are, firstly, the absolutism of certain theses; and secondly, intolerance and contempt for his opponents, who are for him enemies.

Our author bases this character of his on his *profound scientific convictions*. But may not his opponents put forth a like claim? They, however, are more reserved, and do not take it at all that themselves, their pupils, and the public should accept their conclusions, with all the conditions that are presented with them.

But Stoppani is exasperated by the conclusions of others, if contradictory of the teaching of the Scriptures, which he ingeniously interprets so as to harmonize with the henceforth unanswerable truths of science. But I ask, are not these very interpretations that harmonize science and the Bible precisely the fruit of profane truths denied in the beginning by the authorized exponents of Scripture with such positive conviction and such contemptuous intolerance? And why should it be surprising that the learned and the curious, not concerning themselves with Biblical doctrines, should take advantage of every kind of data in order to draw rational conclusions, and should leave to the expositors of Scriptural tradition the task of harmonizing the two ?

It is not only useful, it is honest and right to be prudent, in order faithfully to serve science, which is jeopardized if trammelled by former beliefs extraneous to her. Our author is indignant at the hypothesis of tertiary man ; and excluding or omitting the greater, interpreting the lesser spaces of time attributed to the quaternary epoch, deduced by some naturalists from geological data—none of them very convincing—proceeding in sequence with traditional and archæological elements, he places the appearance of man at an epoch that makes it agree with the words of Scripture. It is a fine demonstration, although, of course, somewhat lame, and will be found interesting both by poets and ladies who care to seek for it at the end of the second volume. But the basis is unsound. For it is in fact demonstrated that it is impossible to prove the existence of man in the tertiary period. Yes, by the author and some others, to his and their satisfaction, and to that of others, perhaps, up to the moment at which he wrote, but can it be so for the future? *À priori* the answer must be in the negative, since mammals are shown to have existed in the secondary period, and the following facts refute such a premature and positive conclusion, albeit accompanied by anathema. Quatrefages, indeed, who is beyond the suspicion of the most orthodox, who at the time that Stoppani's work was published suspended his judgment on this difficult and transcendental question, came later to the conclusion that the existence of tertiary man is proved by the fresh discoveries of the Abbé Bourgeois at Thenay, and those of Professor Cappellini at Monte Aperto. Moreover, he came to the opinion that tertiary man is proved, and not only as belonging to the last period of the tertiary epoch, but also to the middle period, and also he does not hesitate to accept the idea of man as still more remote.

Now, one such proof, if accepted, relegates man to an antiquity with which it is impossible to make the Bible (ransacked to establish an opposite conclusion) agree, unless by means of a retractation like the famous one concerning the immobility of the earth. Such a retractation would be dangerous and scandalous to timid souls and upright minds, in proportion to the fury, and intolerance with which the contrary thesis has been supported.

But the incompatibility of science as the servant of dogma, with science as the servant of truth, is shown most clearly in the question that will henceforth be called Darwinism. Our author here pushes anger and intolerance to the verge of insult.

According to the Darwinian theory, living organisms are the product of progressive evolution in embryonic form, which by exercise of forces of complex kinds, called natural selection, and developed in different directions, with successive subdivisions, has given place to the infinite variety of past and present existing organisms.

This theory, which is corroborated both by fact and reflection, commends itself so strongly to the mind by its simplicity, and to the understanding by its force and depth, that it would probably have been accepted universally, with an immense longing to search into its truths, only that it clashed with the previous cosmogonies sanctioned by ancient religions. The theory was, therefore, received with indignation, when it was extended to the origin of man. The self-esteem of men was appealed to in order to controvert it ; and it was confounded with atheism and materialism, which, although no less worthy of respect than any other opinions, are not necessarily either admitted or rejected by the Darwinian theory. Stoppani even goes so far as to ask whether Darwinians are not ashamed of having been born, now that they renounce their origin from Adam. No ! there is no disgrace in admitting the lowliness of our origin, it is our duty to recognize it, when so it is ; and the vaunt of Themistocles that the nobility of his family originated in himself may even likewise be justified. Man's worth is not to be measured by what he or his ancestors may have been, but by what he is. There is no divine righteousness that can be preferred before the righteousness of the human conscience, and this conscience teaches us that rewards and punishments must be awarded to the man as he now exists, not to a man who existed in the past and is now no more.

What ? Has the Eternal Father who, according to the orthodox, calls to His bosom the souls of those who are like Him, lost all power, and have we lost all merit because the root of our genealogical tree is an organic *monod* instead of an image of clay ?

But such a theory is atheism and materialism ! By no means ! How do we deny God by affirming that a Creating

Power and a Preordinating Mind—instead of manifesting itself by the numerous isolated, intermittent, non-coordinate acts of will which would be necessitated by the separate creation of each of the innumerable species belonging to the vegetable and animal kingdoms—should have created one solitary germ, and pre-ordained for it the laws according to which it should develop in the numberless directions which correspond to the combination and the empire of these very laws?

How do we deny the soul by affirming that the vital force acquires new virtue as it becomes incarnated in progressively higher organisms, until at last it attains to human life, and sees before it the destiny which is attributed by religion to man? Because, in fact, the reasonableness and the justice of this destiny actually reside, according to the declarations of philosophers and doctors and the common consent of mankind, on the faculties by which man is distinguished from other creatures. Now these faculties are not denied by the fact of attributing to them the various gestations of Darwinism.

This Darwinian theory, independently of all metaphysical considerations, and although not exempt from the severity of scientific criticism, presents itself, nevertheless, with such an impress of simplicity, of fulness, of harmony, and of gravity, that it becomes the duty of the learned and the unlearned to study it with profound attention, and to welcome it as a hope that brightens the future of science and of the speculative intellect.

For my own part, I parody the saying on behalf of the existence of God, that "if the Darwinian theory did not exist, we should have to invent it," because the mind and the soul of man may in it find rest in contemplation of the progression and concatenation of organisms, and from that of the irrationality of their existence in such large numbers, if their appearance must be attributed to an equal number of acts of an omniscient and omnipotent will.

We much enjoyed our agreeable and instructive conversation with the gallant colonel, but so soon as the storm, of which the climatological instruments included among his astronomical ones had warned us, had passed away, we decided on resuming our journey, and on the morning of the fourth day we took a regretful leave of our kind hosts, and started for Oran.

CHAPTER XI.

THE CHUQCHO—REPTILES, BIRDS, QUADRUPEDS.

THE poor colonel! An attack of paralysis, brought on by the chuqcho, might have kept him in bed for a long time. But, fortunately, the regimental surgeon, Signor Baldi, from Lucca, a man esteemed and liked by all who knew him, and experienced in this kind of malady, diagnosed the disease at once, and saved him.

The chuqcho is the same as our marsh fever. It breaks out frequently in the summer and autumn seasons in the northern provinces of the Republic, in localities on or near the mountains, where the redundant vegetation, added to a high temperature and a moist atmosphere, determines the production of marshy miasma. The provinces of Salta and Tucuman, and sometimes those parts of Catamarca also that are situate on the plain near hills and villeys, are visited with this scourge. Oran, which is shut in among mountains, and stands in the midst of dense and luxuriant forests, suffers from it to a still greater degree.

It has already been remarked by naturalists that the southern hemisphere suffers less from marsh miasma than the northern ; it exists in the latter as far as 59° lat. N., while in the former it does not habitually reach from beyond the tropic to 24° lat. S. I can add from personal observation that miasma is not only affected by latitude, but by orographical conditions also—which, interfering with the free circulation of the air, and thus causing the atmosphere to be more easily saturated with moisture, constitute, together with the latitude, a region possessing the three conditions mentioned above, viz. redundant vegetation, moisture, and heat. These conditions are thus supplied even more easily than by the great masses of running water and the low-lying plains of the Paraná and the Paraguay in the same latitude. Marsh fevers prevail, therefore, in the Republic as far as 30° lat. S., in the places and under the orographical conditions aforesaid.

From Fort Sarmiento we proceeded towards Oran, a distance by road of thirty-four leagues, but only twenty in a direct line, which is, however, impracticable. We skirted the line of the tropics, and our shadows no longer accompanied us on our left side, but were sometimes in front, sometimes behind, according to the time of day ; and at last we drew near Oran in a W.N.W. direction.

It was the middle of October. The sun was in its dog-days' strength, and the plants, miser-like, after the earliest hours of the day, gathered round them and beneath them all the shade that would have been so grateful to the wayfarer ; while the lizard and the viper, stationed at the edge of the belt of shade, made all approach dangerous.

All was silence, not a rustling leaf heralded a refreshing breeze to play on our foreheads and assuage the burning heat within us ; not a warbling note to encourage our progress from the innumerable singing-birds that were hidden among the leaves, or, with ruffled feathers, perched motionless on the branches, or slowly fluttered, as we approached, from one twig to another.

But, at long intervals, there was a shrill and prolonged whistle, like that of a steam-engine. This was the song with which the *coyuyo*, a large sort of cicada, announces and rejoices over the maturity of the caruba.

As we drew near to the stagnant waters, the frog, hidden under the grass, would suddenly splash in, and for a moment the widening circles would simulate life, as the fetid bubbles rose to the surface; while the stupid toad fancied he was escaping danger by hiding his ill-formed head in the first ostrich egg-hole he saw before him.

Our horses, overcome with the heat, were insensible to the spur ; and the riders, wearied with useless endeavours, left their steeds to their own devices.

Our progress was slow, but not the less fatiguing. At dusk we lighted upon a numerous vanguard of the new flora. These were *chebils*. We were within a little of finding ourselves prisoners until the next day, each step through the plantation, of more than three leagues in length, was so full of difficulty.

We reached our halting-place late at night, having made thirteen leagues. This was an *estancia* called Rosario ; the few inhabitants were already asleep, and, stretching ourselves on the ground, we followed their example. Our slumbers were accompanied by the wailing of women in a neighbouring tolderia, as they mourned over the body of a man who had died of a disease only recently developed among them, and by which they were being decimated.

The next morning the mountains rose distinctly in view, and we could see their crests now and again as far as Fort Sarmiento, standing out against the horizon like immense stretches of landscape suspended between earth and sky. We were at that moment ten leagues away from the nearest, yet we saw it clearly and distinctly. In cloudless weather the atmosphere throughout the Republic is so diaphanous, that European eyes, even when educated to the transparency of southern skies, are often deceived as to distance. I have frequently experienced this on the railway, being able to distinguish the huts of the settlers and the stations at a distance of seven or eight kilometers ; a more delightful prospect awaits me whenever I go to Tucuman and suddenly catch sight of the majestic amphitheatre of mountains by which that province is enclosed on the west and north, while I am still at a distance from it of 200 kilometers.

After travelling for thirty kilometers, we halted for luncheon at the house of a wealthy Spanish *estanciero*, who was said to own more than 10,000 head of cattle. The hour and the heat of the season made the conversation turn on reptiles. We were told of several vipers whose bite is dangerous to man and beast, and of the belief entertained by Creoles and Indians that the skin of a serpent, dried and worn round the head, is a remedy for violent headache. This idea prevails throughout the Republic among the inhabitants of the *campo*.

A virtue even superior to this resides in the lizard and the chameleon, whether raw or cooked, as a cure for syphilis. Some marvellous cures are reported. It is said that if the belly of a living toad be applied to erysipelas a cure is effected. This belief is shared by everybody here, whether civilized or savage ; and the skin powdered and rubbed on the gums is said to be a cure for scurvy.

As to the application of one body to another, there seems no reason to reject *à priori* certain opinions, when accompanied by circumstances that induce reflection. Neither mystic signs nor cabalistic words are in question in these cases. I should add that an ointment of toad-grease, dissolved in boiling oil, and collected on the lid of the stew-pan, has been of proved efficacy in cases of quinsy. A colleague of mine, who was educated in England, Engineer Pardo Saltegno, knew it to be efficacious on two occasions in the case of his brother, a lawyer. Another of my colleagues, Engineer Valiente, had·suggested it to Pardo, who thus escaped the operation he had undergone on a former occasion, and which was impending a second time several years later. My own brother was threatened with the loss of his leg from erysipelas in Italy, but was unexpectedly cured, shortly after binding two live frogs for a whole night on the affected part. He knows how they tortured him! I was a child, but I remember it.

Snakes, including vipers, are very greedy for milk in these parts. There are plenty of anecdotes on the subject, as in Italy. I knew a lady in Rivadavia, the wife of an Englishman, with whom I was also acquainted, who nearly lost a precious infant through a viper that found its way to the child's bed. The mother discovered it one day at the hour of *siesta*, and afterwards, on making a search through the house, its mate was found on the straw roof.

It is wonderful that these vipers so continually glide among persons sleeping on the ground without disturbing them, and do not bite, even when unconsciously touched by the sleeper. This proves not only the intelligence of the creature, but also that it only strikes in self-defence.

The *ampalagua*, so common in the province of Santiago, is very rarely met with in these parts. This snake is four yards in length and about the tenth of a yard or rather more in diameter. Its colour is the same as that of our common snakes. My men destroyed a female containing a number of eggs, with yolks three times the size of the yolk of a fowl's egg. I do not know what stage of pregnancy had been reached.

A coral-snake lying on an iron rod and trodden upon, gave a sort of electric shock to a friend of mine, who felt too much disgusted to repeat the experiment. These vipers are distinguished by coloured rings, white, red, and black, on the back.

There is also a species of animal, half-newt, half-lizard, with a short tail, vulgarly called *sierra morena*, from being marked with a saw (*sierra*) on the back. It is the colour of wood, lives in trees, and is venomous. It is extremely dangerous.

The iguana, on the contrary, is harmless. It is an enormous newt, and is sometimes a yard in length, and in that case is fifteen or twenty centimeters in diameter. It is amphibious, the skin speckled a dull red and green, and changing its colour according to the light. It is eaten by the natives, and the short, thick tail is considered a delicacy.

The turtle is as much honoured in the kitchen here as with ourselves. It is in general very much larger than our turtles, and the shell is superior—being so delicately carved in geometrical patterns at the edge of each octagonal scale that it looks like the work of some skilful engraver.

Venomous insects are not wanting. There are scorpions and tarantulas, like those in the Tuscan marshes, only uglier, and innumerable absurd-looking spiders with bodies as big as a baby's fist poised on the tips of its fingers. They are hairy, extremely prolific, and carry their young astride on their backs when first hatched. They make their nests up trees and in roofs. They are said to be venomous.

In contrast with these ugly and poisonous spiders are the numerous kinds of bees, whose honey—or *milk*, as the Chiccuan word has it (*millsqui*, like the German *milch* and English *milk*)—is so delicious to man and to many wild animals. One kind of bee, called *alpamillsqui*, makes its honey on the ground (*alpa*), in hives divided into several compartments of five centimeters in length and one in diameter, from each of which a different kind of honey is extracted, according to the prevailing flowers entering into its composition. Then there is the *stio-simi*, or sand-bee; the *móro-móro*, that produces a rapidly crystallizing honey in small quantities, but so strong that, on one occasion having taken a little while fasting, I became, as it were, intoxicated. There are many other kinds of bees that, like the two last named, deposit their honey in the trunks of trees. All these are harmless; they do not sting; and look like flies, from which they are only distinguishable by their persistence and viscosity when they alight on the hands and face, and use their trunks for sucking. The two species of *tchiguanas*, on the contrary, resemble our European bees. The larger sort builds a large ball of concentric layers like an onion, and the smaller makes a small, spherical nest, each stratum of which is divided into several open cells, as in wasps' nests. These bees suspend their nests to the branches of shrubs.

The firefly here is much larger than in Italy, and is as useful

P

as it is pretty. It carries on its shoulders two bright and continuous lights, a millimeter in diameter, and which give them
light enough for their purposes. Fair ladies wear them in their
hair at fêtes and parties. This firefly (*pyrophorus punctatissi-
mus*) is vulgarly called *túco* or *tucco* in the north of the Republic,
and it is remarkable that *tuc-cho* or *tuchco*, according to my self-
made vocabulary, means a star in the dialect of the Mocovitans,
who are a completely savage tribe.

Close to the dwelling of our host, and encircling a group of
nests on a tree, were a number of chattering lories, a kind of
parrot, screaming loudly and incessantly *ckié-ckié*, which has
come to be their name among the Mattaccos.

There are two principal families of lories, the *montaráces*, or
wood-parrots, and the *barranchera* parrots, from *barranca*,
which is Spanish for bank. They may be seen in large flocks
excavating their nests in the perpendicular banks, where they
arrange them in rows on different levels like a dovecote. They
make their nests in communities, joined one to the other.
Neither in size nor colouring are they to be compared with
those generally imported to Europe. There are very beautiful
kinds in Brazil and Paraguay, large and admirably tinted.

The birds of the Chaco, as far up as Oran, are pretty much
the same as those found in the centre of the Republic, and
are not remarkable for brightness or variety of colouring. It
is curious, however, that nearly all of them are hooded or
tufted, just as nearly all the plants have thorns either at the
point of their leaves or at the junction with the stalk.

But, if not brightly plumaged, the smaller birds are mostly
songsters, beginning with the blackbird, of which there are
many kinds, larger than ours. They are very tame, besides,
for nobody hurts them ; powder and shot are too expensive, and
the culinary art is not sufficiently advanced to make use of
them.

And then, who would like to deprive his own home, or the
shaded wayside, of the morning and evening concerts provided
by amorous pairs of these little songsters in the hottest seasons
of the year?

The exquisite *colibri* or humming-bird is wonderful for its
small size ; and the *pica-flores* for its habit of sucking its food
from honeyed flowers. It suspends its nest, which is the size of
half an egg-shell, to a straw hanging from the roof of a dwelling.
The lively *cardinal* bird is most elegant and pleasing, with

bright scarlet mitre, grey belly, and white breast. The poetic strain of a Zanella would be needed for its praise.

" How splendid !" one exclaims on seeing the flame-coloured, spoon-billed *flamingo ;* while the appearance of the largest of piscivorous birds, the white and grey *júlo*, reminds one of metempsycosis. The *júlo* remains motionless on the shore, on the watch for prey, for whose destruction nature has gifted him with long and strong legs, a long neck, and an immensely long beak, which is joined without suture to the bald bony head that is not distinguishable from it.

More fortunate than their brethren, in that they can poise themselves in the air, and that as yet the lord of creation has not learnt the art of flying, the smaller wild duck and the wild duck proper, as well as the snow-white swan, which disdains not to be in company with them, delight in circling round in graceful flight and in displaying their strength and their skill in natation, which man has indeed learnt to imitate, but will never equal.

Larger, more expert, and stronger on the wing, but similar in colour and in habits to the turkey, is the *chacá*, which screams its own name along the solitary river shores. *Chacás* collect together in large flocks on the ground, guarded in front, at the back, and on the two sides by sentinels on the wing, who from the tops of the highest roofs look out for danger and give due warning.

The *toucan*, on the contrary, is of solitary habits, and hides in the densest foliage of the woods, attracting attention alike by the beauty and the awkwardness of his many-tinted orange-coloured beak. It is as large as his head, six times as long, and as light as cork, and contrasts strongly with the diminutive size of his body, and with its colouring, which resembles that of a bluish-black pigeon with whitish breast.

Judging from the colouring of the *paloma*, which is like that of the migratory pigeons of Argentaro,[1] as well as from the domestic instinct which makes these birds assemble in large families round inhabited spots, and, alas ! from the taste of their flesh, I conclude them to be the brethren, perhaps the elder brethren of pigeons who, under innumerable aspects and served with innumerable sauces, are one of the most valuable

---

[1] A mountain in Tuscany, on the sea-coast, visited at certain seasons of the year by large flocks of pigeons.

resources of the domestic hearth of the tyrant man, as well as the most striking example offered by the Great Master [2] in proof of his favourite theory of evolution.

I am brought to the same conclusion by the affinity between the domestic cock—disguising his slavery under the glory of his plumage and the pleasures of the harem, unknown to liberty—the *charata* inhabiting the plains, and the *pava*, a larger bird, inhabiting the hills. Both are wild, both incapable of long flight or long running, both flutter from bough to bough, and both are coffee-coloured.

I should like to see every house protected against reptiles and insects by *ostriches* that frequent the fields and thick forests of these Chacos. They do not differ in the slightest degree from those that scour the Pampas, though less than half the size of their African brethren. I am ignorant as to the worth of their plumes or of the down from their breast.

The *chuna* is very similar in the uniform grey of the feathers; it is of moderate size and of the same domestic habits. When attacking a reptile, it avoids a close encounter, and, rising suddenly in the air, falls repeatedly upon the enemy, until the latter, weakened by blows of continually increasing violence, becomes an easy and unresisting prey.

The intelligence of the chuna is surpassed by that of the condor, or great American vulture, of which there are two kinds, the smaller, who frequent the plains near the mountains; and the larger, who dwell on the highest peaks of the chain and only descend into the high contiguous valleys.

The condor is grey, with black feathers at the extremity of the wings, and with a white patch sometimes on the back, which is uncovered when the wings are extended, and can be seen from below as he gyrates in space.

He has formidable claws, a powerful hooked beak, bare and wrinkled throat, and fierce eyes. Standing upright, he measures about a yard, and from wing to wing when outstretched, from two to three yards.

These birds are dangerous, even for adults. They are not of solitary habit, like the eagle, but congregate together on the mountain peaks where they dwell, and do not disdain the company of the *cuervo*, another bird of prey of two species, the larger of which is similar to the condor in size, strength, and

[2] Darwin.

habits; nor of the *carancho*, a hawk frequenting the plains and the hills. Not only do they tolerate the companionship of these birds, but they make use of them for securing their own safety at their expense.

The strength and cunning of the condor makes him a scourge to cattle. With a troop of companions he attacks the cow and her calf; some hover round the mother beating their wings until she becomes confused and wanders away from the calf, which, unconscious of danger, bellows with raised head and open mouth. The rest of the brigade then swooping down drag out its tongue with a sudden stroke of their talons, and then put out its eyes. Thus the mother no longer hears the son, and the latter cannot see the mother, who, terrified by the fierce condors, wanders farther and farther from the poor blind calf, that, without strength to defend itself, soon falls a victim.

If the cow has any previous experience of her enemies' mode of attack, she stands over her calf, and frequently defends herself with such success as to put her cruel foes to flight.

In the case of lambs and kids, resistance is impossible; with two strokes of the talon, all is over.

To get rid of this terrible scourge, the *estancieros* have for some years past made use of strychnine. They insert it into numerous wounds made in the carcase of an animal, either slaughtered for the purpose, or that has been fortunately discovered when newly dead.

At first the condors remain round the carcase, tearing it and feeding from it. But after a while they detect something wrong, and refuse to touch the suspected flesh; and even if it is removed at night to another place, they recognize it again.

In order to convince himself of the truth of his suspicion, the condor waits until the caranchos and crows have thrown themselves first on the prey; if they do not fall dead, the condors plunge down from the mountain-tops and hill-sides, and fall upon the carcase, while, in the contrary event, they remove to a distance.

At present, therefore, strychnine is of no use, except to get rid of a few novices who are ignorant of, or who despise the danger.

The condor, when full to repletion, is slow in flight, and is obliged to throw himself into space from a height like the swallow. Sometimes on these occasions he can be despatched by blows from a stick, but this happens very seldom.

Among the quadrupeds of the Chaco, the *tapir* or *anta* (the

Chicchuan name by which he is called in these parts) is remarkable for its strange structure. It resembles both the horse
and the pig. The Mattaccos, in fact, call a horse *jelatatch*, or
large tapir. Above all, when in a sitting posture, supported on
the forelegs, it looks like a horse, from the waist upwards. The
skin is dark coffee-brown, almost black, and of a texture between
horse and bull. The tail is like a pig's ; the hoofs cloven, with
four front toes and three behind ; the intestines are similar to,
if not the same as those of the horse ; the excrements are those of
the ass. This animal has small, pig-like eyes and ears; the cervix
is armed with a bony projection of immense power. The legs
are short and massive ; body thick and short, of most inelegant
shape, yet with swift action nevertheless. It has a movable nasal
appendage, resembling a diminutive proboscis with the nasal
orifices at the end ; and twenty-four teeth, twelve in each jaw,
arranged in groups of four, of which there is one in front and
one on each side ; the teeth are shaped like the teeth of horses.
The creature is herbivorous ; and being a pachyderm, the hide
is excessively hard and most valuable for harness, especially the
shield-like part along the spine. The liver is large, thirty centimeters by forty, and consists of three lobes ; the centre one
being subdivided at the base into four others, which are partly
placed over it, and into two smaller ones above. The tapir
plunges willingly into and under the water, like the hippopotamus. The one we killed was one yard in height, and
about one and a half in length ; its proboscis measured twenty
centimeters. It was full-grown and was separated from its
female, by which it was generally accompanied, as well as by
another couple or two. It is found in the thickets of the
tropical regions, on the plains, and on the hills. Hence it
abounds in the Chaco and in Tucuman, but avoids inhabited
places, although easily tamed.

The flesh is sweetish, like horse-flesh, and excessively
hard ; the taste remained in my mouth for several days.
Its weight may be about that of a medium-sized horse, or
perhaps rather more, on account of its corpulence and mas-
siveness.

I have given a detailed description of this creature, because
I have read inexact accounts of it, written perhaps by persons
who had not seen the brute. I derive its name from its copper
colour, *anta* being Chicchuan for copper, and not for *large beast*,
as so many writers have, I know not why, asserted. There are

great numbers of dwarf dogs and dwarf fowls in these parts, not from individual defective growth, but the race is dwarfed.

The tiger feeds not only on quadrupeds large and small, but, like our own domestic cat, on poultry in times of dearth, and even on fish. To obtain the latter he stands on watch in some suitable place, often the trunk of a tree that has fallen in the river, and either clutches it with his claws as it swims by, or with one blow of his paw flings it on the bank.

For killing horses and cattle he hunts against the wind, that his prey may not detect him by scent. He springs on the crupper and attacks the head, tearing the creature's neck with his strong teeth and claws. When it has fallen, he prefers the breast, leaving the remainder to the vultures, who are never absent from the festival.

The *puma* is the other large carnivorous animal. The vulgar name for it here is lion, but this is about as appropriate as the name of horse given to the llama by the Chinese when they discovered America on the Pacific side, or that of tapir, given by the Mattaccos to the horse. The American male lion has no mane, nor a tuft to his tail, nor is he as large as the lion of Africa. He is a large cat, if I may say so, entirely grey ; about eighty centimeters in height, and a yard and twenty centimeters in length. He can be domesticated, but even his master must be cautious, while strangers must not go near him. He attacks the smaller quadrupeds, such as goats, sheep, and deer, but he does not like the woods. When pursued, he climbs trees, and dares not descend among the pack of hounds at the foot. The hunters, who have climbed into adjoining trees, then have recourse to the lasso, and strangle him. The puma will attack a man asleep, and even the hunters in extreme cases.

While they are cubs the tapir and the roebuck are striped with white, and the puma has small dark spots. They lose this adventitious colouring afterwards, but it indicates some vanished traits of progenitors.

The ant-bear is a most curious and ugly creature. It derives its name from feeding on these insects, which are found in enormous numbers in the Chaco. They build cities, consisting of thousands of cone-shaped hills about a yard in height, in each of which are billions of these most intelligent insects.

The ant-bear is usually dwarf, and crawls, as it were, along the ground ; it is over a yard in length, with a long, sharp snout, more like a fleshy appendage ; its coat is dark yellow, with stiff bristles. Those along the spine are long and black; the tail has a crook, with which it holds its cub, which clambers on its back. At Rivadavia a cub, whose mother had been killed, refused the milk offered it, unless it was allowed to climb on the carcass of the dead mother. It makes its way about by jumping, with the muzzle on the ground.

The forelegs are armed with claws, and are of enormous strength. They form the bear's sole means of defence; he sits on his hind-quarters, and contends successfully even with tigers. The tongue is excessively long and thin, and used with such twirling rapidity that it reminds one of a venomous asp when in action. It is a prehensile instrument for procuring food.

The wild cat or wood-cat is a great enemy to fowls, both wild and domestic; I killed a speckled one. There are many kinds of deer, and the roebuck, called *corzuéla*, also other lesser ruminants.

I must also mention the *simarrone*, or wild bull, which has escaped from the *estancias*. It is a terrible brute to meet; a man has barely time to seek safety in a tree, when the creature stations himself at the foot, and endeavours to tear it up by the roots. Once, when on the top of a steep and solitary mountain, I saw the Indian who was with me turn pale on hearing the trampling of simarrones.

Hares are very abundant; they are larger than with us, and slightly different. Their speed is great, attaining two-thirds of a kilometer per minute, as I had an opportunity of verifying once in the province of Santiago, when a frightened hare rushed along the metals in front of the locomotive.

An animal called the *biscacha* is part fox, part hare, part cat; its flesh is not very palatable, it is nocturnal, lives in holes, is most prolific, and does great damage in the fields, selecting by preference those near inhabited spots. The owl, called *lechuza* in Spanish, shares in its retreat. I wondered at seeing owls so frequently in the Pampas, because at home with us they live in solitary ruined towers.

Wild rabbits are also excessively abundant; in size and colour they might be mistaken for tailless moles. They are delicious morsels for falcons and vipers, Indians and Christians, as we experienced ourselves after living for months without flesh-meat. But the idea is repugnant to Italians.

Among semi-aquatic, not to say amphibious animals, the largest, though not the most common, is the *carpincho*, a kind of white pig, bristled like the porcupine, with bearded snout, slow in its movements, and which avoids danger by long-continued immersion under water. The flesh is good eating; it weighs about forty kilograms ; it is a pachyderm.

The *water wolf* [3] is of dwarf size, weighing at most fifteen kilograms, the head is cat-like and extremely intelligent; the skin is valuable, and the flesh good. It saves itself from danger like the carpincho, but with more ability, making the most astonishing springs. I have only met with it in the lower part of the Vermejo, where the water is deep and brackish.

In the same localities, and likewise higher up the river, we find the otter, or *nutria* in Spanish. The skin is a most valuable article of commerce; the flesh is good to eat. It weighs from five to seven kilograms. Its movements are slow on land, but it is thoroughly at home in the water, where it gambols and disports itself in view of the hunter. The skin of the otter and that of the wolf, both brown, supply the greater part of winter clothing.

We do not find in the wooded plains of the Chaco the sheep, with its beautiful, almond-shaped black eyes, that lives in deserted fields; or the llama, a beast of burden ; or the untamable vicuna, with its valuable fleece ; or the domesticated alpaca, which represents our own flocks at home, and that lives on the unforested mountains. All these are ruminants, all have long necks frequently curved in artistic attitudes, and all are graceful and stupid in their ways.

[3] Commonly so called ; if not carnivorous, it is certainly piscivorous.

CHAPTER XII.

CHANGE OF LANDSCAPE—PROGRESS OF THE REPUBLIC—
IRRIGATION.

WE were eager to reach Oran, the most tropical city of the Argentines, situate in the midst of a region in which the irony of Fate showers with one hand every requisite for the most astounding fecundity, and with the other restricts the means of fructification within an angle hundreds of leagues from any centre of consumption or of traffic, and subject to volcanic convulsions.

At about two-thirds of our day's journey we came to the skirts of the chain of hills enclosing on the east the basin of Oran, which is bounded on the west by the high chain of the Zenta. This name, like that of Oran, is African, either transplanted here by the pious patriotism of the first colonists, or, as some assert, so named in consequence of their analogous destiny, which was originally that of a penal settlement.

The forests, denser and more lofty, no longer consist of algarrobo, nor of innumerable kinds of mimosa with their minute and deeply-notched leaves, nor of aromatic flowering plants; but sebillos, with knotty and wrinkled bark, begin to predominate, and lapachos with their roseate flowers and hard timber, suitable for all kinds of building purposes; and, further up, the *china-china*, with its fragrant resin, and the purgative *sarsaparilla*.

It is curious that the chebraccio, that flourishes in the very driest regions, should be numerously represented here, and by trees of exceptional height or size.

We ascended the cordon called *Loma de la Embarcacion* by a path that wound sometimes down a deep ravine, and sometimes at the edge of a precipice, the steep sides of which revealed the most capricious stratifications—tokens of the local effects of repeated volcanic convulsions. There are traces

remaining of the earthquake of 1871, when a gulf of some
yards in width, and many leagues in length from east to west,
opened in the direction of Oran, crossing the whole basin and the
hills, and lowering by noontide the surrounding land to the
extent of one yard. Time has obliterated any distinct traces
in the plain near *Tabacal*, but landslips are still visible on the
hills.

Having reached the summit, we easily descended the other
side by a kind of road that had been cut through, and which
led us through a forest vegetation continually increasing in
beauty until, late in the evening, we reached the plain.

The bogs formed by the rains and by the floods of the
Vermejo, which river runs along the western skirt of the cordon
and a few leagues lower down joins the S. Francisco, takes a
curve to the south-east, and begins its course across the plain of
the Gran Chaco—the bogs, I say, formed by the rains, were
filled by an extraordinary quantity of frogs of a thousand
different species. The croaking of these creatures made our
voices inaudible to each other at the distance of a few yards.

The damp, close, heavy, and cold atmosphere made us
anxious to leave these wilds behind us, where every mouthful
of air seemed fever-laden. To this was added the misery of
mosquitoes. Countless, persistent, stinging, greedy, insatiable,
undaunted, they reduced us to desperation. Exaggeration
becomes impossible in describing the misery, the restlessness,
the fury these plagues of nature produce. One must have
travelled in these parts, or, what is still worse, have lived on
board a vessel at anchor, surrounded by forest, in the midst of
a summer calm, to understand the amount of suffering endured
from these tyrants of one's existence. It is necessary to eat
before dusk, to go to bed when the meal is scarcely at an end,
to enclose oneself in a mosquito curtain as in a sepulchral urn,
to endure a stifling heat and an overwhelming perspiration, and
to lie awake till dawn. There is nothing to be done beyond
tossing and turning on the little bedstead of half a yard wide,
while all the time there is a beautiful moon shining, or a starry
sky, and one knows that with two steps out of doors and a fan,
one could spend a night in Paradise. Nor is this all, for
somehow or other a mosquito always finds its way inside the
curtains, followed by several more. One's hands are soon
insufficient for self-defence, and with smarting shoulders, and
face aching from one's own boxes on the ears, and burning with

a childish rage, one must wait seven or eight hours for the early breeze heralding the approach of dawn.

We crossed the river at night on a flat-bottomed boat, and in a few moments were hospitably received at a military post called *La Embarcacion.*

Here we met with an old acquaintance, Colonel Napoleon Uriburu, commandant of the northern frontier of the Gran Chaco, with whom we spent a week or ten days.

This young and able officer holds a distinct place in the military and political life of the country; and there are pages in his life's history that deserve to be known. I am confident that the reader and he will forgive me if I say a few words concerning him. His is a remarkable instance of how men are made. When a lad he worked on his own estancia, and being inquisitive, ambitious, and extremely intelligent, he learnt their native language from the Indians who came harvesting to the estancia, lived among them, and ended by occasionally adopting their mode of life when more convenient, while he worked and studied. Belonging to one of the most distinguished families in the province of Salta and the Republic, he next entered the army, thus adopting the most exalted career afforded by this country, and entered the military college. During the Paraguayan war he had the honour of being chosen to bear the good tidings of victory to the general-in-chief and the President of the Republic, gaining promotion by so doing. Later, he was ordered to make a military reconnaissance of the Chaco from Humaita to Oran, and succeeded to the fullest extent, without even the loss of a single horse, though in the midst of Indians, who are adepts at horse-lifting. He published proclamations to the Indians in their own language, gave them presents, and made friends of them for the time being.

In 1874 he was made lieutenant-colonel, and while in command of the Northern Division, occupied in quelling the revolution which had broken out in that year, he gave proofs of extraordinary activity and ability. Since then he has received various important commands from the National Government, and has been acknowledged as the head of a party in his native province and in that of Jujuy. A few months after our meeting him, General Roca, the War Minister, being in need of an officer whose fidelity was above suspicion for the command of the right wing in the expedition to Rio Negro against the Indians of the Pampas, selected Uriburu, who has now for

eight months been fighting against them. All the heaviest
fighting has fallen to the right wing, which is posted against
the Cordillera, across the river *Nauquen*, and is constantly
attacked with desperation. He has thus obtained the rank of
colonel.

Physically he is the true type of his countrymen. Rather
above middle height, slight of figure, with muscles of steel,
brown complexion, dark and sparkling eyes, jet black hair
and beard, well-bred, and of distinguished appearance.

He likes illustrative conversation. He is studious, hard-work-
ing, and active. He has, if he chooses, a great future before him
in this Republican, democratic, restless nation.

Now, whether it be from race, or climate, or food, or the
freedom enjoyed even by children, or all these together, the fact
remains that the people of the Argentines are remarkably intelligent, and have a truly astonishing quickness of perception.
It remains to be seen whether they possess corresponding good
sense ; but this is acquired in a great measure by studious
cultivation of the intellect, and by living in the midst of fully-
developed and complicated social conditions. Education and
social development are spreading daily throughout the country,
which, in a few short years, has made gigantic strides in
population, in the development of wealth, and of the means of
wealth, and in the progress of learning. Banks, railways,
telegraphs, and other public works, agrarian and industrial
machinery, have come into operation in such proportions as to
remind one of, and even to surpass, Italy in the first twenty
years of her national existence—I say surpass, by reason of the
relatively or individually greater wealth. When we consider
the number of inhabitants is only 2,000,000, and that there is
a corresponding amount of railways and of telegraphs, equal, if
not superior, to the like proportion in North America and in
England.

Then the national system of education and that of the province of Buenos Ayres, has taken root and been regulated and
developed so as to change the face of the country in this respect
within a few years. Two universities, a national college in
each of the fourteen provinces, museums of physics, chemistry
and natural science, might well be envied by many of the
largest cities of Italy. There are numerous Government
libraries, academies, and scientific societies ; and, above all,
general elementary instruction is of obligation in conjunction

with secondary studies, and these, again, with professional studies.   I am speaking now with due knowledge of the facts, for I have been present at the examinations both as examiner and as an interested spectator.   Splendid results must be, and are in fact, obtained from a generation passing through such an apprenticeship as this.   And expectation is the more legitimate, since before the present system of preparation, such self-made men as Sarmiento, Alberdi, Mitre, Rawson, Lopez, Tejedor, to name only the greatest, and the lamented Guttierrez and Velez-Sarsfield, have risen up from among the Argentine people, and would be remarkable in any part of the world.

The next morning our spirits were raised by the sight of an unaccustomed spectacle.   The immense plain was succeeded by a valley surrounded on all sides by hills and mountains, the former clothed with thick forests, and the arid and wild landscape through which we had been journeying for ten days was replaced by a vast chess-board of cultivated fields, growing cereals, oranges, and bananas.   Then instead of the *rastrillada* or beaten track made by the footsteps of animals across the country, like our own *dogane*, traces of which still remain in the Maremma, the road lay across fields flanked by thick and wide quick-set hedges concealing the canals beneath their luxuriant vegetation.

For although the climate of Oran is comparatively moist, the harvest could not be depended on unless the fields were artificially watered.   Irrigation is practised in the Argentines wherever the existence of running streams and the slope of the land make the necessary works inexpensive.   This is the case in the districts adjoining the mountains, or enclosed within them, and consequently throughout the northern and western extremities of the Republic.   In the west the rivers and torrents are few in number and poorly supplied with water, and, for the most part, disappear as soon as they reach the plain.   But it is at this juncture that the industry of man has been applied to dealing with the scarcity of the element, and has worked wonders by adapting the simplest means to his purpose. Doubtless a professional engineer would add many improvements, and perhaps would entirely recommence the work, but the agriculturist is well aware that the extra cost involved in a perfect system would swallow up all his profit, and contents himself with the actual state of things.

The provinces of Catamarca, Rioja, S. Giovanni, Mendoza,

and S. Luigi owe all their prosperity to the small amount of irrigation they are able to effect, the aridity of the climate forbidding the growth of even a blade of grass outside of the irrigated districts—but these, on the other hand, are veritable oases. S. Giovanni is distinguished by wise use of the treasure —for water is indeed a treasure—and Mendoza by the extent of its irrigation, that amounts to 100,000 hectares.

In order to cut a canal for irrigation the country folk use no other level than that—of water! They begin excavating, and as long as the water runs without injuring either the bottom or the sides, the work is considered satisfactory.

It might be supposed that the art of irrigation was introduced into this country by the Spaniards, by whom it was held in honour *ab antiquo*, principally through the works of the Arabs when they were dominant in the south. But it is more likely that they found the art already known to the natives, and that they only continued and extended its practice. All the conquered provinces, in fact, and those of Salta and Jujuy in the north, Oran included, were inhabited by subjects of the empire of the Incas. History does not tell us this, but I assert it, and I believe I can prove it on another occasion. Now, every one knows that the Incas were perfectly acquainted with the art of irrigation, and practised it on a gigantic scale—gigantic, of necessity, because without irrigation not a *poqcha* of maize could have been gathered throughout the whole of the immense empire (a *poqcha* was a measure for grain), and in those very provinces irrigation is flourishing.

It is true that in Tucuman, a province included among those I have named and among other Inca populations, and dependent on them, irrigation is not practised to the same extent, although it is being much extended on account of rice, sugar, and tobacco plantations ; but in the first place we must understand that it is less imperative in regions adjacent to the mountains, and then we must remember that Tucuman maintained a kind of autonomy and held a special position with regard to the Incas. These rulers had not colonized it by expelling the original inhabitants and replacing them by their own legions, because the Tucumans, according to my interpretation of a passage in Garcilaz de la Vega, had offered friendship to the Incas long before the latter were in a position to injure them, and had subsequently facilitated the imperial conquests south of Tucuman. They thus escaped the scourge of the *Mitmacs*, or Inca colonists, who were despatched into conquered countries and very speedily reduced them to their own level.

. . . .

How beautiful is a banana-tree! The stem is from four to six yards in height, with a diameter at the base of fifteen to twenty centimeters; the green leaves are thirty to forty centimeters in width and more than two yards long. They are rolled where joined to the stem, and fall by their own weight into a succession of graceful curves, one above the other, crowned at the summit by immense clusters [of bananas lying on the leaves beneath. The tree lasts three years. During this period numerous shoots spring every year from the roots, each of which bears fruit and dies in the third year, so that one year afterwards the whole of the beautiful plantation has ceased to exist, the soil being exhausted of the aliments necessary for the plant.

And what of the orange-trees? They attain to an extraordinary size, and some trees produce 10,000 oranges. They are planted in rows in the orangeries, and form, as it were, so many porticoes to the leafy vaults, where no ray of the sun can ever penetrate, so that the ground beneath is bare of all vegetation. They form consequently a providential refuge for travellers in this torrid clime.

We proceed onward for another seven leagues, and when half-way we find ourselves in a magnificent forest, surprising us by its density and the variety and height of its plants, which, imprisoned on all sides, dart up in clusters in search of light and air to the height of thirty yards and more.

The forest is succeeded by a stony, barren, and waterless country. At last, on reaching a height, we can distinguish Oran, and are at once reminded of its past ill-fortune and the presages of its recurrence in the future.

CHAPTER XIII.

ORAN.

ONLY nine years ago, a traveller bound northwards could have descried a few miles beyond the tropics, close to the Indian frontier, and a little above the centre of a vast basin, a small but beautiful city, with wide streets lying at right angles, with whitish houses of one and two storeys, surrounded by ever fruitful orange-trees, with numerous canals through which the crystal waters from the skirts of the neighbouring Cordillera brought fertility to the rich lands, which by their produce conferred wealth on their owners, and enabled them to make their homes beautiful and delightful. The basin in which stands the city is slightly undulating in the centre, bounded at the east and north by pleasant hills, and on the west by a succession of mountains, rising step by step to the highest summit of the Andes. They were then fitly crowned by the ancient and dense forests that clothe the greater part of the plain and all the skirts of the hills, reaching at last to the edge of the snowy mantle of the Zenta, and comprising the greatest variety of species, which, growing luxuriantly in this rich soil and favourable climate, interlace their branches and mingle their intoxicating perfumes, while they increase and multiply in marvellous fashion. Then, too, the cultivation of rice, plantations of sugarcane and tobacco, rows of banana-trees, and ever verdant fields repaid the care of the inhabitants, whose labours were sweetened by the ceaseless song of birds, while the perfumed air, laden with a thousand sweet scents, invited all to delicious repose. A sudden shock of earthquake, followed by a second, occurred eight years ago—and great houses as well as humble cottages were shaken to the ground. Perchance nature repented of her crime and would not aggravate it by claiming human victims, with the exception of one young maiden whom she selected to propitiate her wrath. Poor child! she had fled from danger, rushing from her bed at the first alarm, but her mother, ignorant of fate, drove her back with assurances of

Q

safety, and she fell crushed on the very threshold! All was ruin and desolation.

Three-fourths of the inhabitants fled in terror from the sudden and terrible peril; much of the cultivated land and of the plantations ceased to exist for want of the labour required to keep them in order; the neglected streamlets either forsook their recently-constructed channels, or formed into angry pools at their intersection, while numbers of frogs, emboldened by impunity, assembled together, croaking in discordant and never-ending chorus.

It was melancholy to see masses of ruins in every direction; the larger the building, the worse was the destruction. On one side a shapeless mound of earth, on another shattered, broken, or cracked walls; here, door-jambs, rafters, and doors, either overthrown or standing upright like military columns amid the general disaster; and nettles and weeds of all sorts springing up, flourishing and multiplying amid the broken rubbish of what was until recently a human dwelling.

Farther on there are disroofed and dismantled houses, whose walls, bare and split, offer a safe retreat for the amorous embraces of lizards and vipers. Ah! if it be allowable to compare small things with great ones, these ruins recall to mind those of some cities in the Tuscan marshes. There, also, is a fierce sun, a clear sky, a splendid vegetation, mountains on each side, a wide plain in front and a desert within; there, also, perennial shade, among broken fragments, of the evergreen olive, as here, of the orange-tree and the little noisy stream tumbling and frothing until it reaches the plain, where its waters creep slow and neglected about the city walls, carrying death where formerly they brought life and fertility.

Among the houses formerly constituting the town of Oran, there may still be seen a few that escaped the catastrophe. Their dislocated walls seem to be staggering under the weight of the thatched roof, and new dwellings have been and are being built on ready-made and plastered timber framework and wooden lattices, to fill them up again; while behind these, or standing detached in the rectangular fields at the back of the orchards, are solitary and poor little cottages.

This corner of the Republic, however, is an absolute garden. The very atmosphere seems a poem, so fragrant is it with the scent of the gaggio, the brea, the chañar, the thousand species of aromatic plants, the orange-tree, and with the flowers that enamel the meadows and bloom on the gigantic plants of the forest, and the resin that exudes from their trunks. Is it not poetry to admire the lofty mountains, the lovely hills, and the well-watered plain, the astonishing fertility of the soil, and the beneficent sun? Is it not poetry to contemplate the forests with their innumerable species of plants, growing separately in other places, but in this region united and attaining gigantic dimensions, such as the willow, the algarrobo, and the chebraccio —common trees, indeed, but highly useful—the chebil, the cedar, the walnut, the lapaccio, the quinquina, the aliso, and many others. These forests cover the greater part of the plain, the entire hills, and the skirts of the mountains to a great height and for a distance of 4000 square kilometers. Is there not poetry in Yerba maté, in cocoa, in the tea-plant—all of indigenous growth,—in the banana, the *chirimoya*, the sugar-cane, in coffee, tobacco, or rice (all so valuable in commerce), not to speak of other commoner products?

Has this country a future before it? It has an immediate and magnificent future, if the Vermejo becomes safe, periodical, and permanent for commerce. When this is an accomplished fact, the valuable productions of this privileged zone will be obtained at a small cost through the labour of the thousands of Indians who rove through the immense Chaco; and when cheaply transported to the coast will be able to vie with the products of other regions. And Oran, being situate on the skirts of the Cordilleras and possessing the finest harbour on the river, will become, there can be no doubt, a necessary and convenient emporium for the international carrying trade with the south of Bolivia, now carried on at a loss of four months' time, and 1000 francs per ton for transport.

When this shall have come to pass, the traveller in the tropics will find on the eastern slopes of the Zenta, and skirting the Indian territory, a wealthy and prosperous city, risen from its ruins, and surrounded by beautiful country. And instead of feeling called upon to recount a melancholy history of Maremma desolation, he will imagine himself transported to the delightful environs of Florence. In the shade of orange-trees, listening to the song of the blackbird amid the perfumed breezes, and the sweet murmur of the stream, he will rest during the burning heat of a tropical day, and there will come to him sweet dreams of love, country, life, the earth, and— who knows?—perhaps even of heaven!

CHAPTER XIV.

MENDOZA.

THE disaster of Oran reminds me of the still greater misfortune that befell another of the jewels in the belt encircling the Republic—I refer to Mendoza.

This city is the Turin of the Argentines. It is situated on the skirts of the Cordilleras, whose endless ridge of snow-clad peaks can be discerned at a distance of fifty leagues, and is the last trading-point with Chili, just as Turin is between Italy and France.

Railways will bring it into rapid communication with the Atlantic, and when once connected with its harbours, Mendoza will be the richest market for commerce between the two oceans.

The city has had a presentiment of its future destiny, and is hastening to prepare for it.

If you could only see it always in gala dress !

Mendoza is the most beautiful and the most agreeable city in the Republic.

The principal street is a fine avenue, a league in length and thirty yards in width, planted with a double row of plane-trees, poplars, and weeping willows, and watered by two running streams that divide the foot pavement from the road. All the streets are laid at right angles and are fifteen or twenty yards wide, and are also ornamented with trees on each side. The houses are either on the streets, or stand a little way back in pretty little gardens, and are of various kinds, some being simple and modest, and some elegant and picturesque, but all of them only one storey in height, so as to minimize the dreaded perils—alas ! already experienced—of earthquakes.

Mendoza possesses the finest public promenade in the Republic. It consists of a large octagonal garden situated in a piazza of four quadrants. In the centre is a spacious artificial lake surrounded by a labyrinth of paths, kiosks, grottoes, fountains, trees, shrubs and rare flowers both native and foreign.

Yet this city has been in existence only twelve years. She is the lovely daughter of a fair mother, who, while still young and beautiful, succumbed fifteen years ago to a most terrible fate.

It was on the Wednesday of the week that is called Holy by the Nazarenes, in the year 1861 of their era.

The inhabitants were engaged in the customary practices of their religious worship in the splendid and numerous temples raised for the purpose. The priests were preaching to the crowds, who extended to the piazzas, on the Passion of the God whom 300,000,000 of men acknowledge as the Redeemer of mankind. The sun had set, and the contrite crowds were returning to their homes, indifferent to the beauty of the wonderfully clear sky, illumined by a brighter moon than usual, and to the cool zephyr that was seeking to refresh these ignorant children of the soil after a stifling day, when suddenly the earth trembled, darkness obscured the heavens, a loud noise struck on the ears of those who might thenceforth be called the survivors, and the humblest dwellings and proudest temples fell alike in fragments, becoming sepulchres for those most devoted to their God and their Lares.

Fire, water, and repeated shocks increased the horrors of the catastrophe.

The momentary deathlike silence was succeeded by the piercing cries of the wounded, either buried under the ruins that had fallen upon them, or in fear of being crushed by the tottering masonry, or in dread of the river, that, suddenly arrested in its course, was threatening to overflow and drown them. To these terrors was added that of fire, which fed by the inflammable materials scattered about amid the ruins, came forth in volumes of flame to hasten the death of the dying!

How can I describe the heartrending spectacle? Out of 15,000 inhabitants 10,000 perished, and the city was entirely destroyed.

The survivors wandered fearfully for many months round their beloved city, made all the dearer by her misfortunes, and sanctified by the graves of her sons; they hesitated to pitch their tents on such scenes of desolation, and yet were unable to forsake the necropolis of their dear ones.

But affection prevailed; and the new city grew up at the side of the former one, and we may say of Mendoza, as poets have sung of the fabled Phœnix, that she has risen from her ashes with renewed beauty.

CHAPTER XV.

THE BASIN OF LA PLATA—THE PAMPAS AND FOREST REGIONS
—THEIR RELATIONS TO CLIMATE AND AGRICULTURE IN
THE ARGENTINES.

WE climbed the Zenta, whose peak is almost always clad in
snow, at a point near the Tropic of Capricorn, 5000 yards
above the level of the sea; and like Jules Verne, having
provided ourselves with optical instruments, we plunged into
ethereal space on the mighty wings of the condor, and, turning
towards the east, gazed on the horizon.

An immense wooded plain lay beneath us, extending 700
kilometers to the River Paraguay, which itself flows for another
1500, until near the southern extremity of the continent or the
Magellan Strait, where the forests begin to show themselves
again, preceded by dwarf and scanty woods.

The eye instinctively follows the course of the Vermejo, on
whose banks we had lingered so long. We marked its tortuous
course to the south-east, until it falls into the Paraguay almost
opposite Humaita. It turns slightly to the left, and for a
distance of thirty or forty leagues runs parallel with the River
Pilcomayo which falls into the Paraguay at Assuncion.

By attentively watching, we could discern on our right,
but very far off, and looking like a silver thread among the
woods, only visible here and there by the light reflected from
its various curves, the *Rio Salado*, a river running parallel to
the Vermejo, at a distance of forty to sixty leagues from its
right bank until near the mouth of the Paraná, along the side
of which it flows for a long distance, until at last it falls into
it near the city of Santa Fè.

The Pilcomayo, the Vermejo, and the Salado are the three
rivers of the Gran Chaco.

. Directing our gaze beyond the Paraguay, we discern other
plains, woods, and lakes, and some few hills; and turning a
little to the right we discern the Upper Paraná, and still

further off, and more to the right, the Upper Uruguay. Between them lies a chain of lakes, among which, shining in the refulgent rays of the sun, is the famous Lake Ibera, from which the chain takes its name.

It is early morning, and the plain through which run the Paraguay, the Paraná, and the Uruguay, is covered with a veil, transparent as gauze in some places, and in others, near the rivers and lakes, like an opaque and clinging sheet.

In the higher regions, on the contrary, the atmosphere is clear, and on the side of the horizon whence the sun will rise, the crests of the mountains stand out distinctly. Later in the day they will be concealed, and crowned by the white clouds that, having lain all night in mist upon the plains, are travelling from the Equator to the Atlantic in a southerly direction.

Let us lift up our eyes.

Before us is a colossal amphitheatre of mountains that, starting from the higher plains (which here are close behind them, and connect them by other mountain chains with the Cordillera of the Andes still further in the background), turn on our left side towards the Equator, and stand in battle array facing the east, slightly curving in our direction in the shape of a horse-shoe, then extend in mighty ranges to the Atlantic, where they diminish.

Behind us, to the west, the horse-shoe is completed by the chains of the Zenta, of the Acconcha or Tucuman, and of Cordova, which vanishes in the Pampas.

In the amphitheatre before us the harsh and rugged orographical architecture seems to have intended to carve out in gigantic relief three huge fans, with battlemented and intricate edges. The interstices between the ribs appear as if richly silvered, and the fan itself seems to be carved with innumerable patterns, no two of which are alike, and yet all are formed in the same mould; admirable art of the Master! In this grand production, there is not one line, however slight, that does not spring from another more important one; not a silver rivulet unconnected with another of larger size, although an unaccustomed eye may fail to discern as much, among the serpentine meanderings and the boldly cut edges of the capricious and able Artificer.

The sticks of the fans, as we face them, are neither straight nor curved according to any geometrical rule, but twisted, knotty, and roughly broken, like the artificial enclosures of an English garden. At the lowest part, where all the ribs are joined, or rather at the hilt-point, where all the three fans meet, there is a handle of suitable size and glittering like silver.

The mists rose presently to the mountain tops, and the plain lay clear and distinct before us. Wonderful to relate, the three glittering silver handles are the rivers Paraguay, Upper Paranà, and Uruguay. The two first, after hundreds of leagues of separate existence, join in one, under the name of the Paranà, a little below Humaita, and almost opposite the Argentine city of Corrientes. The other, that is, the Uruguay and the Paranà, after 1500 kilometers of an almost parallel course, unite a little above Buenos Ayres and form the Rio de la Plata, or the Mar Dolce, as it was called by its first discoverers, which at that point is thirty kilometers in width, by a length of 270; and at the mouth, where it falls into the Atlantic, between Montevideo and Cape S. Antonio, is 160 kilometers wide.

The immense basin thus spread out before us is therefore the basin of the Rio de la Plata; it is in the shape of a horseshoe, the open part or base lying against the Atlantic, and the upper part towards the Equator, and embracing twenty degrees of latitude from the Equator, equal to more than as many hundreds of kilometers, and fifteen degrees of longitude. The abundant waters of this basin proceed almost entirely from the Torrid Zone, and are precipitated on the slopes of La Plata from the chain of mountains I have described, the opposite sides of which supply the equally large, nay, even more extensive basin of the Amazons.

The basin of the Rio de la Plata therefore includes the greater part of the Argentine Republic, part of South Bolivia, the whole of the Republic of Paraguay, situated between the Upper Paranà and the Paraguay rivers, from the latter of which it takes its name, and the whole of Banda Oriental or Uruguay, which is bounded by the River Uruguay, by La Plata and by the Atlantic, and has Montevideo for its capital, situate on the mouth of the Plata, and also a great part of the Brazilian empire.

The immense plains—perhaps the largest in the world—of the Pampa and the Gran Chaco, the one grassy, the other wooded, lie in the western portion of the basin, on the right and along the estuary of the Rio de la Plata, the Paranà, and the Paraguay, bounded on the west by the Cordilleras, and then by the mountains of Cordova, Tucuman, and Oran.

The Pampa that extends also in a southerly direction for hundreds of leagues along the Atlantic follows the course of the Rio de la Plata from its mouth up, and also that of the Paranà towards the Equator for 600 or 700 kilometers, according to the situation. It is succeeded by woods consisting of algarrobo (carob-trees) and other inferior mimosas, and later, by forests of che-braccio, urunday, lapaccio, palo-santo, and of many other kinds, valuable for the most part for timber, carpentry, or cabinet work.

Is there no evident cause for the marked division of the plains into grass in the south and forest in the north, by a long and sinuous boundary-line from east to west, following closely the parallel of 30°? Or, at any rate, is there no connection between this fact and the climatic phenomena and the nature of the soil in the two regions?

I am not aware that the connection has been observed, but it exists, and I have been able to recognize it in part during my exploration of these regions.

I apprehend that in the region of the Pampa there is one order of climatic phenomena and another in the forest, or Chaco region. In the former the rainy season is in winter, while here in the forests it is in summer. There the climate is less dry, here it is dry to excess. The rains are brought on by the action of the winds. Now, the winds that prevail in the Pampa are not the same as those that blow across the Chaco, or, at any rate, prevail at different seasons. In the Chaco and throughout the centre and northern parts of the Republic, or, in other words, throughout the forest region, the winds are from the south, coming cold and dry from the South Pole, and occasioning the rains, and frequently terrible storms, by contact with the hot and moist winds from the north.

Now, who is unacquainted with the part taken by the winds in carrying and distributing organic germs, whether vegetable or animal? I contend that the forests of the north and centre of the Republic, and the absence of forest in the Pampa are both due to the action of the winds.

I do not propose to trace the origin of these winds, although I believe they form part of the general system of atmospheric currents, albeit considerably modified by local circumstances. I will therefore take for granted that these winds that rage so furiously in summer through the northern regions of the

Republic are the same that in winter blow over the Pampa. This being the case, we shall always be confronted with the fact that in summer the winds of the forest districts may export from the flora of other regions germs that would not exist in winter, when plants are sleeping, or, at any rate, are not flowering, and *vice versâ* with respect to the other hemisphere.

The further properties of climate, heat, moisture, pressure, &c., have afforded the necessary conditions for the development of the germs.

Be this as it may, the analogy, not to say the identity, of the American flora in the regions north and south of the Equator, in Mexico, in Brazil, in the Argentines, and in Chili, is nevertheless surprising.

I have said that in the forest regions of the Republic the climate is drier than in the Pampa, or rather that it is dry to excess.

It is a wonderful fact, this existence of immense forests covering tens of thousands of square kilometers that nevertheless do not produce a climate more moist than that of the Pampa covered with grass only, while every day we hear the changes rung on the influence of trees in procuring rain. So it is, however, and the fact being evident here on a colossal scale should make us perceive the inaccuracy of the contrary opinion, and hence the error of those persons who expect from the planting of the hills and the afforesting of the Pampa an alteration in the climate, and the exaggeration of those others who inform us of the new and abundant rainfall in the afforested districts of the Suez Canal. In truth, whatever influence may be granted to the presence of forests on climate is very small with respect to the various cosmical circumstances, the position of districts with regard to the sun, the existence of mountain ranges, and the presence of oceans. The influence of woods must be limited and local in the extreme, viz. to protect some fields from the action of certain winds, and to purify or vitiate the air of some given locality. The evaporation from the soil is not lessened, neither is its fertility increased. One field is a thousand times more absorbent and fertilizing than an entire tropical forest. The *humus* will teach us this; it covers to a certain depth the surface soil of the Pampa, while it is scarcely ever seen in the greater part of the forest surface soil in the Gran Chaco.[1]

[1] Darwin's latest observations on earth-worms may throw consider-

The climatic conditions in the two regions of Pampa and forest afford us *à priori* a criterion confirmed by fact with regard to agriculture   I assert that agriculture is impossible in the forest regions without artificial irrigation, saving only a strip of land bordering on the Rivers Paranà and Paraguay, which has the benefit of dews and mist from proximity to great masses of water.

I am aware that a learned writer who has lived for many years in these parts has published a contrary opinion; but my statement is not, on that account, the less true.   The writer to whom I allude takes his stand, it appears, on the theory of alternation of crops, which has caused such great improvement in agriculture, and which is based on the well-known fact, that similar plants, nourishing themselves in the soil with the same aliments, exhaust the land, become themselves impoverished, and hence are unable to give the product required for industrial purposes.

Hence the periodical and artificial alternation in husbandry of one crop with another.   Nature follows the same course in the Pampas, but at much longer intervals than the art of man.

However, concerning the substitution of an herbaceous plant for one of forest growth, it would be worth while to examine whether this theory is not only equally good, but is not in fact all the stronger, for the great dissimilarity between the two growths; or whether this difference might not be too great. I concede willingly every latitude in the application of the theory of alternation, but there remains a factor of which either our learned writer is ignorant or which he has overlooked; that factor is the climate.   A tropical climate where the rainfall in summer and autumn is preceded by eight or nine months of complete drought, where there are neither dews or mists, nor under-currents of water near the surface of the soil, is un-favourable to agriculture.   And such are the conditions for the most part of the forest zone.   Irrigation may nevertheless produce extraordinary results, in conjunction with the elevated temperature of the zone.

able light on this question of the vegetable soil of the Pampa and of the forests. The name might even be changed to *animal*, or rather *organic* *soil*, from the concurrence of the two causes.—AUTHOR'S NOTE.

CHAPTER XVI.

THE FOREST FLORA OF THE PLAIN—ITS DISTRIBUTION—CONCLUSIONS CONCERNING THE SOIL, THE CLIMATE, AND AGRICULTURE.

INDEPENDENTLY of the latitude and of other climatic conditions such as drought or moisture, &c., the forest flora of the plain is distributed according to the age of the soil, as we have seen in the case of herbaceous plants.

The heaviest timber grows, generally speaking, on the emerged or original soil, called by the colonists *bordo firme*, and not liable to submersion. The red chebraccio is the best timber for constructions under water or underground or level with the ground; for dyeing, and for tanning leather.; it does not rot, and this, added to its weight, which is greater than that of the oak, makes it above all excellent for railway sleepers, for the weight itself contributes to the solidity of the permanent way. Then there are the urunday and the lapaccio, of similar properties for building purposes, the latter being even superior for carpentering; and the palo-santo for costly cabinet-work; all this wood weighs from 1·20 to 1·50 the same volume of water, and is true hard timber. With them we find the giuccian, the cotton-tree, as flaccid and almost as light as cork, the soft-wooded *chebraccio bianco*, used by cartwrights and for any buildings under cover, with a leaf adapted for tanning leather; it is more lofty and richer in foliage than the *chebraccio colorado*, although there is a certain likeness in the stems of the two trees, but the last named is more like a cork-tree both in leaf and in bough, which are, however, drooping like those of the large olive-tree.

On the land formed by the earliest alluvial action of the river, the oldest and highest land therefore, and consequently very seldom submerged (the level of this, we have already said, is always higher than that of any other alluvial land), we find the algarrobo or carob-tree, of the various kinds already described; the giuggiolo or mistol, the brea (pitch), various species of arome, and others of less importance; all of them being in general ill-adapted for building on account of the slenderness and want of height of their trunks; the algarrobo, however, forming an honourable exception.

The algarrobo associates with the flora of the emerged regions, and visits them in their own domain, while it straightway invades the lands of more modern date than those in which it was cradled, and makes common cause with the beautiful pacara, and other botanical families, and with the chañar, that D'Orbigny takes as the basis of his geographical classification.

At a higher elevation than the algarrobo, but where the ground is sufficiently depressed to retain at least the rainfall, and growing on strips of land from north to south about ten leagues long and a few kilometers in width, we find the palm-tree of the Chaco. The leaves of this tree are fan-like, and grow in a tuft at the top of the smooth, polished stem that is marked with slightly depressed rings, showing where the leaves have fallen off every year. The trunk is ten to fifteen yards in height, and is used for roofing and for beams and telegraph posts; the fruit grows in clusters of nuts, but is not edible by man. Wherever this palm-tree grows, all other trees and shrubs disappear.

On the alluvial lands of still later formation, which comprise the *islands,* so called because they lie very low and are washed by the river on or near which they are situated, the flora is of a different character, and is composed of willows, alders, bobos, and other shrubs. All these are also found along the Paranà in the Pampa, and wherever there is running water. This *flora of the islands* is of an insignificant character, and found within narrow limits.

We also find in the Chaco, but nearer to the mountains, the earlier colonies of sebillos, mulberry-trees, tipas, laurels, and other trees, which, however they may be surrounded, or even intermingled with chebraccios and algarrobos, must not be considered as belonging to the flora of the Chaco, but to that of the mountain skirts, which follows different laws; the case is the same with the cedar, the walnut, and others besides.

The trees above mentioned are not the only ones composing the forest flora of the Chaco; they are, however, the most renowned, and almost the only ones known to commerce. Their dimensions (I am not speaking of those on the mountain-skirts) are far from being extraordinary. In the centre of the Chaco, where the climate is excessively dry, trees are weak and scarce; and even in more favourable localities the trunk is not very tall, a serious, though common, defect in these hard-timber trees.

These groups intersect the territory in all directions, and this is intelligible, since their existence depends on the action of the Rio during the long ages of its capricious course. There is, nevertheless, a kind of cantonment of some less widespread plants. Thus the urunday flourishes in a more humid zone along the banks of the Paraguay and the Paraná, and the lapaccio, after vanishing, suddenly appears again alone and pre-eminent among the flora of the mountain slopes. The palosanto, on the contrary, flourishes in the centre of the Chaco territory, where the climate is much more dry.

But the chebraccio, the foliage of which from afar off resembles that of our lesser olive and that of the green oak, clings to its emerged soil, and follows it through every change of climate, provided only there be sufficient warmth.

The algarrobo is still more eclectic, and, like a creature of spirit and resource, accepts every kind of soil, provided there be no question of mud, or mire, so as to injure growth; and it will live in any climate suitable to forest-trees, while always shrinking from damp and cold. But as if it were the soul of arboreal society, its companion trees do not appear where the algarrobo is absent, yet they will accompany it in its incursions towards the Pampa.

The presence of this tree in all the forests of the plain, its appearance as a visitor in other districts, the vast extent of its own kingdom, its wealth and liberality—for both the fruit and the wood are used on a very large scale—and finally its never completely abandoning its congeners of the forest, since the forest may be said to begin when we see the algarrobo—all these are reasons, in my opinion, for calling the region of forests of the plain by the name of the algarrobo zone.

Yet it may possess a rival in the chañar, especially as the claims of the latter have already been allowed, and have thus acquired some importance; and in truth the chañar of the Chaco holds its head high, so as to rival the algarrobo and the pacara, with whom it is sometimes found, in elegance and majesty, and no one could then take it for the same tree that in colder regions grows so poor and mean. But I cannot make up my mind to give it the preference, because it loves neither the company of the chebraccio, nor on the same soil, nor the higher plains where the algarrobo dwells. The chañar turns away from a very dry climate, which is the natural atmosphere of its vegetable companions; it is among the last new-comers, and stands alone in certain spots; while rickety, barren, and ill-formed, it runs through the Pampa in lines like the beads of a rosary.

Nor can its yellowish seeded berry induce me to change my opinion, although it has often been grateful to my palate when ripened in a torrid clime, and the syrup made from it has frequently cured me of cough; but how can it be put on a par with the berry of the algarrobo, which has enabled me and my horse to defy the desert with a loaf made from its flour in one saddle-bag, and a handful of its pods in the other?

Beyond the algarrobo region and south of it we find another plant called *caldén*, which appears to extend some hundreds of kilometers to the south, as far as, if not farther than the Rio Negro. It does not seem to grow on the actual plain, but on the territories adjacent to the first range of hills (Lomas) that precede the Cordilleras by some score of leagues.

This plant reigns alone, or almost alone; and resembles the algarrobo so closely in bark, leaf, and pod, that it has been mistaken by some persons for the latter. Yet to me the foliage appears straighter, and less ample. The trunk is usually short; the timber is valuable, on account of its veining, for cabinet-work, and is strong enough for buildings under cover; it is very fragile, and retains its native humidity for a long time. The woods composed of this tree are scanty, at least those that I saw.

I cannot give more precise and comparative particulars, because I only explored part of the region where it grows, which begins at a distance of some leagues south of Cordova, and seems bounded on the west by the Pampa. It must be a variety of the algarrobo, and similarly must grow on ground that is at least equal to the highest level next to that of the che-braccio, as we have noted when speaking of the forest region of the plain, of which it must form a zone apart by geological situation, and hence by climate, if not by soil.

From this, we may deduce that the forest flora affords a geological theory which may be stated as follows: Wherever the chebraccio predominates, there the land is either original, or of emersion; where the algarrobo prevails (when hot

mixed with the chebraccio), the land is a remnant from a
far distant epoch ; where the pacara, and still more, where the
chañar predominates, the land is a remnant of a more recent
time, and in some spots may date as it were from yesterday,
according to the complexion of the individual trees relatively
to the atmosphere.   Seeing the uniformity of the geological and
forest phenomena, this criterion may be applied generally from
the Chaco to the rest of the wooded regions of the Republic ;
and by the connection between the lands and the aquiferous
soils, we may utilize such a criterion thus : Where the flora is
of hard timber (chebraccio, &c.), the lower soils are more compact, more clayey, more nitrous ; hence less permeable, and yielding brackish and salt water.   And where the flora is soft-wooded,
still more where it is flaccid, the lower soils are more sandy, less
saline, permeable, in communication with the river-currents,
affording, therefore, good water at a depth corresponding with
that of the rivers.

The inhabitants of the country, without arguing so much on
the subject, act on a knowledge of these facts when they
excavate their wells, as I had occasion to learn when I was
constructing railroads.

I concede that my deductions may not appear strictly accurate
to those who have only travelled by land and through the less
typical regions of the Chaco, but nevertheless, and without
troubling myself about accidents of detail that may eventually
make them appear erroneous, I put them forward with confidence.

We have seen how the forest flora can give us agrarian
criteria, which I formulate as follows : In the algarroba
region, which comprises the whole forest range of the central
and northern parts of the Republic, agriculture is a ruinous, not
to say impossible, pursuit without the help of artificial irrigation, while with it splendid results are attainable.   The banks
of the Paraná and the Paraguay, and their immediate neighbourhood, are an exception, however, as are also some spots
adjoining the mountains, where the earth will bring forth her
fruits without irrigation.

The fate of agriculture and of pasturage must depend on the
immigration of men and of capital, or colonization.   With
regard to the Chaco, the conditions of productiveness and of
economy may be summed up as follows :—

The littoral of the River Paraguay within the torrid zone is
favourable to the highest industrial agriculture when applied to

R

sugar-cane, tobacco, and coffee, and backed up by the large capital necessary for raising water for irrigation, for defence against the Indians, who, for good pay, will help in the work, being able to resist the extremes of their native climate, and for the cost of the plant and machinery. The remainder of the land, as well as the portion just mentioned, is adapted for pasturage and for colonization by families. The water-highway, the proximity to centres of production and consumption already in existence, the forests to subdue and utilize, the land given gratuitously, or nearly so, are all very advantageous conditions for the culture of these districts. The centre of the Chaco, on the contrary, where the hot climate is noxious to colonists, and where the Indians attack them and carry off their cattle, is favourable to pasturage only in some scattered spots, and to the formation of roads only along the banks of the rivers ; but the dry and hot climate, and the presence of the Indians, will always prove sources of annoyance to colonists. The cost of raising water from the deeply-imbedded rivers would not be recouped by the produce or crops. Within the frontier-line, which lies at a distance of 500 kilometers from the Paraguay and the Paranà, the danger from Indians no longer exists, but the best lands are already allotted.

The districts adjacent to the mountains and near the rivers that run from them, are adapted for the highest culture of the same crops I have already mentioned when speaking of the littoral, but not without large capital, which is, moreover, required for the purchase of the land. The Indians will supply, as they do now, the necessary labour, but the enormous distances for transport offer difficulties that can be lessened only by the navigation of the Vermejo, if ever this becomes an accomplished fact. On the above-named spots and in the rest of the aforesaid districts, colonization and pasturage prudently carried out has succeeded and will succeed, although with the economic disadvantages of long distances for transport of goods, and the high price of the land, and with the physical drawback of dangerous fevers and ague.

At the present time the littoral of the Paraguay and the Paranà, with the numerous intersecting streamlets (*riachos*), is best adapted, both physically and economically, for the outlay of large capital, and for the labour of colonist families, who, however, must be emigrants from countries that are neither cold nor mountainous.

CHAPTER XVII.

FOREST FLORA OF THE MOUNTAIN—ITS DISTRIBUTION—CONTRAST
BETWEEN THIS AND THE PRECEDING FLORA—CONCLUSIONS
AS TO ALTIMETRY, CLIMATE, AND SOIL.

THE afforesting of the mountains that bound the Gran Chaco
on the west is subject to these three fundamental conditions :—
1. Exposure to the south and south-east winds.
2. A humid atmosphere.
3. A warm atmosphere.
These three act reciprocally on each other. The south and
south-east winds bring on the rains by cooling the atmosphere.
Humidity is necessary in order to supply the rain, and heat,
besides being required to provide the necessary thermal conditions for any given species of plants, is necessary also to
hold in suspense a larger amount of vapour, and to allow of its
precipitation into rain by sudden cooling, which, on contact
with the said winds, will be the greater in proportion to the
elevation of the temperature.

There is a fourth condition, viz. height above the level of
the sea. But this influences the species of the plants solely,
because the three conditions first mentioned are always essential
to the existence of forest on the mountains.

It follows, therefore, that in the parts farthest from the torrid
zone the mountains will be less wooded, and plants of the same
species will be either different or less numerous, or altogether
absent ; and that in the lower and backward ranges the same
phenomena will be observed. In the first case the temperature
is not sufficiently high, in the second the winds I have named
do not reach the more distant mountains, but are stopped, as it
were, by a wall formed by the first mountain range.

It also follows that those spots where the mountains form
a semicircle under the conditions I have named, will enjoy,
on a larger scale, the results I have indicated, because heat

R 2

and humidity will be more concentrated, and the winds will be moistened and arrested in their course.

What I have said concerning the mountains on the western edge of the Chaco is true likewise of those other mountains that bound on the south the *forest region*, situate in the north and centre of the Republic. It must be remembered that we are in the southern hemisphere, and that consequently the south being nearer the Antarctic Pole is the colder, and the north, which is nearer the Equator, the warmer region. I take this opportunity of remarking that it would prevent confusion if, at a suitable time, geographers were to adopt a nomenclature better adapted to the analogy between the climatic conditions of the two hemispheres.

The influence of the above active causes extends not only over the mountain-slopes, but also over the adjacent table-land, and this in proportion to the energy with which those three causes are put into operation.

The spots in which Oran and Tucuman are situated are therefore highly favoured on account of the semicircle formed by the mountains, Oran in particular being nearer the tropics.

The southern portion of the Tucuman range, on the other hand, and the whole of the Cordova range are unfavourably situated for the opposite reasons, and thus are almost completely bare of forest growth.

The Oran or Zenta range, that of Tucuman or Acconchica, and that of Cordova (I use the popular names for the sake of clearness and conciseness), situated respectively farther and farther from the torrid zone, consist, each of them, of various parallel chains of mountains, divided by deep and narrow valleys called *cañons* on account of their shape.

Now, the difference between one range and another by reason of its position with reference to the three causes I have named is palpable, remarkable, and most surprising. Thus the declivities directly exposed to the winds—that is, the eastern slopes—are much more wooded than those on the opposite, or western side; and the foremost range is more wooded than the second, until passing from one range to another we exchange a humid zone of magnificent forest for another of excessive aridity and bareness.

The Pucará region, of which I shall treat presently, furnishes us with a remarkable instance of this, within an extent of a few kilometers from east to west.

We may thus account apparently for the barren desolation of the mountain-ranges standing behind those I have mentioned, and farthest to the east, and of the Cordillera itself with its peaks of 7000 yards in height, although situated many hundred kilometers west of the above. In any other way their denudation would be inexplicable, since such mountains belong geographically to the forest zone as we have defined it.

Meanwhile the phenomenon of a *flora of the plain* existing and being developed in a dry climate, and another similar one *of the mountains* needing humidity for its formation and development is no less extraordinary. Both require the same conditions of heat. The most salient difference in the aspect of the two is that the flora of the plain is smaller in the trunk, and especially less lofty, and that in general the leaves are deeply notched and very small; while the mountain flora is of large and lofty trunk, and with larger leaves, thus bearing a resemblance to the European flora. It is singular that, generally speaking, the timber of the flora of the plain resists the action of water better—being, in some cases, absolutely incorruptible—than that of the flora growing in a damp climate. Is this a caprice, a compensation, or a law of nature?

Having set forth in the preceding chapter the principal conditions on which the presence and development of the arboreal flora depend, and having roughly defined the superficial extent of the forest region, let me say a few words on its vertical distribution.

I will proceed as before on the data of personal observation made while exploring the mountains and plains of the forest region, and I will permit myself some few repetitions for the sake of clearness.

As with us the zone of the oak, that of the chestnut, and that of the beech, are vertically distinguished,—a nomenclature which has served since in agronomia, and in practical agriculture, to divide the mountainous regions into so many agrarian zones, to which corresponds a climate and soil of certain known properties; so an analogous distinction may be made in these parts with the same results, although the state of cultivation in the country renders it of less practical importance than among ourselves. Still, it will help us to place our ideas in order.

The forest region of the Argentines—I speak of that portion of it with which we are occupied; that is, the north and centre—must be divided, in the altimetrical sense, into three zones, which, being named according to the plants distinguished by their greater respective expansion united to their importance, ought to take the name of the algarrobo or carob-tree zone, the sebil zone, and the aliso zone.

In the regions where the pine is found, a fourth, the pine zone, must be added. It lies between the sebil and aliso zones.

The algarrobo zone includes, as we have seen, the whole plain; it begins at a height of 50 to 100 yards, above the level of the sea, and ends at a height of 300 or 400, according to the latitude. Most of the hard timber is found in this zone, viz. the red chebraccio, the urunday, nandubay, palo-santo, palo-ferro, guajacan, iscajanta, and others whose specific weight, generally speaking, exceeds that of water.

The presence of the algarrobo mostly indicates a dry climate; its forest companions nevertheless, or those trees that must be included in this vast zone, admit of differences which may give room to sub-zones, like that of the somewhat humid urunday, or of the palo-santo and the excessively dry *patai* algarrobo.

With regard to agriculture it is unfortunate, but as we have seen, not the less certain, that throughout the great algarrobo zone, unless irrigation be employed, the climate forbids any great prosperity, owing to the absence of rain and of atmospheric moisture, except in the sub-zone of the urunday and likewise in that of the nandubay, or in localities very specially situated. But wherever irrigation is practised, splendid results are obtained ; and the sub-zone of the patai algarrobo is singularly favourable to the culture of the vine and the olive, when duly irrigated. In that of the palo-santo, and the conterminous zones, on the other hand, the chaguar *testile*, of which we have spoken elsewhere, and the *aji* or pepper-tree grow spontaneously.

Wherever there are rivers in the algarrobo zone, we find what may be termed an island zone, going up the valleys among the high mountains, whose flora consists principally of various kinds of willows, of seibos and bobos. Only certain kinds of willows that are almost like forest trees, and form beautiful groves along the banks of the river, are available, and that to a limited extent, for building purposes.

Next above the algarrobo zone comes that of the sebil, which, in its lower part, shelters some of the inferior flora, while supporting among them numerous colonies of its own. This, zone comprises the lands adjacent to the mountains where the climate is sufficiently moist, and the slopes to the remarkable height of 1000 or 1500 yards above the level of the sea, according to the latitude, diminishing towards the south on account of the excessive dryness of the climate.

This is the region of the timber most valuable for its size, its adaptation to various uses, and the large number of trees. The sebil, of which there are three kinds, is at the present time the basis of one of the most important industries in the interior of the Republic, viz. the tanning of skins. Growing with or near the sebil, we find the two cedars, the white and the pink; the lapaccio, that we have remarked likewise in the sub-zone of the urunday, the walnut, the laurel, the tatané, the pacara, the mulberry, the tipa, the male oak, the orco-moglie, the fragrant china-china, the palo-lancia, the palo-blanco, and many others, including the biscote, whose wood resembles ebony. It is very scarce, requiring both dryness and heat, so that but for its altimetrical situation it should rather be classed with the flora of the algarrobo zone.

It is in the sebil region that we find the colossal trees, of numerous kinds, and in immense quantities, that have made tropical forests so famous. Tucuman and Oran bear away the palm of wealth in this flora.

In the lower part of this zone, that is to say on the plain or table-land adjoining the mountain skirts, and particularly in the provinces of Tucuman, Salta, and Jujuy, agrarian industry has been developed to a certain extent in the cultivation of sugar-cane, rice, and tobacco. In the section nearest the tropics we find the requisite conditions for a great development of agrarian industry, in the numerous and abundant streams which, flowing from the neighbouring heights, make irrigation easy, and likewise afford a gratuitous motive power; making amply remunerative the large capital employed, where transport does not imply vast expense.

Agriculture scarcely exists in the upper part of the zone I am describing, on account of the excessive labour required for the cultivation of the declivities of the hills, and of the quantity of excellent land in more advantageous situations.

The cultivation of the vine and the olive will not be successful in general in all the sebil zone, because of the rains and humidity, which are excessive for these plants, and prevail at unsuitable seasons, that is, at the setting of the blossom, and at the maturity of the fruit. Pasture, on the contrary, would be very suitable, notwithstanding the large portion of the land occupied by trees, for the grass grows beneath their foliage owing to climatic influences, including that of light, which is admitted by the incline of the mountain sides.

CHAPTER XVIII.

FOREST FLORA OF THE MOUNTAIN—THE ALISO ZONE NOMENCLA-
TURE—FUTURE DESTINY OF CERTAIN FLOWERS.

As we come forth from the splendid vegetation I have briefly
described, we meet after a short interval with the first representatives of the forest zone of the aliso, which after a while,
are succeeded by extensive and dense woods, consisting almost
exclusively of that tree. The spectacle they present is entirely
different from the last, and resembles that of European forests
of a single species of tree.

The aliso is found at the height of 2000 or 2500 yards
above the level of the sea, according to the latitude; and
consequently crowns many of the lower ranges of hills, and
clothes the sides of the higher mountains. It has a tendency,
in my opinion, to push its way farther into the lowlands, and on
comparing it with the preceding flora, it would seem that the
latter begins to extend itself from below, while the aliso works
downwards from the heights, and the two are thus endeavouring to come into contact.

The aliso (a variety of the alnus) is our alder, and is of two
kinds, which are much alike in appearance and in properties.
It is lofty and upright with a diameter from twenty to forty
centimeters; it is very abundant and scattered, holding the
same place in the flora of these parts that is held by the beech
in the European flora; and the timber also is similar. It is
little known, nevertheless, if not absolutely unknown, and for
this reason I will say a few words on the subject.

The timber is adapted for building under cover and will
resist water. In the church of Santa Maria of Catamarca, a
master-beam of the roof, more than seventy years old, was
found the best for replacing; 1800 years ago, Pliny declared this timber to be indestructible, and builders inform

us that the lacustrine cities of Venice and Holland have the greater part of their houses supported on stakes of aliso, otherwise alder, driven in below the water.

The height, therefore, of the aliso and its lightness, make it admirable for building, because, generally speaking, timber that will resist water in this country is very deficient in length. The difficulty of access to the regions of its growth would not constitute any serious obstacle if the system of transport by water, as practised in the Alps and in North America, were adopted. Such a system would be quite practicable here by reason of the numerous streams running through every mountain pass, and by this means, the other forests that form the wealth of this mountainous district could be utilized.

The aliso is only met with on the summits of mountains, or on the declivities exposed to the south and south-east winds. At an equal height, but on summits and declivities sheltered from those winds, we find pasture-land, provided there is moisture sufficient.

Grasses grow freely under aliso-trees, because in general there are no climbing plants, nor even shrubs about their roots, the temperature not being sufficiently high.

This region or zone of the aliso is favourable, therefore, to pasture-land, and together with the region of natural meadows lying above it, offers immense advantages for *estancias*, for summering cattle.

Between the sebil and the aliso zones, we occasionally find interpolated the pine zone, which seems to fill the void we have noticed where the pine is absent. This tree appears to like very tropical latitudes, at any rate they seem to be the centre of its diffusion, since it is not met with until the north-west of Oran and on the hills of the Upper Paranà. I am told it grows also at Tafi, north of Tucuman.

A curious and very unexpected mountain vegetation is that of the reed-cane, or *caña brava* as it is called here. We suddenly come across it in the aliso zone, on the more marshy spots, which are nearly always dark and miry, in bushes consisting of hundreds of high reeds, that entangled with each other and with those of the neighbouring bushes, form an archway under which a man may pass on horseback. They frequently make quite a labyrinth of galleries through which one may wander over immense mountain tracts.

A similar reed cane, called *caña tacuára*, growing along the rivers, in the lower plains of tropical Chaco, attains such dimensions that it is used for props in roofing.

On the heights of the aliso zone, we also wonder to find the arborescent *salvia* and the *sambuco*, called *sauco*, the leaves of which are said to have medicinal properties.

The zone of the mountain flora above mentioned may be subdivided into sub-zones. But besides the absence of sufficient data from which to generalize, I have already said enough to indicate the characteristic features of the forest zone, especially with regard to climate and consequently to agriculture and pasture, which was one of our principal objects.

Many of the plants I have named serve for dyeing and tanning purposes, and some, besides those I have noted here and there, are fruit-bearing; among which we may remark the *mato*, bearing a cherry that is good to eat raw, and which makes also a fermented drink, and the *arrayan*, a shrub bearing a kind of currant which can be used in the same way as the *mato*. Besides these there are several *enredaderas*, including the *tasi*, with a hairy, milky fruit like an egg, and another plant bearing a kind of bean, and which has supplied the Mattaccos with a name for our beans. The leaves of many plants, especially of the large family of *moglias*, yield a fragrant scent when rubbed; the same with the flowers of the numerous varieties of acacia and mimosa, particularly the *tusca* and the *ciurchi*, which are the same as our cassia (*gaggio*).

Scientific Nomenclature of the said Plants.

Asi (pimento)	Capsicum microcarpum.
Algarrobo	Prosopis algarrobo.
,, blanco	,, alba.
Aliso	Alnus ferruginea (var. Alisus).
Algarrobillo	Acacia moniliformis.
Arroyán	Eugenia uniflora.
Brea	Caesalpinia praecox.
Cedro	Cedrela Brasilensis (var. Australis).
Ciaguar	Gurliaea decorticans (delle papiglionacee).
Ciaguar (textile)	Una Bromeliacea.
Ciugoio	Nierembergia hippomanica.
Ciurchi	Prosopis adstringens.
Chebraccio blanco	Aspidosperma Chebraccio.
,, colorado (red)	Loxopterygium Lorentzii.
,, flojo (shrub)	Iodina rhombifolia.
Cortadera	Gynerium Argentinum.

Garabato . . .	.	*Acacia tucumanensis.*
,, shrub .	.	,, *subscandens.*
Giuccián (*Yuchán*) .	.	*Chorisia insignis.*
Guayacán . .	.	*Caesalpina melano carpa.*
Jume (delle salicornia) .	.	*Spirotachys vaginata.*
Lanza . .	.	*Myrsine marginata.*
Lapaccio . .	.	*Tecoma (gen. belonging to the Bigo·gniacee).*
Laurol . . .	.	*Nectandra porphyria.*
Mato . . .	,	*Eugenia mato (belonging to the Mirtacee).*
Mistól . . .	.	*Zizyphus mistol.*
Moglie or Mojé .	.	*Belon ging to the Terebentinacee.*
Mora . . .	.	*Gelso Americano.*
Niandubay (Nandubay) .	.	*Acacia cavena.*
Nio-Nio (venomous herb)	.	*Baccharis cordifolia.*
Nogal . . .	.	*Yuglans nigra (var. Boliviana).*
Ombú . . .	.	*Pirconia dioica.*
Pacará . . .	.	*Euterolobium timbavva.*
Palm of the Gran Chaco	.	*Copernica Cerifera ?*
Palo blanco . .	.	*Belonging to the Rubiacee.*
Palo-santo . .	.	*A Zygophyllea.*
Pino . . .	.	*Podocarpus angustifolia.*
Roble (male oak) .	.	*Belonging to the Leguminose.*
Salcio (willow) .	.	*Salix Humboldtiana.*
Sambuco (*sauco*) .	.	*Sambuccus Australis, S. Peruviana.*
Salvia . .	.	*Salvia matico.*
Sebil . . .	.	*Acacia Cebil.*
Seibo	.	*An Erythrina (Christa-galli).*
Soconto (coloured, climbing) .		*Galium hirsutum.*
Tala . . .	.	*Celtis Tala.*
Tasi (climbing) .	.	*Morrena Brachystephana (Asclep.).*
Tatané (Espinillo of the North)		*Belonging to the Leguminose.*
Tipa . . .	.	*Machaerium fertile.*
Tuna . . .	.	*Cactus.*
Tusca . . .	.	*Mimose fam. (Acacia aroma ?).*
Vinal . . .	.	*Prosopis ruscifolia (Mimose family).*

The question may be asked whether the flora of these regions is in a state of progression or on the contrary, either stationary or retrograding. There are indications in some species, of one of these three conditions. For example, in the sand of the arid Bacino di Belen, after long journeying across bare and saline land, we come suddenly upon a magnificent forest of *patai* algarrobos, of ancient growth and large bulk, not a young tree among them. I have no hesitation in saying that this flora will not be renewed and must disappear.

In the forests of Tucuman, within the sebil zone, it is extremely rare to find a young cedar, although there are plenty of ancient cedars of stupendous size. I do not think we can refer the destruction of the young trees to cattle, which do not exist in sufficient number. The same may be said of the chebraccio in the centre of the *chebracciali*. This, however, may be explained by the famous "struggle for existence;" air and light, if not soil, are wanting to the young shoots in the thick of the forest. But even on the skirts, young trees are very scarce in the chebraccio and cedar forests, and among the other trees in the sebil zone, and do not seem to exist in sufficient proportion to replace the former growth when it shall have perished, although in general the growth is excessively slow, and hence the decay of the individual tree very remote. But these remarks show us that where the axe anticipates the destruction of Nature, while it cannot hasten its productive power, it would be well to regulate the felling of timber, and to fill up the vacuums thus created, so as not to exhaust the forest long before the period popularly assigned to its duration.

We have already seen that the chebraccio of the Chaco has a tendency to become scarcer as the lands of emersion disappear. The danger, however, is remote, on account of the vast extent of the territory, and it is probable that the conditions of climate and of vegetation suited to its reproduction will previously alter. But on the hills (Lomas) of the provinces of Santiago and Catamarca, even this danger does not exist, and there yet remains territory for this tree to invade.

In the sebil zone the forest has already spread over almost all the available territory, only leaving part of the strip dividing it from the aliso. The latter, on the contrary, has still a vast territory before it, which it is hastening to conquer by visible forward extension every year. The aliso is in the period of expansion.

I have not remarked in the sebil and algarrobo zones any tree with a tendency to predominate over the others. It is not impossible, however, that some that may be imported into the still virgin forests may produce that result. I have spoken of territory to be conquered; but then do not the forests spread all at once over the ground they occupy or will occupy? My answer is this: afforestment seems to have proceeded by irradiation, as it were, from various nuclei of isolated woods, ever increasing in size, until uniting together they have constituted immense forests.

Certain isolated forest centres are still frequently met with, both in the Chaco and in Santiago, the expansion of which, by irradiation, seems established not only by ratiocination, but by the facts as narrated to me by some timber contractors, that in the heart of these so-called *islands* the trees are of older growth and a large average of them split under the saw, or are defective in other ways, and that, on the contrary, the outside trees are smaller and younger, and exempt in larger proportion from the defects I have mentioned. These circumstances appear to justify me in an assumption that is based on reason, and is moreover confirmed by the habits of the aliso.

CHAPTER XIX.

THE PUCARÁ COUNTRY.

At a height of 2500 yards above the sea, on the range of mountains that divides from north to south the two provinces of Tucuman and Catamarca, and at a point where they join other ranges that turn east, west, and north, we come suddenly upon a large basin, twenty kilometers by thirty, surrounded by a circle of mountains of various heights, among which the Aconguija rise majestically, nearly always crowned with snow for a distance of 5000 yards downward from the summit.

This basin contrasts greatly with the surrounding landscape, and is itself in strong contrast with its condition in the past.

It still retains the name by which it was known to the aborigines, who inhabited it in large numbers, and is called the country or campo of the *Pucará*. The word means *strength* in the Aimará language, and *red* in the Chiqchuan, both of which appellations are appropriate, the one on account of the general colouring, and the other on account of formerly existing fortifications, of which some fragments yet remain.

The explorer who, crossing the mountain range at this point, delays his steps for a while, may find here an opportunity of acquiring special information.

On his right hand there is a narrow range of hills 2000 yards in height, the eastern slopes of which, facing the south-east winds, are clothed with magnificent forests that spread out at the base and form splendid wooded skirts to the fertile plain of Tucuman lying at his feet. The western and steeper declivity is thick with beautiful woods, which, however, betray their recent origin by being chiefly grouped where a line of counterforts has sheltered them when still young from the prolonged heat of the sun, and the spray of a precipitous torrent has charged the atmosphere with moisture. Then comes a second range, higher by 1000 yards than the first, with wider crest, with the lower part of its eastern slopes comparatively denuded of forest, and the higher parts clothed with woods of aliso-trees, while the summit is crowned with meadows.   The western declivity of this range, entirely bare of arboreous plants and with very scant pasture, encloses on one side the campo that lies beneath at a depth of 500 yards.

On the west of the Pucara the horizon is bounded by low-lying barren hills; beyond a bare and rocky precipice 800 yards high, lies the vast Bacino di Belen, enclosed on all sides by high mountains and by the Cordillera, whose snow-clad Famatina can be discerned from an immense distance. This mountain is rich in mines; the table-land is extremely arid and for the most part sandy, but with some oases of ancient algarrobos (carobs), which, however, are not reproductive. In the concave centre of the mountain there is an immense tract of whitish hue, thirty leagues by three, consisting of salt-mines. During the brief season of light rain these become an immense marsh or bog.

The *Campo del Pucara* is the turning-point between the grassy ranges on the east and the bare sand-banks of the west. It is itself arid and burning, but affords sustenance to cattle during some months of the year.

Its elevation, however, and the encircling hills, among which the Alpine Aconquija on the north is like a star surmounting a diadem, would seem to promise at first sight a climate more favourable to the vegetable life that only a few steps further is so luxuriantly developed on the eastern slopes.   There is, in fact, less than the distance of a league between the ridge of the Tucuman mountains and the eastern extremity of the campo, and only five leagues from the same point to the sandy basin of the Belen.

Here the action of the winds is evident; as is the inference from the position of the mountains with regard to them, and here again we have the same teaching, repeated in less concise language, but much more rigorously by the other immense circuits of the Republic.

The parallelism, or in other words the uniformity of direction in the mountainous system of the Republic, joined to the uniform direction of the atmospheric currents, and to the seasons in which they prevail, in that region at least which is comprised within a limit a little beyond the Rosario and the northern extremity of the Republic, afford us an anticipated knowledge of the climates of the country, and assist us wonder-fully in verifying the theory of atmospheric circulation excogi-tated and demonstrated by the most learned modern climato-logists.

Meanwhile a magnificent spectacle is presented to us during the summer season in the Pucara Campo. A hot, still, and unpleasant air, accompanied by a diminution of twenty to twenty-five millimeters of atmospheric pressure, is succeeded first by a light breeze that veers rapidly from north-east to south-east, and then by a furious wind, raising great clouds of dust from a soil burnt up by eight months' drought, darkening the clear sky, and tormenting any one exposed to violent contact with the grains of sand that are driven before it. Our tent is loosened by the repeated shocks of the aerial current, and soon affords an insufficient refuge, as does also the humble *rancho* which owes its own safety to the numberless fissures that allow of a passage to the gale through which it strikes the powerless inhabitant. On the outside of the crest of the circle of mountains there now appears a subtle vapour which almost immediately vanishes into space and is succeeded by light white clouds that also evaporate, followed by others rather denser; these seem to shrink from resting on the ridge of the mountains and disappear almost as quickly as they come. I do not know whether they turn back or vanish away.

The south wind now blows furiously, and the air becomes colder, and behind the white cloudlets are big clouds, dark at first and black, that rise up and intermingle, advance and recede, seeming to roll up the steep incline like another Sisyphus, and when they have reached the top to be thrust down again to the depths whence they first rose.

To the shrieking and raging of the wind is now added the noise of the thunder and the flashing of the lightning, the battle waxes fiercer, the combatants can now scarcely be dis-tinguished; the dense phalanxes on the heights are hardly to be discerned as they clash together, intermingle, and form at last a compact dark mass that advances slowly and heavily over the face of the *campo*. This mass is constantly diminish-ing; it is whitish and vaporous towards the west and is con-stantly renewed by black clouds from the east; now it halts, anon draws back, obeying I know not what occult, mysterious force, until at last the storm has conquered every mountain summit. Then a leaden pall covers all the heights like an

s

enormous bell, and after remaining for a long interval will often vanish harmlessly away. Sometimes through a rent in the edge the sun can be seen shining in imperturbable splendour on the Belen basin lying beneath.

The dryness causes the evaporation of the clouds, which, when the atmosphere is saturated on the side of the eastern Tucuman declivities, are driven by the wind into fresh space above the ridges of the mountains. Hence the rainfall in the Campo of Pucara is very slight, and still less in the Bacino di Belen.

Nevertheless, there are large remains of Indian habitations, which are built in clusters, looking like so many separate villages. They are situated not only on the plain, but on the mountain-skirts as well.

If the campo were formerly under the same conditions of natural productiveness as are now existent, it could not have afforded subsistence to so many human beings. Can a change of climate have occurred? If this has been the case it has not been due to any change in the accidents of the mountains; there is no indication of such having taken place, or any tradition on the subject. It is more probable that the local conditions have changed by the drying up of some large reservoir of water in the neighbourhood, some lake, in short, of which the fish afforded food, and the water was used for agriculture, while it supplied the first necessity of material life. And, in fact, north of the campo, in the lands of recent formation, there is a passage for the watercourses of this basin, and its name of *Cortadera* expresses both its aspect and the phenomenon indicated by it, just as among ourselves we call the openings of former lakes *incisa* (a cut), *rotta* (a break), or *ripafratta* (broken shore). Tradition or popular acuteness having bestowed these appellations, or else we may infer that either during the conquest of the indigenous tribes of Catamarca by the Chiqchuans, or that of the Americans by the Spaniards, the primitive inhabitants of the land sought refuge there as in a stronghold, and protracted their defence, although amid serious privation.

However this may have been, a country which once swarmed with human life is now almost a desert, useful, perhaps, to the antiquary and to the dilettante traveller or scientist.

CHAPTER XX.

TUCUMAN.

I ,CANNOT refrain from recording here the impressions produced by my visit to Tucuman, the garden of the Republic, after a long period of absence. I had been received there with the most flattering kindness during my first visit of eight months, in which I explored its wildest and most picturesque parts, spending the winter on the ·peaks, I may say, of its lofty mountains. In the course of this book I have mentioned it frequently as one of the privileged cantons of the Republic, so that to return to it now will not be entirely out of place, or unintelligible to the reader. I will add that I claim to be accurate in all essentials, notwithstanding the poetical form in which my description is cast in order to do honour to the subject, and to make it more attractive to the numerous readers of the *Operaio Italiano*, in which it first saw the light.

O Tucuman! thou the most beautiful among thy sisters, all hail to thee! Whether I contemplate the level plain or lift up my eyes to the lofty mountains encircling thee on the side of the Circolo Massimo or the Occaso, my soul is thrilled with delight and admiration. Nature, who has been somewhat niggardly to thy companions, has lavished her gifts on thee, her favoured one, because thou wert beautiful and beloved! To thee she has given the vast plain of the Pampa, and bounded it with a semicircle of hills so as to welcome the *Alisian winds*, that in return for thy hospitality, enrich thee with the life-giving elements gathered in their wanderings over numberless Alpine heights, and fraternize with thy river, called by thee the *Fondo*, but changing its name over and over again, according to the caprice of the friendly lands whose bosoms it fertilizes. And if the sun shines on thee with burning rays, his heat is tempered by the moisture dropping from the clouds as they are rent by electricity, with sudden explosion, or prolonged thunder.

Hence thy soil is verdant in the winter, and in spring is
adorned with innumerable flowers—a treasure-house of exotics
—giving place one to the other for thy embellishment during
half the year ; and in the summer and autumn thou gatherest
abundantly the fruits of a few growths. Nature has not
bestowed on thee the algarrobo, nor is the *mistol*, its comrade,
abundant with thee, nor yet the *chañar*, that emulating the
tamarind, buds forth in primitive Santiago, on thy southern
borders. But instead of these she has given thee the *tuna*, the
prickly pear-tree, the *arrayan*, and the *mato*, growing on thy
sierras ; and grants thee, with little trouble, the orange, the
yam, rice, potatoes, wheat, corn, barley, and other cereals, in
such wise as to make her storehouse within thy borders. Thy
climate refuses to give any industrial advantage to the culture
of that fruit which is first mentioned in connection with sin,
that, according to Biblical teaching, was fatal to its unconscious
inheritors, the pre-destined inhabitants of unfruitful Africa.
But thou, yielding the glory thereof to thy western neighbour,
sober, laborious, and honest Catamarca, art compensated by the
cana, that while bestowing on thee the principle of the vine,
enriches thee with sugar, and is guiltless of the shame of Noah
or the punishment of Cham. Thou dost not fear the envy of
proud Salta, lying close against thee on the side of the seven-
starred Ursa Major, nor the unrecognized claims of distant
and neglected Jujuy. Meanwhile thy pre-eminence is assured
by thy many fine *establecimientos*, by thy highways crowded
with waggons, the clamour of the husbandmen, the creaking of
the presses, the bubbling of the boiling caldrons, the hubbub
of all kinds, the ovens, the buildings, the heat, the smoke, the
feast of peeled cane with its fresh juice and syrup, which, at
harvest time, constitutes a *fête champêtre* worthy of Arcadia.

And how shall I fitly praise the soothing herb that in mani-
fold guise bestows such bliss on man—tobacco, which is to thee
a boundless source of wealth ? Until now it has crossed the
Cordilleras in large quantities, and its progress has only been
stopped by the seashore, where it is unable to compete with the
produce of other lands. But when its culture ceases to be a
monopoly in the hands of the representatives of the first
inhabitants, and science and art take it under their protection,
it will become thy special honour and glory.

The iron-fibred chebraccio, which is wealth to thy sisters,
finds no hold on thy plains, nor are they shaded by frequent

woods, but thy mountain is clothed with primeval forests stretching to its very base, and rich in magnificent cedars and graceful walnut-trees with their ashen bark, *orcomollos,* the two kinds of cebils, whose bark is used for tanning, the . pacara with its saponaceous properties, the lapaccio with its rose-coloured blossoms, the two kinds of alders (alisos), which, with many others, crown its alpine heights, and daily push forward towards the barren coast. All these trees afford building materials or food to thy *aserraderos,* while at different altitudes grow among them the early-flowering cassia (*churqui*), its sister-plant, the tusca (black vine), the garravato, and two kinds of wild orange, mingling the perfume of their innumerable blossoms with the arrayan, the mato, and the molli, whose leaves give forth fragrance when bruised, or are of medicinal value.

The borracho, with its barrel-shaped trunk and lemon-like fruit, which, when ripe, is full of cotton, flourishes as far as thy southern limits, but refuses to grow in a more humid climate.

The *salvia* likewise enlivens the forest, and in the form of a tall shrub is found on the topmost altitudes, and is rivalled in its braving of the elements by the alder, the elder, and the peach-tree. And there, where tree and shrub can no longer live in the cold and rarified atmosphere, strong herbaceous plants, food for cattle, take their place. But why endeavour to describe thy flora since the life of a man would not suffice to enumerate and distinguish their kinds. Pride thyself on thy virgin and impenetrable forests, and on the graceful convolution of thy climbing lianas twining and intertwining undisturbed, and numerous lesser flowering shrubs, the home of numberless wild bees' nests, some hanging from branches, some underground, some hidden within the trunks of decayed trees, of round, oblong, or cup-like shape, and stored with as many different kinds of honey as there are varieties of bees, and with flavours as various as the flowers from which they were culled, each kind filling a separate and special cell.

Nor may I dilate on thy teeming insect life, nor on thy numerous reptiles, among which is the tricoloured viper—black, red, and white—its terrible power forgotten in the beauty of its bright-coloured rings or continuous spirals.

Rather would I speak, if competent, of thy feathered inhabitants whose trills make musical the mornings of thy spring,

although I am heretical enough not to care for the beauty and
brightness of their colouring. Nevertheless, I cannot be silent
on the tiny emerald-coloured humming-bird, whose swift flight
leaves one in doubt whether it be bird or insect, nor on the
green *catas* and *lorys*, and the cardinal-bird, and the variegated
carpenter-bird. I admire the mason-bird, with his little
mud-built house, contrasting favourably with those of the men
around him ; and the pelican and the ibis—the one with its
motionless aspect, the other with its slow movements remind me
of pensive philosophers ; and the white or black piscivorous
birds, all beak, neck, legs, and wings, varieties of wild ducks
and geese, and a few others. The pigeons, with their pretty
ways of wooing, the *ciaratta*, and the mountain peacock, the
first inhabiting the wooded plain, and the last the forest on
the hill, appear, the wild brethren of the dove, of the domestic
fowl and the turkey—the boast of housewives in both hemispheres—to whom I must not fail to recommend the gray *chuña*
that disports itself in large companies, turning round and round
with ceaseless clamour, and the *suri* (ostrich) with its enormous
eggs, both these birds ensuring cleanliness from vermin and
safety from reptiles in the houses where they are kept.

I must not omit the yellow and gray *carancho*, and the black
crow (*avvoltoio*), feeding on putrid flesh and indicating the
proximity of its prey whose end it sometimes hastens by tor-
turing it while yet half alive, an unconscious instrument of
hygiene on plain and hill.

And shall I forget the inhabitant of the heights, the great
gray or black condor with its white back, the terror of heifers
and of inexperienced cows, whose first calf they tear to pieces in
the sight of its mother, regardless of its cries for help ?

I will not stay to describe thy amphibious animals, or I might
dwell on the great slow-moving iguana-lizard, liked as food by
the aborigines, or on the croaking multitudes that people thy
marshes, and with strange, hoarse sounds offend the ear and
overpower the monotonous cry of the grasshopper. And I will
not describe my abhorrence of the moscardon causing gangrene
in horses and cattle, nor of the gnat, or the many mosquitoes
which infest the forests and the cool banks of thy rivers.

I do not blame thee in that thou permittest the degenerate
lion of thy wild fauna to satiate his hunger on thy flocks scattered in their solitary pastures, and that the ferocious tiger finds
an asylum in the recesses of thy mountains, although I cannot

forget my soul's alarms when in the darkness the tracks of the savage beast told me of its neighbourhood, or when I saw the heifer or the playful colt that only a little while before had been overflowing with life, lying dead with their neck rent with its talons and their breast torn by its teeth. And I still feel a longing to discover the tapir or ant-eater, whose thick hide is so much valued by the horse-tamer, the sight of his den at the foot of a riven cedar on the crest of thy unclimbable hills not satisfying me, nor his bear-like tracks and dung like that of a horse.

But it grieves me that thou affordest no home to the deer and the lama, to the hare and the rabbit, while the prolific biscacha becomes ever more and more hurtful to thy lands, and that the vicuna with its precious wool shrinks in horror from thy hill-side forests so destructive to its fleece.

Thou art glad, however, over thy happy flocks of tall, rounded, slender goats, each with three sucking kids, and worthy of breeding with those of Cashmere; and glad, too, over thy many sheep, whose wool is preferred by thee to that of the merino, with which they were formerly crossed, but which are now beginning to be discarded. These numerous flocks browsing by the sides of thy rivers or in the shade of thy woods, seldom or never suffer from drought. The ground is covered over with savoury grasses, serving as food for the many horses with diseased hoofs, to which flints are injurious.

And why should it be forbidden me to mention thy dark-eyed daughters, their shining raven locks, their slender figures, their natural grace, their fascinating manners?

They are fond of dancing, music, and lively conversation when quite young girls, but when married they may justly boast that they devote themselves to domestic duties. I speak of thy *señoritas*, whose anger I fear to excite by naming the *cholita*, who, presuming on the whiteness of her colour, considers herself on a level with them, although her crisp hair betrays a recently mixed breed. She is humiliated by the contempt of the aristocratic class, and this causes, in time, a real degradation. Her own scorn for the clay-coloured *chena* does not suffice to console her—the poor *chena*, the most miserable representative of the daughters of Eve in a land where once she reigned as queen, *nigra sed formosa*.

To the grace and beauty of thy women I must add the courtesy and generosity of thy gentry, and the kind-heartedness of thy country folk, so gracious is their hospitality towards strangers.

But if thou art privileged by nature, O Tucuman, be not proud thereof, nor lift thy desires too high. The labour of man has been hitherto defective, and can only operate slowly in the immediate future. The land is too thinly populated, and the want of capital forbids any sudden development of thy natural wealth; large numbers of workmen cannot find adequate pay for their labour, and there would be no home market for the consumption of any large produce, while it would be impossible to contend with distant and foreign producers. The climate of the most fertile portion of thy territory is hurtful to colonists during part of the year; thy mountains, so integral a part of thyself, and so abounding in wealth, and the fertile valleys they enclose, are without roads; thy laws and the rights they confer on the masters of indebted operatives, sanction a disguised slavery that excludes the services of free European workmen. The treasures of thy waters are in the power of the first occupier, a probable cause of conflict, and thy capital city, though enriched with many educational institutes, is wanting in every hygienic contrivance for the alleviation of life.

Proceed cautiously therefore; endeavour to open streets, to regulate irrigation, to procure liberty for the workman, to make the lives of thy children healthy and pleasant, to maintain thy liberal traditions, and to carry them still further in politics, in religion, in every civil and social relation: *sic itur ad astra!* Then both men and capital will come to thee, and from their mutual increase will arise immediately a greater prosperity and progress.

Meanwhile, I salute thee yet once again, O Tucuman!

Part III.

ON THE LANGUAGE OF THE MATTACCO INDIANS OF THE GRAN CHACO.

~~~~~~~~

CHAPTER I.

JUAN M. GUTTIERREZ'S ADVICE—MY FIRST LESSONS IN MATTACCO
AND THE SPEECH OF THE TOBA CACIQUE MAKE ME DESPAIR
OF SUCCESS—HOW I TRIED TO PLUCK AT THE FRUIT—
FAUSTINO IS MY MATTACCO MASTER— EXPERIMENT WITH
NATALIO ROLDAN—THE OPINION OF THE MISSIONARY FATHERS
IS CONFIRMED—HOW I DISCOVERED ONE OF THE FUNDA-
MENTAL CHARACTERISTICS OF THE LANGUAGE—FUNCTIONS
OF THE PREPOSITIVE PARTICLES *nu*, *á*, *lu*—GREATER FACILITY
FOLLOWING ON THIS—ADVICE TO AMATEURS OF PHILOLOGY.

WHILE waiting for the succouring party, which was destined
to be greatly delayed, I knew no better way of employing part
of my time than by learning words from the Indians by whom
we were surrounded.

I had often been told that their language must be poor both
as to the number of the words and their forms; and although
from the little I had read on philology, I was disposed to come
to quite a contrary conclusion, I was desirous of personal experience before forming a decided opinion and communicating it
to others. On the other hand before leaving Buenos Ayres, I
had seen Dr. Juan Maria Guttierrez—the same to whom Mantegazza dedicated his fine work, *Teneriffe e Rio de la Plata*, in
which the only fault is that the beauty of the style may cause
the reader to doubt the truth of the narrative, which I have
found to be strictly exact, and he had said to me,—

"If you have leisure, study the language of the Indians; in the absence of all tradition and of all archæological data with regard to them, philology is called upon to play a great part in interpreting their origin, and explaining their connection, if any, with other peoples in very remote times, remote at least with regard to the history of existing mankind. The study of language, will henceforth be raised to a science that will in due time shed marvellous light on the history of humanity."

And then he added, in order to encourage me, "The soil of linguistic research is still virgin in many parts, and on this account, promises an abundant harvest to whomsoever will cultivate it; take advantage of it, and you will succeed."

How could I neglect advice coming from such a quarter? Although conscious that I should only be able to add an insignificant little stone to the pyramid of philology, yet I felt stimulated by his words, and as it were, pledged to the task. And afterwards, while I was puzzling my brains to wrench a rule of some kind from the medley of sentences that I had gathered together, and when I appeared to have done so successfully, the delight I felt was increased by the thought of how, on my return to Buenos Ayres, I should hasten to Guttierrez on the very first night, show him the results of my endeavours and talk them over with him. A man of powerful mind and profound erudition, he had a love for art and science, and a tolerance in accordance with his vast knowledge and the extreme liberality of his views. His manners and appearance were agreeable, he was a self-made man and had experienced the greatest changes of fortune. At the age of seventy and in the high literary and administrative position which he occupied, he yet knew how to speak a word of encouragement to the most modest student, and to converse with cordial deference with the least important visitor, a very rare thing with men of his age and attainments.

But this joy was not to be mine! The first paragraph that I read in the first newspaper I met with as I stepped from the vessel on my return, was an account of his burial on the preceding night.

May thy memory, Guttierrez, be embalmed in the hearts of thy fellow-citizens as vividly and lastingly as in that of him who writes; may the earth lie light upon thee! and let me dedicate to thee and give the shelter of thy name to the few lines on the native languages which I shall write on the follow-

ing pages; for they are due to thee, and without thy patronage
I should not have courage to publish them.

My first attempts gave me but little hope. We had on board
an Indian, who called himself a Mattacco, for whom I sent at
once in order to learn the names of our garments and of the
surrounding objects. But after a few words the man grew
weary. It was evident that he was not capable of intellectual
effort, however slight. If, however, I asked a second time,
either inadvertently or on purpose, for the same word, he would
make signs that he had already told it me, and taking my note-
book, would look through the few written pages and point the
exact place where I had written it down. And yet one would
have thought that he was looking in another direction while I
wrote. So that when we Italians say *far l' indiano* to describe
assumed ignorance, we are expressing an actual fact.

I therefore made little or no progress.

But when, a few days later, we were harangued by a Toba
cacique who seemed to be barking at us rather than speaking, the only appropriate course was to conceal my want
of comprehension, since it was useless to attempt to construe
his yells.

However, man proposes and circumstances dispose. For
some days we were aground, and being unable to push on, I
had a great deal of time to dispose of as I pleased ; the Indians
remained grouped round the vessel, and many of their caciques
came to visit us. We could understand none of them; in short,
the longed-for fruit was there ; I attempted to gather it.

The Indian is so suspicious that he dislikes any one learning
his language; but Faustino the Christian was with us, and I
began questioning him in secret, unknown to the Indians. At
first, however, I was dissatisfied, finding so much difficulty in
resolving phrases into words, which I attributed to his want of
knowledge. Finally, I succeeded in establishing better relations
with the Indians, and the openness of our behaviour, the per-
severance I showed in repeating their words, as if they were
something precious, whenever the opportunity offered, and
finally a few presents, removed their suspicions, especially
among the younger ones, who vied with each other in telling
me the name of any object that I pointed out to them.

But it was curious how a word on being repeated appeared to
change without any discoverable reason. Sometimes it was the
slightly double sound of a diphthong, one vowel or the other

being the more marked, but often a syllable was actually changed, and sometimes a syllable was added to or subtracted from the word.

One morning, Natalio Roldan and I endeavoured to come to a conclusion on the matter. For a quarter of an hour we tried to decide which was the actual sound to be reproduced by the Castilian alphabet, and which of two sounds had been intended in a word that had been taught us. The uncertainty confirmed Roldan in his opinion that the Mattacco language was an enigma, that it was impossible to reproduce it, that it had no rules, and could not be acquired, and that he agreed with the missionary fathers on the Christian territory near the frontier, who had always said so.

My ear, however, was becoming cultivated, and I was beginning to believe that the Mattacco language was not, after all, such an intractable Bucephalus ; yet, although able to distinguish the sounds, I could not fathom the reason of the change in certain syllables.

I made up my mind to avoid every pretext for a discussion, and to continue accumulating words, and then after examining and comparing them, and writing them down according to their apparent pronunciation, to deduce some laws for my guidance.

I caught hold, one day, of the son of a cacique, and began asking him the names of the various parts of his body. Nude as he was, there was no danger of misapprehension between humanity and clothes.

But I had hardly ended my inquiries before I perceived that each of the fifteen or twenty words began with *nu* or *no*, the *u* and the *o* being frequently substituted the one for the other by an almost imperceptible gradation of sound.

Good Heavens ! I muttered to myself, this *nu* must be either an article or a particle expressing affinity, because it is morally impossible that so many words should have a common root. It seemed unlikely to be an article ; nevertheless, I bethought me that had any one, when I was a boy, asked me the name of any of my features, I should have touched the part mentioned and replied, for example, the *eye*, the *mouth*, &c. Why should not these young Indians do the same ?

But it soon became clear to me. I resume my questions, asking the names of the various parts of my own body, and these are repeated to me, with the *nu* changed into *a*, and sometimes some

OF THE ARGENTINE REPUBLIC.

of the succeeding letters changed. This was a flash of light, but I still felt uncertain, and to clear away my doubts I took advantage of having captured a kind of hawk, to ask the names of the same parts of the bird's body. In the replies I received many words began with *lu* or *lo*, and the rest remained the same, or nearly the same, as the corresponding. parts in man, minus the *nu* or the *a*.

The following conclusion appeared to be almost certain. In Mattacco the principal words are preceded by a variable particle which expresses relationship. But of what kind ?

I look through my notes, especially through the phrases I had collected, and I find that whenever reference is made to the person speaking the word begins with *nu;* when the person addressed is referred to, with *a*, and when a third person is in question, with *lu* or *lo*.

This was a revelation. It gave me the key to the understanding of a great number of words ; it was the mariner's compass leading me through a great part of the labyrinth !

. Great was my delight !

Moreover, these particles are placed not only before nouns, but also before verbs and adjectives when necessary. They are used redundantly and in pleonasm, just as is the case in Italian conversation, and still more in vernacular Italian, with certain particles.

Continuing my search for the reason of these particles, I found my previous induction confirmed. *Nu* is an abbreviation of *nuch-cá*, meaning my ; *a* of *ach-cá*, thy ; *lu* of *luch-có*, his, of him (*ch* being pronounced as in German, or like the Castilian *jota*) : before substantives and before verbs they may be considered as abbreviations of *noch c-lám*, I ; *am* or *ham*, thou ; *lutzi* or *toch-lutzi*, they, them. Before verbs, however, *lu* is less used than *toch*, which, standing alone, means these (near me), while *toch-sam* and *toch-lani* mean those (near you), and *toch-licné* and *toch-lei-tzi* mean those (yonder).

Besides simplicity and convenience, is there not also clearness and beauty in the relation between the personal pronoun, the personal adjective, and the particle of personal relation ? And was it possible that such a language should be without rules ? I felt encouraged, therefore, to carry on my researches.

Being accustomed in our languages to find the root and invariable portion of the part of speech at the beginning of the word, it was truly confusing to meet continually with the contrary before discovering the law. Therefore this fundamental rule must be borne in mind. Whoever wishes to study languages that are without written rules must dismiss from his mind all those rules that govern his own, or it will be as difficult for him to enter on the right road as to recognize a person wearing a mask.

CHAPTER II.

NAMES GIVEN BY THE MATTACCOS TO IMPORTED ANIMALS—HOW I FOUND OUT THE ETYMOLOGY THEREOF—IMPORTANCE OF THIS DATUM—AUGMENTATIVES AND DIMINUTIVES—CHANGES IDENTICAL WITH THOSE IN ITALIAN—NEGATIVES—THEIR COLLOCATION—EXAMPLES—ABBREVIATIONS—ANALOGY WITH ITALIAN.

ANOTHER thing over which I cudgelled my brains was the names of the domestic animals imported into America from Europe at the time of the discovery or conquest of the former.

It is well known that in those countries where new things are suddenly introduced, their names, as a rule, accompany them. It is equally well known what an important advantage this is, not only to the philologist, but also to the ethnographer —in a word, to all who study the distribution and description of the human race.

Now, it so happened that when I asked the names of the horse, the ox, the sheep, which in Spanish, as it is here pronounced, are called *cabaggio*, *vacca*, and *ovécha*, the names given me in answer were entirely different.

It still makes me laugh when I think of the efforts I made to reduce Mattacco words, by my own fanciful alterations, to their Spanish roots.

But one fine day I found myself killing two birds with one stone.

We had a handsome bull-dog on board. Now, *sinoch* is Mattacco for dog. The creature's name was Palomo (dove), which the Mattaccos translated literally into *Ucquinatac*. But one day, while caressing it, an Indian said to me, as if praising the dog, "Sinoch-tach!" instead of sinoch or ucquinatach. I began then to understand that the particle *tach* expressed size or superiority, that it stood apart, and could be added to, or taken from a word in order to modify its signification. I

hasten to fetch my note-book, I turn over the pages, I read
through all the names, adding *tach* to those that have it not,
and all at once, to my unspeakable delight, I recognize the true
and beautiful, and philosophical and scientific etymology of
my chinnassetach, my jelatach, my cionatach, in *chinasset*, stag,
jelách, tapir, *cionách* gamma, with the suffix *tach* aggrandizing,
ennobling, extending, and exalting them.[1]

And then all at once dozens of words ending in *tach* became
clear to me.   By cutting off this syllable, as well as the continually recurring *nu*, *a*, *lu*, and by fixing both eye and ear on
the essential syllables of the word, I not only seized the meaning
more easily, but discovered its origin, laws, and variations more
easily also.   I stood on the threshold of another.

The reader must not deride my enthusiasm.   In my place he
would have felt the same.   For man is the creature of his
surroundings, and a minister of state who should become a foot
soldier would feel pleasure if his corporal showed approval of
his manner of presenting arms, and a philosopher would be
gratified at a woman's praise for disentangling her skein of
wool.

How could such a tyro as I fail to be delighted when a
beautiful and complete language sprang up, as it were, between
my fingers?   And a language both methodical and elegant,
instead of the exact contrary, as I had been led to expect?

Meanwhile, these Mattaccos possess augmentatives in *tach*
both for physical and moral relations.   Thus *icnú* is a man, and
icnu-tách a great man, *inót* is water, and *ino-tach* fire-water or
spirits.

As diminutives, on the contrary, they use the particles *quuach*
and *chiach;* for example : *coló*, a foot ; *colo-quuach*, a little foot ;
quei, a hand ; *quei-chiach*, a small hand ; and this last word
also means a one-handed person.   Thus a cacique who was
called *manco* in Spanish because he was deprived of one hand,
was called in Mattacco, *quei-chiach*.   And they can also modify
their pronouns at pleasure in a manner that cannot be rendered
in Italian or English, although it has an equivalent in Spanish,
viz. *esa*, that, and *esita*, a diminutive of that; and very
frequently used by country people.

Tach, *quuach*, and *chiach*, although distinctly particles, may
be, and perhaps must be, considered henceforth as inflections

---

[1] The pronunciation of these words is guttural.

because they are never used alone, and more especially because they are declined instead of the words to which they are joined.

It is very usual for Mattaccos to change the sounds of *chia, chié, chii, chió*, and *chiú* into *tzá, tzé, tzi, tzo, tzú*, and into *kia, kié, kii, kió, kiú*, and *vice versâ*, and also into *tiá, tié, tii, tió*, and *tiú* reciprocally. Thus for *sheep* I may use indifferently *tzonatách, kionatách, chionatách*, and for *bird* I may say either *huenkié* or *huentié*. Nevertheless, the more frequent use of one form than the other distinguishes the different dialects. Thus the Mattaccos on the Toba borders say, *tza, tze*, &c., and those on the Christian borders *chia, chié*, &c. These variations that up to a certain point, and in polysyllables, or even in dissyllables, are easily seized by an attentive observer, cause terrible misapprehension when they occur in words of one syllable only. Who would imagine, for instance, that the *tzac-dái* (imperative of *give*) of one dialect was equivalent to the *kiach* or *kioch* of another?

Nor is it uninteresting to notice how certain phonetic deviations are, as it were, instinctive in man, since we meet them among ourselves also. The Milanese, for instance, call their *chiesa* (church) *ciesa*, and Spaniards say *cucciara* (they write it *cuchara*) for *cucchiara* or *cucchiaia* (a large spoon or ladle), and very many other words are altered in the same way, viz. *meticcio*, Italian for half-caste, is *mestizo* in Spanish, and *schiacciare* (to crush) and *stiacciare* are synonymous. Thus those inhabitants of Santiago who can speak Chiqchua make frequent use of *ná* in cases where the Coyas inhabiting Bolivia say *gná*. For example : *once* is *na* and *gna, I* is *nochca* and *gnocha*, just as in Castilian, Portuguese, and Spanish, viz. *nina, niña* (the Spanish *n* representing *gn* in Italian) ; *farina, farinha* (*nh* in Portuguese = *gn* in Italian).

Next as to the inversion of letters and syllables. Does it not happen sometimes that in speaking quickly we alter a word by inverting its letters? Now, this is instinctive and becomes habitual until certain words of one language sound ridiculous to persons speaking a tongue akin to it. For example : *ghirlanda* (a wreath) is *guirnalda* in Spanish ; *bribone* (a ruffian) becomes *bribon = virbonus !* in Latin. But to reach the climax of exaggerated inversions we must go the Galliziano dialect, two-thirds of which are Portuguese and the rest Spanish. Now, these Mattaccos likewise invert their words : *melón*, for instance, *nelóm*, and so forth.

T

The Mattacco language has many negatives, but they are diversely used. On another occasion I may perhaps be able to show an unexpected similarity in this with other languages spoken by South American tribes who apparently are in no way akin.

The principal of these negatives is *ka* = no, which is used alone, and is also prefixed to adjectives, thus reversing their meaning; for example : *mátt*, true, *ká-matt*, untrue. It is curious that the Akkas, the apocryphal dwarfs of Africa, have the same word for "no," if one may believe the statement of the Abate Beltrame di Verona.

Another negative is *tdé*, always placed at the end; for example : *matt*, true, *matti-tdé*, untrue. Note the addition of *i* for the sake of euphony. These additions and withdrawals of letters are one of the most desperate difficulties in the study of this language, and, in truth, make one despair of mastering it. Thus : *nu-huen*, I have ; *hueni-tdé*, I have not.

Next comes *am*, which is prefixed to verbs. For example : *n'amhuen* or *namuhen*, I have not ; then *jach*, interrogative and imperative, and prefixed to the verb ; it is the Latin *ne*, but in a different position. Then *lácha*, which also means *without*. Example : *jach-lón-nu*, do not kill me ; *jach-á-hémin-nuja ?* Dost thou wish me well ? *lácha-ciécuó-ja*, a widow, that is, *without* a husband.

Prepositions in this language, as in others, form in a great measure the basis, and I may say, the philosophy of the language. When united to a verb, they attribute to it a relative signification. They are, nevertheless, so undefined and so unfixed, that a little while before writing these lines it seemed to me, and I marvelled at it, that this language contained only a very few. The contrary is the case in the Chiqchua language, in which the prepositions are beautiful, melodious, detached, and always in the same place, i.e. after the nominative case, so that they should rather be called postpositions.

In Mattacco, likewise, the prepositions are postpositions, but sometimes, instead of being placed after the noun, they are placed after the verb, and then they may be mistaken, as happened to me, for a form of the conjugation. At other times they stand between the root of the verb and the inflection expressing tense, or between the root of a noun and the inflection indicating number or case. One can imagine the horrible state of confusion into which one is thrown on finding in a perfectly new and strange language a number of expressions in which one and the same word seems to alter the sense of a sentence without the shadow of a reason. For my own part, I must admit that for a long time I entirely failed to understand it, and even now I must confess that I have only mastered very few of the rules that are concealed in several hundreds of sentences in my possession.

For example: *cue* means *with;* *nu-hén* is an abbreviated form of *us;* *with us* is rendered by *nu-cue-hén.*

There would certainly be no great difficulty in the matter if you could ask an Indian for a single word and he could answer you as simply ; but, in fact, he must always refer the word to something else. Thus, if you ask him to name the foot, he will answer *nuccoló* if he touches his own foot, *accoló* if he touches yours, and *toccolo* if he touches that of a third person. Next, the difference of construction is puzzling. For example, take the case of *nucuchen:* if you ask your teacher which part of the word means *with,* and which part means *us,* if he is a *ladino,* i.e. intelligent, and acquainted with the language, he will reply with great ingenuousness : *nuc* means *with,* *cuchen* means *us,* turning the words, in fact, topsy-turvy.

Therefore the best plan is to go on by degrees, and from the known to the unknown, first asking for single words, then for simple and clear phrases, then for others less simple but still clear. After this it is well to repeat the same sentence, changing only one of its words or one of its parts. Then, by comparing and eliminating, there is a likelihood of arriving at a word-for-word translation. And even this is not enough ! because on account of the conditions I have indicated in the language, of the great intellectual disparity between the two interlocutors, and their diverse and mutually unintelligible points of view, the unhappy learner suddenly finds a word entirely changed without knowing why or wherefore, and is left in doubt as to which is the right version. He multiplies his questions to his own greater perplexity and the whole thing ends in a regular Babel.

Talking of Babel, among the Vilela Indians the word for "speak" is *Mbabelon!*

But to return to our prepositions. I have said that they modify the sense of the verb ; it would be truer to say that they complete it. For example : *toll* contains the idea of motion. When used alone it may mean *to sprout;* the grass

T 2

sprouts, will be, the grass *toll;* with *ca* after it, it means *to come from ;* with *ppe* after it, it means *to fall.* There are other words expressing the same thing, but if you wish to use the word *toll,* you must add the aforesaid particles which are placed as postpositions to the substantives.

When these are placed after the verbs, it might seem that they are in reality prepositions placed before the direct case; but although there are some true prepositions, nevertheless in the case I have mentioned they are postpositions with regard to the verbs also, because they modify their terminations so as to agree with the sound, because the verb thus modified can stand alone, and because between it and its preposition and the direct case other words may be interpolated ; thus proving it to be bound to the verb.

The principal particles used like our prepositions, or at least those with which I am acquainted, are, *cchia,* until; *tamennech,* wherefore ; *appé, pé* or *ppé,* upon ; *icchió,* under ; *cue, chié, jcche, écche, éch,* with (these are probably modifications of the same word for the sake of euphony) ; *uuith* or *uuitd,* and *c-loja* also meaning *with,* that are placed as prepositions, but are rather cumulative conjunctions ; *op* or *ob, hót, hlót,* by, for—I have only met with these last as equivalents of why or because ; for example : *op-toch,* because (through this) ; *op-chi-lá,* why? meaning, for what object? while in order to say *why,* meaning, for what motive? *atddejeche ?* is used. This word is composed of *atde,* how? what? and *jecché,* with. Then there is a postposition *ei,* which is like the Italian *da* and the French *chez,* and is used to express movement to or from a place ; it is often omitted and is variously placed. This *ei* or *iei* forms an extremely gracious verbal expression, viz. *mi-ei = vai-per,* composed of *móh* or *mmoh,* signifying *vai,* and of *ei,* with one of the numberless variations that bring me to despair over this language. Thus in order to say, " Go and fetch me some fire " (*itóch,* fire) ; they say, *Miei itóch,* or " Go for fire," just as the verb *to go* is used in elegant Italian. At first, and for a long time I mistook this for an inflection.

Another important postposition is *ca,* meaning *of* and *from.* It is placed after verbs and substantives. Together with these it forms a kind of genitive, but it is seldom used and only with proper names. Added to personal pronouns it forms the possessive pronouns *my, thy, his,* which are genitives, if I may say so, in this language, and follow the same rule as in ours, in which we may say either *my* or *of me*. Thus from *nú* (the abbreviated form of *nochlám*, I) we get *nuch-cá*, my; *ah-cá*, thy; and *luh-cá*, his, of him.

There are other prepositions besides, viz. *cqui*, within; *lácha*, meaning without, and placed before the word it governs, but this is rather to be considered as a negative, because I have always found it before words, the termination of which indicates possession, which is thus negatived by *lácha*. For example: without a wife, is *lácha cequó-já*, that is, unwived.

There are very many others that I do not recollect.

The words that express *with* (*ech*, *je-che*, &c.), lead me to think that some prepositions govern certain cases, and that their apparent alteration is due to the different terminations of those cases. For example: *me* is *nuja*; *with me* is *nujecche*; it is easy to perceive here a rational alteration of *nuja-ech*.

CHAPTER III.

THE reader will not fail to observe that in Mattacco the position
of the preposition is the exact reverse of what it is with us;
and our custom should seem the most remarkable to him,
because that of placing prepositive particles after the noun or
verb must be looked upon as a characteristic that at one epoch
was probably universal in all languages.

In German and in English, especially in the former, the
transposition of the preposition is very frequent, and constitutes
an element in the language as conducive to its elegance as to
the difficulty with which it is acquired and spoken by those
whose mother-tongue is one of the so-called Latin sisters.   This
was the case at least with me after allowing for the dissimilarity
of words.   It is the same in the Slavonic languages and in
other languages belonging to the Aryan family.

Further; in Latin, which is said to be our mother, but is not
so, except as to polish, in the absence of some grammatical
forms and of some parts of speech; in Latin, I say, we find
examples of the transposition of prepositions in *vobiscum,
nobiscum, tecum, mecum,* and in the varying places of others
either before or after the noun, as for example, *versus* towards,
may be indifferently, I go *Romam versus,* or *versus Romam.*
Conjunctions follow the same rule; whence I can say, *Senatus
atque* (and) *Populus Romanus,* or *Senatus Populusque Romanus,*
the famous motto that is now used by the municipality of
Rome.

In the Italian language *meco* and *teco* is used in place of *con*

me, con te (with me, with thee). The Spanish seem to have
lost sight of the etymology of *migo* and *tigo*, for they all make
use of the pleonasm *con migo, con tigo. Migo* and *tigo* are of
course no other than the Italian *meco* and *teco*, the *c* being
changed into *g*, as in *amigo* and *amico* (friend). Other examples
of this may be found in Italy, at least in Tuscany, in the
vernacular. They are eloquent of one of the greatest factors
in the transformation of languages, i.e. whenever the origin and
the sense of a certain exceptional form is lost sight of, it comes
to be treated under the general rules. Thus also, when foreign
words are introduced in their full force into another language,
that is to say, when they are pronounced and written as in the
tongue to which they belong, after the lapse of little more than
one generation they become assimilated in every way with their
new family. The lower orders, especially, who are ignorant of
the genealogy of their guest, alter the word at once and treat
it as one of their own. Hence those well-known Gallicisms,
Teutonisms, and I know not what besides, that so often break
the hearts of purists, but which are in truth a real manna
raining down and enriching the language that adopts them :
for my part I should welcome such rain every day, in spite of
any opposition—provided indeed there were national reciprocity
in the matter.

Meanwhile, the examples I have adduced may be looked
upon as the remains of pre-existing forms.

In the native languages of South America, postpositions are
employed commonly in place of prepositions ; the contrary is
the exception, at any rate in Chiqchuan and Guarany, which
possess postpositions only, and in Araucan, which possesses both.
These tribes, with the Mattaccos and the wild Indiadas of the
Chaco and the centre, occupy the whole of South America.

May not this grammatical form be superior to ours, and
hasten the perception of ideas by suddenly fixing the terminations of words on which the relation expressed by the particle
is to be thrown ? Certainly one of these particles cannot greatly
retard the perception of the relation between the terminations
and the relative object ; but if we revert to the epoch when
language or languages were formed, does it not seem more natural
to name the objects in the first place and then to express their
inter-relation ? It is probable also that the phonetic symbol
expressing relation was of later growth and was due to the
progress of intelligence, and still more to practice in the use of

the instrument, if I may call it so, that had been adopted, the speakers being helped at first by a conventional collocation of words, or by modulation, or in some other way. In such an order of ideas the preposition would seem to be of later date than the postposition in the genesis of language; and the postposition would be later again than modulation. Modern languages, nevertheless continually make use of both conventional arrangement and of modulations in order to distinguish relations.

The declension of words, while complicating grammatical forms, is a great aid to clearness; and this superiority is possessed by the Spanish language, in which the accusative is pointed out by the preposition *a*, and by the French language also with its nominative *qui* and accusative *que*. But is this an absolute progress, and more especially is the process anterior or posterior to the declension of substantives? To discuss this would carry us too far. I will limit myself to stating that in my opinion, the simplest language, if equally expressive with others, is the best, and that, on the other hand, certain individualized forms that are necessary for what I will call a material intelligence, gave way probably to simpler forms owing their strength to the relative positions of words, when intelligence had become more capable of apprehending such relations and of apprehending syntheses.

Meanwhile a language that is characterized by formulating by means of symbols that which we express by means of relative positions and by modulation, is the Chiqchua, in which we have the declension of nouns and the enfeoffment of particles expressly for the interrogative form. viz. *ciù* after a verb, and *tach* after a noun. Examples: *wilt thou*, is *munánchi; water* (acc.) is *jacútta; Wilt thou have water?* is *Munánchicciù jacútta? thou callest thyself*, is *suticchi; how*, is *ima. How callest thou thyself?* is *Imátach suticchi?* Modulation is thus avoided, as also the sign of interrogation in writing.

It must be observed that in Chiqchua all particles are placed after conjunctions, prepositions, interrogations, and declensions. Thus it is an exceptionally typical language.

I have not met with any disjunctive conjunctions in Mattacco, such as *or, neither*, &c.

Instead of *or* they seem to use *if not*. For example: *Give me water if you have not wine*, instead of, Give me water or wine. And instead of saying *neither*, they repeat the verb. For example: *I have no water, I have no wine ;* instead of, I have neither wine *nor* water.

But they have many words to express the copulative conjunctions, *and*, *also*, &c., which as with us are placed before the direct case. The following are the principal words: *uuith*, or *uuith* and *c-loja*, which they use also for our *with*, as we have seen; and *útcuei*, *isichiei*, *tdéui*, for, and. *Tdéui* is especially used for interrogation; for example: *I am going, are you ? Nu-jiche tdéui-am ?*

It is curious that as to conjunctions Mattacco is the reverse of Chiqchua, which has no word for *and*, instead of which they use *with* placed after the subject or object; whereas they have *or*, placing the particle *ciù*, which expresses it, after one of the two alternatives presented.

The following analogies approaching to identity are curious also: *uuítd* with the English *with ; op* with *ob*, and *op-toch*, meaning *also*, and *for this*, with the Latin *ob-hoc ;* and *utquei* with the Latin *atque.* We shall take an opportunity of noticing other analogies as we go on.

The conditional conjunction *if*, is *chiá* or *cchiá.* When placed before the proposition conditional on the principal proposition, this last is joined with *uuítd*, like the *so* in German after *wenn ;* for example : " If thou wilt not tell me," *cchiá*, thou wilt not ; *uuítd*, tell me.

CHAPTER IV.

ADVERBS—RATIONAL FORM OF ADVERBS OF TIME—SUN AND EARTH, DAY AND NIGHT—THE HEAVENS—ADVERBS OF PLACE—APPEAL TO THE READER—ADJECTIVES—COMPARATIVES AND SUPERLATIVES—FORMS FOR CONTRARY SIGNIFICATIONS—FOREIGNER AND STRANGER—ETYMOLOGY OF CIGUÉLE CHRISTIANS.

THEY have one adverb of space, but their adverbs of time are remarkable for their rational formation and their analogy with our own; for example: *day* is *squala, sun,* a sun; month is *iguelách,* moon; *tem-lo* means, *at the side of;* *náche* or *nachi* or *nach* means, *past* and *after* in the sense of bygone time; *nen-ná* and *ná* mean the present time, now. Now then: to-day is *icuálanná,* that is, the present sun; to-morrow is *icuála* and *chiicuála,* for the same reason that in Spanish *mañana* means both morning and to-morrow; yesterday is *icuálannáche,* the bygone sun; the day before yesterday is *icuála elláche,* i.e. another bygone sun, *el* meaning *other,* and *láche* having the same meaning as *nache,* the change being due to a desire of harmoniousness and to the genius of the language; the day after to-morrow is *tem-lo icuala,* i.e. at the side of to-morrow. It is curious that *tem-lo* should stand before *icuála* to express the day after, and that *náche* should stand after, to express the day before. These may seem caprices of language, but they probably indicate an etymological, or even a philosophical cause, presiding at their formation.

I explain myself thus: They make use of the words *hunát* or *hunná,* meaning *earth,* to express night; for day, on the contrary, they say *the sun;* seeming to have understood the contrast between them. It is not unlikely that this contrast represents to them a kind of philosophy in which the earth and sun might represent two opposite principles, darkness and light, good and evil. I have not, however, been able to detect this philosophical system in their ideas, although as we have seen, some of their religious forms would seem to express it.

Moreover, is not their way of using the sun and light in order to express time, an intellectual link with the Aryan, who from the Sanscrit *dyu*, light, has passed on to the Latin *dies*, the Spanish *dia*, the Italian *di*, all these words meaning day?

For *this evening*, they say *hunná* and *chiahunná*; and for *this night*, meaning last night, the *anoche* of the Spanish, they say *hunna-tzi-nna*; analogously to the form used and the sequence followed in the distribution of words for expressing *to-morrow*, *to-day*, &c.

Moreover, for sky they say *ppe-le*, which I think may be translated, " that which is above," from *ppe*, above, and *lé*, syncopated from *lél-lé* or *chéllé*, a patronymic word which serves to express origin and country.

It is said that savages have no abstract ideas, but I ask you whether ideas of *ever*, *never*, are abstract or not? Without waiting for an answer, I say that these tribes have the words *ic-ne-mid* for *never*, and *ch-lam-mech* for *ever*.

It may be argued that these expressions are composed of words having in themselves a limited meaning; quite so. But the French also make use of *all-days*, *toujours*, to express *for ever*; therefore they express an indefinite and infinite idea by means of a word signifying a limited time, viz. *day*.

I take the opportunity of remarking that the particles *nache* and *nenna*, of which the latter is sometimes changed in the second or third syllable, and the vowel altered from *e* to *i*, form two tenses of the verbs; *nache* being used for the Perfect Tense, and *nenna* for the Imperfect. For example : to return, is *tapil*; I returned, *tapil-lache*; and I was returning, *tapil-lé* (the second *l* is in place of *n*, for the reason already given).

For noon, they say *icuála ichni*, which in my opinion means the *sun is high*, or *above*; and for midnight, they say *hunnat-chiú-uech*; I think this means *under the earth*. *Inatach* means quick, and *hunach*, slow.

There is one syllable, *tdé* or *dthé* or *ntdé*, which is the basis of very many adverbs of place and time. For example : why? *atdjeeche*; where? *tdene*; whence? *dtel*; how? what? *atde-tzu*; how much? *tde-hote*; when? *tdé-nách-hoté*; (*hoté* by itself means *how*, and the *nach* indicates that the question refers to a somewhat remote time). It must be observed that where the *a* comes first, it probably refers to *thou*, owing to the question

being asked in the second person. This proves how necessary
it is to establish clearly the circumstances of time and person
before writing down the reply.

Though I fear to weary the reader by dwelling too long on
the Mattacco language, yet I feel bound to impart the little I
have learnt; for I devoted the short leisure I could snatch
from my professional duties to studies, often prolonged to the
small hours of the night. And if in order not to weary him,
I begin to digress, I am afraid of being too discursive, while
if I keep strictly to the thread of the narrative, he may
find it too dry. I am puzzled. Will any one suggest a way
out of the difficulty? No one? Then I must remain as
I am. But then, O my reader, if indeed at this time there
still exists one for me, be compassionate to me and my poor
book! I ask it for the sake of the affection I feel towards
you, and the desire I have for reciprocity! for the sake of the
hours I refused to Morpheus while thinking of you, and endeavouring to disentangle the hitherto inviolate tongue of
Mattacco! For the sake of the ridicule that I feel already I
am destined to encounter for omitting the exact mathematical
root, in this uncertain philology! And then there is some
possible gain for you, if you ever care to study, in whatever
degree you please, the prehistoric history of this South American
population, for with the light shed by philology we might well
try to discover if the Redskins were once as closely related to
each other as ourselves and the Croatians at the least. And
if this does not suffice thee, have pity at least on an unfortunate author plunged in a slough of difficulties whence the
strength of Hercules would be needed to extricate him!

I am still confronted by adjectives, comparatives, superlatives, numbers, declensions, and verbs. I know not which to
select first, but I will begin with the first-named.

Adjectives seem to have resembled isolated buds, needing
but a touch to open them. But such is not the case. There
are many with roots and intricate branches, that we must accept
in order to understand them.

But as for hypotheses, I give due warning that we must clear
them with a jump.

There are a goodly number of adjectives of which I can tell
neither whence they come nor whither they go, and these perhaps are the majority. But there are others of which the
derivation is obvious. Among these are the possessive adjec-

tives formed from the root of the pronoun with the addition of the particle *ca*, of, which is also a genitive postposition, and *co*, which must be considered as a variation of *ca*. Besides *co* and *ca*, they also make use of *lo* in possessive adjectives, but principally, I think, with *my* and *thy*. *My*, therefore, is *nuch-cá*, *nuch-có*, and *nuch-lo* ; *thy*, is *accó* and *al-lo*.

Another way is with *tzac*. Example: fear is *uai* or *huái* ; frightened, is *huáintzách*. And another form is with *já*. But this would seem rather to be a present participle. Example : *Nuhuái-já*, I am frightened, I am afraid ; *accecuója*, thou who hast a wife, or a husband.

Another way is by adding the proposition *ech* to the substantive. Example : hunger, *na-in-ló*, hungered, *na-in-lo nech*, i.e. with hunger ; now, *cchia*, fresh, new, *cchiá-jéch*, i.e. with or of now. Such forms as these are rational, surely, and reveal a process of agglutination.

Comparatives and superlatives proceed likewise by agglutination, *hom* or *chom*, meaning more, being placed before the word, and *tach*, expressing superiority, after it. The comparative, however, is not followed by *than*, as for example : Peter is handsomer *than* Paul, is rendered even with agglutination, "Peter is handsomer, as is not Paul." It is a somewhat odd form, but I find it repeated very often in my notes. The particle *já* frequently follows comparatives, for which it seems to me there are other laws which, however, I have not discovered.

As superlative they use *ntocq*, most, as is the case in many other languages, and sometimes the sound is prolonged by a syllable. For instance, far, is *toquéj* ; very far, is *toquéej* ; the word being accompanied by a gesture. This form is also used by the Araucanos, and by ourselves in some cases. It is a natural form.

As I said before, they have augmentatives in *tách*, and diminutives in *chiách* or *quách* ; these are postpositions and are declinable, while the preceding substantive remains unaltered ; the declension consists in changing *ch* into *ss* for the plural.

In order to say *less*, they say *jách-lom*, which is the same as *jách-chom*, i.e. not more. The agglutinative form must be noted here ; it is common to all these adjectival forms. This language seems to me extremely logical, and once having taken a certain direction goes on to the end. The difficulty is to grasp it at first, and then not to be bewildered by its sudden turns.

While on this subject let me observe that almost all adjectives expressing the opposite of a good quality, are composed of the adjective expressing that quality and of a negative particle either preceding or following it. For example : true, *matt ;* false, *ka-matt* or *mattidé,* i.e. untrue. Good and fine, *hiss* and *tzi ;* ugly, *ka-tzia* and *tzitdé ;* far, *tocuej ;* near, *tocuei-tde ;* instead of the last word, *ca-tu-ta* may be used ; now *catú* means the elbow, and metaphorically, a bend or curve, &c. This form extends sometimes to substantives. For example : a remedy is *ckiá,* a poison is *ka-ckiá.* We find the same forms in our own languages when we say *uncertain* for not certain, *scortese, descortés* in Spanish for courteous, discourteous, &c.

It may seem, nevertheless, that these Redskins lack certain shades of meaning that are possessed by our language, in which, for example, there is a formal distinction between false and untrue, between far and not near.

It may be so ; nevertheless they do possess certain shades of meaning, such as a distinction between foreigner and stranger ; the first being *achlú-tách chle-le,* that is, one who comes from a great distance ; and the second, *icchiomchlé-lé,* that is, one who comes from lower down. With regard to these Mattaccos, strangers do, in fact, live lower down, near the mouth of the river and of the Paraguay. Above them dwell the Christians, whom they call *Chiguéle.*

Whence this name of *Chiguéle ?* Not from their colour, because *prelách* means white, and *jaccatdé* means yellow, i.e. notblack, showing that to them the opposite of black is yellow. They have no word for blue or green, and it may be they are so far colour blind. And if they intended to call us *red,* which is *icchiott,* there seems to be a wide gap between that word and the word *Chiguéle.* Therefore ?

I have it ! *Chiguéle* means "fine men !" *Chi,* as I have already said, is the same as *tzi,* and would be the same as *chj.* Now *tzi* is a root found in *katzia* and in *tzi-tdé,* meaning ugly, not handsome, as we see in the word *tzilatách,* also called *chilatách ;* thus the Christians, having partly corrupted the former word, pronounce it *chilátta* and *catchia. Chilatách* is composed in the first place of *tách,* an augmentative particle, and of *chila.* In *chila la* is a particle that, as we have seen in the case of *lo, ca,* and *co,* forms adjectives when placed after the root. *Chi,* therefore, is the root giving signification to *chilatách ;* but *chilatách* means fine or handsome in a high degree, therefore *chi* expresses beauty.

We have seen that the patronymic word *chelelé* means "which is 'of," or "belonging to." Now there can be little difficulty in admitting that in a language like this one, which sacrifices so much for the sake of euphony, *chlele* may have been changed to *ghuele* or *guéle,* either to soften the sound, or in accordance with a rule not yet ascertained. Hence *Chiguéle* is equal to *Chichléle,* that is, equivalent to *those who are fine,* i.e. *the fine men.*

I may be allowed to congratulate myself on an etymology that gives me a share, unworthy though I be, in one of the four qualities that a Greek philosopher has declared to be necessary to earthly happiness, viz. competence, faithful friends, a taste for music, and either to be handsome, or to be thought so, which is practically the same thing !

Now, among these Indians, even if one is rather ugly, one is considered a fine man.

CHAPTER V.

THE INDIANS OF THE CHACO CAN COUNT ONLY UP TO FOUR—
QUATREFAGE'S OPINION—THE VALIANT DEEDS OF A CACIQUE
RELATED BY HIMSELF—SLAUGHTER NEAR FORT AGUIRRE—
INCOMPATIBILITY BETWEEN CIVILIZATION AND BARBARISM—
MANNER OF COUNTING OF THE MATTACCOS—ANALOGIES.

MOST of the Indians of the Chaco can only count up to four.
These include the Mocovitos, whose lands are contiguous on the
south to the provinces of Santa Fé and Cordova, and on the
west to Santiago; the Mattaccos reaching on the west to the
provinces of Santiago and Oran; the Tobas lying between the
before-mentioned races and the River Paraguay, along which
they inhabit part of Bolivia; the Vilelas and Ciulupos, who
now only exist in tribes and families, dispersed among the other
races, or absorbed by them.

The Chiriguans, however, and possibly other peoples dwelling
in Bolivia, on the great wooded plain called the Gran Chaco,
can count indefinitely; and the other Indiadas of the Chaco
nearer the north can count beyond four, if I may judge by my
first teacher on board, who, although a Mattacco, was able to
give me words for higher numbers. This was a result of contact,
as we shall see in due time.

With regard to the power of counting only to four, I see by
Quatrefage's last work, La Specie Humana, that he appears to
throw doubt on this statement, interpreting it differently, but
without giving his reasons. He seems to admit at the utmost
that expressions are wanting, but not the idea of larger numbers.
But even if we accept his hypothesis psychologically, it is con-
tradicted philologically; and knowing, as we do, the relations
between words and ideas, we must own that where the former
are wanting, the latter must at any rate be in such a confused
state as not to admit of fixing by words; just as among ourselves any one unacquainted with an art or science is unable

to use the technical terms thereof, although he may recognize and appreciate the works of either.

For my own part I will relate a personal anecdote, as it will help the reader to form an opinion on the matter.

I was conversing one day with a cacique, and as it was for the first time, he began recounting to me his deeds of valour.

On my asking where these took place, he answered me at once :—

"*Num, maittá, ntócq, Téúch, tocuej !*" thrusting his right arm towards the north, and drawing it back again.

I stared at him and interrupted, "*Ntdé-hiche*" (where ?), for I understood him to be telling me of a people on the Teuco, called Umaità, like the people of Paraguay at the mouth of the Bermejo, and my interest was intense at the thought of an ethnological discovery !

But he had meant, *yo (nu) maté*, (I killed) great numbers on the Teuco, far away ! hence he answered, "*Nu ilon ntocq*" (I killed many of them), and began counting in Mattacco from one to four, holding his right hand in his left, and lifting one finger at a time, but not the thumb. But when he had reached four he was puzzled, and sitting down cross-legged on the ground, he began making marks on the earth with his finger, exclaiming at each one, "*toch*," i.e. this, raising his head each time as well as his hand, the thumb of which he held in his left hand, and looking at me, he added, "*uuitd toch*," meaning, "and this one too," and so he went on until he reached about a score, always, however, turning towards me that I might understand that, besides these, there were also the four fingers, until at last I was almost tired out with *ntocq, ntocq* (many, many).

It was quite true. That particular cacique had been for a time the pest of the Christian frontier and the scourge of his Indian enemies, until at last, having grown old, and being beaten besides by the Christians, he made peace ; and, receiving rations from the Government, he and his greatly diminished tribe were reduced to Fort Gorriti, on the left bank of the Vermejo. Now it so happened that near Fort Aguirre, on the right bank of the Teuco, about fifty kilometers north-west of Gorriti, some other Indians, who had attempted an invasion, were surprised in their tolderia ; some were killed and some taken prisoners. These last were bound together with their hands behind them, so as to form a chain of thirty or forty

men ; and my cacique was called upon to despatch them, which
he accordingly did, spearing the most of them with his own
hand.   The greater part of them remained dumb during the
slaughter, others uttered cries as in their religious ceremonies.
These were probably the priests.

Five years later I visited the scene of the massacre.   Not a
bone remained of the unburied corpses ; the waters of the flood
season had washed them away and the winds had covered over
the rest.   It was with difficulty that with the help of a soldier
who had been present, I succeeded in excavating three skulls
from under certain shrubs.   The Government intended to
punish the officer of the Aguirre garrison on picket duty, and
perhaps did so.   But it should be clearly understood that there
is no possible compatibility between civilization and barbarism ;
and all individual philanthropy, all *à priori* arguments from a
distance, are bereft of any practical utility on the scene of the
struggle, and amid the battle of races.   To every one of these,
the destruction of the enemy appears the most natural, and
the simplest expedient in the world.   Hence the destruction
of the Redskins by the Christian weapons of iron and fire, by
transportation, and by dividing them like herds of cattle is
inevitable.

To return to our arithmetic, we must not take for granted,
except in jest, that these Indians are unable to perceive that
ten fish are the half of twenty.   The dog who seizes on a
second bone when flung to him, and yet growls if another
attempts to take the first, has that much perception.   But the
absence of adequate expressions reveals, in my opinion, an
insufficient power of abstraction.   The development of this
mental faculty is followed by development in language, and by
an alteration of words with due regard to the original sounds.

As to the Mattacco names for the first four numbers I was
struck by their length, and by the gestures accompanying them.
Each of them, it seemed to me, should contain an entire sentence in order to account for the gesticulation.   After a long
time I believe I discovered the meaning of this, and that my
intuition was correct.

In effect, an Indian says *hoté-quaach-hi,* and lifts one finger ;
or, at the same time, he may say likewise, *hotecki* and *hotécoaki.*
Now, *hoté* means *how,* *quaach* means *finger,* *hi* (*h* nasal) is a
particle indicating possession, containing, &c.   Thus, disregard-
ing the slight difference only too natural in every language, and

especially in one so liable to change as this one, we have the translation of *hotéquaki* in *as my finger holds* or *contains*.

Two, is *hoté-quoasi*, and two fingers are lifted ; *quoas* is the plural of *cuoach ;* thus the translation is : *as my fingers hold*.

Three, is *lach-tdi-qua-jél*, and three fingers are raised, the last finger—the little finger—remaining close against the left hand. Now, *lach* means *without* or *not, él* means *another ; quai* is too like *quoacki* not to suggest its own meaning ; therefore I translate it " without the other finger."

Four, is *tdi-qualéss-hicki*. I cannot render this literally, hence I will not attempt it ; but I recognize a plural form in *qualéss*, and in *hicki*, a word often found in conjunction with *hi'*, and in phrases containing the idea of permanence or similar meanings. It is probably, therefore, expressive of the action of the hand ; "the fingers are."

This action of the hand was not confined to the cacique, but was used by the other Indians in the centre of the Chaco, and even by the Christian Faustino, who knew how to count as we do. Hence, it must bear some relation to the words. The etymology that I put forward seems to be a more satisfactory explanation than that usually afforded by philology in similar cases.

The elegance of the original forms must not be estimated, however, by a literal translation. How inelegant would not the greater number of composite Greek words appear if translated literally into the vulgar tongue !

As to the intellectual worth of these renderings of numbers, their origin is very natural. The Guarani follow a similar fashion, at least for certain numbers, such as ten or twenty, for which they say " two hands," and " two hands and two feet." And it is probable that by analyzing the words for numeration used by other Indians and other nations we should find some analogy. Roman numeration, in fact, represents the fingers as far as three, and the palm of the hand in V. (five). The palm, less one finger, is IV. (four), and two palms reversed, one over the other, represent X. (ten). It is clear that Roman numerals represent in cipher that which is represented by hieroglyphics in writing, and by Mattacco expressions in words.

It is natural to man to seek the nearest instruments for the expression of his wants and for the development of his ideas.

CHAPTER VI.

DECLENSIONS—SUBSTANTIVES—PERSONAL   PRONOUNS—APOSTRO-
PHIZING PARTICLES PLACED BEFORE NAMES IN MATTACCO,
GUARANY, AND AKKA—GENDERS—COMMON AND ·ABSTRACT
NOUNS—OBSERVATIONS.

WE have frequently mentioned declensions and plurals; it is time therefore to say a few words on them.

I was so strongly persuaded that the inhabitants of the Chaco would have the plural formed by the addition of a word expressing the notion of plurality, such as *much* or *many*, that I was always seeking for it. Nor was this extraordinary; for the Guarani do, in fact, add *heté*, many, to the singular, in order to form the plural; the Chiqchuans add *cuna ;* these two tribes are or were bordering on the tribes of which I am treating. Many other nations follow the same rule, which is known as agglutination or aggregation; among others, the Akkas of Africa.

It seemed very natural therefore that the lesser should do as the greater. Besides, it is generally acknowledged that the stage of agglutination is proper to a less advanced language.

It is true that in such case the people speaking it should also be less advanced, but this is very far from being proved. In short, every theory is found to halt in one place or another without thereby losing its substantial excellence, or being less binding on its adepts. We may therefore accept, as a whole, the above philological theory.

The replies I received to my questions respecting the plural were unsatisfactory. Some words were terminated in the plural in one way and some in another; while *ntocp*, many, might always be used. If I named a certain number, the same uncertainty pervaded the replies. For example: two horses? They would answer, horse two; two men? two *icnú* or *icnúl* or *icnúil.* The terminations seemed slightly varied by different modes of pronunciation, and not for any other reason.

I note down all these things because they will be a guide for some of the numerous travellers who nowadays wander among the tribes of Africa or America. They may be useful to an explorer who does not rely too presumptuously on his own knowledge or penetration.

I was surprised to find that *we* and *ye* are formed from *I* and *thou* by means of the same affix. Thus: *noch-lám,* I, becomes *noch-lam-il,* we; and from *am,* thou, we have *am-il,* ye. But this refers only to pronouns, and may easily therefore be exceptional. Nevertheless, by calling my attention to this definite form, I obtained a clue to the mystery.

The Mattaccos have the plural form, not only by the addition of *ntocq,* many, but also in various other ways, by inflection; in short they possess different declensions, which they use almost exclusively, and which seem to fall under the following rules.

- Words ending in *o* and in *é,* take an *i* in the plural. Ex: *colo,* foot, *coloi,* feet; *huentié,* bird, *huentiéi,* birds. Words ending in *ach,* change the *ch* into *ss;* all the augmentatives in *ach* and diminutives in *chiach* follow this rule. Ex: *iguelach,* moon, month, *iguélass,* months; *jelatach,* horse, *jelatass,* horses. Words ending in *n* take an *l,* which is pronounced by placing the tip of the tongue against the palate, and sounds almost like *il.* Ex: *cannu,* a needle, *cannyl* (almost cannuil), needles. Those ending in *t,* in *och,* and other letters, change them into *ess.* Ex: *jáhset,* a fish, *jáchsetéss,* fishes; *tdoch,* hide or skin, *tdochess,* hides. Those ending in *l* often take *iss,* and sometimes drop the *l.* Ex: *tzet,* paunch, *tzeliss,* paunches; *jél,* a sick man, *jiss* (or *jéliss*), sick men. This last is a good specimen of alteration.

There are many exceptions and probably other rules that I omit for the sake of brevity.

I am doubtful as to whether they have the dual number like the Araucans and the Guaranys, and like the Greeks among ourselves, but I am not certain. Yet I have noted: the hand, *cbuéi,* both hands, *cbuéjai;* we, *noch amil,* we two, *nochlamáss;* you, *amil,* you two, *amáss;* but I repeat, I am uncertain whether it is a dual form.

When numerals are used, the nouns following them are indifferently in the singular or plural. Adjectives seem to me to remain in the singular, and they are placed after the noun.

I have not met with sufficient examples to authorize me in attributing declension to cases also, unless indeed we may thus denominate the occasional addition of *ca* in the genitive. For example: Peter's people, *Péilo-ca Uicchj*. Their method of using prepositions may suffice instead of cases.

The personal pronouns *I* and *thou*, however, at any rate in the singular, are declined, while only *toch*, these, seems to have an accusative in *tocha*.

The declension of pronouns is as follows:—

SINGULAR.	SINGULAR.
Nom. I. *noch-lam. nu, no, ni.*	Nom. Thou, *ám* or *ham*, and *á.*
Gen. Of me, *nuch-cá.*	Gen. Of thee, *ach-cá.*
Dat. To me, *núho.*	Dat. To thee, *ámu* or *hámu.*
Acc. Me, *núja, nu.*	Acc. Thee, *ama* and *ái.*
Abl. With me, *nújech.*	Abl. With thee, *ámech* or *ámchie.*

PLURAL.	PLURAL.
Nom. We, *nochlam-il, ná,* and *inát.*	Nom. You two, *amáss, á.*
Nom. We two, *nochlamáss* and *inamáss.*	Nom. You, *amil, á.*

The finals *l* and *il*, may be due to an alteration of the word *él*, other, originally used to express the plural; it would therefore be merely an ancient form, agglutinated, set aside and varied by successive changes.

The apostrophe is much used in this language, for the sake of harmony most likely; but by altering and confusing the words, it leads to mistakes and to difficulty in securing the right word. Example: Dost thou wish me well? *jácháémin nuja;* (i.e. *jach-a-hemin nuja*); I wish thee well, *nai* (i.e. *nu ia*), *hemin.*

In the formation of nouns, as in that of verbs, they make use, as I have already said, of the possessive particles *nu, a, lu,* my, thy, his, which are placed before most substantives. In asking a question, therefore, one must determine exactly the *nu* which refers to the person speaking, who, if asked the word for house, will reply: *nuhauet* or *nu-hepp,* i.e. "my house." And thus with the apostrophe, which is easily hidden in *na, ne, ni, no, nu,* and is mistaken for the root letter, with consequent misapprehension and confusion when the same word reappears in an altered form in other or identical expressions.

I draw attention to this because it is not improbable that the same rule may exist in other languages. The knowledge might be useful to some other traveller who may chance to read my notes. In Guarany nouns are preceded by *cie* or *cce*, my ; by *nde*, thy ; and various particles for *his*.

The Vilelas have many words with *beyp* in the centre, expressive of some relation no doubt; but I have not sufficient materials from which to form a judgment.

So far for America !

I see in the Abate Beltrame's *Saggio Grammaticale*, on the language of the African Akkas, that all their verbal infinitives begin with *k*. It is morally impossible that this letter can be a root. It must therefore express a relation. But which ? Probably a pronominal one. Guided by this idea, I find on examining the personal pronouns, that the third person plural is *kaé*, those. I have no doubt that the *k* of the infinitives comes thence ; their root must be sought therefore in words without the *k*.

The substantives do not seem to me to have genders ; but in the pronouns and demonstrative adjectives I have remarked sometimes certain changes which led me to suspect a distinction of gender. But the suspicion is of the slightest.

The names of female animals, however, are followed by *tziná*, meaning female ; the word for woman is used by itself. For example: a mare, *jéla-táck-tziná ;* and for males, the names are sometimes followed by *asnach*, which means male.

There are common names, already including an idea of abstraction, as we have seen with regard to bird, fish, tree, for which they use words that I have found applied to the species. And it is noteworthy that they possess also abstract names, because, besides *never* and *always*, they have others, such, for example, as fear, *uái*, with which they also express trembling. An earthquake is *hunát uai*, i.e. "earth-trembling," as in the Spanish *tiemblor de tierra*. For these Mattaccos therefore are fear and trembling the same thing ? And were not our abstract expressions for the most part formed in a similar way, i.e. by taking a part for the whole ? Now, trembling is the most common manifestation of fear.

I contend that these Indians possess to the full, the intellectual faculties of man, and his power of reasoning, and in so high a degree that they are like ourselves both as to ability and antiquity.   The distance between us is that of the actual world of facts and of the ideas relating to them, but it is disproportionate to their faculties and ours.   This is intelligible.   For long ages there have been numberless individuals among us enjoying the intellectual advantages of a scientific, moral, and polite education.   Yet they are few indeed in comparison with those of ancient history or with mankind at large.   The influences therefore of hereditary physiology must have had little or no effect on mankind throughout the world, during the period of barbarism.   It is by overlooking these considerations that the public in general is led to wonder at the relative inferiority of the wild races.

The very small intellectual and moral distance between them and us, is an eloquent proof of the immense antiquity of man, necessary to bring him from the state of rational anthropomorphism into that of the existing savage.

CHAPTER VII.

CURIOUS EXAMPLES OF THE FORMATION OF NEW WORDS—ETY-
MOLOGY OF *iúccúás*, TOBACCO—HAIR, WOOL, LEAVES—THE
TREE AND ITS FRUIT—NAMES OF KINDRED—ANALOGIES—
REMARKS—DEMONSTRATIVE PRONOUNS—INTELLECTUAL HAR-
MONIES—NO, NOTHING, NOBODY—COMPOSITE NAMES FOR
OFFICES—VERBS—DIFFICULTIES THEY OFFER—EXAMPLES.

IT is interesting to note how these tribes form words in their
language to express some new object. Observation is the
great teacher. For instance, for bell, they say spider-paunch,
chiu-hút-tzel ; for musket they say, as did our forefathers, arque-
buse, i.e. fire-bow, *itóch-letzech*, from *itóch*, fire, and *letzéch*, bow ;
ammunition is, as in Italian, little balls, i.e. *c-lóquass*, from *c-ló*,
a balla, and *quuach*, a diminutive ; a steel for striking a light, that
they had never seen before, nor had they seen the other under-
mentioned objects, they call *itóch-cchia*, i.e. "a means or instrument for fire ;" flint is *ten-thé*, a stone; a match is *itóch-léss*,
from *less*, bundle, union ; family is *c-ló-hi*, from *c-ló*, a ball, and
hi, a particle expressing holding or containing ; a mirror is
tope-jach-hi, *topejach* meaning image and shadow ; a stocking is
ccoló-búth, from *ccolo*, foot, and *bhút*, a bung or cover—in short,
a covering. A shoe, on the contrary, they call *nissót* or *sót*. i.e.
a cone, indicating that they already knew of shoes, and in fact
they sometimes wear a kind of sandal like the *osectas* worn by
the inhabitants of the campo, and made of a piece of leather for
the sole, and two strips of the same that, after passing between
the great toe and the toe next to it, are fastened at the ankle.
A lucifer match is *itóssass*, an abbreviation of *itoch-quass*, meaning small fires, and the match-box is *itoch-hi-huass*, i.e. the care-
taker of matches, or match-guard.

One word has always awakened my curiosity as to its etymology, viz. *iúccúas*, tobacco, which does not exist in the Chaco ;
I believe I am not mistaken in deriving it from *iú*, burned, and

cúas, to bite, to tear, to sting. Now in these two actions consist the manner of using tobacco, and its effects.

Another analogy as to power of judging, in addition to what we may deduce from the foregoing words, is found in the use of *tei* both for eyes and for countenance, just as in Italian poetry and in accordance with the etymology of the Latin *visus*, which means eyesight.

The doorway is *hlappé-bhut*, i.e. the door-cover, a clearer and more precise expression than ours.

The same word, *huolei*, preceded by the name of the object to which it refers, is used for fleece, wool, and hair.

They use the same word for foliage, showing that they look upon the leaves as the hair of the plant; and this is no forced analogy, if we remember that mimosas with deeply indentated leaves predominate in these parts. The botanical term for these indentations is *pinnated* or *bipinnated* (feathered), thus justifying the Mattacco expression.

Their manner of distinguishing between the plant and the fruit by means of flexure is worthy of remark. Example : *mistol* (jujube-tree), *ohó-jucche*, the fruit of the mistol, *ohójáche ;* the *vinal*, *attécche*, the fruit, *attáche ;* the black algarrobo, *uóssot-etzúche*, the fruit, *uóssot-etzáche*, &c. Here we see the *u* repeatedly changed into *a*.

Names of kindred vary according to sex. This is not surprising, for have we not ourselves father and mother, brother and sister, &c. ? It is curious that all languages are alike in this matter, and the American are no exception to the rule. In these latter the names of kindred vary, not only according to the sex of the person addressed or spoken of, but also with the sex of the speaker. For example : in Araucano the father calls his son *fotúm*, and his daughter *gnahue ;* but the mother calls her son *cogni huenthu*, and her daughter *cogni domo—cogni* meaning offspring generally in the mouth of the mother. In Chiqchua the father calls his son *cciuri*, and his daughter *ususi ;* the mother calls her *guagua*.

In the Chinese language, according to the teaching of my interpreter, *Ajao* of Pekin, whom I engaged lately for two francs an hour, son is *Tsae*, and daughter *Pnoé ;* father is *Lu-tao*, mother *Loúmuú*, brother *ghoo-séi-lou*, and sister *tta-i-tzi é*.

In Mattacco we find the following names : father, *chia ;* mother, *ccó ;* son, *locsé* or *lotsé ;* daughter, *lectzá ;* brother-in-law, *quajenécche ;* sister-in-law, *ticchié ;* brother, *lecchiíla*, or *cchulá ;* sister, *cchiinno ;* uncle, *uitoc ;* aunt, *uidoché ;* nephew, *lec-chié-ios,* an abbreviation probably of "the son of the brother;" niece, *cchiáió ;* father-in-law, *chioti ;* mother-in-law, *catelá ;* cousin, *huoclá.* I remark, moreover, that for son-in-law and daughter-in-law, they use the same words as for brother and sister-in-law, and for brother-in-law the same word also is used as for son-in-law ; which, however, I am sure is an error.

The different words employed to express the same degree of kindred, according to the sex of the speaker, are due in my opinion to the method of aggregation originally adopted to determine that degree, although subsequent changes have obscured etymological origin. It is clear that in the case of husband and wife a nephew will be the son of a brother of the one and of a brother-in-law of the other, or of a sister and sister-in-law.

By agglutinating or aggregating the words expressive of these diverse relationships, we shall secure the same degree of kindred, a nephew, in four different ways.

An equally interesting form is that of the demonstrative pronouns, which resemble the French because they are formed by the pronoun *toch,* these (in French *ces*), *licué,* those (yonder), and *letti* and *lani* for those (near you). There are others besides, among which is *tzi,* these ; *tzi* is the same as *cci* and *cchj,* and is of importance because we meet with it in Araucano. These words, when used as demonstrative adjectives, are divided : *toch* is placed before the substantive, and *licné, latzi, tzi,* &c., are placed after it, remaining indeclinable, while *toch,* on the contrary, is declined. Now, is not this just the same with French demonstrative adjectives—*ceci, cela,* for example, which in the plural are *ceux-ci, ceux-là,* and can be divided ?

Do not these forms reveal a grand harmony in the human intellect, which makes use of the same means, among widely separated races, of expressing similar steps of relationship ?

The following genesis, which reveals an order of things, deserves special mention. *No* is *ká,* nothing is *kiá,* nobody is *kiái ;* here we see the root clearly and constantly shown.

And what can be more elegant or methodical in philology than the Mattacco words expressing possession, capacity for holding, and the accomplishment or execution of an office ? The letter *ḥ* (*h* with a dot beneath is pronounced nasally) appears in a very great number of words, if not in all, expressing to have, or to hold. Now, we have *hi* and *huú,* expressive of that which contains, and possesses, and does a thing; and we have *huét*, meaning house, a place containing things. For example: a fish, *jácsét;* a fish-pond, *jácsette-hi;* shoes, *nissóhéss;* a shoemaker, one who sells shoes, *nissohésse-hi;* shoemaker, one who makes them, *nissohésse-huu;* a shoemaker's shop, *nissohésse-huét*. The same plan is followed in all similar cases. In what respect are other languages superior?

But the verbs are a serious matter, and I must confess my ignorance. I am not able to give one infinitive; one, that is, that I could conscientiously so describe. I might be able to find some, had I leisure for the necessary study, but at present this is not the case. In justice to myself, however, I must say that the fault does not lie entirely in my want of intelligence; the greater number have all the intricacy of this language, joined to a complete absence of the least glimmering of intuitive grammatical form in my Indian interpreters. If I asked them, for instance, how to say "to eat," they would either not know how to answer me, or would give me each time a different answer. It was needful to say to them, "How do you say, 'I wish to eat'?" and "How do you say, 'Let us eat'?" and so on. And then one falls at once into the difficulties of the language, because the two ideas of eating and wishing to eat will be included in one special form, and so forth.

Next come the various forms and dictions. For example: "I have," may be translated with the French form, "il est à moi," or the corresponding Latin form, "id est mihi." Thus one incurs the danger of mistaking *est* for *have*. Now these people appear to possess some of these forms.

And if I were to say that I have not even discovered the plurals of the verbs? The particle *en* or *hen*, according to the termination of the preceding word, certainly expresses the plural; but I do not know whether it is pronominal, or whether, on the contrary, it is a real plural inflection of the voice of the verb. Example: "Dance thou!" *catin;* "Dance ye!" *catinen*. One might succeed at last, were it always like this, but let us see. "Let us dance," *inát-catin;* the *en* has already disappeared; *inát* means "us." Yet it will reappear in another similar case. Example: "Strike up (thou)!" *hén-chié;* "Let us strike up!" *inénhechién*. Here there is plainly a change for the sake of harmony and for convenience, yet it is easy to discern the *en* that vanished from "Let us dance!" Still this would be comparatively nothing—it might only imply two forms of plural

The rub lies here; that, complicating the example with the subject and the object, it would seem that *hen* or *en* agreed with the object and not with the subject, although we find no passive or neuter form in the verb, as in certain Latin verbs, *videor, loquor*, &c. Example : " Kill the sheep ! " is *llón tzonatach ! Llon* is kill, *tzonatach* is sheep. "Pietro has killed the sheep," will be, *Pietro ilón tzonatach*. ".Pietro has killed the sheep " (plural), will be, *Pietro ilónen tzonatass*. Where now is the meaning introduced by the *en* in "Dance ye !" "Let us dance," &c.?—and we meet with such difficulties by the dozen.

With regard to *en* or *hen*, however, I may say that this particle is found mostly in the plural. I say mostly, because it is not always the case. Example: " The Christians have killed the sheep," will be, *Tsiguéle ilon tzonatách*. This plural form *en* is apparently only used in the verb, either when the object suffering the action is plural, or the plural subject itself performs it, as in " to dance."

CHAPTER VIII.

CONJUGATIONS—VARIOUS FORMS OF PAST TENSES—REFLECTIVE
VERBS—RETENTION OF THE ROOTS—POSTPOSITIONS AND
VERBS—VERBAL POSSESSIVE FORM—THE VERB *TO BE*—TABLE
OF AN INDICATIVE MOOD—PASSIVE VERBS.

JUDGING from the heap of verbs before me, I think I may affirm
that there are sundry conjugations in this language.   In this
respect it resembles Guarani, which has a very great number,
and is unlike Araucano, with its one conjugation for its many
thousand verbs; and Chiqchua, that in like manner has but one,
albeit extremely complicated in the compound tenses.

From the preceding pages the reader will understand that I
am unable to offer him one or more models of verbal conjugations on account of my own ignorance.   But I can give some
of the forms of various tenses.

One of the most precise is the Future Tense, which consists
of the Present Tense augmented by the syllable *lá*.   Example :
He returns, *tapil ;* he will return, *tapil-lá*.   This is the Future
Absolute, for there is another, that I will call Doubtful, *pbije*,
" perhaps," being added at the end of the sentence.

The Past Tense is formed by the addition of an *e* preceded
by a repetition of the last letter of the Present form—double
letters being in the nature of this language, as in the Italian and
many others, excepting the Spanish.   Example: " He arrives,"
jom ; " he arrived," *jommé*.

The Remote Past, however, is formed by adding to the Present
the adverb of time, *náche* or *náchi*, and changing the *n* into
another letter, especially into *l*, when the ear requires it.   Example : " He kills," *ilón ;* " he killed " (Remote Past), *ilonnaché*.
Sometimes *áche* is used.   Example: " He eats," *théucque ;* " he
ate," *theuquáche*.

Another form of past time, resembling the Imperfect Tense,

is by adding the word *nenná*, either whole, or one of its two syllables, according to taste.

These two words, *náche* and *nenná*, are the same that we have seen used in "yesterday" *icuála-náche*, and "to-day," *icuála-nenná ;* so that these savages are logical.

It would seem from the above examples that there are no terminations to the verbs according to *person*, although there are some depending on number that have the addition of *en*. Nevertheless, either from a casual difference of pronunciation, or intentionally, I remark that in the first person singular of the past tenses the *e* is changed into *i* in the following examples : " I arrived," *jommi ;* " I returned," *tapini ;* " I ate " (Remote), *tdeucquáchi*. However, it is not necessary, since each voice of the verb is preceded by the pronominal particle *nu*, *á*, *lo*, *inat*, " I, thou, they, we," with various changes such as, *no* and *ni*, *lu* and *li*, *inné*, and I forget the rest.

In the negative, however, which is formed by adding *tde*, "no," to the root, it may seem that the word suffers a flexure ; but this is due merely to euphony. Example : " I see," *nu-huenn ;* " I do not see," *nu-huenni-tdé*, instead of *nuhuenntdé ;* " I cut," *nu-issét* or *nissét ;* " I do not cut," *nu-jissti-tdé*, instead of *nuissettdé*. " Is he dead ?" *jách-iil ;* " he is not dead," *jigni-tdé*, instead of *jill-tdé*.

I do not enter into further particulars because I should necessarily stumble over forms for the differences in which I could not account to myself ; and the greater the difference, the more complex is the relation denoted. Let us take one elementary example : " Did the (my) chief return ?"—*Jachtapil-é nu-canniat*. " He did not return," *tapini tdé*. In this simple example why is there *l* in one place, and *ni* in another ? The interrogative form merely affects the phrase by affixing *jach* at the beginning. I feel convinced that the change is merely due to euphony. And *ab uno disce omnes*.

Some reflective verbs seem to be formed by the addition of *chlam* to the active verb. For example : " Pietro killed himself," would be, *Peiló tilonne ch-lám*. Can this *chlam* be the Latin *met*, and the Italian *stesso* (self) ? In that case the personal pronoun, *no-chlam*, might be *egomet*, I myself, thus harmonizing with the other pronouns. I must observe that when I quote Latin, either on this or on other occasions, I have no intention of establishing any analogy ; I do it merely by way of explanation.

It is to be remarked that certain verbs retain their common root, while their signification is modified. Example : To go, *opil ;* to return, *tápil ;* to come, *nom ;* to arrive, *jóm ;* to die, *iil ;* to kill, *ilón ;* to cry, or shout, or say, *ohn, hón ;* to speak, *hon-chié,* i.e. to say with, just as we say, to *con-verse ;*—all this shows both acuteness and logic, to my mind. These expressions may give us the key of the modifying power of some particles, to the advantage of the philosophy of the language, as in *hon-chói,* and to that of comparative philology, as in *ta-pil,* in which *ta* represents a repeated action, such as "returning" after " going," and we meet with it again in the same sense in the Araucano language.

Postpositions, however, are the great means in the manufacture of verbs. I have already noted, for instance, *toll cá,* to come from ; *toll-pé,* to fall from ; *toll icchiot,* to fall ; in which *toll,* expressing movement, is the common root. And I feel sure that if, in accordance with this rule, I were to say to these Indians, *toll-chié* (*chié* = with), meaning, " to accompany," they would understand me. Here are some further examples : " Pietro is dying of hunger," *Peilo ill-ech na-in-ló ; ech* meaning *with,* the instrument. That *ech* in this case is probably a preposition before *nainló,* hunger, we may see by the following example : " The Indians are dying of hunger," *Uicchj jil echión nainló,* that is, *jill-ech-en ; éch* standing before the *én* signifying the plural number of the verb, which is therefore attached to and placed after *éch,* and not placed before the substantive ; hence it is not a preposition, as we have already said, when speaking of prepositions.

This same use of postpositions, together with the other changes I have already deplored, are not the least causes of confusion and difficulty in the study of the verbs. For what action can in fact be expressed without a verb for signification of the principal idea, and a postparticle to define relationship? Very few, surely. Very few, too, will be the words free from one of these disguised wedges, either on one side or the other, and in various shapes, according to the requirements of the ear, without the slightest consideration for the student, who remains astounded and confused before certain inexplicable alterations.

One verbal form for actions including possession is the addition of *já* to the word denoting the object possessed. Example : Wife, *ciequa ;* to have a wife, *ciequaja ;* fear, *huái ;* to have fear, *huája.*

They omit the verb *to be*. Example: "I am ugly," *nu-tzi-tde ;* that is, "I handsome no."

I will conclude the weary subject of verbs—as wearisome to the reader, I imagine, as to myself—with an attempt to set out a model of the Indicative Mood of a verb. I do not guarantee the details, for reasons already explained, but it will serve to sum up my ideas.

<table>
<tr><td>*Ilón*, to kill.</td><td>We have killed, &c., *inat, há, tochéss-ilonnehén.*</td></tr>
</table>

INDICATIVE MOOD.

Present Tense.	*Remote Past.*
I kill, *nú-ilon.*	I killed, *nu-ilon-náché.*
Thou killest, *há-ilón.*	Thou killedst, *há-ilon-náché.*
He kills, *li-lon* and *tilón.*	He killed, *l-ilon-náché.*
We kill, *inát-ilón.*	We killed, *inát-ilonnachién.*
You kill, *há-ilón-én.*	You killed, *ha-ilonnachién.*
They kill, *tochéss-ilon-én.*	They killed, *tochéss-ilonnachién.*

Imperfect.	*Future.*
I was killing, &c., *nu, há, l-ilon-nénna.*	I shall kill, &c., *nu, ha, l-ilon-lá.*
We were killing, *inát, há, tochess-ilonnennahén.*	We shall kill, &c., *inát, ha, tochéss-ilon-lá-hen.*

Perfect.	*Imperative.*
I have killed, *nu, ha, l-ilonné.*	Kill (thou), *llon.*

It must be remarked, however, that the remote form with *naché* is very seldom used, and that with *nenná* still more rarely.

Have these people a passive form of verb? I cannot solve this question. I have observed, however, that many of their verbs when formulated in Italian can be reduced to an active, or at least an intransitive form. For example: "Paul was killed by Pliny," can be formulated thus, "Pliny died by means of Paul," or even, "Pliny killed Paul."

After all, I do not consider this an inferiority.

The model conjugation I have set forth must not lead us to attribute simplicity to the verbs of this language. The reverse of this is the case, and therefore I cannot give other moods or tenses, for they seem to me so complicated that hitherto I have not been able to grasp their laws.

x

CHAPTER IX.

THE *r* OF THE MATTACCOS AND OTHER INDIANS—LABIALS AND
THE *l*, *ua*, *ue*, *ui*, &c.—ARTICULATION OF THE MATTACCOS
AND THE CHINESE—CURIOUS ANALOGIES—PREDOMINATING
SOUNDS IN THE TWO LANGUAGES—MATTACCO ALPHABET—
Onomatopéiche WORDS—RESEMBLANCE BETWEEN MATTACCO
AND ARYAN WORDS—I TAKE LEAVE OF THE READER.

AMONG the peculiarities of this language we must note the
complete absence of words with *r ;* it is a letter, in fact, which
the Mattaccos can only pronounce with great effort and imper-
fectly.

Their neighbours—Tobas, Ciulupos, and Ciriguans—however,
possess this letter.   The Mocovitos are the link between, as it
were, pronouncing the *r*, like the French, in the throat, almost
gh-r.

To many persons, perhaps, the French pronunciation appears
rather an exaggeration of the *r* than a suppression ; but I am
of a contrary opinion, and it is confirmed when I see that a
Mattacco succeeds more easily in saying *Peghro* than *Pero* (for
Pietro, Peter), and *Peilo* than *Peghro*.   In any case the ability
to pronounce the letter more or less correctly proves that the
absence of the *r* in Mattacco is not owing to an innate
physiological defect in the vocal apparatus, but to conventionality,
or, at least, to a tendency in the language.   The fact of not
using this letter during the lapse of ages is the reason that the
vocal organs have, by physiological heredity, become inapt to
produce the sound of *r*, and by degrees the power of doing so
may be entirely lost.

Yet it may be attributed to the ear, which, being unaccustomed to the nasal sound, cannot seize upon it, and hence there
is a sympathetic difficulty in reproduction on the part of the
vocal organs.   Every one has experienced this on beginning
the study of a foreign language.

Nevertheless they can pronounce *d* with clearness, although they have many words with approximating sounds, but only at the beginning of words, and with a resemblance to the English *th*. Example: How? *tdé hoté?* He eats, *théucque;* tirador (*ventriera*), *tilalól*.

I have yet to hear a Mattacco pronounce *b*, *d*, *f*, *g*, *p*, *t*, joined with *l*, or with *r*. A great alteration in words is consequently occasioned. They become, in fact, unrecognizable; thus: *ccailá* instead of *cabra* (a she-goat), *Pailó* for *Pablo*, *hléno* for *freno* (a bit), *huéiló* for *pueblo* (people, country). Another peculiarity is that they cannot sound a labial before *uá*, *ué*, *uí*, *uó*, *uú*, in one syllable, and substitute an *h* aspirate. This defect or deviation is also found among the people of the Campo in this Argentine Republic. Thus, in place of *bueno* (good), they say *huéno*, and in like manner *huego* instead of *fuego* (fire).

While on the subject of articulate sound it is curious that, according to the pronunciation of my Chinese master, *Ajao*, a most intelligent cook, who can write Chinese, his countrymen not only have, as is well known, no *r*, but are unable to pronounce the very same combination of letters that are found insuperable by the Mattaccos; they cannot even pronounce *d*, besides so many others. It often happened to me when I was discoursing with Ajao, that I forgot I was not talking with a Mattacco, so alike are they in colouring, oblique eyes, hair, and flattened nose. Thus, for *adios* (adieu) my Chinese says *alio;* for *tres* (three), *tles;* for *proprio* (own), *lópio;* for *señora*, *señola;* for *teatro* (theatre), *teetelo*. It is often impossible for me to understand the Spanish word he is endeavouring to pronounce—as, for instance, *teetelo* for *teatro*, *oléchalo* for *oreja* (ear), *liálio* for *diario* (diary), *poole* for *pobre*, *huelo-liá* for *buen dia* (good-day), *huela-loche* for *buena noche* (good-night). I note that an immense number of Chinese words end in *lo*. It is also noteworthy, in my opinion, that *l* is the letter generally found replacing the *r* and the other combinations of letters that are of difficult pronunciation. But with regard to the Chinese *r*, I have found one word among the 200 I had in my collection containing an *r*. The position of this letter, therefore, may make its pronunciation more or less possible, as is the case with the Mattacco *d*. The word to which I refer is *tai-hi-ro* (theatre), in which the *h* is so sounded that it takes away much of the energy of the *r*—which is the alien?

But if certain sounds are wanting to the Mattaccos, others are abounding. Among these the most prominent are *kiá, kié, kii, kió* and *kiú, ckia, ckié*, &c., and are so frequently used with others of similar sound that one remains in doubt whether it may not be the same syllable repeated over and over again with different meanings. We have already seen that *kiá, kié*, &c., change into *tzi* and *tzé*, into *chia* or *tcia* and *tcié*, &c. They are also added to the augmentative *tach* and to *lo* or *la* to form adjectives.

I do not want to make absurd comparisons, but, as a curiosity, I may remark that in Chinese we find the following syllables predominating : *tziá, tzié*, &c. ; *sciá, scié*, &c. ; *tzá, tzé*, &c. ; *ttai* or *tai*, meaning large, and *lo*, of the meaning of which I am ignorant, but which I always find in the root.

These facts, combined with an almost identical pronunciation, may be worthy of the serious consideration of linguists.

In studying these languages, and in making use of the sounds[1] of our five vowels for the pronunciation, it will be seen that the diphthong, or coupling of two or more vocal sounds in one simultaneous utterance, is inevitable. Natural diphthongs are those which, if we imagine them to have been fixed in writing, would give way, when time had caused inevitable changes in pronunciation, to conventional diphthongs, like the French *ou*, the Latin *oe* and *ae*, and the German *eu*. I note, however, that in a written language diphthongs must be considered as symbols of a former different phonetic expression.

In these studies we become aware also of the insufficiency of a single alphabet, which has to alter according to the various languages, unless we adopt a rigmarole of letters as long as a litany. Our Italian alphabet is besides one of the poorest, especially in the absence of a guttural symbol and of an aspirate, representing sounds that are exceedingly common in most of the languages of the world.

If we want to write Mattacco with our alphabet, we must use the following modifications, which will apply in general to most other languages. *Gh*, as in German ; *j*, the Spanish *cota* would serve also, but would be confounded with our Italian *j* ; an aspirated *h*, as in some French words, and at the beginning of German words ; a sign to express the lengthening of a vocal sound, but not the doubling of the consonant—*h* might be sufficient for this, as in German, for the prolongation seems to correspond with the physical act of pronouncing the *h* ; an

[1] This refers to the Italian language.

English *th*, but with a sound between *t* and *d*—this would be a consonant diphthong; a diphthong *ou*, the *u* not pronounced, as in French, but both vowels rapidly sounded; the diphthongs *óéú* and *éú*, pronounced as they are spoken; an aspirated and nasal *h*, that I distinguish by a dot underneath; and an *l*, so uttered as to sound almost like *il*. *Vice versâ;* abolish *r*, *d*, *f*, *v*, and almost *b*, which never occurs but in diphthong with *p;* and *p* singly, which occurs only with *b*, or as conveying a special sound which can be approximately rendered by the addition of *h*, so as to form the diphthong *ph*.

In this manner, and without introducing foreign characters difficult of retention, and having to be learned beforehand, I have written down specimens of Mattacco, Guarany, Chiqchua, Aimará, Mocovito, Ciulupi, Toba, and Chinese. I substituted, however, as I was writing in Spanish (when I made my notes), *j* for *ch*, and *y* for *j*. These letters are sufficiently well known for us (I mean, the reader and me, who are not learned in languages) to be able to read the words without any marked difference in pronunciation, and thus we can satisfy the curious, if not the scientific.

I must draw to a conclusion, if I would not sicken my reader with American languages; I will merely complete some details on Mattacco, concluding them, against the usual grammatical order (for who, indeed, would have had time to write a grammar, and who the patience to read it?), with a few native words that we may consider as *onomatopéiche*, i.e. imitating natural sounds—an action to which some thinkers attribute the origin of language, afterwards developed by human intelligence.

To shout, to call, *óhn;* light, *chlepp;* dumb, *huó-haó;* a cough, *ccocóchtáss;* a cricket chirping, *li-tzil;* *loro*, a kind of parrot; *quécchié*, pelican, vulgarly *ccia-cá*, and a kind of large, wild turkey, *tzá-coch*—in both cases from the noise they make. There are very many other words of a like nature.

I will conclude with some Mattacco words resembling others belonging to European languages.

Hié, Mattacco; *yes*, English; *si*, Italian; *ja*, German; *giá*, Italian. No, *ka*, Mattacco; *cché*, Tuscan; *kein*, none, German; (*káe*, Akka). Son, *tse* or *ssé*, Mattacco; *tze*, Boemo (*tzae* and *ize*, Chinese). Ill, *iell* and *jéll*, Mattacco. *Op*, Mattacco; *ob*, Latin —*p* and *b* being frequently substituted, the one for the other, in all languages. The country, or campo, *achlú*, Mattacco; *agro*,

Latin and Italian—note that the Mattaccos use *l* instead of *r ;* thus *achlú* might be *achrú*. Dog, *sinoch*, Mattacco ; *kinos*, in *Greek*—inversion of letters, as in *melon* and *nelom*. Cock, *húh* or *cúh*, Mattacco ; *coq*, French. Grasshopper, *li-tzil*, Mattacco ; *zillo*, Tuscan—some crickets and birds are so called from their cry. House, *hauét*, Mattacco ; *haus*, German ; (*huasi*, Chiccina). With, *uuitá*, Mattacco. And, *utquei*, Mattacco ; *atque*, Latin.

These are all I recollect.

In the formation of compound words they follow the German and English manner. For example : gloves, *hand-schuhe*, in German, meaning, shoes for the hand ; in Mattacco, *cquéi-pbut*, meaning, hand-cover. And similarly as to negatives. Example : "I do not see," *Ich sehe nicht*, in German, and in Mattacco, *nuihénni-tde*, that is, *I see no ;* a construction frequently used by the Milanese.

We have already noted other analogous constructions.

And here I pause for the present and take leave of the reader. My hope is that as a practical, though indirect, result of our studies, pursued with difficulty and interruption, he will be convinced that mankind is potentially the same in every corner of the earth. We behold man mastering with singular ability the complicated instrument of speech, and showing himself to be the possessor of every quality corresponding with the most able intellectual development, provided circumstances will admit of civilization, as it is understood at the present day.

If the modern Indians rebel against civilized society, they do so as individuals, on account of habits acquired during the individual life of each ; but they possess the *natural* aptitude, as is clearly shown by their children when brought up in our midst. These children grow up with abilities fully equal to those of our own offspring, as might have been inferred by any one who had dwelt among savages.

Yet I have no wish to deny the effects of heredity, or to assert that man is born into the world armed at all points, like Minerva. On the contrary, I contend that in the series of evolutions by which man has reached his present condition, so-called civilization represents an imperceptible atom, both by the short time (the few thousand years) that it has existed in any part of the globe, and the limitations of the individuals and nations enjoying it.

It follows from this point of view also, that we must date the origin of man from that remote period already indicated to us by the science of geology, a period measuring a greater number of years than we can measure days between ourselves and the Adam of Scripture.

THE END.

LONDON:
PRINTED BY GILBERT AND RIVINGTON, LIMITED,
ST. JOHN'S SQUARE.

www.ingramcontent.com/pod-product-compliance
Lightning Source LLC
Chambersburg PA
CBHW020808060726
47498CB00017B/947